DEAD BURN

An Emily Stone Novel

by Jennifer Chase

Also by Jennifer Chase:
Author Blog/Website: http://authorjenniferchase.com/

Emily Stone Series:
Compulsion
Dead Game
Dark Mind
Dead Burn

Fiction:
Silent Partner
First Watch (a short story)

Non-Fiction:
How to Write a Screenplay

JEC Press

ISBN: 978-0-9829536-9-3

PRINTED IN THE UNITED STATES OF AMERICA

Praise for the Emily Stone Series:

"[COMPULSION] is truly a top notch mystery-thriller of a read." - **Midwest Book Reviews**

"The tension, twists, and turns in [DEAD GAME] are perfect! This thriller was truly a read through in one sitting. I've just added Chase to my list of 'must read' authors!" - **G.A. Bixler, IP Book Reviewer**

"[DEAD GAME] is a deftly crafted piece of writing!" - **Simon Barrett, Blogger News Network**

"DEAD BURN is a gut-wrenching, nerve-wracking thriller that will keep you glued to the edge of your seat from start to finish." - **Readers Favorite**

"An intriguing alpha-female heroine...impressive action scenes and taut suspense." – **Kirkus Reviews**

"Chase's use of a very clear and descriptive writing style allows a reader to `cognitively experience' the emotions and events that take place `within' and `between' the different characters within this particular gripping and absorbing story." – ***The Secret Writer***

" The attention to detail in regard to the crime investigation is first rate, the author utilizes her experience in the criminology and forensic areas to provide a story that diehard crime thriller fans crave." – **The Jersey Girl Book Reviews**

"Comparable to the likes of Lawrence Sanders' Deadly Sins Series. [COMPULSION] and the books to follow are sure to generate a loyal following." - **Bengal Book Reviews**

"... [COMPULSION] is a fascinating story of serial murderers, pedophiles, and the one amazing woman who is able to bring them all to justice." - **Sarah Moore, Writers in the Sky**

In [DEAD GAME], Chase brings us another exciting Emily Stone adventure. Any mystery fan will enjoy this follow-up to[Compulsion]. Highly recommended." **Tracy Winters, author and publisher**

" Dark Mind is an electrifying thriller complete with police corruption and unthinkable crimes readers won't forget." **– Beach Bound Books**

"DARK MIND is written with a sharp attention to detail and a commanding knowledge that Jennifer Chase lends to the readability and believability of this book. " **– The Kindle Book Review**

"DARK MIND is a rollercoaster of intensity. I could not put it down. (I read the entire novel in one sitting) EMILY STONE is nobody to fool with -- I'll be back for seconds! " **– Douglas Wickard, Best Selling Author**

"DARK MIND, the latest novel in her Emily Stone series, again demonstrates why Chase stands out in the crowded field of crime authors." **– B. Sobieck, author**

"Jennifer Chase has released yet another heart thumping mind blowing novel with her Heroine Emily Stone." **– Yvonne Mason, Best Selling Author**

"This [DEAD GAME] is a must read for those who want high action in their crime thrillers. An amazingly, talented author. " **– N.Silk, author**

For all the police officers and firefighters who put their lives on the line every day for all of us – thank you for your unwavering service and dedication.

"You will not be afraid of the terror by night, nor of the arrow that flies by day, nor of the pestilence that walks in the darkness, nor of the destruction that wastes at noonday."

PSALM 91:5

PROLOGUE

"After thoroughly reviewing the evidence of this case, the court has determined that there's *insufficient* evidence to proceed."

Low muffled cries filtered throughout the courtroom.

Judge Christensen peered over his reading glasses at the defendant and his high-priced attorney. Disdain was evident in his voice inflection with the distinct syllable emphasis on the word *in-suf-fi-cient*.

He took a stilted breath and continued, "Timothy Devlin, you are released from these proceedings, and free to go."

The young man grinned and eagerly shook his attorney's hand. He stood up, dramatically turned to the courtroom gawkers, and raised his hands in a cheesy victory salute. His sinister grin turned into a full-faced smile. It was obvious he loved every minute of the attention he garnered. He had beaten the system with the help of his pit-bull lawyer.

A commotion broke out in the courtroom galley among onlookers. A few angry voices boomed above the escalating noise, "Rapist! Rapist!" and "Evil shouldn't be allowed to go free!"

Murmurs, gasps, and cries continued to echo throughout the courtroom. It made it difficult to differentiate statements between the angry words and oppositions.

The prosecutor tried to compete with the crowd's outbursts as he stated to the court, "With prejudice your honor."

"Noted," replied the judge. He stood up. "Clear the courtroom now!"

Four sheriff's deputies moved from their strategic vantage points to guide the men and women from the courtroom. It took a few minutes, but they accomplished their arduous task.

Assistant District Attorney Joshua Richards bypassed most of the crowd, skirted out of the courtroom, and did not pause to hear more critiques about his job performance. There were a few additional shouts of profanity and evil doom-wishers before the only remaining occupants were the defense counsel and the defendant.

The noise level instantly ceased to that of an abandoned classroom.

Chad Bradford slipped the rest of his court notes back into his designer brief case, still with a look of smug satisfaction on his face. That made fourteen rape cases acquitted in the past six months. It didn't matter that this case was pro bono; more high profile cases with a heavy price tag would soon follow. His smile still radiated as he slipped the lucky gold pen back inside his jacket pocket.

Everything that any halfway decent attorney needed stared right into their faces; they just had to know where to look, and how to slant it to their advantage. It was simple. He had the best job in the world – power, money, and an endless supply of sex.

Who could ask for anything more?

A cell phone buzzed from inside his pocket. Quickly he retrieved it, and the text read: *Baby meet me – u won't be sorry*

"You off to celebrate?" The newly freed defendant asked.

"Maybe for an hour and then it's on to the next case," reflected Chad. "You going to be okay getting out of the courthouse without being mobbed? I could have a deputy escort you."

"Nah, I'm outta here." The young man smoothed his hair, which seemed to stoke up his smirk once again. "It's been real." He shook Chad's hand again and then sauntered from courtroom.

Chad took a moment to breathe as he gathered his thoughts on some of the upcoming cases currently sitting on his judicial plate. He had an interview at Soledad State Prison with a serial rapist charged in seven cases, and the victims kept mounting; it could be as many as thirteen by the end of the week. Without DNA evidence, the case did not scare Chad in the least, but amped his adrenaline with a new manipulative courtroom challenge. He would have his private investigator Zig Rodriquez gather dirt on all of the female complainants. By his estimation, the district attorney's case would soon crumble and blow away in the wind. He would play the criminal justice system and win once again.

His cell phone buzzed again.

This time the text message instructed Chad to an address in the downtown area. It made him smile. A quickie in the afternoon was what he needed to refocus his energy.

He left the empty courtroom.

* * * * *

Chad eased his sleek black BMW up to the curb and kept the engine idling, his GPS directed him to an abandoned location. He stretched his neck precariously as he leaned across the passenger's seat and peered out the window, trying to get a better vantage of the dilapidating building.

The business had been an independently owned hardware store throughout the late eighties and into the mid-nineties, but remained vacant ever since. They couldn't compete with all the super stores and Internet sites monopolizing the consumer market.

The storefront windows, which once housed large displays, were now boarded up with heavy plywood and swathed with flyers of lost items and pets, work at home scams, and black and red graffiti emblems from rival gangs. Adjacent storefronts, torn down five years previously, had only chain link fences marking their once existence.

The only other car on the back alley was a rusted Toyota truck missing the back tires and driver's side window. Some flyers had scattered along the broken sidewalk and continued to tumble down the street. The breeze kicked up another notch as more litter blew along the pavement.

"What the hell?"

Chad looked around and double-checked the address once again from his phone. He was at the correct location, at least according to his phone application.

He dialed Abby's number and it went immediately to voice mail. He listened for a moment to hear her sexy voice apologizing for not being available before he ended the call. It must be some kind of kinky game.

Well okay, I can play too.

He finally turned off the engine and sat a moment before he disengaged the door locks. This place would definitely take his mind off work. He could use some down time with a little adventure to feed his soul. He hoped that no one would jack his car in the meantime.

Chad opened his door and stepped out, he still monitored his surroundings, but it was quiet and deserted. He shed his suit jacket, grabbed his brief case, and put everything into his trunk, except for a small handgun he casually dropped into his trouser pocket. He didn't want to be another crime statistic, and this was one instance being a lawyer could get him killed.

As he walked back to the front of the car, he caught a brief refection of himself in the window, and it always amazed him that he was so handsome with dark brown hair and a medium muscular physique. No wonder Abby found him so attractive and many others for that matter.

"How the hell do I get into this place?" He muttered to himself.

Chad secured his car alarm with a gentle push of a button from the gold keychain.

Nothing had changed on the quiet street, no one appeared, no slow moving cars checked out his expensive ride, and no homeless people materialized from tucked away locations in the alleyway asking for spare change.

It was dead quiet.

One of the sections of the chain link fence was broken and forcibly curled backward, as if a huge wind had transformed it. He decided to scope out the building and easily squeezed through the metal barrier.

Pieces of trash, rotten food, various sized recycling cans, and weathered cardboard littered the empty lot, but didn't mask the unappealing sweet-sour stench.

Chad tried not to inhale too deeply as his stomach churned the more he thought about the snaking filth all around him. He hoped that the interior of the building was clean and sanitary as he unconsciously wrinkled his nose and pursed his lips tightly together.

He made his way around to the back of the building, carefully examining each step in order not to soil his Italian, handmade loafers. A metal door caught his eye. It led directly to the alley and it appeared strangely out of place. The doorknob glistened bright silver, sparkling clean, without smudges or fingerprints. It imbibed the late sunlight and expelled a star shadow trail with long sliver points, reflecting around the alley.

The high-tech door stood out against the run down building. There were no available windows, just more disintegrating pieces of plywood bolted onto the building, layer after layer, from the years of neglect.

13

Chad swallowed hard as his mouth went dry, licking his lips in nervous tension. He blinked his eyes several times to try to stop the slight dizziness that crept into his view. It made the door and the crumbling building vie for his attention.

He stared at the doorknob for what seemed like an hour, but in reality, barely five seconds had passed. Finally, with his right hand, he reached for the grip and twisted. It turned easily in his grasp.

He let go and backed up two steps, still staring at the closed door.

Something deep inside told him to retrieve the .22 from his pocket.

It could be so easy to leave and return to his car, but an unseen force pushed him to move forward, if not for some great sex, then at least out of fundamental curiosity.

Chad was out of his element and he liked the feeling of being in control of his destiny in a foreign setting, and never knowing what could jump out at him. The adrenalin surged through his veins, down his arms and legs, and pumped in unison with his heartbeat in an orchestras' tempo. It kept perfect time.

Chad grabbed the door handle, turned it, and pushed the door inward. A whoosh sound from the suction of the tight weather stripping dulled the ordinary outdoor noises. A crazy heartbeat now hammered in his ears. He felt the small gun in his left hand, smooth, precise, which made him feel invincible, like a superhero in an action movie.

He entered.

The door automatically closed behind him with barely a sound.

The long corridor was almost completely dark, but low lights appeared from the molding along the bottom of the walkway. The windows were now part of the building, and not even a crack of daylight shone through the haphazard boards.

"Abby?" Chad announced.

He was surprised that his voice seemed weak and small. He wasn't expecting to play hide and seek in an old building, and now his nerves had transformed into anxious energy.

A thought suddenly occurred to him, this place would make a perfect location for a surprise party. His birthday was next week. That welcoming thought soon faded. He licked his dry lips, moved his chalky tongue, and he realized that his palm left a sweaty residue around the pistol.

"Okay, you got me." He tried to sound casual. "I followed the bread crumbs."

Silence greeted him.

Chad glanced down and noticed that the floor looked clean; it was as if someone had meticulously swept it, and he thought he could smell a hint of industrial floor polish. Odd, he considered as he continued to move forward, deeper into the building.

The corridor led into another part of the structure through a doublewide doorway, which once housed a holding area for inventory merchandise as well as the main hub for shipping and receiving.

His eyes adjusted to the darkened rooms.

Several plain brown boxes sat in the far corner.

The two heavy doors slammed shut with such an incredible force that made Chad jump, goose bumps instantly raised on the back of his neck and down his arms. He quickly moved toward the closed doors, but there weren't any doorknobs or handles to open them.

"Okay, you can come out now." He didn't care that his voice sounded nervous.

"Mr. Bradford" A calm man's voice with disturbing clarity filled the room.

Chad spun around, but there wasn't anyone in the room with him. The voice seemed to materialize from nowhere, and yet everywhere.

"Mr. Bradford, do you know why you're here?"

"What is this? Who are you?" He kept turning slowly expecting to see someone enter, but no one did.

"It's your sentencing."

"What? I don't understand…"

"You have sinned and now you must pay the price." The voice changed to a higher pitch.

"You're out of your mind! Open the doors now!" He remembered that the gun was in his hand. Jabbing it out in front of him, he moved it in jerky motions from corner to corner.

"That isn't going to save you." The eerie voice narrated like a parent reprimanding a naughty child.

"Is this some kind of sick joke?" Chad moved around the room, even though there wasn't anywhere to go.

"It's no joke."

The monotone inflection of the voice wormed inside Chad's head, and deep within his core. He knew it was human, but he pictured a futuristic robot presiding over him.

"I said open the doors now!" The lawyer demanded.

"Do you know how ridiculous you look? You're weak and pathetic. You had much more confidence spewing lies in the courtroom."

Chad felt his heart pounding faster as he gasped for air. It was years since his panic attacks had surfaced, due to work related stress, but now in the darkened room that familiar dread of anxiety crept back into his body.

"C'mon Mr. Bradford, you know exactly why you're here."

Chad waved the gun to each dark corner and squeezed off two shots, bullets zinged around the room. He realized that there were small speakers in each corner where the phantom voice emitted. He aimed the gun and fired several more shots at those general areas, but the blasts only managed to hurt his eardrums.

Chad dropped his empty gun on the floor. "What do you want from me? You want me to apologize for my job? Is that it?"

"Your greed spreads more filth. You covet, commit adultery, and most of all... you knowingly defend rapists and murderers."

"Oh, so *I'm* guilty. Guess you just skipped over something called the Constitution, due process, and innocent until *proven* guilty."

"You have free will and you've chosen your sins... so now you've sealed your fate."

"Who are you?!"

No response.

"Hey, I'm talking to you!" Chad kicked his gun and the weapon slid across the floor to a couple of stacked boxes. "Coward!" He managed to say. "Show yourself!"

In desperation, Chad tried to find a way out of the room. He ran his fingers over the doors and down the walls. There weren't any gaps, cracks, or hardware that would allow him to pry it open to escape.

Chad caught the distinct odor of smoke and spun around to face the boxes. The cubed cartons began to burn. A small flame ignited from each of them and cast a macabre light around the room. He could see wires and small plastic boxes, along with what he counted to be six small speakers.

"Let me out of here!" Chad beat his fists on the doors, but it barely made an audible sound. The doors were steel reinforced and heavily insulated.

Within minutes, smoke filled the room, and floated effortlessly in ghostlike apparitions.

Chad coughed and gagged.

He dropped to the floor and slowly crawled to one corner. He tried to breathe in a normal manner, but gasped for air in between violent fits of coughing.

After three minutes, he faded into unconsciousness and slumped against the double doors. He never heard or felt the explosion that obliterated the one room in the old hardware store.

The carefully orchestrated burn completed its job.

The intensity of the blaze ripped apart Chad Bradford's bones, and it included a quick decapitation, which left few charred human remains.

The fire had burned down to a smoldering, smoky remnant before the fire department arrived on the scene.

CHAPTER ONE
Saturday 2300 Hours

The black SUV sped down the dirt road in the middle of the night, bouncing left and right from each uneven dip in the broken pavement. The gravel and dirt battered the undercarriage with a high-pitched sputtering noise. Dust encrusted the windshield distorting the view ahead, but the neglected street conditions didn't slow the urgency of what was at stake.

Emily Stone rode shotgun, solemn, spine straight, with an unwearied attention. She stared straight ahead at the rushing road, but her mind remained only on the two nine-year-old twin sisters abducted from a neighborhood playground only three days earlier.

Anxiety rolled through her mind, but she didn't externally show it, not even to her partner. Her biggest fear was arriving at the rural compound too late. It was something that she would not allow herself to contemplate in her covert pursuits – ever.

She worked tirelessly to piece together the clues from the playground, family members, and the surrounding camera technology, which eventually prompted her in the right direction. The rest was pure intuition and dogged experience.

"How many more miles?" Emily asked, tapping her fingertips nervously on the armrest.

"Rolling up to sixteen-five." Rick stated as he turned his head to look at his impatient partner.

Emily double-checked her cell phone again on the directions – it was approximately nineteen miles to the location. She knew that the rural site wasn't marked on the digital map and that they were relying solely on technology updates, and some much welcomed luck to find the exact location.

"Maybe we should have alerted authorities?" She said.

"Em, your instincts are always right on. The police would have stormed the location in military formation and both of those girls would be dead before they even got out of their cars. The best plan of attack is to find and rescue the girls, and once they're safe, then call in the local cops." He looked at her. "It's been *our* protocol and it's worked well."

She looked at Rick's profile and admired his tough exterior and dark good looks, but she knew that he felt scared too. He gripped the steering wheel with purpose, biceps strained, and his jaw remained set in stone. He was her rock in these types of searches. His eyes kept a serious watch on the road as they took an unsuspected tight right turn.

The SUV skidded precariously. She felt it would tip to one side, but the rear of the vehicle swung back and forth in the loose gravel, and then found its proper groove on the road once again.

Seconds counted.

"Mile eighteen-four." Rick announced.

"Look for some kind of back road or path." Emily instructed.

She turned her attention out the passenger window to the overgrown trees and giant bushes for some type of road they could access unseen. They hadn't passed any homes or barns for more than fifteen minutes. They were completely alone, in a rural territory of central California, and only had one chance at a surprise attack.

"There!" He said.

Emily looked to the left past Rick's view and saw a narrow roadway with a single, rusted chain across it. If you blinked, it would have been easily missed in the darkness.

Rick cranked the steering wheel to a hard left, guiding them into the driveway and abruptly stopped.

"Got it." Her hand grasped the door handle and she gave a quick tug.

Emily jumped out of the car. She hit the ground running and easily unhooked the chain and pulled it out of the way, as Rick maneuvered their vehicle through. She attached the barrier once again before jumping back into the car.

The cut-through appeared to be a county access for water and drainage, but it hadn't been used in quite some time. It was overgrown and the SUV barely eased through the pathway, as branches scraped down both sides of the vehicle.

Rick extinguished the headlights and inched to a snail's pace.

Emily's eyes had adjusted to the darkness as the roadway narrowed to a dead stop. They couldn't pass the thick obstacles to continue any farther. Safely tucked away, the SUV left no visible view, both from the road and from the air.

Rick killed the engine and unhooked his seatbelt. "This is it, we go the rest of the way on foot."

Emily had already squeezed her small frame out of the passenger door, pushing branches away from her face and body. She moved to the rear of the vehicle. Opening the hatch, it revealed carefully organized boxes in color-coordinated sections. Dark green were guns and ammo, black were all types of knives and cutting tools, dark blue were extra batteries, walkie-talkie headsets, an endless supply of heavy-duty zip ties, and all types of flashlights.

"Ready?" Rick asked softly as he double-checked his weapons.

"Wouldn't be here if I weren't." Emily secured a Glock 19 in her hip holster and rolled up the right leg of her jeans where another small holster waited for a smaller caliber pistol.

For the first time since they had left their home that evening, Rick smiled. His handsome face lit up, which accented his dark eyes. "Maybe we should've asked Jordan to come along?"

Emily playfully rolled her eyes and said, "He'd be pissing and moaning about the scratchy bushes and biting bugs." She laughed as she inserted a loaded Beretta into her ankle holster. "Jordan is a brilliant profiler, but he's a pain in the ass in the field."

Rick quietly continued to ready himself for the challenging hike ahead.

Emily didn't mind the idle chitchat because she knew that any one of these covert missions could be their last, whether it was a dangerous rescue, stakeout, or a crime scene investigation.

Light banter between the couple helped to relax the situation. Death was just seconds away and precise focus was the key to any successful rescue mission. She quickly put any fatal thoughts out of her mind and continued to arm herself.

From experience, Emily now made sure she had at least one hunting knife at her disposal. It was easier to handle and conceal than a firearm. She slipped the seven-inch blade into a sheath on the outside of her right thigh against her dark jeans.

Rick handed her a small hearing device that fit snugly into her ear and hooked the receiver just inside the neck of her long sleeved t-shirt. Emily secured the communication device. She stopped and stared at him for a moment. She never knew exactly what to say before they ventured into the unknown.

Emily shut the SUV's hatch.

Rick checked his portable GPS. "Let's go. It's about three-quarters of a mile."

The couple proceeded northwest from their vehicle into the dense brush, Rick taking up the lead. They moved steadily, but slowly, in order not to make any unnecessary sounds or alert the kidnappers that they approached. They kept their flashlights low and just out in front.

The countryside was uncomfortably quiet. Not a single noise from any night dwelling critters filled the night, and not even the wind rustled through loose leaves and branches.

The air was cool and unusually dry, but Emily felt a trickling perspiration on her scalp that meandered down the center of her back. She anticipated several scenarios in her mind as she crept ahead, but knew if they kept their wits and stuck to the solid plan that everything would work out.

It seemed that they trudged through the thickets for an hour making considerable progress, but Emily glanced at her watch and only twelve minutes had passed.

Faint voices cut through the quiet night.

Emily and Rick stopped and listened, barely breathing.

For a moment, it seemed that the human sounds came from all around them. The rural landscape played unexpected tricks on the ears as the sound bounced along the ridges.

Inching forward in a crouch posture, the couple moved slightly to the left and up an incline to try to gain a view of the property. Through the overgrown bushes and approximately two hundred yards away, two men stood smoking cigarettes, engaging in a casual conversation.

Emily wriggled her body lying on her stomach as close as she dared in order to watch the men. She spied through a pair of mini infrared binoculars and immediately saw the handguns tucked into their waistbands.

One man, unshaven and his body adorned with anti-sematic tattoos, lit up another cigarette and took a long puff. His expression hardened by years of criminal activity, and he had the definite imprint of prison experience upon his face. The other, shorter man appeared to be ex-military with tightly cropped hair, tidy clothes, and a posture that lent itself to years of obeying orders.

Behind the so-called guards were three manufactured homes trucked along the property, two of which were small and seemed to be a place that housed supplies, and one main house or headquarters. The larger house remained dark, while a dim light illuminated in one of the smaller buildings.

A radio played somewhere inside the compound. Two radio voices chattered and the sound was eerie as it echoed around the landscape like in a strange dream.

"We're in the right place." Emily whispered and handed the binoculars to Rick. She continued in a quiet tone, "I get the feeling that there's one more." After pausing a moment, she continued. "Maybe the boss is offsite somewhere else?"

He nodded and continued to study the land and overall layout.

There was only one way in and out by a single dirt road. A partial barbwire enclosure in between farm-like fencing was the only barrier around the property. It was still quite a hike back to the safety of the car, and it worried Emily.

"No sign of the girls – at least from here." Rick whispered, clearly frustrated. "One truck, two guys."

"Wait until they split up?" Emily suggested.

He nodded.

"I think we can enter the camp from that farthest corner." Emily pointed in the general direction. "Let's move."

24

Rick pushed his body up slightly and away from their initial view of the property. He followed Emily through some tough, winding vegetation until they reached the camouflaged location for entry. They kept their flashlights off, which made it more difficult to push through the brush. As luck would be on their side, the rotten wooden fence had an opening just big enough for a single, averaged-sized person to climb through.

The sound of a gunshot broke the dead silence.

CHAPTER TWO
Saturday 2345 Hours

Bile flooded his mouth. He choked back the repulsive liquid, clenching his jaw as the fluid scorched all the way down his esophagus. His stomach churned and felt like a hollow, burning cavern preparing to erupt. There was nothing to worry about; he had killed countless times before, more than three hundred, and mostly repulsive victims of their own circumstances.

By society's standards, he was a clear-cut psychopath. It was easy to fulfill the psychological label, deprived of any remorse or sincerity, and exhibiting antisocial behavior from the most criminal standpoint – at least that was what so-called civilized people believed.

Still, his long career of killing had now turned his heightened excitement and adrenaline into a mild stomach discomfort of irritable bowel syndrome. Nothing slowed down his work or ambition, and he managed to keep his concentration no matter what occurred.

He knew more about the human behavior and what made people tick than most highly trained psychologists with their PhDs, just by studying the subjects carefully, looking for their weaknesses, strengths, and fears. Emotions and feelings revealed insight from people's common expressions. It was all in how they carried themselves and how they interacted with others. The subtle moves were not perceptible by most, but to a trained killer, it was painfully obvious. The human condition was not that difficult to figure out. You just had to know where to look.

Intensified perception was key.

He watched and waited.

The subject's fate was in his hands now, along with the help of a high-powered rifle and accurate scope. He liked to be up close and personal with his kills. Nevertheless, tonight for some reason, Mr. Bishop wanted it to be different.

The cool, damp night chilled him. His right hand stiffened, which caused him to straighten and curl his fingers in a slow, painful manner. That familiar clicking noise in the joints only proved to annoy him even more. The increasing chill of the night air wreaked havoc on the muscles and tendons in his hands, arms, and hips.

He watched through the eyepiece as the short man moved from his kitchen to the living room dressed in a sloppy, stained t-shirt with some 1980s band logo, and baggy sweat pants. His slovenly appearance reflected the same feeling he had for his young victims when he repeatedly violated them.

The portly man absently wiped his hands on the front of his shirt as he reached for more food from a bright yellow mixing bowl. Like a well-rehearsed machine, he shoved his hand into the container and filled his mouth, crumbs falling down the front of his already soiled shirt. He continued this procedure nonstop.

It did not matter that the target was the brother of a well-known senator. All jobs were the same – take out the target.

Then, the heavyset man moved from easy view and stayed away from any of the windows for more than half an hour.

It was now time for the plan.

The killer had to move quickly; otherwise, he would risk someone seeing him in the neighborhood. This contract was to be fulfilled immediately and with strict instructions – no questions, no mistakes, or easy clues for the cops to piece together. Forensics my ass, he thought as he quickly broke down the rifle and left the property.

The street remained quiet and deserted. It was not the typical suburban road, each home had a minimum of an acre, and many houses could not see all of their surrounding neighbors. One home in particular was in bank foreclosure and provided a perfect hiding place.

The methodical assassin casually took his time returning his rifle into the trunk of his four-door sedan that he conveniently borrowed from a nearby dealership. Nothing would ever be traced back to him and, even if they had seen his face.

The cops would not be able to identify him from fingerprints due to years of excessive cutting and peeling of the skin on his hands. His fingerprints were probably on file somewhere in the big uncoordinated database called the government melting pot. It really did not bother him. He had joined the Army at seventeen after running away from his foster home, too many years ago to count, but that was where *they* had found him.

As he quietly made his way back to the home of his target with an untraceable handgun, a familiar twinge within his gut greeted him again. This time, it was anticipation. He slipped on a pair of snug fitting gloves just for comfort from the cold.

He was excited like the old days and the eagerness of the kill filled him with joy. He stood at the side door to the garage where it was impossible for anyone to spot him or hear his movements. A long row of unkempt hedges further helped to block him from any potential collateral complications.

The side door was locked.

A basic tumbler deadbolt proved only a slight distraction and a loss of a minute or two. He could kick the door in, but did not want to leave any more clues than necessary. Within seconds, the assassin inserted the slim tension tool into the bottom of the keyhole, while he used another apparatus with an uneven tip. It only took a little bit of pressure with an in and out motion, and he easily unlocked the door.

The garage interior was warmer than outside, but smelled of old, dirty clothes and mothballs. A few boxes were stacked chaotically at the far corner. He walked to the door leading into the house, which was unlocked. He slowly opened the door, the heat from inside brushed past him along with a sickly stink of filth and garbage. He could see through the darkened kitchen into the messy living room.

A faint sound originated from a television somewhere else in the house.

With purpose and a relaxed ease, the assassin walked toward the hallway. He continued forward as the sounds became louder.

The bedroom door was slightly ajar. A flash of light flickered around the doorframe and down the hallway at an odd angle from the TV. It became clear that a homemade movie played on the television of a crudely taken video of the molestation of a young child.

The killer stood for a moment at the doorway – the horror of the video did not elicit any reaction as he then looked to the child predator. The heavyset man, now stripped of his baggy sweats and underwear, slept like a baby on top of his bed with the yellow snack bowl at his side. Eyes closed, softly snoring, and a barely audible whimper from some pleasing dream was the only aspect that represented any human identity.

Walking to the bed and standing over the sleeping man, the assassin retrieved his gun from under his jacket. There was no silencer because this hit was to look like a suicide. The cops would not look any farther into the case of a registered sex offender and a three-time acquitted child molester who decided to take his own life.

A few seconds passed before the assassin shoved the pistol into the man's mouth slightly at an upward position. He looked into the wide-open, shocked eyes of the bastard, and easily pulled the trigger.

Brain and bone matter spoiled the pillow, linens, and headboard. Blood slowly pooled around his head and almost instantly seeped into the mattress. His eyes open, glazed, as the life ran out of them.

Carefully taking the pedophile's right hand, the killer slipped the man's index finger through the trigger and his palm around the grip. He stepped back and let both the gun and hand fall limply to the side.

The scene looked perfect, just like a suicide. The one gunshot sound would not alert anyone in the neighborhood. He took a small digital camera out of his top pocket and snapped two frames, one portrait angle and the second a landscape view.

It was the proof of death.

He knew the cops would never take the extra time to have the fat man's hand tested for gunshot residue.

Forensics... what a useless crock of shit.

The hit man mindfully backed up from the bedroom and retraced his steps toward the hallway, watchful not to disturb or leave anything behind. His energy drained and the killer suddenly felt tired because his newest assignment did not evoke any inspiration.

He walked slowly down the hallway when he heard a low guttural growl.

He stopped.

The snarl grew louder with a bark in between heavy breaths.

The assassin turned and saw a brown and black stout dog at the end of the hallway. The canine's eyes flashed an amber glow. It was difficult to tell the exact breed, most likely mixed, but the dog weighed at least fifty pounds and meant business.

This was the exact reason why he painstakingly surveyed all of his targets for any potential complications, before he completed any contract to prevent needless problems.

The dog inched his way closer, hackles pronounced, and spine low to the floor.

It was either, run or stand firm; either way, the assassin was not going to make it safely out of the home before the animal sunk its teeth into his body. The only weapon he had to protect himself was lying in the bedroom next to the dead pervert.

The dog gave one last growl before it charged.

CHAPTER THREE
Sunday 0105 Hours

Another two gunshots exploded before Emily got her bearings to think clearly. Catching her breath, she dared to inch forward to look toward the compound area.

Rick grabbed her arm and motioned for her to stay still. His eyes, even in the shadows, said so much more than the simple gesture. She respected him and his expertise. Even though he had retired early from the Santa Cruz County Sheriff's Office as a homicide detective to join her in covert investigations, he still had the sharp intuitive factor when it came to bad people and human behavior.

Heated voices argued and continued to escalate.

Emily peered through an opening in the bushes. She could see the two men engaged in a spirited argument over which gun packed more of a punch in a hand-to-hand combat situation.

After listening to their rants and loud voices, it was clear to Emily that they had been drinking and the scene was nothing more than obnoxious horseplay between two men. This situation worked to the couple's advantage.

Emily watched as the heavyset, tattooed man swayed back and forth, and then shuffled away to sleep off his booze indulgence. He opened the front door of the larger building and went inside; the indoor lights flashed on, and then went off seconds later. The radio voices abruptly quieted as well. Emily gambled that the two girls were inside that house.

It was as if Rick had read her mind. He stated. "Go find the girls, I'll take the guy on watch."

She nodded and whispered, "Send all info to the local sheriff's department right away. It'll take them some time to find this place."

"Already on it." Rick used his cell phone's touch screen, moving pertinent information around with his right index finger, and attached all the information to send to the county police dispatch, watch commander, and the detective division.

Emily squeezed Rick's shoulder before she backtracked around the property to enter the compound. He looked at her with concern, deep respect, and love.

Emily quietly retreated from the safe position and made her way to the farthest side of the compound. She brushed her fingertips to her holstered gun and knife out of anxious habit, but also as a way to calm her nerves and keep focus on the rescue.

She could smell stale alcohol along with the pungent sewer leaching from the old countryside. Usually the smell of the country would relax the nerves, but the reek reminded Emily of death creeping in closely at her heels. She kept her effort on the task and stealthily proceeded to the small building with the dim light. For an instant, she thought the light blinked, like someone tried to turn it off, but then it reignited again.

* * * * *

Rick watched Emily silently disappear into the darkness. He knew that she was savvy and had the spirit of an entire police force inside her, but even still, he continually worried about her safety.

Moving forward through the density of the landscape, he slipped his phone back into his pocket. He had the ability to hone his cop senses at one particular bad guy in an instant, and could anticipate what they would do next. It was easy to figure out the average thug's motivation of greed, but it was also one of their biggest weaknesses.

Rick heard soft murmurs of complaints and realized the military-looking man still protested his views on guns – only to himself. His words slightly slurred, indicated that he wasn't up to his usual game, and Rick would take full advantage of it.

Out of his peripheral, he saw Emily skirt around the small building. He took her lead and headed toward the front of the compound to detain the first man; careful to stay within the shadows, he kept his steps continuous like a stalking panther.

A lighter sparked up another cigarette as the intense man took an exceptionally long pull from the filter-less cylinder. The embers glowed in the darkness and appeared to almost bob and weave as the man paced with an unbalanced gait. The entire time the captor kept his back to Rick.

Hesitating out of intuition rather than fear, Rick paused against the building waiting for the perfect moment to strike. There was no use of jumping into a situation that could go sideways in a heartbeat. He wanted to wait to hear form Emily to verify the girls were stashed and safe.

Patience was a virtue. Rick paid it homage and waited.

* * * * *

Stretching her body as tall as she was able, Emily ran her fingers up to the window's edge, which still had the original price sticker affixed in the right corner. She peered into the partially lit structure. A few boxes and bags of tied garbage sat undisturbed. From the looks of it, no one had entered the building in quite some time. It seemed strange that the light was on inside, but time continued to tick away and Emily needed to locate the little girls.

After quickly looking through a window of the other small building, Emily found the same results.

Empty.

The girls had to be inside with the tattooed man by the process of elimination. At least his drunken stupor could work in her favor. Emily thought a moment about waiting for Rick in case of trouble, but the drive of rescuing the sisters was far too great to ignore.

Every second counted.

She stopped to listen for Rick, but did not hear any voices or sounds of a confrontation.

She whispered into the headset, "Both small structures are clear. Proceeding to house." Emily didn't expect Rick to reply, but she wanted him to know the updates as they became available.

She walked around the manufactured home and came to the side sliding door. The small deck sat empty. Darkness loomed inside, but the little voice inside her head urged her to move on.

She slowly slid the glass door open.

For a brief instant, she thought she saw a dark shadow lurking inside, but it was only her imagination combined with an accelerated heart rate. Her vision clouded a bit under extreme stress, but her adrenaline never disappointed her in her time of need. She had learned to moderate it with breathing and intensified concentration for her next move.

The house was in complete disarray with newspapers, magazines, overflowing garbage bags, and dirty dishes. The stench inside proved worse than outside. At first glance, the living room was a decent size with a sofa and two large chairs, but in the dim lighting the furniture resembled marauders waiting to pounce.

Emily stepped inside and pulled the sliding door shut, leaving a couple of inches to let light and air inside. Her eyes quickly adjusted to the indoor lighting. She moved forward as even her slight weight made a creaking noise on the loose linoleum.

Once her heartbeat returned to normal and wasn't pounding loudly in her ears, she heard the soft snoring of the man lying on the couch. The whiskey and beer smell hit her senses causing her stomach to shift on the queasy side.

Emily walked over to the couch and looked down, the man slept on his stomach with his face turned into the back of the seating area. She watched him breathe peacefully in his alcoholic stupor. He would be out for probably the rest of the night, and she decided not to restrain him.

Her hand touched her Glock as the image of the man stayed suspended in her mind. She desperately wanted to press the barrel of the gun to his temple and pull the trigger. Emily quickly snapped back to reality and to the two little girls that desperately needed her.

She took another quick look at the snoring thug. Then she headed down the hallway where there were three shut doors. Without wasting any more time, she opened the first door and it was empty.

Then the second door, she pushed open and peered inside. A queen-sized bed pushed all the way against the wall, absent of linens or pillows, had the two little girls tied to the headboard. Their dark, long hair, matted and dirty, jeans and t-shirts looked soiled as if they were dragged across the countryside. When they saw the door open, the girls immediately became agitated and whimpered softly.

Emily quickly put her fingers to her lips and smiled. She looked nervously over her shoulder and then entered the room, leaving the door slightly ajar not to make any more noise than necessary.

Working quickly, she took their gags from their mouths and began untying the ropes.

"It's okay, I'm here to help you. Shhh... be quiet, okay?" Emily gently coaxed the girls. She didn't want to think about what they had been through earlier.

In her headset, she whispered to Rick, "I've got them, they are in a bedroom, south side, in the main house. I'm coming out in three..."

Tears streamed down the children's faces as they obediently complied to Emily's reassurance. She could see some deep scratches across their faces and on their arms.

The little girls looked to her for safety, like so many other children from other rescues, with the frightened, horror-stricken faces, and a questioning of why did this have to happen.

Emily retrieved her knife because the ropes were triple and quadruple knotted. She sliced the blade back and forth, careful not to accidentally cut through their skin.

"Who are you?" The thick-necked, tattooed man demanded. His body filled the bedroom doorway as he held a machete in his right hand.

CHAPTER FOUR
Sunday 0135 Hours

Before the dog hit top speed, the assassin grabbed a flimsy metal handle on the hallway linen closet and pulled with all of his strength. The thin pine door flung open just as he sidestepped the narrow gap.

A loud crack walloped the door followed by a yelp.

The killer, as if propelled by an unseen force, carried himself with lightning speed to the kitchen, where he grabbed a plastic garbage can that sat next to the refrigerator. Beer bottles and soda cans scattered out onto the floor with a thunderous clatter. He picked up the lid in one hand, and pushed the empty garbage can out in front of him with the other.

It was a matter of seconds before the dog had regained its senses and composure. The killer heard the familiar growl. The dog stalked him and stood at the edge of the kitchen floor. Eyes direct and determined with a curious expression mixed into the defensive canine behavior.

Two dirty butcher knives rested in the kitchen sink, but that would be messy and make the bedroom scene of suicide appear unusually out of place – even for the most inexperienced police detective.

The dog managed top speed. It leaped through the air with gleaming teeth barred.

The cool contract killer punched the garbage can lid forward with a perfect jab movement and smacked the dog directly in the chest. With a departing dull thud, the dog crashed on the slippery linoleum, furiously scrambled his four legs, and then tried to ready itself for another attack.

This time the assassin thrust the empty can over the squirming dog. Within seconds, he managed to secure the dog inside the recycling plastic can and fastened the lid. A muffled bark and violent shaking bounced around inside the garbage receptacle like a deranged rat in a cage.

Thoughts of what he would tell Bishop raced through the killer's mind. He rarely had trouble with any of the hits he executed over the years. His situation tonight made him seethe in rage. His demeanor showed lack of any of the usual frustrations, but feelings and emotions festered deep within his soul. With every experience of hate and discomfort, he had filed those incidents away quietly, until the time in which they would serve him.

As he dragged the garbage can down the hallway that reverberated with snarls and growls, his mind gathered momentum on all the tortuous ways to kill Bishop, including slicing, tooth pulling, and punctured eyeballs, were just a few that came to mind. Those thoughts kept him company as he paused a moment to look into the molester's bedroom. The man was still in the exact position as ten minutes earlier with a stunned expression staring into nothingness – a fitting end.

The killer continued his cleanup duty and he was not worried if anyone would arrive unexpectedly. It would only mean that he would have to stage a murder crime scene, instead of a suicide. Nothing worried him anymore; he had been shot twice, blown up, and even pierced through the solar plexus with an arrow. These things never worried him. It was just a job – nothing more, nothing less.

He opened the last bedroom door, which doubled as a small storage room filled with boxes and included a brightly colored dog bed. He dragged the bouncing garbage can into the middle of the room, loosened the top slightly, and left it lying on its side. Quickly slipping out of the bedroom and shutting the door before the dog had a chance to get out, he left the dog where it belonged.

The kitchen was already messy, but the assassin decided to sweep the cans and beer bottles to one area to give it a more true-to-life disorganized appearance.

The dog kept a rapid barking tempo in between furious scratching on the bedroom door, which soon quickly lost steam.

The killer took one last look around to make sure it looked like the pigsty that the predator had kept. Everything looked legit. He knew that the cops would not give any scrutiny to the appearance of the house.

He exited and quietly closed the door behind him.

CHAPTER FIVE
Sunday 0210 Hours

Emily watched the drunken man stare her straight in the eye. He still swayed from the evening's booze flowing through his veins, but his basic faculties were still intact. Up close and awake, the man looked like a hardened criminal with a propensity for extreme violence. She could see the jagged scars on his tattooed arms and down the right side of his neck, which only slightly overshadowed the glint of the machete he held.

"I'm not going to ask twice." He snapped, words slurred slightly, and spittle dribbled from his mouth.

The two girls, now freed from the restraints, cried as they slipped down into a corner of the bedroom. They made their already little bodies as small as possible.

Emily slowly stood up, standing her ground, as the man eyed her sidearm as well as lingering a second to admire her body. There was no escape or easy way to diffuse the situation unless she pumped several rounds into his chest. She couldn't take the chance of any stray bullets hitting the girls. She tried to estimate the distance from the doorway to the bed, about ten feet, if that, and how fast the man could wield the primitive weapon and make direct contact.

"Don't even think about going for it." He grunted.

"There's some misunderstanding here, don't make it worse than it already is for you." Emily realized as soon as the words escaped her lips that her plea sounded weak and contrived.

The burly man laughed – a loud maniacal burst.

It wasn't the reaction she had expected and that made her even more uneasy. She tried to block out the whimpers and stifled cries of the two little girls that counted on her to save them. If she failed, they were dead too.

* * * * *

Rick's stomach plummeted as he heard the words that Emily spoke and he could hear the monstrous laugh in the background from what sounded like a demon. It wearied his mind on the dangerous scenarios they both now faced.

He had to move now; otherwise, he would be of no use to Emily. For a split second, he squeezed his eyes shut and opened them to precisely dial in on the other captor.

With little regard to what may or may not happen, Rick hurried forward in a half crouch, half sprint position, with his Glock firmly planted in his right hand.

Just before he reached the man in the compound, the kidnapper turned in his direction. Their minds were in sync.

Rick squeezed off two rounds.

* * * * *

As Emily's fingertips touched her gun, the beefy man took his opportunity to strike out at her. He waved the machete with an erratic swiping motion, back and forth. It was obvious that he had never used the weapon before; it must have been the only available offensive instrument he could find.

Emily took the chance, pulled the Glock from her holster, and pushed it forward just as two shots were fired from outside.

Both combatants stopped for a fleeting moment, turning their heads slightly in the direction of the shooting from the front of the compound.

42

"Rick?" She managed to utter. Emily knew that Rick had no other choice but to shoot the kidnapper, at least she hoped that was the case.

Emily gave the huge man one more chance to surrender and ordered, "Stay right there!"

The man only scoffed at such a request and took another step toward her, swinging the thick blade side to side with extreme exaggeration.

She stepped toward him squeezing the trigger twice, just as the hulking man slammed into her arm with the back of his massive bicep – but she managed to hold onto the gun.

The bullets hit the ceiling.

The two hundred and something pounds of the drunken man shocked her system, shook her bones, as the impact thrust her backward onto the bed. The weight broke the box springs underneath them. Her ears rang with a peculiar buzzing noise. The smell of sickly sweat and last night's stale booze invaded the available air around her.

The man groaned and strangely contorted his face, as he lay halfway on Emily and atop the cockeyed mattress. Her arm and gun were beneath him and she tried to pull it free. She quickly turned her gaze on herself and half expected to see the machete sticking out of her chest or cut across her carotid artery; but instead, it seemed to have vanished.

The machete had struck the captor's shoulder separating the meat from the bone. The ghastly open wound wasn't mortal, but it took his immediate strength away.

Emily swung her left leg and pushed the moaning man onto the floor. He appeared helpless writhing in pain, a completely different person than just a moment ago. She pressed the gun into his face, hands now shaking. Anger infused every cell of her body. She wanted to blow his brains all over the walls, but knew that her mission was to diffuse the situation at every means possible before the use of deadly force. This kept her mentally and physically in check, and kept the chasm between what these people do, and what she did.

"Get up." She ordered, her voice steady and direct.

Emily could hear the small, fragile whimpers of two innocent girls as they watched in horror; she couldn't compound their already traumatic experience with more senseless violence.

The tattooed man crawled toward the doorway on his hands and knees. Emily picked up the machete with a piece of paper and tossed it out of the way. She looked down. His blood had splattered across her shirt and speckled the carpet.

One of the little girls dared to emerge from her hiding place and grabbed Emily around the waist.

"Stay back honey, in just a minute we can get out of here."

Emily knew that she couldn't look into the girl's eyes because she'd lose her concentration. They weren't out of danger yet.

With the sound of vomiting, Emily watched the burly man violently eject some of the cheap alcohol he had consumed. The repulsive mixture of vomit and blood engaged her gag reflex. She held her breath and swallowed hard. She brushed her hand up to her nose to induce any other type of odor.

She stepped forward over the barfing man and pushed him down flat on the floor. Quickly retrieving a couple of heavy zip ties from her pocket, she slid them easily over his wrists and ankles. Pulling hard, she secured them.

The man moaned and whined with incomprehensible words, now mixed with spit, blood and vomit smeared across his face.

Emily leaned him against a wall in the hallway, not worried that he'd escape or hurt anyone else. She quickly went to the little girls and made sure that they were okay and not in need of an immediate doctor.

"Rick?" She said into the headset.

No answer.

She kept moving. "C'mon, let's go." She gently instructed to the girls.

"Geez, what stinks?" Rick stood at the doorway grimacing, relief was evident in his eyes.

"Bad guys." Emily's flippant answer didn't slow her down. Relief washed over her that Rick was safe.

"You okay?" He stopped her for a moment to examine her shirt.

"I'm fine, I'll need to take a shower for a week though." She tried to sound like nothing was wrong, but the gravity of these types of situations ate away at her, losing a bit of her humanity with every incident.

Emily began, "Is the other guy…?"

Rick solemnly nodded.

Emily and Rick escorted the girls down the hallway as they made their way to the front door when they heard a helicopter swoop overhead.

"They're here faster than I thought." Rick said.

"Let's get the girls to the entrance of the road."

The group sprinted as fast as they could to the main entrance driveway.

"Stay here and the police will take you to safety." Emily instructed with a definite tenseness in her voice.

"No…" Spoke one of the girls attached to Emily.

"Honey, the police are here, you're safe." She looked directly at the little girl and her heart broke.

Sirens quickly approached with cops at least two miles away.

They didn't have much time if they wanted to leave the girls and then retreat back to the SUV without being caught.

Rick grabbed Emily's arm and they ran back into the compound using the buildings as cover just as the helicopter made a sweeping pass again. A spotlight shined across various areas of the property and then stopped on the little girls waiting for them. Dirt and debris spiraled all around.

The brief reprieve gave Emily and Rick just enough time to disappear into the thickets and trees. The duo waited deep in the brush and watched as the emergency vehicles arrived.

First, patrol officers secured the area after finding the two little girls safe and the dead man in the compound. The local cops did a quick look around before they called in detectives and crime scene techs.

Emily let her eyes wander around the darkened area, something didn't look quite right to her. Previous experiences culminated her gut instincts and something told her to move toward an enclosed area behind them to have a closer look.

Rick mouthed the words with a quiet whisper, "What are you doing?"

Emily smiled, which was in direct contrast to her blood stained shirt and hair.

A few more patrol cars arrived on the scene as well as an ambulance and fire truck. No one ventured toward the outer, darkest areas of the compound – at least for now.

Secluded behind some dead trees and overgrown brush, a path meandered to a clearing away from the police zone. It was an area tucked away that Emily and Rick didn't see or stumble upon when they had first arrived.

Emily stood upright, muscles in her back tightened from the scuffle.

The helicopter overhead took one final perimeter of the property and then headed off toward the city.

After the leaves and dust settled, Emily scrutinized everything she could visually see in the nighttime lighting.

The area was approximately fifteen foot square and relatively flat. The earth had been disturbed recently, it was an unnatural occurrence and definitely not caused from nature or natural erosion.

Emily stayed on the perimeter of the small clearing and studied everything, the foliage, soil, level of the dirt, and made a crime scene grid in her mind. A reflection in the evening moonlight caught her attention. She flicked on her mini flashlight and beamed it over the area. A decaying skull still partially protruded. It still had some hair strands attached to the decomposing scalp.

Emily gasped. She kept her composure as Rick's eyes meet her own.

"A burial ground…" Her voice drifted off.

Emily didn't have her familiar digital camera for documentation, so Rick's phone would have to be sufficient. He stood next to her as she photographed the scene. She didn't want to take a chance that the cops might not find the location.

A few clicks and Emily shot an overall view, medium vantage, and a close up of the bones. She stayed in place and only moved around the small perimeter to gain a better view. She didn't want to disturb any more of the area, but knew in her gut that there were more bodies just beneath the surface. With a few more snaps of the camera phone, Emily had a decent documentation of the area. She posted some notes of where the area was on the property and estimated dimensions using an Internet map and GPS.

Voices grew louder as law enforcement personnel roped off areas to wait for detectives and the coroner. Conversations about what had happened sounded more like idle gossip than police work.

"We better get out of here." Rick whispered. His eyes looked troubled in the dim light.

Emily handed the phone back to Rick so he could send the information to the detectives and forensic division of the local sheriff's office. It may, or may not be connected to the girls kidnapping, but now at least the bodies could be identified and cold cases closed.

Rick sent the new photographic evidence with a few well-placed buttons and screen maneuvers. The information flew out into cyberspace and almost instantly, the phone reported it sent successfully.

Emily and Rick retraced their steps in the dark and made their way back to the SUV without incident. The covert rescue was a success, but it left a heavy weight upon Emily's shoulders that would never quite go away.

The ride home left more raw emotions and little time to heal until the next case.

CHAPTER SIX
Tuesday 1030 Hours

The sun spilled through the large bay window into the dining area, which cast its appealing streaks across the hardwood floor. A large black Labrador retriever rested strategically on his side with just paws warming in the direct sunlight. The large feet twitched every few seconds to reflect the enjoyment of a wonderful canine dream.

The sound of computer keys pecked away in a manner that lent to the urgency of the operator. In between the pauses of the keyboard, a distinct dog snore filled the momentary gap.

Emily worked diligently on her open cases, her tireless efforts paid off almost ninety percent of the time. These particular cases had gone cold for most police departments, but she persevered and searched for the next break in order to solve the case. Important clues discovered only by the relentless pursuit of the truth made for Emily's strong investigative integrity.

Learning from experience and from dangerous cases of the past, she didn't store her investigations on paper or in the house anymore. She didn't leave any type of evidence that could be found by others, either accidentally or by any law enforcement agency. All files, reports, profiles, forensics, and photographs were stored in an online, heavily encrypted file that was known to only three other people. This file resembled a type of hidden file found in the mass clutter of innocent website information. It was simple, but highly effective.

Even though the case of the abducted twins was over and the criminal justice system had to clean up the loose ends, she took the time and typed out all of the information of what took place. It was her way of closing another file. This case made one fifty-seven.

Emily paused from her report writing and looked down at her sleeping Labrador, smiled, and then typed out the current date and time that sealed the case. Taking a sip of coffee, she dragged her finger across the mouse pad and opened a file that simply read: FIRE

It was the most complicated investigation with what seemed like endless reports, profiles, and photos of the crime scenes, scanned newspaper articles, excerpts from criminology researchers, and even quotes from incarcerated arsonists. Not one bit of information proved particularly useful, but in the right combination, all of the records told a very specific story. It was her challenge to find the answer.

This case dated back to almost ten years and the police were no closer to solving the cases; in fact, they didn't link all the cases in her opinion. With each incident, there was only one, specific victim in a carefully executed fire.

Was it a different kind of serial killer?

It intrigued Emily and her borderline obsessive behavior. She searched her victim files as faces of people flashed across the screen, both men and women of different ages and races. Most didn't have anything in common and wouldn't have crossed paths with one another in any kind of interconnected order. She had viewed their faces and backgrounds, for what seemed like a million times, and knew everything about them. She could draw every line of their face from a skilled photographic memory.

The computer screen showed a photo of a handsome attorney by the name of Chad Bradford. His well-rehearsed smile, sparkling teeth, perfect jawline, and dead grey eyes reeked of a high-priced lawyer that commanded a hefty retainer.

She toggled to an article from a few months ago of the last known arson victim, which had highlighted the attorney's career of getting child molesters, rapists, and murderers acquitted.

There was no doubt plenty of people who wanted him dead, thought Emily sourly.

She knew that this murder wasn't a copycat killer by the behavioral evidence of each crime scene she had studied.

Emily leaned back and sighed. Her mind always reset itself back to this serial case after a closure of a tough investigation. In a strange way, going over this file helped her to cope with the work stress, and increasing depravity of society.

"You're looking at the case Dead Burn again?"

Emily turned her gaze from the computer monitor to Rick. He stood in the dining room, barefoot, wearing loose sweats and a black t-shirt with the word S.W.A.T. imprinted across the front.

"I like to clear my mind." Emily replied.

"Looks like you're cluttering it if you ask me." He leaned in and kissed her, lingering a moment. Emily stole another kiss before he straightened up.

"I think this is the one case I'm not going to be able to solve." Emily's gaze went back to the computer where the smiling face of Chad Bradford stared back at her. It was as if he had a secret to tell her. "I knew there would be one sooner or later."

Rick grabbed her coffee cup and headed toward the kitchen. "It's too early to contemplate any worldly wisdom of cold serial murder cases."

The large Labrador stood up, yawned, and stretched into his usual downward dog pose before he padded after Rick.

Emily laughed. "You too Sarge? I thought you were on my side."

The dog hesitated, looked directly at her with his dark eyes, and then turned his large head toward the kitchen at the sound of the refrigerator door opening and the clatter of dishes. It was too much for any dog to dismiss when food was part of the deal.

Emily watched the dog saunter around the corner, and the tip of his tail disappeared before she returned her attention to the open computer files.

Her cell phone toned with a downbeat from an 80's slasher movie.

She immediately picked it up and saw that it was a text message that read: *Chk in howdy hi over and out*

It was exactly eleven in the morning on Tuesday – right on time. With a few quick keys, she responded with: *A-OK closed talk later*

Before she put down the cell phone, another text came in: XO

"Jordan?" Rick said as he downed a half glass of orange juice.

"Yep." She put her phone down on the corner of the desk.

"Did he send you a love poem?" Rick smirked.

"Funny. No, he's checking in and I think it's a great idea."

"Does he think that we're going to get murdered, buried, and no one will ever know what happened to us?"

"I think its great protocol."

Rick finished the glass of juice in one gulp. "What then if we're missing? He's going to track us down?"

"Something like that." Emily closed down her computer. "There's nothing wrong with being careful *and* organized."

Rick put his empty glass down, pulled Emily up from the chair and held her tight. "I suppose careful is good sometimes."

CHAPTER SEVEN
Tuesday 1115 Hours

Jordan still had a subtle smirk etched on his face as he pocketed his cell phone. His entire life had changed the day he ran into Emily Stone, and he would never forget that chance encounter. His days of working for the FBI in the Behavioral Science Unit as a criminal profiler was over, and he knew even before he had met Emily that there was something more important out there waiting for him.

Jordan's last assignment with the FBI was an undercover assignment into a computer game company. It had changed his life forever. Not only meeting Emily, but also understanding how he could really make a difference without corporate politics, favoritism, lack of trained agents, and hidden agendas. His perception about life and law enforcement did a one-eighty, things now really made sense to him.

Computers and technology kept Jordan entertained in the meantime. What started as a side job to keep him employed until he figured out what to do with his life; he had turned into a full time and lucrative security consulting business. The money was good, great in fact, but the benefits were even better with incredible places to vacation and influential names to fill his secret little black book.

He watched his latest client Mr. Bishop, as he was introduced, stroll around his lavish veranda speaking quietly to one of his trusted minions. The dark, wavy hair and the general nondescript alpha male appearance kept the sharpness of his reptile-like eyes in check. His lean body structure of a middle-aged man didn't lend itself to just eating right and plenty of exercise; it seemed oblivious to the gaining years.

Jordan gave him the usual speech about security. It was the effective *blah, blah, blah* version of safety and security that the world demanded, especially for the ones who could afford it. He never thought of himself as a salesperson, sometimes a profiler and covert investigator with Emily, yes, but rather someone who had turned his charm into information of interest. It worked most of the time. It didn't take much prodding to convince a mega billionaire that there were people who wanted them dead.

The current assignment involved a huge security undertaking. The house was enormous with just under nine thousand square feet that sat right in the middle of three acres. It opened up all sorts of security nightmares with unannounced point of entries.

Jordan worked many hours on the security details of the house, roamed the grounds locating various options for cameras and alarms, and searched for every possible breach. The detailed layout that he carefully scrutinized looked more like a drawing an architect would render in a sci-fi movie than a home security system.

The glint of the mid-morning sun directed Jordan's gaze to a beefy bodyguard. The suit jacket had stretched its limit over the gym-induced physique as the skewed lines of the garment compensated the bulky frame. When the jacket flopped open slightly from a quick breeze, Jordan could see a fully automatic weapon tucked neatly into a holster against the ribcage.

Jordan turned his attention back to the huge windows and breathtaking vista of the garden just as two more of the armed bodyguards came into view. He knew that Bishop ran a background check on him, probably for the tenth time. It was the beautiful thing about technology that kept everything on the upscale, but it still didn't delve into the deep, dark secrets of anyone's true mind and motivations.

Sitting down at an antique writing desk, Jordan slid out his laptop from his briefcase, flipped it open, and clicked a few keys. He waited for some information to come back on two of the assistants and one bodyguard on Bishop's staff. It amused him while he waited for his potential new client to return to their meeting. It demonstrated a big test, a game of sorts, for the wealthy and powerful types to make a service person wait for as long as they wanted.

Jordan had the inexorable gift for sarcasm and spewing out whatever he felt like saying among a group of people. Today, he had to rein in his tongue, get through the gauntlet of professional niceties, and then move onto the next client.

"Mr. Smith, thank you so much for waiting. I can tell you're a patient man." Bishop forced a smile and never left his sights from the security specialist.

"It's my pleasure. I was thinking of ways to break into your beautiful home while I was waiting." Jordan's confidence spilled through his classic all-American good looks.

Bishop purposely walked to an armoire, dated easily from the 1600s, opened the left door, and retrieved something that Jordan couldn't quite see from his position. In his mind's eye, he imagined the scenario as how a movie would unfold, and this was where he would be bludgeoned with a baseball bat.

"Mr. Smith, your report on security was quite impressive and very thorough." Bishop turned and lit a cigarette with well-rehearsed precision. "But I am a bit surprised though."

"By what, may I ask?" Jordan thought he would play along with the game already in progress. He quickly tightened his jaw to keep from saying something more colorful and off beat.

"You being an F.B.I. profiler, rather an ex-F.B.I. profiler."

"Things change."

"Ah yes, don't they? You see, I like to know who I'm dealing with." He exhaled the cloud of smoke that meandered around his head and then dissipated.

"Perfectly understandable. Do you have any more questions that I can answer?" Jordan stood up and slipped his laptop back into the leather briefcase, just as one of the shorter bodyguards with a permanent distasteful expression on his face took a step toward him.

Jordan lifted his hands with some slight drama and said, "Nothing but boring paperwork in here."

Bishop took a step closer to him. His smile had faded, but the predatory look in his eyes remained focused and keenly aware of Jordan's slight nervousness. "You've answered everything and more. Your fee for services has already been transferred into your account."

"Thank you for the opportunity and prompt payment. I wish every client was so diligent and gracious." Jordan realized he was spreading it on a little too thick, but what was said had already left his mouth. No other client had ever paid his fees before he left the meeting before, now he genuinely wondered about this meeting and the motivation of Bishop. He chose initially to ignore it before because he had a job to do, but now he wasn't so sure.

A smile spread across Bishop's face as he spoke, "No need to express thanks, it's all about business… Jordan."

That little voice which kept Jordan alert in dangerous situations screamed at him now. There was more to Bishop's business dealings than just security. "It certainly is…" Jordan made a move toward the front entrance as Bishop stepped abruptly in his path.

"If I do have a question, I will call you. Or, perhaps one of your colleagues?" He watched Jordan closely.

"Nope, it would just be me." Jordan flashed his signature smile.

"Are you sure? I thought there were a couple of *other* specialists you frequent with."

"Not that I'm aware of." Jordan flipped a business card onto the antique desk. "Feel free to contact me anytime. It's been a pleasure." He shook Bishop's hand.

Jordan eased his way to the foyer struggling to keep a calm and professional composure. He exited through the front door. He could still hear Bishop's tone resonating in his head when he said *Jordan* and *specialists*. It actually thumped in his ears.

He began to question this man. When he had searched the corporation "TSL, Inc.", there was not anything listed, or any record of the man who easily transferred a substantial security fee into his account.

Dummy Corporation? Phony front business? Mafia boss? A terrorist cell? All of these thoughts tumbled through Jordan's mind faster than a speeding freight train. If he had to do a profile on what he had just witnessed, it would read more like a British spy novel and not about some enterprising executive.

Relieved when he sat behind the wheel of his car again feeling the steady support of the leather seat behind him, and no bullets pierced through the back of his head. Jordan doubled checked his bank account from his phone, and indeed, the money was deposited.

He took another second before he inserted the key into the ignition – the car hummed as usual, without any glitch or hesitation.

CHAPTER EIGHT
Wednesday 0945 Hours

As the elevator doors shut, a quiet numbness of the confined space made the assassin uncomfortable and conspicuous. A low buzz of the circulated air trickled to that of a leaking tire. The obscure security cameras remained nestled at two corners of the passenger car.

No music played idly to pass the time.

It remained disturbingly quiet.

He knew they watched him.

He kept a steady watch forward and could see his own distorted reflection from the steel exterior of the doors. A deranged killer came to mind from the out of focus features of the man staring back, known only to a select few as Red.

Black jeans, black shirt, black boots, and a black leather jacket were his personal uniform of choice no matter what the temperature or occasion. As usual, his jacket looked too tight on his lean torso, and it gave the impression of someone who wasn't comfortable in his own skin.

Appearances were deceiving.

The brief solitude gave him time to reflect on his own inner demons and the value of his work. Inside, he raged with violence and craved revenge – his kind of revenge. The previous rushed contract, still made him seethe, and he wanted to unleash the mayhem he felt to set things right in his eyes.

The elevator ascended the floors with ease. The upward movement progressed in a floating motion that almost lulled Red into a false sense of security - almost.

As he stood stationary, his fingers painfully curled into tight fists, one at a time, and on cue. The more he thought about how he had been manipulated into a situation that wasn't his usual code of operation, the more unsettled his stomach became.

His imagination kicked into high gear about all of the slow ways to kill a man. It wasn't something that was out of his capability or code of ethics. Killing was a part of his daily routine, like eating, drinking, and paying the bills. How to kill a person was the more creative side of his profession.

He remembered fondly the expression on the child rapist's face as he left him in his pornography lair, never again to watch his aberrant videos. Vacant, dumbfounded, and even surprised was among his last emotions on earth before his brains obliterated into tiny pieces, only for the coroner and crime scene techs to scrape up.

A pleasant bell chimed as the elevator prepared for the thirty-ninth floor. The doors slowly opened.

Red crossed the threshold seconds before the elevator doors shut. His boots compressed the plush burgundy carpet, slightly slowing his gait. Walking down the long hallway with several wooden doors, the assassin never averted his attention from the large, double doors at the end.

No identification, letters, or numbers were on any of the doors, but it was clear that the point of interest were the heavy metal doors. An electronic noise above his head moved and focused the camera directly on Red's face. A few moments passed before the lock disengaged and the killer entered.

The heavy door closed automatically and secured the triple titanium locks.

It smelled of freshly cleaned carpets with a pungent pine and lavender scent, which made Red's stomach take a jolted sour turn. A barely palatable taste entered his mouth and he swallowed several times to keep it at bay.

Another long hallway welcomed him with two rows of offices on each side. A few of the room's windows had bulletproof glass, along with sparse, monochromatic desks, chairs, sofas, and tables. A middle-aged woman in a dark suit sat at a desk typing on a laptop computer, she never acknowledged Red, even if she saw him.

There were still no identifying names or numbers of any kind. There wasn't a pleasant receptionist to guide you where you needed to go, or to inform someone you had an appointment.

The air conditioner was on full force because Red could feel his right shoulder and left knee complain with a dull stiffness from the drastic drop in temperature. The cooler temperature kept minds sharper and more efficient to carry out the duties of the GATE.

Every few months, sometimes six months to a year, Red reported to his boss. Most assassins did not have any direct contact with their so-called bosses. GATE was different, more hands on, and more lethal than any other contract government agency. GATE was an abbreviation for Government Anti-Terrorist Enforcement. It wasn't as candy coated as it sounded. GATE worked on its own agenda, for its own reasons, and was headed up by a ruthless director known as Mr. Bishop.

Red stood in front of a stainless steel wall and waited. His internal impulses competed for something different from his cool, aloof demeanor. Finally, the wall slid open and revealed a huge room filled with computers systems.

Several nondescript employees diligently worked with high-tech searches and background assignments. Other staff members listened to phone conversations of taped intermissions of cell phones from persons of interest. Every word spoken, carefully coded and cross-referenced, and then entered into an even larger database that created more lists of suspects.

No one looked at Red as he entered the control room. The assassin looked oddly out of place in contrast to the office employees in starched white shirts and blue or grey suits.

The low buzz of the electrical devices and state of the art technology made Red feel like he would undergo some type of radiation treatment. He wondered if his chances of contracting cancer were even higher now.

A short, heavyset man with sagging jowls and droopy eyes approached Red. "This way." He led Red into another office.

Once away from the hum of computers and florescent lighting, the only sound was Red's leather jacket that made a rhythmic squeak as he crossed the threshold into a much more modern office. All of the plush amenities and furnishings were that of a wealthy stockbroker, instead of the head of a covert, contract agency.

"Would you care for anything?" The pudgy man asked Red, but clearly wasn't interested in what he had to say.

"No."

The man left.

Red looked around the room, nothing had changed much since his last visit eight months ago. The heavy antique desks, credenza, and filing cabinets were typical of most offices. It was the extent of the lavish fixtures, computers, overhead projector, and crystal decanters filled with expensive scotch and brandy that made the office seem oddly out of place.

The dark brown leather chairs were imported and most likely handmade by someone in a small village in Italy. Red chose not to sit down in one of the comfortable chairs, it made him feel more secure if he stood.

"Nice to see you Red. I trust you are well." Bishop said.

62

"Fine." Red replied sourly.

Bishop walked to the opposite side of the room and took a seat behind the desk. He looked like he was navigating the helm on a star ship cruiser. His hands moved in the smooth, quick manner of a politician before he spoke again, "It's nice to know that you can improvise when necessary." A smile settled on his face as he waited for Red to respond.

"I thought I had made myself clear." Red flatly stated.

"Sometimes things just work out that way."

"Not for me."

Bishop leaned back in his chair. "Please have a seat, relax."

"I'll stand."

"Very well. I appreciate your work ethics and exemplary record, and now I have a different assignment for you."

"Meaning?"

"Your usual fee will be doubled, plus a generous bonus of the extra time you spend." Bishop paused as he studied the hit man.

Red thought about grabbing Bishop's throat, if he would struggle, and how long it would actually take him to die.

"You seem troubled."

"I don't like changes." Red grunted.

"I understand your position, but times change, people change, and often plans change. It's a fact of life." The steely eyes of the director rested on Red's arthritic hand. "It's my job to make sure that the right people are doing the right job. You see, I had to make sure that you were still sharp, and in top shape when unsuspecting events arise."

"Like what?" Red clenched his jaw as his breath became somewhat stilted.

"Don't worry, you're still the best contract man in the biz. This assignment is for someone of your, let us just say, experience." He watched Red's reaction.

"Who's the mark?"

"This time I need for you to run an op."

"I don't work with anyone."

"This is a babysitting job, just until *we* get what we need from the person of interest. A simple job and good money."

Red sighed. He hated everything about the thought of running an operation with others, they were usually inexperienced, trigger happy clowns. There were too many variables to consider, and too many things that could, and most likely would, go wrong with an op.

A moment passed before Red spoke. "What do you need from me?"

"Excellent." Bishop pulled open a drawer and retrieved a thick, dark manila envelope. He tossed it across the desktop. "Everything you need is inside. I trust you won't have any questions."

Red took a step forward and picked up the packet. It was unusual to get anything on paper. "Fine." He turned to leave.

"You can take your time to get everything just like you like it before you proceed. I'll leave it up to your discretion." Bishop smiled. He was a snake in civilian clothes. "Make sure you destroy everything after you've completed the job."

Red left the office and retraced his steps back to the elevator. He hated the administrative aspect of his job. He wanted to do his work – alone and uninterrupted.

As he waited for the elevator to drop him back at the basement level, he opened the one-inch thick envelope, and slid out the top photograph of his mark along with a zip file. The photo was a beautiful blonde woman running at the beach. The image was grainy due to the telephoto lens of the camera, but her face was clear enough to identify. Killing a woman was not a problem for Red, but there was something about the particular woman that troubled him.

He quickly skimmed the remaining photographs, explicit instructions, in-depth background, addresses and contacts before he tucked the packet into his jacket. The anger he felt inside about Bishop was about to explode, but he would soon direct this rage at his new assignment – Emily Stone.

CHAPTER NINE
Wednesday 2210 Hours

The old building remained intact from the front view. The back area had a burned out portion that left a complete cavernous opening, which gaped profusely and left a deep impression. Even though the structure was in the middle of the city, it was quiet on the street, without any voices or passing cars encroaching into the midnight hour.

The chain link fence, haphazardly dismantled, from the trampling of the fire personnel, waited ominously. The emergency group had moved quickly, from the street side to the old building, in a rushed effort to extinguish the blazing fire.

Of course, they were too late.

Water had drenched the empty adjoining property, which left a muddy trail and standing pools of sludge. Twisted wire let go from the top and sides of each fence section. There remained sharp hooked snares for anyone who entered, and a twisting gauntlet path to the back entrance of the building.

Tattered crime scene tape fluttered in the wind and caught up in muddy clumps between the scattered garbage. Several paper coffee cups arranged next to the building in a neat pile, were obviously overlooked by law enforcement's cleanup crews.

A flashlight beam led the way for Emily and Rick to navigate the sloppy pathway to the point of interest.

Emily took the point position when it came to studying a crime scene. Even though emergency personnel from the fire department, patrol officers, a fire inspector, several police detectives, crime scene technicians, bosses in charge, and any curious onlooker had bombarded this particular crime scene, it still had important clues that waited for discovery.

Emily trudged through the muck and garbage, but scrutinized everything in her path from impressions made from equipment and footprints, to tossed garbage, and all various access routes. She estimated two to three dozen sets of work boots, and two or three sets of casual shoes, most likely from the public.

Rick remained quiet and gave Emily space to evaluate the scene.

Standing at the back door entrance and turning slowly in a three-sixty degree turn, Emily studied the area. Her eyes moved slowly and took a mental inventory of everything around her. It seemed strange to her that there was a heavy fireproof steel door. It appeared newly installed and stood out unscathed against the building skeleton.

"Who do you think installed this door?" Emily asked as she took a closer look.

Rick must have been thinking along the same lines. "This isn't your normal heavy back door... it's fireproof and would cost some serious bucks."

"Not to mention the installation cost. There must be a record of purchase and installation."

Emily handed the flashlight to Rick. She took photographs of the door, building, and the various accesses that someone would have to gain entry to the back door and to the property. Keeping the digital camera level, she panned around so that she could connect the photos in a real view of the crime scene when she got back to her computer. It gave the investigation a flowing interpretation to study, and often many times new clues emerged from this simple reenactment technique. She continued to follow the protocol at low, as well as, higher angles.

Emily softly spoke as she studied the surroundings. "I know that this isn't the normal serial case we investigate, but this killer is targeting very specific victims and then somehow leading them to a place where they are then killed." Her voice trailed off before she continued. "These victims don't necessarily lead a perfect life."

"What do you mean? Well, I know this guy was a criminal lawyer and was able to get judges to acquit rapists and child molesters."

"I think," Emily explained, "He has an agenda… we need to figure out what that is…"

"All the arson cases I've seen and investigated had to do with revenge, insurance scams, teenage nonsense, or covering up another crime."

"This guy isn't the usual arsonist. He's complicated."

"Aren't they all?" Rick poked fun to lighten the mood.

Emily smiled. She loved to watch Rick's face light up when he was more relaxed. "You know what I mean. The usual profile is a single, white male, teens to twenties, low education, antisocial tendencies, anger retaliatory, and they're usually against some type of societal norms."

Emily eyed a fence post and an electrical box adjacent to the ally wall. "This guy is the exact opposite of the usual profile, and extremely efficient, almost to the point of … obsessive compulsive … psychopathic…"

"Great, we're looking for an anal, psycho intelligent guy who could be a member of Mensa."

"If I didn't know better, I'd think you've been hanging around Jordan." Emily clicked more images around the building to complete the views.

"Yeah, just what I need more Jordan."

"What's this?" She asked.

Rick stood next to Emily and examined the control box used for electrical, and the wires appeared new. The bright red, green, and white wires hooked into a small camera, and then into a small black box about the size of a deck of cards.

"There's no electricity to this building, right?" Emily surmised as she held the flashlight at various angles to see if there were any fingerprints or specific tool marks left behind.

"This building has been vacant for years, there wouldn't be any power. Besides, if there was, the city would have definitely turned it off before addressing the fire."

"It's been wiped clean, no impression print of any kind, not even a scratch from manufacture or installation. Strange..." She studied the box a little more.

"What do you think it is? A new smart meter or something?" He watched her with curiosity.

Emily took more photos. Then she said, "Okay, so then they wouldn't mind if I do this..." She took a small screwdriver from her pant pocket and carefully freed the mysterious black piece.

"Would it matter if the city did care?"

"No, but..." She put the small pieces into her lower side leg pocket. "Maybe..." Her voice trailed off.

"What?"

"I think that this murder was carefully planned for quite some time, calculated down the last second." Emily turned, faced the building, and mentally calculated how many steps to the door. "I think there's more to this scene that has been so painfully overlooked by fire inspectors and detectives." She took the flashlight from Rick and waved the beam toward the building.

"The cops are looking for criminal access into the building, accelerant used, and even a blatant message of revenge left behind." Rick explained.

Emily pried away crime scene tape and two pieces of plywood haphazardly nailed in place. She entered. "There has to be some type of receiver that connects somewhere in this building." She disappeared into the darkened structure.

"Em... wait..." Rick's voice stressed.

Emily pushed forward as her curious mind and unrelenting determination drove her. Her ambition could also be her greatest weakness. Her main objective was to solve the case and stop the arsonist before he killed again.

The stench of burnt wood and stagnant water made it difficult for her to breathe. She quickly cupped her left hand over her nose and mouth to try to gulp some fresh air.

The interior area of the structure unnerved her, and cranked up the creepiness factor the further she ventured into the blackened den. The burned out area looked like a macabre haven for the undead and Emily half expected to see zombies.

"Dammit Em..." Rick sounded annoyed. "Wait... it's not safe..."

Emily could hear his footsteps quickly approaching from behind. "I'm fine Rick... I'm taking careful steps so that..."

As she took a right step, the floor felt peculiar under her weight. She quickly took a left step to balance her body weight. A splitting noise cracked loudly in her ears. The structure tweaked a high pitch, and finally exploded under her footing. Falling effortlessly into an abyss, Emily flapped her arms to grab hold of anything within her reach.

It was too late.

She fell through to the basement floor.

CHAPTER TEN
Wednesday 2250 Hours

The familiar glow of the computer screen cast an eerie light on the small one-room studio. It was one of three newly purchased laptops, which sat on a foldout utility table. Each computer was open to various chat rooms; different Internet crowds matched the three different screen names of the voyeur's identity. All of which had youthful, even hip nicknames. It was like casting a fishing line into a large pond and waiting for the first fish to bite – and someone always took the bait.

The apartment, almost empty and absent of the usual furnishings, made for a convenient office. No couch or dining table resided. There were no toiletries in the bathroom, no pots or pans in the kitchen, and no artwork on the walls. It was a husk of a living environment, and suggested of something more threatening.

The dingy apartment was located in the one of the most crime-infested areas of the city, but it was only one of the temporary accommodations of five low-income residences. It made it easier for him to move around freely, and it helped to keep the people away who wanted him dead. The cops did not know about most of his places and that suited him just fine.

Timothy Devlin, careful and overly confident, still didn't hamper his enjoyment of his odious fetishes and addictions to adolescent relationships. His dead lawyer had put a temporary kink into his free lifestyle, but he would deal with that situation when it came time to go to court again. He really did like the guy and respected how he handled all of his cases. It gave Timothy a class of distinction – even some decency.

A computer alert interrupted his contemplations.

SugarGirl17 responded to his request to chat privately.

That proverbial tingle began to ignite and move through his body; he needed something warm and young, and soon.

He smiled and quickly typed out a message.

FanBoy1996: *looking 2 party*

SugarGirl17: *up for anything*

Timothy focused in on the conversation. He knew that he had a lovely little girl in the chat room, ready for him, and ready for discovery in every way. He slowly typed out his response.

FanBoy1996: *what do u like?*

SugarGirl17: *sniff and hard drink*

FanBoy1996: *How old are u?*

SugarGirl17: *old enough*

That's what he wanted to hear. He quickly glanced to the other chat rooms, and the conversations talked about movies and teen celebrities, nothing that interested him. He knew how to weed out the pack to gain the trust of one, special girl. It was one little girl that didn't belong with the group, and wanted so much to be accepted and liked.

FanBoy1996: *do u know where to party?*

SugarGirl17: *can party and crash at rock farm*

Timothy thought for a moment, where had he heard that name before.

Rock farm?

He suddenly remembered; his fingers twitched as he hesitated to type out his next words. It was in a rural setting surrounded by trees and a lake. There wouldn't be anyone camping or enjoying the lake this time of year. Everything fell into place.

FanBoy1996: *what do u look like?*
SugarGirl17: *long blonde hair, thin*
It was perfect. It sealed the deal in his mind and he couldn't wait.
FanBoy1996: *meet u at 1:30?*
SugarGirl17: *see u there*

CHAPTER ELEVEN
Wednesday 2330 Hours

Blackened pieces of debris, some jagged and others splintered, along with clouds of heavy dust, showered on top of Emily. She protected her head as best as possible, and cupped her nose and mouth to keep from inhaling anymore of the building than necessary.

She waited for the deafening noise to stop.

During that terrifying moment, one thought raced numerous times through her mind. She knew that someday she would become a part of the crime scene. It was somehow her destiny in a crazy, twisted way.

The ear splintering noise stopped abruptly.

Only quiet resonated. Stunned, Emily thought that she had gone deaf from her fall. A few more creaks, groans, and powdery mist fizzled overhead.

Emily let out a quick sigh of relief, and then quickly focused on the damage she caused to the crime scene. From the impact, her back and right leg speared a hot pain, just enough to take her breath away, and then subsided. The black box she had inserted into her cargo pants felt imbedded into her leg.

"Em!" Rick's voice shouted from above with a peculiar echoing sound. "Emily!"

"I'm... I'm okay..." Emily tried to sound like her usual tough self.

"Don't move." Rick had maneuvered himself to peer down through the gaping hole at her, shining a small pin flashlight. His face looked haunted and concerned. "I'll get a rope. Don't move."

"No." Emily slowly got to her feet, wobbly at first. "I'm okay. This must be the basement and that means there's a way out."

"Em, I don't think that…"

"Just give me a minute…"

Emily searched the immediate area, and moved a few pieces of charred boards that had dropped. They were light and easy to move. From the extreme heat, it left hollow shells of timber in its wake. She spotted her flashlight and it looked intact. Immediately, she flipped it on, and the area lit up like an underground cavern.

Emily said with more authority, trying to lighten the mood, "Great flashlight. I'll have to write the company and tell them how durable these things are."

"The building isn't safe. Don't move." Rick insisted.

"No, I think it is. Apparently, the one room up there was designed to burn quickly, leaving everything else mostly intact. Careful and precise planning…" She said more to herself than to Rick.

"The extreme heat had to weaken the rest of building." He persisted.

Emily ignored his comment. "Not a lot of downtown buildings in California have basements like this, except historical buildings I suppose."

"Which means what?"

"I think the killer used this basement access into the building to move around and set up his elaborate trap."

Rick stared at her for a few tense moments, as if he pondered her revelation. "Then there should be an outside entrance. But we didn't see one."

"It's well hidden, but I know it's here. Look for an area that looks too tidy, or well-groomed, and I'll find the exit from this side." She explained.

Rick muttered something Emily couldn't quite hear, as he carefully retraced his steps above to the original entry point.

Emily took a deep reassuring breath, and hoped that her theory was correct.

She directed the flashlight beam from the dirt floor down a narrow hallway. Even though the building had burned recently, the basement still had the typical musty, damp smell.

Emily's skin felt clammy and chilled, as she moved slowly, and deeper into the underground passage. She was aware of the dirt floor, but could not see any visible footprints. Incredibly, it looked as if someone had prudently raked the floor.

Part of the basement had reinforced walls. The barriers steadily narrowed, and Emily couldn't tell what direction she headed. Keeping her focus on locating an exit, she tried not to let her mind fall prey to claustrophobia.

The flashlight flickered.

"Don't fail me now." Emily muttered.

A strange scraping sound reverberated along the long corridor. At first, it sounded like the building may just implode into itself. As she studied the noise further, it reminded her of an old squeaky gate at the entrance of a graveyard.

With a slight shiver, Emily kept moving forward toward the noise.

A slim ray of light crept into her immediate view, about twenty feet in front of her path. It did not light up the basement, but the illumination gave a little more visibility to the dank dwelling.

The screech ended with an odd plunking noise.

She quickened her pace, hobbling slightly as she went.

"Em?" Rick's body came into view, and he was dramatically backlit by the evening light. He looked like a hero coming to rescue her.

"I'm here."

Relived, Emily squeezed through the slim opening that was once an entrance to the underground room.

"You okay?" Rick examined her leg.

"I'm fine. I want to get more photos because the fall smashed the camera. Well... it actually broke my fall." She laughed. "Hopefully the internal card is still okay, but I want to be safe and get more photos."

Rick retrieved his cell phone and gave it to Emily. He grabbed her arm with his usual intensity. "You've got to be more careful."

Emily turned her full attention to him, even though her mind was several steps ahead in the investigation. "It's okay, I'm fine." She touched his cheek, and let it linger for a moment. "We would have never found out about this basement entrance if I had not fallen." She smiled.

"You always turn situations like this around to the case, instead of your safety."

Emily decided not to argue, but at moments like this, she realized how much she loved him. She didn't know what she would do without him.

She took his cell phone and photographed the underground entrance. Hidden by old grocery store pallets and crates, it took cover in plain view. With inside and outside shots, she retraced previously taken photos.

Emily now realized that she had one of the important missing pieces, but she just had to figure out which one.

CHAPTER TWELVE
Thursday 0130 Hours

Feeling like a teenager that had just sneaked out of his parent's house to go to a party, Timothy Devlin drove his car slowly down the dirt road. He relished the warm current pulsating throughout his body.

He needed warm flesh.

It was almost more than he could bear, but he kept everything under control because of the amazing rewards only minutes away. The hollow promises and compliments he had rehearsed relentlessly for the unsuspecting girl, shot through his memory with acute clarity.

Everything played out perfectly in his mind.

Casual greetings and nervous laughs pressed into his psyche.

He had once spoken to a therapist at the request of the court, during one of his trials, and she told him that he suffered from a borderline personality disorder compounded by an extremely immature outlook on life.

Whatever the hell that meant?

All he remembered from those meetings was that the therapist had fair-hair and a hot body, if only she was fifteen years younger, he might have done something about it. She had tried to get him to open up about his childhood and previous relationships.

So typical, when all else fails, ask about the childhood.

He slowed the car as the road narrowed slightly, and clicked up the headlights. The trees and bushes seemed to bend into the street with a macabre arch and claw, leaning toward the car, taunting him.

A little unsure if he should continue, Timothy decided to go for it, and punched the accelerator. The car lurched forward. The trees and brush scraped the sides of the car with a high-pitched tone. For a moment, he cringed, and pressed his back deeper into the seat half expecting something unearthly to creep into the vehicle.

Rolling down the window halfway, he took a breath of air. The breeze had a hint of humidity imbued with the autumn saturated earth. As he approached the location, he sighed with relief when the roadway widened again, as if to welcome him home after a long journey.

He had remembered the infamous barn. It was the remnant of another time, and it still stood vacant, and abandoned, as it had for so many years. It loomed, uninviting to visitors. It was a place for kids to party and hang out. Everyone knew about it, but no one really cared, until there was a murder a couple of years ago of a homeless man. Even that incident didn't provoke the county to tear it down.

The dirt road dipped as the car bounced from the deep potholes, and the narrow lane broke into a fork in the road. The unevenness worked in every direction. Both lanes looked the same, long forgotten and ignored.

Timothy pressed the brake; the car hummed an unusually high pitch and sputtered. He looked in each direction. Traveling left pointed toward the pond area, and heading right must lead up to the barn.

He contemplated his decision.

With a quick jerk, he turned the steering wheel to the right, and pressed down enthusiastically on the gas pedal. The engine hit another gear. The car lurched, tires spun slightly in the loose dirt and gravel, until traction took hold and then headed up the hill.

Once at the top of the hill, the landscape changed slightly. It transformed into an open and flat terrain. The trees and overgrown foliage were set back and away from the barn. Weeds had grown snugly around the structure, but a well-worn walkway from so many sets of footprints back and forth exposed the path.

Empty beer bottles and soda cans reflected supernaturally from the evening moon.

A single light shone from the second story of the barn. It flickered with a hypnotizing effect and seemed to become brighter when the wind blew through it.

Timothy eased the car up a little bit closer and cut the engine. He watched the upper open window, and strained to see anyone moving around before cutting the headlights.

What a perfect place to party.

He opened the car door and quickly stepped out. The ground had an unevenness as he stepped to the back of vehicle and popped the trunk.

His custom-made party kit.

The organized overnight bag consisted of, hard alcohol and beer, cocaine, blanket, condoms, and his secret weapon of *Rohypnol*. It had never failed him yet. He slipped the drugs into his pocket for the right time.

Grabbing the duffel bag, Timothy walked hurriedly to the barn entrance. The two large doors had been spray painted dozens of times, and the wood warped from age, giving it a secret clubhouse feeling.

The hinges creaked as he opened the right door. Once inside, more spray paint and useless profanity abounded, but there seven white candles were lit, sitting on a metal plate.

How cozy.

A thick layer of fresh hay littered the floor, up a ladder, and led to the loft… and to his prize.

"Hello?" He said with confidence.

A faint female voice replied, "I'm up here. C'mon up."

"I can't see you." Timothy scanned the view to capture a glimpse of the girl. She sounded cute and ready for him.

Again, she repeated, "C'mon up."

He stood for a moment. Usually, he would practically fall over his own feet to get to a party girl, but something felt different this time.

"Why are you hiding?" His voice didn't sound as confident as before.

"C'mon baby..." A brief few seconds passed before, "C'mon baby..." She repeated.

Timothy gave his caution a rest and walked directly to the ladder. Before he reached it, a loud crack clamped onto his left ankle with such a force, he instantly crumbled to the ground in agony. Flailing around in the newly dispersed hay, he groaned, screaming out in pain.

Blood darkened the straw beneath him.

He tried to direct his attention and to make sense of the situation between gasps. A bear trap, used primarily to catch large game, had caught him before he reached the ladder. Purposely set and strategically centered, it had waited for him. There was no doubt that it would take him down and hold him like a wild animal.

What the hell?

"Who are you?" He screeched. "I... I... need a doctor!" For the first time, he examined his ankle looking down at the shattered appendage, broken, cut deep to the bone, and gushing blood. "Please... why are you doing this?" His fearful thoughts turned to the possibility of a severed artery and dying in a couple of minutes.

A small tape recorder flew over the railing from above and landed next to him. Still running, it said... "C'mon baby... C'mon baby..." It kept repeating the same words, and sounded more like the rant of a crazy person with each fevered request.

"Help me!" Timothy screamed in agony.

The candles blew out.

Darkness fell over the interior of the barn.

Footsteps moved from one side of the loft to the other.

"Help! Help me! Please!" Timothy screamed.

* * * * *

Standing in the clearing, barely fifty feet away from the barn, a dark, slim figure watched. He observed the destruction as the light became brighter with profuse shades of yellow, orange, and red. It overflowed into the night. It burned bright and deep, cleansing away any remnant of what remained behind.

A new beginning would soon reveal itself.

The man pushed his hands deep into his coat pockets, nervously pressing the thumbs against the forefingers, each time with more force, staying in the moment, wanting to experience life dwindling from another person, but not just any person – *a sinner.*

The screaming had stopped. It was unclear if he still felt the scorching heat peel away his skin from the bones, or if he had succumbed to the smoke before the transformation occurred. The pleads and agonizing screams made it more enjoyable, but still, the outcome was always the same. A long, drawn out death, or a quick one, it did not matter.

The burning building captured the man's soul and deep seeded emotions with the hypnotizing and inviting spirits. It amazed him each time with a wondrous performance.

A sin repaid.

DEAD BURN

The arsonist patiently waited for a hidden message to exit from the fire to commend him on his sacrifices of righteousness, but it never did. He did not grow weary of waiting; it was only a matter of time. The deeds piled up, and once he reached the appointed number, the words would push him to the next level.

The flames gained an impressive momentum that engulfed the building, crashing and exploding inside with a magnificent symphony. It incinerated everything within its path, until it reached through the windows like fingertips from the afterlife, clawing for redemption, and some sign of recognition.

No one would grieve Timothy Devlin.

CHAPTER THIRTEEN
Thursday 1930 Hours

A camera flash illuminated the corner of the restaurant where a table of three friends congregated over drinks and dessert. Several more bursts from the camera phone in rapid succession finished the impromptu photo shoot.

"Knock it off Jordan." Rick grimaced and rubbed his eyes.

"What?" Jordan smirked as he scrolled through the images on his camera phone. "Rick you take really nice photos, even with a nasty scowl on your face. We're talking high fashion model here."

"Take another photo and I'll break your phone."

"Ricky...Ricky... after everything we've been through?"

Emily interrupted. "I almost forgot. I have something for you Jordan."

"Me?" His voice raised an octave.

"Don't get too excited." She reached into her leather handbag, and retrieved a flat white box with a red ribbon tied around it.

"Wow, you really shouldn't have." Jordan replied dramatically.

She handed the box to him. "Don't open it here, it's the device I was telling you about from the fire scene."

"It might be over his head. Maybe we need to send it to an expert." Rick interjected with a half-smile on his face.

Jordan took the box and held it close like a child not wanting to give up a toy. "I'm hurt. I'll take a look when I get home, and give you my *professional* diagnosis." He beamed the usual toothy grin.

The waiter stopped at their table. "Would anyone like another cocktail?"

"Please." Jordan quickly piped up. "All around, thank you." He tossed a hundred dollar bill on the table.

The waiter smiled, gave a courteous nod to the group, and left to get their orders.

Jordan searched his phone using the touchpad, and brought up some of the photos that Emily had taken at the crime scene. "I've been thinking…"

Rick grunted in annoyance.

"I have been thinking… that this crime scene doesn't have the usual MO that most burn scenes have…" He lowered his voice. "This guy…"

"We don't know it's a man." Rick interrupted.

Emily said, "We'll just assume for now that it's a man, until evidence dictates otherwise."

"Thank you." Jordan continued, "*Anyway*, most arsonists are angry and retaliatory in nature. Right? Basically, they are people just pissed off at the world around them. But this guy, a totally different serial anomaly."

Emily listened and she knew that they were on the same page. "The only motive or purpose that seems to fit from all the crime scenes is that he's choosing his victims selectively."

"What's the worst kind of criminal?" Emily watched the two men.

"Child molesters and murderers." Rick stated. He paused a moment and then said, "What about any other high-profile cases tried in the media?"

Jordan added. "Like the Devlin case. He's a serial criminal that rapes, tortures…"

"And..." Emily added. "Anyone who helps the perps, like attorneys, special interest groups, judges, social workers."

A young cocktail waitress arrived with their drinks on a tray. She smiled and swiftly served their drinks.

"Thank you." Jordan smiled.

Emily took a sip of her drink, wrinkled her forehead. The alcohol was distinctly stronger than the last cocktail. She quickly focused back to her train of thought.

Leaning forward at Jordan, she continued. "I forwarded you my profile, new findings, and questions about the latest scene."

"Got them."

"What confuses me are the fire patterns, and how it could burn so hot, and just destroy the one and a half rooms." Emily mused.

Rick explained. "Usually you can detect some type of accelerant, or find pieces of the incendiary device, but there was nothing."

"There wasn't any unusual odor that would indicate a controlled burn or accelerants." She leaned back in her chair. "I know that there's something that we're missing."

"Hmmm... a case that Emily Stone can't crack." Jordan laughed.

"Yeah, well, more people are going to die if we can't figure it out." She looked seriously at Jordan, right eyebrow raised. "You still have contacts at the courthouse?"

"Sure, why?"

Rick took Emily's hand, and squeezed it gently. "It would probably be a good idea to find a casual way to warn the judge and prosecutor in that Devlin case. Just as a precaution."

"Will do..." Jordan turned his attention to Emily again. "I briefly went over your notes and photos. There was something unusual at the scene."

Emily took another sip of her drink. "What's that?"

"The shoe prints. I know they were muddled, but there was one set of work boots that seemed to be distinctly apart from the others." He laughed. "I know that's like a needle in a haystack, but it still bothers me."

Rick didn't make eye contact with Jordan, he stared at Emily. "You think that it was someone impersonating a firefighter, moving through the crime scene where no one would notice."

"Something like that..." Jordan downed the rest of his drink.

"The cops only have bits and pieces of the body, and very little to go on from the actual fire." Emily's mind spun. "Is there a solid way to connect the evidence? All of the forensics and behavioral evidence in order to flush out the killer?"

"We'll just keep digging until we do." Jordan replied.

The group sat silent for several moments.

Emily let out a sigh. "I don't know about you guys, but I'm exhausted.

Rick pushed back his chair. "It's time to get home and get some sleep."

"Oh, yeah, sleep..." Jordan said with a sarcastic tone and a dramatic roll of the eyes.

"Jordan are you ever going to get a girlfriend?" Rick equaled his mocking tone.

The group stood up to leave.

"Yeah, well, most of the women I know can't handle me." Jordan grumbled.

Emily grabbed her bag and slung it over her shoulder. "One of these days Jordan..." She patted him on the shoulder in a friendly gesture.

Rick headed out of the restaurant first, followed by Emily and Jordan.

Jordan slipped his arm around Emily's, and spoke directly into her ear. "I have something for you." He padded his hand into hers. "It's a little something that will help you, if you're ever lost."

"What?" Emily looked in her hand, and revealed a silver locket in the shape of a heart on an intricate chain. She looked at him with a blank expression.

He laughed. "It's a tracking device. You don't have to worry about activating it. It's always emitting a low signal." He tapped his cell phone. "I can track you with a simple application. It is something I'm working on to take to a big company. Cool huh?"

"Thanks Jordan." Emily smiled, and thought it was a nice quality for the jewelry version of a low jack. She slipped it into her jacket pocket.

* * * * *

As they drove slowly down the quiet street, the evening remained serene and dark, and the only lights illuminating were motion lights affixed to neighbor's houses. Most residences had at least one car parked in front of the house as well as one in the driveway.

Rick eased the Explorer into the driveway and cut the engine.

Emily jumped out of the vehicle, and proceeded up the cobblestone walkway when Rick caught her around the waist, pulling her close to his body. She returned the affection, leaned in and kissed him. They lingered for a moment enjoying each other, the warmth of their bodies, and the quiet moment on a clear, crisp evening.

"You managed to make it through another dinner with Jordan." Emily teased.

"I'll let you in on a secret."

She nuzzled his neck. "And?"

"I really don't mind him, he's like some of those stand-up comedians that you flip by on the television, but you wind up watching them eventually."

Laughing, Emily replied. "He is, isn't he?"

Rick kissed her again.

A deep dog bark boomed from inside the house. It continued in rapid succession.

"Oh, I left my purse in the car." She wiggled out of Rick's comfortable embrace.

He tossed her the car keys. "See you inside. I better go and let Sarge out before he tears down the door."

Emily walked back to the car and opened the passenger door. As she reached inside to retrieve her purse, the low glow of Rick's cell phone caught her attention. It had fallen out of his pocket and now rested on the seat. She quickly picked it up, and saw a recent text from a local law enforcement agency that read: *Nothing new to report on escape of Leo Brown*

Emily stood up straight, still staring at the phone screen, dumbfounded, which quickly turned to anger.

How could Rick have kept this from her?

The man responsible for several deaths that almost cost her life, not to mention the man who killed her parents when she was twelve years old, was out roaming free to kill again.

So many questions rifled through her mind with lightning speed.

When?

How?

A crash from inside interrupted her endless loop of irritation. "Sarge..." She mumbled. Rick and the dog were probably roughhousing again, she thought to herself.

Emily grabbed her purse, slammed the door shut, and engaged the locking mechanism before returning to the house.

Still reading the message, Emily pushed through the front door, walked over the threshold, and demanded, "Leo's not in prison? Why didn't you tell me?"

The house sat quiet.

"Where are you guys?" Her voice confronted.

Emily stomped into the living room, when an intense pressure squeezed her neck and upper right arm. Her breath caught in her throat, chest tightened, just as she fell to the floor, in what seemed like, extreme slow motion. Her vision dimmed, wavered in and out, as the room spun like a carnival ride with a sickening ripple effect.

She heard two, maybe three men, talking in low tones as they stood over her with authority and confidence. She could not see them, and had no way of knowing if they were young or old, cops or burglars. The last thought that muddled through her mind was of Rick and Sarge, before she succumbed to unconsciousness.

Everything went black.

CHAPTER FOURTEEN
Friday 0830 Hours

What had once been a large barn sitting on top of a beautiful hill, now smoldered with lingering smoke billowing in low clouds. A few surrounding trees with scorched leaves, and gnarled trunks, made the entire site chilling. It sparked a supernatural scene that inspired urban legends.

Detective Bobby Duncan stood twenty feet from the scene, uncomfortable and stressed, as usual. He watched the crime scene techs methodically sift, search, and photograph any item from the debris that did not belong at the location. The seasoned detective hoped to find some truth this time, and some solid answers before the next one.

The secured area doubled the size of the standard fire crime scene. At least until it was determined an arson act or not. Due to lack of evidence from previous scenes, Duncan decided to extend the search area this time.

The burnt body freshly extracted from the center of the structure, shrouded in a black body bag, was laid to rest on the gurney.

The detective did not need to see the body; he knew the typical conditions of the charred form, contorted in a ghastly manner, teeth and bones protruding in between any skin that had not burned completely off the body. Sometimes, enough grisly matter oozed from the victim, which transformed into sickening chunks. This condition made the body appear mannequin-like, or something that would be dangling during a haunted house ride.

These images made the long, two and half decades as a cop, still shocking to the detective. No matter what any cop

91

conveyed about homicide investigations, there were always murders and crime scenes, so disturbing, that it couldn't be erased from memory.

The wheels of the gurney screeched and churned in the uneven dirt pathway as two coroner technicians maneuvered the metal contraption to the van.

Evidence markers scattered over dozens of areas around the location. Every item with an identifying number that coincided with pieces of evidence discovered, photographed, and collected. Some burnt fragments deposited into containers, jars, and plastic bags filled the forensic van.

The mood and energy remained somber and quiet. Each technician worked diligently and there was little conversation, which usually consisted of casual topics to lighten the attitude of the team.

Moving with the great effort of an overweight physique, breathing heavy, Duncan wanted a closer look to determine, and possible locate, anything that hid underneath the body. He puffed for breath, not because of increasing anxiety or overexertion, but for the sheer effort of the extra bulk taxing his middle-aged body.

The large bear trap, mostly intact, extracted carefully from the ashes, made the detective ponder. It wasn't clear if the victim was caught accidently in the device, part of a killer's plan, or if it was just another item from inside the barn.

The first thing he noticed about the crime scene was that it differed from the others, this time the entire structure burned.

Could he be changing his M.O.?

Was his psychological need escalating into something else?

Duncan knew in his gut that it was the same perpetrator as the other arson sites over the past several years.

So many questions lingered and haunted him, day and night. Chasing after a serial killer was not anything new to the detective. In fact, he gave talks and workshops based on some of his previous solved serial cases. There was always a thirst in the law enforcement community for answers, and for new insights into solving serial murder cases.

Duncan distanced himself from other detectives on a certain level. He had a secret that he couldn't tell anyone at the department, or even anyone in his personal life. A phantom investigator sent him anonymous emails with information about various serial cases. It wasn't idle gossip among the blue code, but a real vigilante detective that provided evidence. He had met her in person, almost two years ago, and everything changed. It transformed how he conducted his investigations, how he looked at evidence, and ultimately, the closed murder cases steadily increased at the police department. He felt a sense of pride and admiration for Emily Stone, and protected her identity at all costs.

Even with a potential hovering angel at the crime scene investigations, it still didn't ease the detective's mind about the arsonist. He checked his phone with regularity, waiting for some piece of evidence, or in-depth profile to solve his problem – but nothing came.

Kneeling slowly at the exact location where the body was discovered, he took a ballpoint pen from his top pocket, and moved some of the ashes with a circular motion. Not expecting to see the final puzzle piece that would break the case wide open, but he wanted to make some sense out of the scene.

Why this barn?

Did the victim know the killer?

"Haven't solved this case yet?" The voice came from behind the detective.

Duncan grunted before he hoisted his cumbersome body in an upright position again, not showing the sharp pain he felt in his knees. He knew the voice, which had a hint of sarcasm infused into a perfectly innocent question.

The detective turned to face Lance Myers, the arson investigator. "Just making sure you don't get *all* the glory."

"This one is different." The tall, extra lean investigator stated as he casually looked around. He towered over the police detective. Both professionals looked like the perfect odd couple.

"Accelerant?" Duncan asked.

"Yep. Won't know the exact chemical components, but my guess, it was gasoline used in the loft area."

"What's his motive?" The detective asked rhetorically rather than waiting for answer.

"That's your job detective." Myers scoffed. "You'll get my report." He walked away without another word.

It unnerved the detective that an investigator with little experience, about eighty hours to receive certification, made him feel unworthy of solving an arson case. He watched two technicians chat for a moment. Suddenly he barked out orders to them in frustration. "I want everything gone over twice, everything needs to be documented! Now!"

The two forensic techs jumped at his deep tone, kept their eyes down, and stepped with great care around the area in order to finish their duties.

Duncan retrieved his cell phone from his pocket, agitated, anxious, and annoyed with his progress. He stared at the screen. It was still the same - no messages.

CHAPTER FIFTEEN
Friday 0945 Hours

The silence inundated Emily's ears as she awoke and found herself lying on a king size bed, all alone, in a colorless room. Slowly rolling to the side, she swung her legs over the edge of the bed and gently sat up. Wavering as she strained to focus on the room.

White imprisoned the comfortable bedroom. The bedspread, pillows, two nightstands, tall dresser, small round table with a scarf draped, and the ornate closet doors shared the same starkness. If it were not for the high priced pieces of furniture professionally arranged, the room could easily double as a cell for the criminally insane.

Extreme nausea washed over her, lobbying from her head to her stomach. Her eyes, dry, and with each blink made the room appear grainy and impressionistic.

She wiped her forehead with the back of her hand. Her skin felt damp to the touch. The black t-shirt she wore felt cool, wrinkled, and her jeans looked like someone else had dressed her. The urge to take a long, hot shower overpowered her, as her stomach grumbled with the same emptiness as the room.

The events of the previous night knitted its way into the daylight.

Dinner with Rick and Jordan, and then she arrived at home. She remembered her conversations, along with details discussed of the last arson scene.

She ran her hand down her right leg and could feel the tenderness of the bruises from the fall at the burn site.

A raging headache ensued. The harder she tried to remember, the more pain it caused.

Emily stood up, faltered from side to side, before she sprinted for the bathroom. Within seconds, she heaved several times until her stomach was completely empty and her muscles left sore.

Overpowered and drugged in her home, the thought made her angry. Her hands shook slightly, along with a dizziness, which seemed a side effect as the drugs left her system.

She sat down on the bathroom tile, waited for the spinning to stop, and noticed that she was barefoot. Strapped tightly around her left ankle was a tracking device, similar to the ones used for house arrest. It was a small black box, the size of a matchbook with a tightly interlocked strap.

It seemed futile to try to pry it loose.

A green light blinked every two seconds.

Emily watched her ankle accessory, hypnotized by the exact timing. She wondered what would happen if it changed to red.

She stood up, using the wall to steady herself. As she positioned her body in front of a white pedestal sink, she splashed water on her face and gargled with the cool water. She saw her reflection staring back. Gaunt, haunted, with a hint of fear, was the expression that filled the center of the mirror. Dark circles under her brown eyes enhanced the petite features of her face, and accented the subtle battle scar she wore on her cheek. It was a constant reminder of the danger she put herself in to rescue a child.

Emily splashed more water on her face, running her fingertips through her hair. It didn't help her appearance much, but she managed to steady her floating nausea, and began to feel better.

She rejected the obvious thoughts.

Where was Rick?

Was he okay?

Denial in her line of work was useful because it allowed her to focus on stressful situations without any unnecessary conflicts – at least for a short period of time.

Feeling more human and present of mind, Emily approached the bedroom door. Her hand turned the knob.

It was unlocked.

She half expected to hear a blazing alarm, along with a crew of armed guards to burst into the room.

It remained unusually quiet.

She pulled the door open.

For the first time since she awoke, it felt strange to be barefooted. The bedroom carpet felt plush, until she stepped into the hallway where the cool tile was accented by European rugs. The smooth tile pressed against the balls of her feet as she warily stepped down the long hallway.

Absent of her usual arsenal of weapons, feeling vulnerable. Emily steadily, but cautiously, walked toward the large room not knowing what, or who to expect.

Cameras installed at various angles above the crown molding tracked her movements. Emily counted six. She kept moving forward.

Silence escorted her.

She stood at a threshold that opened into a large living room area. Heavy European furniture rambled out in front of her.

Quickly discerning her self-defense options, Emily took a mental inventory of the accessories of lamps, candlesticks, and interesting knick-knacks.

Quickly she rushed through the room toward an outside door, which led out into a large patio. Before she could reach the glass French door, the locks engaged automatically with a harsh clunking sound. She tried the door anyway, but it remained locked.

Before she grabbed a silver candlestick to smash the door, the distinct click of a firearm hammer cocked in her ear.

"Put it back." A monotone voice ordered.

Her heart sank as another wave of nausea caught her by surprise. She gently put the candle stand back down on the end table, and turned her head in the direction of the voice.

With a quick wave of the gun, the severe looking man dressed completely in black said, "Sit down."

Emily knew the man would kill her without any hesitation, and no one would ever find her body. He never took his gaze from her, but it was difficult to get a solid read on him. It meant only one thing; the man knew psychology or had psychopathic tendencies. Her guess, he was a hit man, or some type of specialized security guard.

Emily's mind spun in so many directions as she sat down on the sofa.

Another middle-aged, extremely severe looking man entered, carrying a tray. "Ms. Stone, nice to see that you're awake." He set down the plate with a tall glass of orange juice and a buttered bagel.

"Who are you?" Emily wanted immediate answers. "Where's Rick?"

"Slow down Ms. Stone. One thing at a time." He smiled like a snake with a devious secret.

"Why am I here?" Emily noticed another heavyset man loitering on the far side of the room within earshot; no doubt, her host had more than one hired gun at his disposal.

"My name is Mr. Bishop and you've already met Red." He gestured to the man in black. "Well, maybe you don't remember you're first introduction to him." He took a seat across from her.

"Why am I here?" Emily was scared, but her anger tried to disguise the fear. She struggled desperately not to show any vulnerability.

"Ms. Stone I have wanted to meet you for quite some time. You're not an easy person to find... since you've been very, very busy." He never looked away from Emily as he spoke. His eyes flat, dense, as he stared right through her. He gestured to Red.

Emily didn't believe that her life was in immediate danger, but there was something terrible that she was about to learn. Her body chilled just below the surface. Call it an instinct of a former cop, but she had been outmaneuvered, and would soon pay a high price for her mistake.

Red holstered his gun under his leather jacket, walked toward a tall cabinet, and slid open the top portion to reveal a large flat screen television. In a few seconds, the display showed a photograph of Emily when she was a deputy sheriff in Indiana. A serious expression painted on her face, hair pulled tightly back, eyes eager to make a difference, and all from a rookie's naïve perspective.

Bishop stood up and dramatically wandered the room as if making sure he would hit his marks in a well-rehearsed movie scene. It was clear that he was going to tell a story. It was going to be a tale that Emily didn't want to hear.

He began, "You see, as you probably know, every single law enforcement agency in the United States report their crime statistics to the government. Every crime incident, every arrest, and every solved case in order to record and analyze crime statistics." The older man who seemed to control his deep seeded anger smiled at Emily. He continued. "Something interesting has happened here in California over the past few years. Do you know what that is Emily?"

Emily sat motionless and quiet, as she narrowed her eyes in extreme focus. Her adrenaline radically pumped every ounce of energy she had left.

"There was a spike in *solved* serial cases and child abductions. Much more than statistically possible. Now, it's been long documented that the average murder, solve rate is around fifty percent, and usually less for any given department."

Red stood quietly. He stared emotionless at Emily.

Emily didn't know which man was more dangerous. Both men ticked all the right boxes for the psychopathy checklist used to evaluate incarcerated offenders. Red unnerved her, and Mr. Bishop reminded her of the quiet man next door that had fifty bodies buried in the basement.

Bishop smiled. "So I did some digging, and you know what I found?"

Emily gritted her teeth and took slow deliberate breaths.

He nodded once again toward Red.

The television screen flashed through photographs taken from satellite images and other security cameras of both Emily and Rick. Some of the pictures showed them searching remote areas, while others were of them entering into various buildings and conducting basic surveillance.

It shocked Emily to see her covert investigations documented. A new perspective of her life's work emerged. Seeing it in black and white made everything surreal and unbelievable, it probed through a hidden eye instead of from her own personal view.

"I found you shadowing the investigations and helping the police. Quite impressively, I have to admit. Of course, not one detective ever refused your assistance, even though they didn't know where the information was coming from. But of course, you weren't acting on their behalf, so they could use your evidence legally." He sat back down in front of Emily, leaning back in the grand chair. "So pathetic cops are, but you... you are a different breed. I have never met anyone like you, with such drive and dedication. Not wanting any recognition, or money, for your good deeds." He turned to look his associate. "Interesting... isn't it Red?"

The hit man looked bored with the entire scenario.

Emily's nerves and anger had reached its limit. To Bishop, she demanded. "What do you want from me?"

"I want you to work for me."

More photos flashed on the screen. Some were close up shots of Emily's face, somber and fierce, as she worked the grid of a murder dumping ground.

"What do you mean?" She tried not to let her panic override her demand.

"You've probably figured out that Red here does a variety of contract work, and he's very good at it." He leaned forward. "I need someone like you to compliment *his* work, and he's so graciously accepted the task to be your mentor."

"It's never going to happen." Emily felt sick at her stomach, an uncomfortable churning. She wasn't sure if it was the aftereffects of the drug in her system, or the thought of being a hired killer.

He laughed, a broad, deep belly laugh. "I hoped you would say that." Like a sudden flip of light switch, his face turned taunt and serious.

She watched Red go to a desk near the window, and he picked up a laptop computer. He walked up to Emily, flipped it open on the coffee table, and turned the screen toward her.

Emily gasped in horror. She leaped up and lunged at Bishop just as a searing pain pierced her left ankle. She crumbled to the floor in misery. The agonizing burn teleported up her leg, and immediately caused her stomach to contract. Her breath stayed trapped in her belly.

"Don't forget, I know *everything* about you." Bishop said as he kneeled on the floor next to Emily. He showed her a remote in his hand. "This is the one time where you can't fight your way out of it." He grabbed hold of her hair and forced her to look at the screen. "You will do *exactly* what I say."

Emily saw every horrifying detail in real time. The live video recorded from a small room that looked more like an archaic prison cell. Rick sat helpless and strapped to a chair. A dark bruise had begun to appear on his jaw and cheekbone, accompanied by dried blood staining his nose, side of his right eye, and mouth.

A man's back stepped into camera view. Careful to remain away from his victim's sight, as he slammed his fist into Rick's face. The pain and anguish captured with every shocking detail on the remote webcam. The torturer's identity conveniently remained out of view, while he roughly shoved a hood over Rick's head that ended the beating.

CHAPTER SIXTEEN
Friday 1145 Hours

The distinct metallic taste spilled into his mouth as parts of Rick's body went numb from the fierce beating and tightened restraints. He knew that his nose was broken, but that was the least of his worries.

Every nightmare scenario of what had happened to Emily, where she was, continually pushed its way to the forefront of his mind. Despite how heinous it was to imagine, it kept him acutely aware of everything around him. If he were to survive, he was going to have to stay focused.

Even from inside a canvas hood, the room's rank odor of body waste and rotten garbage came in repulsive waves. Rick swallowed frequently to keep from retching.

The most important mind control to uphold in desperate situations was to remain calm, and keep the psyche absent of any unnecessary thoughts and feelings. Solid judgment and options depended upon a clear head – easier said than done.

It was exceedingly difficult, but Rick switched psychological gears and began to retrace the entire experience from the previous evening, starting with dinner. Gently clearing his mind of thoughts of Emily, he pieced together the previous evening's events in a cohesive sequence.

Arriving home after dinner, he had entered the house to let Sarge outside, but noticed that the dog was locked in the bathroom. Before he could investigate, his arms were forcibly wrenched behind his back and securely tied, his body slammed down, and his head held against the hardwood floor. Instantly a gag pushed into his mouth and tape over his eyes.

He didn't have time to react, or fight back. The person that ambushed him was a pro, and knew exactly when and how to act.

The events turned to a speeding blur after that, but he had managed to stay conscious as he rode silently in some type of cargo van. He never heard Emily, or felt her next to him. He wasn't sure if she was even in the same van.

Counting quietly in his head, he managed to estimate that it took thirty minutes to arrive at the current location. The van drove constantly and only stopped a few times, which meant that he travelled most of the journey on the freeway, about thirty to forty miles.

What Rick didn't know was which direction he had gone. He envisioned possible scenarios, and came up with either the direction of north or east from his home. It was one of the two disturbing theories; he would be a murder victim, and dumped at a remote location, or held as a prisoner.

The locks rattled at his cell door.

He heard his captor enter again.

Rick braced for another beating, or the final bullet. Instead, the unknown assailant released him from the chair and shackled him with prison issue restraints. Without a word, the captor blindfolded Rick and ushered him out of the room. It took a few minutes before he was loaded into another vehicle. He held his breath, counted the travel time, and listened for anything that would give him some solid answers.

* * * * *

Red helped Emily to her feet. It was as if he had lost the art of speech, and was an android going through the motions for his master.

Silent.

Intense.

104

Red's hands were strong as he kept hold of her arm and guided her from the living room. Emily could smell the subtle fragrance of his spicy soap mixed with the aroma of the leather jacket he wore. She had the feeling that he had only black clothes in his closet, so it made it easy to throw on something coordinated every day.

The pain subsided from her ankle and leg, but it still managed to cause her difficulty in balance and coordination. Anger reverberated throughout her body, while anxious thoughts came flooding back.

How could she have been so careless?
Would she be able to find Rick?
What about Jordan?

She hobbled back toward the bedroom where she had emerged a half hour earlier. There were white bath towels, miscellaneous toiletries, including a toothbrush, toothpaste, hairbrush, and as well as her shoes and jacket laid out on the bed.

"You have fifteen minutes to take a shower and get ready." Red spoke and stared directly at her.

Emily knew that she couldn't challenge the assassin, especially in her condition. She didn't have any other choice but to grab everything, limping toward bathroom.

Red followed.

"I think I can handle this by myself." Emily said as she tried to shut the door.

Red blocked the door. "Fourteen minutes."

"Fine."

Emily undressed as Red stood guard at the doorway. He didn't look at her directly, but she knew that if she tried to escape, or got the upper hand, he would do whatever was necessary to stop her. She used her time wisely and mindfully examined her available options.

She hoped that time was on her side.

* * * * *

Jordan drove down the main boulevard to his next security meeting with an up and coming rock musician, and his wannabe, supermodel girlfriend. So cliché, he thought. He had been referred by another one of his other clients, sworn to secrecy, and promised a hefty fee for the job.

As usual whenever Jordan was stuck in traffic, annoyed by bad drivers cutting him off, or wasn't focused on the security layout of a home or business, he thought of Emily. It was stupid to think that she would drop Rick and run into his arms. He knew it would never happen, but still, it made for nice mini vacation during his boring days.

With roadwork up ahead, he sat in a lane directed by an inept flagger.

Jordan pushed one of the memory buttons on his cell phone.

The phone rang three times, then an electronic voice said, "Please leave a message." Beep.

"Hey Em, just touching base. I had some more thoughts on the burn scene that I want to run by you. Also had a chance to look at the black box too. Call me, or text me. Bye."

Jordan was disappointed, but knew he would hear from her soon. Out of curiosity, he pressed the cell phone tracking app to find out where she was at the moment. The software still had a few glitches and updates needed, but it eventually directed the smiling face icon to the vicinity of the intended target. It zeroed in on the closest location.

The software locked onto a position and gave the closest address.

Jordan erratically pulled his car to the side of the road and stopped. He ignored the honks as a couple of ticked off motorists gave him the middle finger, and then drove on through the busy intersection.

He double-checked the address again. He punched a few more keys. It produced the same result.

"What the hell?" Jordan's heart rate increased, hammering in his ears. He actually felt sick in the pit of his stomach.

His new phone application clearly read out the address of Mr. Bishop's estate, where he had been earlier in the week.

CHAPTER SEVENTEEN
Friday 1245 Hours

Emily sat in silence as Red drove toward the downtown area. She felt much better after a hot shower, but her spirits still plummeted as she watched the occupants of the cars pass by on the freeway. She wondered about their lives, friends, family, what they did for a living, and how they most likely did not realize how lucky they were to have structure and security – sanity without imminent danger.

It was the first time in Emily's life that she experienced real defeat when lives were at stake, not only Rick's life, but the unsuspecting target. If she weren't so outraged by the entire situation, she would break down and cry, and probably wouldn't be able to make the tears stop for days. But, she maintained her composure and kept calm, mind alert.

Emily glanced at Red. Quiet, severe, hands perfectly placed on the steering wheel as he weaved in and out of traffic. Her handler looked in his mid-fifties, lean, no doubt an expert in weapons and hand-to-hand combat, extremely focused to the point of obsessiveness, and he obviously hated his current assignment of babysitting her. He was capable of killing a person, probably in mere seconds; this man now had Rick's life in his hands. He would look for any excuse to kill her.

As a guess, Emily mused over in her mind that this man hated Mr. Bishop too. Taking orders from a man that looked down upon most of society. She saw a few subtle twitches when Bishop asked him to do something. She had to figure out a way to play one against the other.

She tried to gain more of a personal profile on the assassin to find any weakness that would benefit her situation. His extremely subtle actions, clenched jaw, few words spoken, showed that he believed in strong convictions. He had some integrity too, in that he didn't ogle her naked body in the bathroom.

Emily searched him from her peripheral vision and ran familiar profiles in her mind, but found nothing that proved hopeful in her experience.

She didn't know where they were headed, only that it was her first killing assignment. At least she had some time to figure out how to save the intended target, and find out where Rick was held captive.

The simple fact was if she didn't complete the assignment, Rick was dead.

The delicate balance of lives weighed on Emily's every move.

Red eased the car into the far right lane, carefully merging in front of cars, then exited, and made a left under the overpass, heading west.

Emily noticed a sign indicating the Amtrak train station with additional parking about a mile up ahead.

Red parked.

For the first time since the drive, he looked at Emily. Cold grey eyes without an ounce of fear or uncertainty behind them, scrutinized her actions. The man behaved like a well-practiced killer, and he had the resume to prove it.

Emily asked, "Where are we going?"

"San Diego." He replied flatly.

It surprised Emily that they would take a train instead of driving, or flying.

Red unhooked Emily's seatbelt. He ran his hands down her left leg. As a reflex, she grabbed hold of his hand and began to struggle with him.

"Do you want your ankle cuff taken off or not?" He snapped with annoyance.

Emily stopped reacting. "What do you think?" She scoffed at him.

"Give me your foot."

Emily complied. She pushed her foot in his direction. Red quickly used a special key device, releasing the anklet. Instantly, her leg felt better without the tight restraint. She massaged her tender ankle and her entire leg actually felt lighter.

Red leaned close to Emily. She felt his breath on her neck. "If you try to escape or do anything that I don't like, he's dead. Understand?"

His voice reflected a monotone that hit all her senses at once, down to her primal core. She knew he wasn't threatening her; he would kill without any hesitation due to years of expert practice and conditioning.

"Understand?" Red said again. He waited for her answer.

Emily's heart sank at the mention of Rick. "Yes."

"Get out." He grabbed the device and opened his door.

The wind had picked up, sending a chill down Emily's spine. The coldness in the air with the combination of her damp hair made her shiver. She stuck her hands in her jacket pockets. Her fingertips touched the cool silver pendant that Jordan had given her at dinner. She gently wrapped her fingers around the piece of jewelry like a lifeline. Of course, she thought to herself, Jordan would know something was wrong when he couldn't get a hold of her or Rick. Jordan's clever tracking device would eventually force him into some type of plan to action.

Emily's optimism rose.

She watched Red take one small carry on suitcase and a metal briefcase from the trunk, before slamming it shut.

110

He walked briskly toward the Amtrak entrance, not bothering to wait for Emily, or explaining anything further. He expected her to follow.

The electric doors whooshed open as Emily trailed the assassin inside where people patiently waited on uncomfortable benches. Most were lost in newspapers or electronic e-readers, and didn't pay any attention to the unlikely couple.

An uneasy pang rose in Emily's fight or flight response, which caused her muscles to twitch and an unsteady dizziness to emerge. Her vision dimmed making the angled corners of the room appear warped. It took every ounce of courage and determination not to turn and run. It had deadly consequences.

Emily stood next to Red as he retrieved two tickets from inside his jacket, ready for immediate boarding.

A printed sign on a silver stand next to the exit door read: Coast Starlight departing 1:00pm.

Emily had never been on a train before and it made her situation seem more surreal. As she casually glanced around, she noticed commuters and vacationers. Everyone busy with their own itineraries. No one bothered to look in Emily's direction, but she felt conspicuous to everyone around her.

The conductor looked at their tickets. He politely directed Red and Emily to the designated area, which occupied the private sleeping cars.

Red motioned for Emily to climb the steps and board the train ahead of him. She felt his eyes surveying everything around them, and then his gaze settled on the direction of the narrow hallway ahead. To the left and down below were for some travellers and handicapped passengers. They moved steady through the car that occupied several sleeping rooms, with two or four seats facing one another.

People settled into the cramped quarters and chattered incessantly.

Red took Emily's arm, guided her to compartment #16, and gently pushed her inside the room. Immediately shutting the door, he secured the two small pieces of luggage.

"Sit down." He ordered.

Emily took a seat to gaze out the window at the flatness of the land, which had only slight rolling hills of a dry and brittle landscape. It was difficult to believe that during the rainy season the same area would be green and lush, and full of native wildlife. For now, it resembled how Emily felt inside, lost, forgotten, and in desperate need of a miracle.

Red checked everything inside the quarters, every compartment, and every amenity from coat hangers to the daily newspaper. After he was satisfied, he sat down across from her.

Emily fidgeted in her seat. Her knees barely inches away from her captor, moved from side to side. The room's already tight depth shrank, the generous length of six feet seemed to morph into a coffin-like facade. Her covert work and demanding investigations had turned into something she had never imagined, a tomb aboard a train, heading to a murder assignment.

The train lurched. It settled into a slow mode as it left the station. The engines grinded before it caught the correct gear, quickly building momentum. The ride was surprisingly smooth and the vista looked more inhabitable when they moved away.

Emily interrupted the silence, "I'm thirsty."

Red stared at her, but remained quiet. She couldn't get a read on his reaction, eyes cold and without lack of any expression, or a facial muscle movement. Her advantage and chance for escape rested on being able to read him.

"I'm dehydrated. I need to get some juice or water, or something." She persisted.

He looked out the window as the train gained speed. "Go ahead."

"I need some money." She held out her hand.

Completely irritated with Emily's request, he dug into his pocket and pulled out a couple of five-dollar bills. He finally showed some emotion, which lent to the distaste of babysitting.

"Thanks." Emily rose to leave the compartment. She was surprised that Red didn't attach himself to her, but rather, he continued to look out the window even as she closed the door.

Once in the hallway, her feet glued to the floor, Emily didn't know which direction to proceed. She figured that the dining car should be toward the front of the train. She willed her legs to carry her.

Moving through the cars, she glanced at the passenger's faces, some serene and eager, while others were uncertain and questionable. Everyone had a story. Emily's story unraveled more like a movie, than real life.

A group of teenage girls, giggling while texting on cell phones, entered from the adjacent car, blocking the passage for anyone else. It took Emily a couple of steps to maneuver around the gossiping girls.

Suddenly the train cut its speed rapidly and slowed down. All travellers who weren't sitting, ended up thrown to one side, or in an unsuspecting passenger's lap. Two girls lost their balance, tumbled to the floor, backpacks and purses with all of the personal contents rocketed to the other side of car. Pens, books, lipsticks and other items clattered with a musical tone in between the seats.

Emily regained her balance and eyed a hot pink cell phone neatly tucked under an empty seat. She leaned down and covertly pocketed the phone. No one paid her any attention as the commotion ensued. She had some ammunition now, quickly moving on to find a quiet place to send a text to Jordan.

Emily took the stairs leading toward the changing rooms, and swiftly shut the door behind her. Her hands shook as she pushed the buttons through all the messages and goofy photos of teenagers.

As she began to punch in Jordan's number, the door flew open, and all she could see at first was a black blur. No outline, just a force that didn't appear to be human.

The pink phone smashed against the barrier. Bits and pieces hit all four walls at once.

The air seemed to disappear from Emily's lungs as she found herself pinned halfway on the floor of the small room. Red expertly held her against the wall with his thumb at her throat. His eyes raged like a predator staring at his prey, just before the fatal attack. The assassin bore down and paralyzed her with his excessive strength.

Red showed his own cell phone screen with a message directly at Emily's view. He read the glaring words to her with conviction in his voice. "He's dead."

CHAPTER EIGHTEEN
Friday 0145 Hours

His exhalations inside the hood made it almost impossible to breathe in a relaxed manner, the air restriction and stiltedness contorted in his lungs. The rise and fall of dizziness swept over him, and the general overall weakness of hunger made him fight even harder to concentrate.

It had been an hour since Rick waited in a new holding area, hands and feet shackled, tingling numbness prevalent throughout his body.

No sounds from his captor, no shuffling of feet or muffled voices, just the silence.

He felt the room's dampness, which penetrated deep into his bones, leaving a loneliness and despair in the pit of his stomach that inched up toward his psyche. Pushing any negative thoughts from his mind, he concentrated on his approximate location with every detail that his senses could muster.

He fought the urge to sleep.

The door opened with a crash, causing Rick's adrenaline to surge.

The barrel of a large caliber gun pressed firmly against his temple. He felt the captor's hand shaking from anger, frustration, or having to kill someone.

Helpless, Rick waited for his fate.

The reluctance infuriated Rick. With a calm voice he stated, "What are you waiting for?"

For the first time since the abduction, the captor spoke, "Looks like your girlfriend didn't do what she was told." There was a winded quality to the voice. He sounded young, which surprised Rick.

The man tore the hood from Rick. He stared him in the eye. A monumental mistake for the captor and a brief reprieve for Rick, but now the job turned personal, instead of an order.

The light burned Rick's vision for a moment as he blinked rapidly. His eyes adjusted to the dim lighting of the holding cell, everything still looked blurry.

Rick pushed the conversation as he kept his eyes focused on the young man, "She knows what she's doing." His voice replied raspy.

The man stepped backward and released the gun from the side of Rick's head. He paced, raising the gun up and down, as he wrestled with his conscience. "Why can't she just do what's she's supposed to do?" The question was rhetorical.

Rick forced a laugh. "Have you ever had a girlfriend? Especially one that's determined to get her own way?"

The man stopped and stared. "What?"

Rick estimated the guy to be mid-twenties. He still lacked the emotional wherewithal to handle deadly situations, or any type of stressful confrontation. It was obvious that he had never killed anyone before as the anxiety rose by his erratic movements.

"Look, it's some kind of misunderstanding." Rick treaded lightly and didn't want the young man to see right through his subtle attempt to diffuse the situation. "I'm sure that she's just being combative."

The captor pulled a cell phone from its case; he read the instructions again. It was obvious that he knew what it said. From the desperation wiped across his face, he wanted it to say something different.

Rick felt relieved that Emily was alive, but worried for her safety. He had no idea if she was captive, hurt, or what the intentional motive was for the kidnapping. It drove him crazy thinking about it.

"Just ask whoever is with Emily to verify. No big deal." Rick sounded casual, but he knew that it teetered on his swift execution.

The young man studied Rick for a moment. Without warning, he swung the gun in a hook-like fashion and it landed squarely on Rick's jaw. "Who the hell do you think you are?" He spat the words out in anger as his demeanor changed.

Rick had considered that this wasn't the same man who had beaten him, but that thought soon diminished. He watched the eyes of the man, dead, darting from side to side, almost that of a caged, starving animal.

The room darkened.

Rick knew his life could end in a dingy holding cell. For now, he ran out of ideas.

As if a voice had willed the young man, he erratically punched the keypad on the cell phone.

There was nothing for Rick to do, but wait.

* * * * *

The breath quietly escaped Emily's lungs. She didn't want to think the unthinkable, but her only thoughts were of Rick as her eyes rolled back in her head. Her body went limp in Red's grip. Fighting for strength due to the lack of food, and the effects of the drugs filtering out of her system, Emily blacked out.

"Hey…"

In Emily's mind, a nice quiet place to rest as her body floated through the gently swaying currents. It was a place she could stay forever, no killers, no crime scenes, and no kidnappers.

"Get up!"

A faraway voice tried to get her attention, but she was comfortable sleeping.

A sharp pain stung the side of Emily's face. A strong jerk of her left arm made the world come into view again.

"Wake up. You fainted."

Emily replied slowly with a slurred speech. "What do you want from me?"

Nothing mattered to her anymore.

Red let out a frustrated sigh. He sat Emily on the floor, leaning against the wall. Gentler this time, he slapped her face several times. The rush of blood flooded her cheeks. The assassin's face came close to hers. He leaned in and studied her face, which appeared like he wanted some sort of answer from her.

He slapped her again.

"Stop... Stop it!" Emily jerked her head and faced Red.

"You're lucky." He stated without compassion.

Emily felt the blood pump through her arms and legs again with a strange tingling sensation; she clenched her fists allowing her strength to recuperate.

Her vision sharpened.

The tight quarters instantly made her self-conscious. It surprised her how strong the killer's grip had latched onto her body, unable to move with such a severe force that she could not fight back. At the same time, he proved an interesting study for a textbook.

"Lucky?" She managed to say.

He showed his cell phone to her again. "It's a reprieve. Do you understand?" The text message clearly read: *confirm kill y/n.*

Emily didn't know what to say. She searched his desolate eyes for anything that would explain the nightmare.

As if he read her thoughts, he continued. "It means that the person overseeing him wants clarification."

Clarification?

Rick was still alive.

"Please…" She said.

Red glared at Emily, but it didn't seem to register to him by his expression that love was the most important thing in the world. It was nothing more than an emotionless reaction from the psychopath.

"Please don't kill him…" She tried to find anything in Red that resembled kindness and understanding. Her tormented expression softened as she continued to plead with her eyes.

Nothing registered on his face.

Red relaxed his posture and typed on his cell phone. He turned the small screen for Emily to see the order: *Negative*

CHAPTER NINETEEN
Friday 1600 Hours

Jordan called, left messages, and sent texts all afternoon to Emily and Rick. They never responded. His heart raced as the old scenarios of working at the F.B.I. flooded forward. He held his phone close, rarely taking his eyes from the security icon as he drove. He watched Emily's necklace move steadily south toward the Los Angeles area.

Of course, it had to be a day with some of his most important client meetings. His mind relentlessly wandered back to Emily during his lectures on security. Difficult to ignore the absence of his friends, but he pushed through the last meeting.

Jordan wasn't the type to panic. He had performed well under pressure during undercover operations, but in some ways, it had felt more like a game, a performance with an endless audience. He loved the challenge of the work, but as with anything in Jordan's life, it grew boring and lacked any purpose if the excitement stalled.

Being a part of Emily's life meant that nothing was ever boring.

Instinct and experience made Jordan pull to the side of the street and park several houses away from Emily and Rick's house.

He sat a moment, staring through the windshield.

Looking to the left and right, nothing seemed out of the ordinary. A few cars were home in various driveways, SUVs and compact cars, but nothing screamed unusual to him. The daylight dwindled, but it did not obscure the view of the entire neighborhood.

He followed his instincts.

Jordan waited until the streetlights came on as the dusk turned into early evening. Luckily, the bright lights were sparse, and he could still move around unnoticed.

For good measure, Jordan tried both the house phone and cell phones before exiting his car. He obtained the same result, no answer. Emily's necklace still headed south, past Los Angeles, at least according to his security application.

It wasn't like Emily and Rick not to check in. Jordan tried not to worry too much.

The house next door was dark and provided a perfect cover as Jordan crept in the darkness to get a better view. The well-trimmed and manicured yard with the evergreens made his approach that much easier, without a gopher hole to fall into, or noisy leaves to alert anyone.

He continued to wind around the yard with a purposeful pace.

Part of him thought with some sarcasm that the couple just wanted some privacy, and wouldn't appreciate Jordan's commando approach. Maybe they would all have a good laugh about it later.

Jordan flipped up the gate latch, paused a moment, and then slipped through. It was dark where he stood as he observed his surroundings. A lamp was on the living room, which gave a dull glow through the shut curtains.

He almost felt silly embracing a cloak and dagger entrance, instead of just waiting for a call back. His suspicions quickly were realized as he peered through the small kitchen window, and saw two unidentifiable men searching the living room.

One tall man pulled out desk drawers, flipped through bills, various pieces of paperwork, and continued throughout the room by tossing books from the tall bookshelves. The shorter, stockier man pulled out magazines from the shelf underneath the coffee table, quickly turning pages, but not finding anything that interested him.

Jordan leaned back against the side of the house and out of the view of the men. The good news was that he couldn't see Emily or Rick inside, but the bad news was something had happened to them. Otherwise, why would two goons search the house?

Sucking in a deep breath, Jordan dared to move forward and peered inside once again. The two men disappeared, but returned moments later from another room. In low tones, they spoke to one another. Jordan strained to make out the words, but they were muddled through the wall.

With Emily's insistence, Jordan helped her devise a computer file storage system that couldn't be hacked or stolen – at least by traditional means. No secret hiding place under the floorboards or inside the wall was safe. It was the age of technology, and using it wisely to hide classified information was the best opportunity.

She stored all of her cases, both closed and ongoing serial cases, in a file on an unadvertised, dormant website. It was simple, clean, and extremely effective. Her laptop only had a few software programs and access to the Internet, which wiped clean every time she powered her computer off. Certain files she emailed to Jordan. He kept them in various security files with a system that only he knew, and no one else would connect the files.

Jordan surmised that the men looked diligently for her files, or anything that she was currently working on. A small smirk turned the corners of his mouth upward because the men still didn't have a clue about Emily Stone. They weren't going to find anything.

The front door slammed.

Jordan slipped around the corner and saw the two men get into a van, which was parked across the street. He waited a few moments until he heard the vehicle drive away before entering the house.

He quickly checked the home for any kind of scuffle, blood, or anything that would appear that Emily and Rick had been taken by force. Nothing. The furniture, tables, and lamps sat intact and centered in the correct positions.

Upon further inspection, Jordan noticed Emily's wallet, cell phone, and jacket were missing from the usual location on the table next to the front door, which seemed logical if she went somewhere. He quickly opened the hall closet to discover that the suitcases were neatly stored.

The entire situation wasn't right; they wouldn't leave for any length of time without telling him.

A strange scratching sound came from the bathroom at the end of the hallway. Of course, he thought stupidly to himself. He never checked the bathroom; Emily and Rick could be tied up.

Jordan hurried down the hallway and turned the knob for the bathroom door. Instantly a big, black blur knocked him backwards. He tumbled down hard onto the hardwood floors.

Sarge locked in the bathroom, was now excited to see someone, and he licked Jordan furiously.

"Uggh…" Jordan managed to say as he caught his breath. He wasn't a dog person, or even a pet person for that matter. Not because he didn't like animals, he didn't like the mess and the disgusting things that they did – especially the smells.

The large Labrador ran back into the bathroom, took several slurps of water from the toilet bowl, and came charging back to Jordan, water droplets flying everywhere.

"That's disgusting!" Jordan scrambled to get to his feet, furiously wiping the sloppy mess from his face and shirt. "Sit! Stay! Go away!"

The dog charged up and down the hallway with unbridled happiness.

Jordan got a distinct whiff of urine from the bathroom and could see that the dog had to relieve himself on the bathmat. He looked at Sarge with a renewed respect on the innate survival instinct to pee in just one spot. "How long have you been in there buddy?"

He followed the dog into the kitchen where the canine looked longingly into his stainless food bowl, and then up at Jordan. Quickly Jordan found a large bag of food in the pantry closet and dumped a fair amount into the bowl. Instantly the dog ate, gulping, and smacking until the bowl was spotless.

Jordan estimated that the dog had been locked away between twenty-four to forty-eight hours. It implied that whatever happened to Emily and Rick, it was planned, and perps knew that there was a dog in the house.

Jordan projected the timeline from the last time he saw the couple, which was at dinner night before last. He had the loose timeline and the necklace – at least, it was a solid place to start.

He looked down at Sarge's big brown eyes, which searched his face for some type of indication of where his masters had gone.

Jordan said flippantly. "And what are we going to do with you?" The dog moved forward, licked Jordan's hand, sat obediently in front of him, waiting and watching.

"Oh no, you can't come with me. I don't entertain dogs…"

CHAPTER TWENTY
Friday 1730 Hours

Letting out a relaxed sigh, Judge Christensen sat comfortably in a leather chair located in his study – his favorite room in the rambling estate. He finished the weekly docket early and took full advantage at home. As he swirled the ice cubes in his glass and hoped to wash away the gruesome images of the cases paraded in his courtroom over the past couple of months, he breathed easy.

His waking hours consisted of murderers, child pedophiles, rapists, and even a serial killer, which had found its way into his courtroom. After a while, all criminal cases merged, and the faces of the defendants morphed into one living, breathing, wicked entity.

With all of the justice he dealt out in his court, he remembered every single person he sentenced over the years. In fact, it remained burned into his memory. Their faces, some smug, others showed remorse, but most were emotionless when the years piled up for multiple offenses.

The judge rose from his chair and filled his glass again. The smooth sound of Scotch against the sides of the tumbler glass swilled among the ice cubes. It entertained him. His day slowly faded, but was never completely forgotten.

He paused to gaze at a group of framed photographs of his late wife and their three children, along with six happy grandchildren. He was proud of all of his children, but only three years from retirement, he was lonely rattling around the large estate without someone to share it with him.

Walking to the tall bookshelves with his glass tucked under his fingertips, he scanned for a new book to read for the evening. He prided himself on brilliantly organizing his volumes from classic titles to contemporary fiction. Tonight, he thought only a classic fiction story would improve his mood and solitude.

His arms and legs felt strangely weak. His vision burred and then focused again. He knew that he needed to eat dinner, but it could wait a little longer before he heated up some leftovers.

Running his left hand over the spines of the books, the room began to rotate. The titles jumbled into a dark, muddled abyss.

His glass dropped to the floor and spilled out tiny streams of Scotch.

The judge's body crumbled forward. He made a weak attempt to catch himself on the books shelf for support, but succumbed to the darkness on the floor beneath the library of his favorite books.

CHAPTER TWENTY-ONE
Friday 1810 Hours

"Where she's going? Is Rick's with her?" Jordan muttered to himself as he glanced to the computer. "Did the arsonist find them?" He was not expecting an answer out of thin air, just a clue to which direction he should venture.

The big dog watched the laptop screen with mild curiosity where a small icon blinked, indicating Emily traveling South on Interstate-5. With a yawn, Sarge rested his large head on Jordan's lap.

"You'd never last on a stakeout buddy."

Jordan couldn't help himself, and petted the dog, scratching him behind the ears. In an unexpected way, he felt closer to Emily in the company of her favorite four-legged companion.

Pulling out a yellow steno tablet from his desk, Jordan jotted down what he knew for sure about Emily and Rick:

Not answering phones.
No sign of abduction at house.
SUV in driveway.
Missing her purse, cell and coat.
Laptop not found.
Left dog without care.
After dinner with me went home?
Two guys tossed house looking for something. But who, and what?
Last case Emily worked – arson crime scene. Dead lawyer, Defendant, Judge next? Connection? Those who worked on the cases?

Necklace tracker showed address of Mr. Bishop. How? Why?

Necklace tracker travelled south to Los Angeles. San Diego? Mexico?

Jordan paused to run several scenarios, but nothing logical clicked, or seemed to have a plausible motivation for the abduction of Emily and Rick.

Everything that he came up with screamed abduction, planned, organized, and very specific.

Extortion?

After doodling around the list with goofy drawings of people, Jordan circled the names of Mr. Bishop and the Judge on the sexual assault case.

"Well, Sarge…"

The dog sat up straight, ears perked, and his tail thumped on the floor three times.

"You ready for a road trip?"

The dog watched with increased interest as his tail fanned in enthusiasm.

Jordan went to his closet, retrieved two handguns, and made sure that they were fully loaded.

CHAPTER TWENTY-TWO
Friday 1845 Hours

Heaviness exploded inside his skull, squeezing the front and back of the head with a vice intensity as he fought to open his eyes. It took every ounce of strength for the judge to lift his chin and to process what he saw through the one-way mirror.

Horror twisted his soul.

His breath caught in his throat like a hard knot, he felt his blood pressure rise to a critical level, the rapid booming of his heart quickened, and his stomach churned in acidy discomfort.

He was inside his own panic room, staring into his master bedroom through a glass window, merely mirrored on the other side. A room he had long since vacated because he had chosen one of the more comfortable, smaller rooms to sleep and shower.

The judge tried to stand but found his body tied securely to a metal chair. He dared not to take his eyes away from the bedroom. Still not entirely believing what he saw. The will of hope flooded deep inside. Surely, it was an appalling joke, or a bad dream.

In the same type of metal chairs, a man and woman sat, tied with heavy twine, and duct tape pasted across their mouths. Their eyes told the entire story, horror and panic. Terrified and uncertain of what fate had in store for them, the couple pleaded with their eyes, tears flowed down their faces.

The judge couldn't pry his eyes away from them. It was his only daughter, and son-in-law, helpless and alone.

129

They must have paid him a surprise visit. There was nothing he could do for them.

Everything he had witnessed and heard inside the courtroom for decades didn't compare to what unfolded in his home, his supposed safe haven. He kicked in frustration at his chair to loosen the ropes, but it only pulled them tighter across his chest, arms, and legs.

A dark figure entered the bedroom.

The unknown man, tall and painfully thin, wearing a black running suit with the hood pulled firmly around his face. A glimpse of pale skin and sharp features obscured by the athletic wear, gave the only indication of who was behind the macabre performance.

If there was an existing grim reaper roaming the earth, he resembled it. He moved with agility and purpose, as his hands swiftly checked and double-checked the restraints on his victims, never looking directly at their faces, or reacting to their pleas.

A strangled cry escaped the judge, but no words formed from his lips. Anguish and misery lent to more inaudible sounds. No one could hear him, and no one would rescue them in time.

The dark shape left the room for what seemed like an eternity, and when he returned, he carried a large plastic container with a pouring spout. With a quick flick of the wrist, the top of the container dropped to the floor, and the man poured the liquid on the two victims.

As hard as they tried, the judge's daughter and husband couldn't escape the foul smell, and then everyone knew what horror was about to happen.

The only thing that the judge could think was NO, NO, NO, repeatedly in his mind. He continued to watch in horror, unable to pry his eyes away. His thoughts scrambled. Not his baby... not the little girl that he had taught to ride a bike... and the young woman who graduated from Harvard.

It was not happening.

The unknown assailant calmly left the room, and returned, wiping his gloves with a white hand towel. He took painstaking care to wipe each finger, palm, and then the back of his hand. After he was satisfied, he neatly folded the towel, and gently laid it on the edge of the bed.

For the first time, he turned to the mirror and stared into the judge. Even though he couldn't see him, he knew exactly where the judge sat. The killer's gaze bore into the judge's direction. He walked purposely to the mirror, stood for several seconds, only inches from the barrier, and lifted his left hand with a small object tucked between his thumb and forefinger. He moved gracefully, like a professionally trained dancer as he wrote three large letters: S I N

That one word hit the judge with an unprecedented power, which jolted his entire body and shocked his spirit.

The man that stood at the mirror, stared, never blinking, never moving, as if to telepathically express all of the sins of the world onto him.

The judge saw him clearly and could identify him, but the killer's face wasn't one he had seen before. Expressionless, dark, and average was the best description of attacker through the window. Racking his brain, the judge tried to dig deep into his file of defendants, but nothing surfaced through the hundreds, if not thousands, of criminal faces.

Who was this young man?

Turning with grace and perfect timing, the intruder effortlessly dropped a lighter while he exited the room.

Flames burst into full force within seconds.

The fire flipped and dove in unison as it gained more momentum, burning hotter with light and dark orange colors. The two victims scorched, bouncing and writhing in the chairs, before the intensity toppled them. The skin curled from their bones in charred pieces.

A dull buzz accompanied by a fading view distorted the judge's perspective. Not willing to acknowledge the horror, he stared straight ahead.

The gruesome display took minutes, but time stalled for the performance of terror to end, and allowed the carnage to take center stage. Bones of the contorted limbs remained as the fire danced from the carpet to the drapes, walls, and everywhere around the room. It fed on the available oxygen, craving it, and easily igniting available cotton, paper, and wood to keep up its incredible strength.

Judge Christensen sat slumped in his chair, dead from a massive heart attack. He never felt the heat of the explosion as the mirrored window splintered into millions of pieces, or that his body shredded upon impact. His house continued to burn with a magnum force, everything he had worked for melted, burned, exploded, and soon transformed into ashes.

CHAPTER TWENTY-THREE
Friday 1945 Hours

High on a hill in between a dense area of trees, Jordan peered through his digital binoculars at the darkened estate belonging to Mr. Bishop. He had taken a roundabout route to make sure that he wasn't seen, or recorded on well-hidden surveillance cameras. He hated feeling completely out of the loop and deep into the unknown factor of mysterious disappearances. It left him without an appetite with his nerves tattered.

It didn't make any sense to him that the huge estate was dark and vacated. He continued to look for any sign of life or someone residing inside the house – but no one appeared. It looked as if no one had been in the house for months, but he was there only a few days ago.

Retrieving his cell phone, Jordan watched the pendant icon blink and travel past the Los Angeles area. So many questions flooded his mind of why the necklace was first at Bishop's estate, and how and why it travelled to southern California.

For as long as he had known Emily, it was the first time he felt that this might be a situation where they couldn't get out of before something really bad happened. Jordan's stomach took another low dip as he steadied his body against a tall Pine tree. He closed his eyes for a moment to take in the fresh air and clear his mind.

Something cold and wet touched his left hand. With a start, Jordan took a defensive stance only to see a curious dog face staring at him. The brown, almost black, eyes of the most loyal animal on earth, waited for a command from him.

"Sarge…you are such… a bad dog… for scaring me…"

The faithful canine sat, stared at him, and patiently waited.

"How did you…?"

Jordan realized that the dog was out of the car and he quickly walked back to the vehicle. He looked at his ride after an extensive detailing and saw the dog slobber all over the driver's window and headrest. The back window remained halfway down and judging by the streaks of saliva, scratch marks, and some black tufts of fur; it was the escape route.

"See, this is why I don't have pets. Oh man…"

Opening the back door, Jordan grabbed a grey sweatshirt and wiped the slobber off the window and seat. "Get in, and quit nosing around and licking things." The dog obeyed and easily jumped in. He leaped up to the front passenger seat, sitting straight, and readied himself for the ride.

"Uh, I don't think so… C'mon, get in the back seat." Jordan lamely gestured to the back of the car.

Sarge glanced at him and then turned his head back to peer through the front windshield.

"Fine…" Jordan got behind the wheel. "You're just as difficult as your owner is, you know that?"

Inside the car, his remote police scanner kept a background noise, which sometimes proved useful. It also offered him some company in addition to his new canine friend. He heard an address reported for a request of fire trucks and ambulance.

Immediately turning up the volume, Jordan recognized the address in a very exclusive neighborhood, and from his recent search of court personnel. The location belonged to the judge that preceded over the case where both the lawyer and defendant ended up dead, and on Emily's radar of victims.

Now the judge's house burned to the ground.

Jordan knew that the serial arson cases and Bishop had something to do with what happened to Emily and Rick. Unfortunately, now he had more questions than ever, and no solid answers – yet. He started the engine and drove back to his apartment to dig deeper into the situation and to call in some favors from old colleagues at the bureau.

The beginning of a long night set in for Jordan.

CHAPTER TWENTY-FOUR
Friday 2020 Hours

It was the longest ride of Emily's life aboard the train to San Diego. At least she had hydrated her body with water and two different juices, and tried to eat a cold chicken sandwich, but only managed a few bites. In between waves of nausea of the drugs still floating in her system and the constant dread that inundated her mind about Rick, she willed herself to move forward with the assassin's plan.

Every move she made became Red's top priority. She had received a reprieve for Rick's life, but paid the price on anything she did and every wrong gesture she made. If the perfect time came up and she found out where Rick's location was, Emily would make her move and hope that it proved to be the right decision for his survival.

She tried not to look directly at Red. He seemed to have three specific locations where his attention focused with practiced expertise, on Emily, the window, and mostly the door. As the speed of the train changed every so often, it caused the door to rattle and gave the notion that someone would burst inside. Emily wondered if the hit man would quietly take out the person with a snap of the neck. Or, if he would open fire blasting out the windows, taking a few bystanders down as he escaped with Emily by jumping out of a moving train.

Emily sighed as she stared at Red. He didn't seem to care, but kept his obsessive attention on all three areas of the cramped room. She waited for him to look at her again and tried to find something in his demeanor or behind his eyes that would show some insight into his weaknesses.

* * * * *

There were many other contracts and killing assignments that Red found appealing and even soothing, one bullet through the brain from a high-powered rifle, or up close and personal with a hunting knife through the solar plexus.

However, sitting with a wildcard of a woman who impressed the government as a serial killer hunter wasn't one of them. It aggravated him that she could stare right into his eyes and didn't flinch, and he knew that she would fight to the death if the situation called for it.

Sedentary in a cramped room on a train for several hours, unable to move around freely, caused his joints to pain and seize up. At least his stomach maintained control and didn't burn a path up to his mouth.

The door rattled as the train down shifted nearing the station.

Red's eyes darted to the door, not expecting to see anyone, but again nothing proved ordinary in his work. He glanced at his watch, appeasing his displeasure that the train arrived in San Diego on time.

Emily stood up.

Red followed her lead and met her strong gaze, hooking his hand around her arm. "Stay put." He guided her to sit down.

It would be fifteen minutes before the train completely stopped and allowed passengers to disembark.

Imagining the quick end to Emily Stone by twisting her neck and leaving her to gaze aimlessly out the window, Red almost broke into a smile. Her body left in the compartment for some sorry-ass Amtrak employee to discover.

He looked at her, trim, petite, and attractive. It amazed him that she could locate all of the serial killers under extreme hostile situations. Apparently, she prided herself on criminal profiling and crime scene techniques. It seemed impractical.

Forensics is a bullshit manipulation by law enforcement to close cases.

Red fought the urge to end the growing farce of the babysitting job as his arms tensed. It wouldn't take much to press his fingers around Emily's pretty neck. From years of exercised breathing, he could accomplish anything, which included restraint no matter how long it took.

Emily slowly turned her head and looked directly at Red, eyes steady, jaw relaxed and secure in her position. It intimidated him to a certain degree, it was as if she could read his thoughts – or at least try.

* * * * *

Emily stepped from the taxi followed closely by Red carrying the two small suitcases. She was extremely surprised as they headed into a ritzy downtown hotel lobby. The assassin casually approached the front desk where a polite young woman greeted him that sported a short bob hairstyle and oversized eyes accented by blue eye shadow.

"Hello, welcome. How may I help you?" She smiled.

"Checking in. Mr. Townsend." Red stated, neither with contempt nor with warmth.

With her fingernails clicking on the computer keyboard, she quickly found the reservation. "Yes, your suite is ready Mr. Townsend." She continued typing in information and asked a few amenity questions.

Emily casually surveyed the lobby, suddenly felt a little conspicuous in her jeans and rumpled t-shirt. She desperately needed a change of clothing as she pulled her jacket tighter in front of her.

Turning her head to observe the large palm, she noticed her reflection in a huge mirror. Drawn and pale, Emily tried to smooth her shoulder length hair in a more flattering manner, and tugged at her leather jacket's collar.

A woman carrying a fluffy Pomeranian headed toward the registration desk with a bellhop tailing her. Business executives as well as couples moved freely through the lobby and into elevators. Noise resonated from the bar and restaurant area, laughter and clapping ensued. The sound of clinking of glasses made Emily remember a wonderful evening and a night out with Rick.

"Let's go." Red said and interrupted her fleeting lapse into a fond memory. He guided her toward the elevators.

He picked up the two suitcases and exited the lobby through a large area where a waterfall cascaded; several people laughed, dressed in upscale clothes, and hurried into the restaurant almost colliding into them.

Red hit the call button for the elevator.

Emily saw the room number on the keycard in his hand: 1821

No one was in the elevator car; Emily pushed herself to the back corner and felt her time running out like an hourglass. Her energy zapped and dwindled with every passing minute.

What hoop did she have to jump through now?

Her mind melted into a blur of past events, and nothing gave the impression of what was right and wrong anymore.

The elevator chimed as the doors opened to the eighteenth floor.

They stepped out and paused. Red quickly oriented himself to the room numbers. They headed to the right.

Emily curiously watched each room number count down to their room. Surprised by how narrow the hallway appeared. She took special notice of the small security cameras at each end. Most people wouldn't notice the technology, but it made her wonder why Red chose this hotel if they were recorded on those devices.

Without a second to lose, Red inserted the card key and opened the door. He ushered Emily inside and shut the door behind them.

Incredible views from the spacious seating in a living room, along with a kitchen, and a large bedroom made Emily, for a brief moment, marvel at the plush surroundings. As fast as she became impressed, doom set in at what she must endure in Bishop's plan. Red wasn't giving any clue to her assignment until the absolute last moment.

Red put one small case on the desk, shed his leather jacket, and then walked to the bedroom with the other overnight bag. Opening it, he said. "Get dressed."

"What?" Emily wasn't sure if she heard him correctly.

"Get dressed. Red dress, brown wig. You have half an hour."

Emily stared at the contents inside the suitcase neatly folded and organized in sections.

Red didn't wait for an answer or even a question. He swiftly left the bedroom and shut the door behind him.

Weak and fighting defeat, Emily sat on the bed rubbing her forehead and hoped a fantastic idea would emerge. Nothing came. Planning, searching, discovering, and even fighting at times was the usual comfort zone for Emily's work, but tonight her outlook mirrored that of a wounded victim.

One question tormented her mind.

Would she be able to save a stranger and Rick?

She stared at the closed bedroom door, not because she was afraid that Red would enter, but because it shut out everything that she didn't want to process at the moment.

Pain and self-pity only proved ineffective under the circumstances.

From inside the suitcase, Emily pulled out a beautiful cocktail dress, simple and tailored from a high-end couture designer along with a bra and panties. The dress and lingerie were her size as well as the three-inch, strappy heels. She shuddered at the thought of someone measuring her body as she lay in a deep, drug-induced sleep. Everything about Bishop and Red made her shudder, but she had to move forward.

Rick counted on her.

Her fingers touched the brunette wig with long wavy hair, the strands felt like real human hair against her hand. Several smaller zippered pouches contained makeup and various toiletries, everything needed for an evening out.

She remembered the pendant that Jordan gave her and quickly retrieved it from her jacket pocket. Squeezing is tightly in her hand, she sat for a moment, wondering if it worked at all. Almost willing it like a magical talisman where he could hear her thoughts.

Emily stood up and studied the room for anything that resembled a weapon. The room contained nothing except the basics, and the absent of a phone.

It bothered Emily that the murder fit a perfect plan with exact timing and precision. There would be little room for error or surprises. It concerned her as she quickly took a shower, hoping that the steam and water gave her a solution.

* * * * *

Red set up the laptop. He readied the camera and microphone for Emily. Two small caliber handguns lay on the desk, one fitted with a silence suppressor. He knew that she could prove to be quite useful, but never a willing participant. What a shame, he thought. The agency could always use a woman to get to certain targets with much more ease than a man. Most people hardly ever suspected a woman to effortlessly take their life.

Glancing at his watch, two minutes before he checked on Emily. Red was not worried that she'd escape because they were eighteen stories up, but she could have assembled something to catch him by surprise. No discussion or pleas this time for anyone, he would kill her.

The bedroom door opened.

Emily crossed the living room as Red blinked in surprise. A half hour revealed a stunning brown-haired woman that looked more like a celebrity attending a cocktail party, rather than someone who stalked killers.

She demanded, "Are you going to clue me in on the plan?" Her dark eyes dared him, and even stirred some buried emotions.

"Sit down."

Emily pulled up a chair and sat down across from Red. He knew she eyed the guns, and casually took inventory of everything he had on the table.

Red kept control of his usual conduct, but internally it angered him that he liked Emily's intelligence and demonstrated abilities.

It would soon end.

CHAPTER TWENTY-FIVE
Friday 2100 Hours

The strong canine snoring with intermittent whines from a deep doggie slumber didn't interrupt Jordan's quick pounding of the keyboard as he searched for more information on the Internet.

Two state-of-the-art laptops and one older, diehard clunky desktop computer surrounded him, like a techie command center. His eyes darted from one screen to the other. One computer could crash or take too long loading a file; three computers were the workhorses to his business.

He kept a watchful eye on the cell phone app, tracking Emily's position. It had not moved from the San Diego location. A few glitches kept Jordan from pinpointing exactly where she was located. It was somewhere in the downtown area, most likely a hotel or restaurant.

But why?

He had no other choice, but to forge ahead with the arson investigation and hope something pointed to Emily and Rick's whereabouts.

It amazed him how many things he could find out even though he didn't work for the FBI anymore. With less restrictions and protocols as a licensed private investigator, he had made the right decision getting the license for his security business.

The thump of the Labrador's otter-like tail now kept a constant beat along with the snores.

Jordan continued his search. He added a few potential things to Emily's profile on the arsonist, hoping something would break.

143

He typed out:

Overachiever, never completed a degree(s), wronged by society, believed "he" is smarter than police and society, obsessive/compulsive, tech savvy, EMT or firefighter or investigator experience?, washed out of fire type of job or didn't make the grade?, sales job?, makes for flexible schedule, multiple residences, no family, no close relationships, won't surrender, watches law enforcement closely, may even know someone in law enforcement.

A new email notification chimed on one of Jordan's working accounts.

A list of suppliers for security doors appeared, specifically for the one mysteriously installed at the location at the abandoned hardware store. Attached to the email were the most recent catalogues, complete with photos and specifications.

Jordan swiveled his chair to compare the photo that Emily took of the door to the catalogue items. Back and forth, he compared the size, color, depth, and hardware, until one emerged. Luckily, it was an unusual model, extremely high end, and originally developed in Germany.

"Gotcha." Jordan stared at the door image.

He mumbled. "What does this mean? How could someone afford something like that?"

He studied the door, the layers of steel, the weight, and the usual subcontractors that installed something of that caliber.

Jordan realized that the killer wanted to show off his expertise and arrogance with the door, but someone had to have sold it and installed it. With fast keystrokes, he contacted every distributor who sold that particular door, twenty-two places in all.

It was like locating a needle in a haystack, but Jordan felt that every investigative avenue should be covered. He left his email and contact phone for them to respond. Of

144

course, he gave the pretext of a major security client's needs for the company; otherwise, they would not give him the information he needed.

Jordan glanced at his cell phone, the blinking icon still showed the same location in San Diego.

That means something, but what?

Pushing his office chair backward and running his hands through his hair in frustration, Jordan scrutinized all the running computers, and what kept pushing to the surface was Bishop's house.

Sarge had awakened, sat next to Jordan, and plopped his big head on his lap.

Scratching the big dog's ears, "Yeah, I know. I miss her too."

* * * * *

The last time Jordan did a covert reconnaissance at a location for a person of extreme interest, it turned ugly fast, and left behind a trail of dead bodies. He tried not to think about it as he entered Bishop's estate from the far northeast corner.

The cameras on two of the corners of the estate were not in operation yet. He had surveyed the property first and found that these two cameras weren't running, and the electronic eye wouldn't see him scale the rock wall to drop into the garden.

Jordan didn't waste any time at his apartment to make the rash decision to break into Bishop's house. He knew that the elusive man was miles, if not several states away from the house. The lavish home waited for something other than his personal home base.

Damn.

Jordan hated when he missed the obvious, but he had focused on the huge security assignment instead. He loved the challenge of the business and missed the subtle cues of the intended motivations of something much more sinister. Like a clever illusionist's performance, Jordan looked one way as Bishop worked his dark magic with unidentified motives the other way.

Somehow, Emily became snared in the web.

The ground in the garden squished with a wet suction on the bottom of his boots. He quickly searched for the timer that directed the sprinkler system. On the corner of the house, a small box hung with simple buttons to set at specific times – nothing out of ordinary.

No controlled gunfire spattered the walls.

No bullhorn announced that he was trespassing on private property.

Jordan stopped in the darkness and listened, not only for a henchman straggler, but also for that tiny internal voice telling him to run away as fast as he could.

A soft breeze blew through the foliage. A subtle nudge kept him focused.

There was no turning back now.

He knew every inch of the estate, how many windows, doors, and rooms.

Unhooking one of the straps of a specialized fitted backpack, Jordan retrieved a small black box from a zippered compartment. He pushed a button to jam all signals for cell phones and any wireless computer connections. It also included the motion indicators for the cameras. The cheap device purchased from any tech-oriented store proved extremely useful in so many situations, and should last for the length of time Jordan needed. It also meant if something went wrong, he wouldn't be able to contact the police for help on his cell phone.

A low hum interrupted Jordan's illicit thoughts.

He stopped.

With nerves at an all-time high, he realized that the noise he kept hearing was the filter system for the pool.

It was now or never, go or stay, so Jordan kept low and approached the back entrance where the main security keypad was located. It was time to disarm it. He also knew that this area of the house opened into a long hallway with four bedroom suites.

The back door had plain glass panes halfway down in sections of three. Strangely, the door looked like it belonged in a standard three-bedroom home in modern suburbia, instead of a multi-million dollar property.

Dim outdoor lights burned along the walkway and along the bottom of the building to illuminate the outside of the structure.

With a quick elbow movement, Jordan smashed one of the windowpanes.

A red light flashed from inside. No alarm sounded, but if it wasn't deactivated in thirty seconds the police would arrive, more likely a group of hired guns with the attitude of shoot and ask questions later.

The red light flashed like a warning beacon from the underworld.

Twenty-five seconds...

Jordan jimmied the lock open and slipped inside, not bothering to shut the door.

Twenty seconds...

Quickly taking a control device, about the size of eyeglass lens, it held a mini keypad and a USB cord used to plug into any of his systems as an overseeing administrator.

Fifteen seconds...

Hands shaking, he managed to plug in his device and typed his commands.

Ten seconds...

The code consisted of numbers, symbols and letters. Jordan clumsily entered the overriding combination with his mini-flashlight in his mouth. He waited. There was always a slight delay; he hoped that he punched in the correct cypher.

Five seconds…

"C'mon… c'mon…" He jumped up and down, deciding whether or not to run. "Crap!"

Three seconds…

Two seconds…

Green light…

The alarm successfully stopped and waited for an operator to reset it.

Jordan stared at the box for a few extra seconds, expecting it to activate again. The box remained the same, quiet and unassuming, without some unknown source controlling its destiny.

Jordan snapped out of his perceived twilight zone. He slipped on a thin pair of gloves, careful not leave any fingerprints or anything else behind.

Systematically he searched the house, not sure exactly what he was looking for, but he would know when he found it. Something in the estate had to tell him if Emily had been there, or if there was reason to believe that Bishop had something to do with her and Rick's disappearance.

The first two bedrooms didn't reveal anything unusual, except sparse furnishings that resembled more of a stage instead of a comfortable home with guest bedrooms.

Jordan almost skipped the next two suites, but thought better and entered the third bedroom. Compared to the other two, the room decorations looked more appropriate for someone who didn't like color, or had issues with anything bright and cheery.

Upon closer inspection, someone had slept on top of the bed. The linens were wrinkled. The shower was recently used with a still damp towel on the floor. Nothing hung in the closet. The small trash receptacle had an unused plastic zip tie. Innocent enough, but something more threatening lingered in his mind. He picked it up. Jordan turned the simple but sturdy maintenance implement over in his hand. Absently, he pocketed the strip. The first thought in his mind raced to Emily. Zip ties were one of the standard work tools that Emily and Rick carried in their investigations, but there could be a million reasons why it was in that particular wastebasket.

Retracing his footsteps, Jordan reached the doorway to continue his search just as a heavy fist walloped his face. He careened into the doorframe, fell hard, and hit the stone floor as he felt every piece of the house architecture slam into his body.

Jordan groaned as he slowly moved his buzzing limbs. Blood flowed from his lip. Quickly he checked all of his teeth with his tongue, making sure that they were all counted for before another blow hammered down.

Not the face.

He sneaked a peek from under his right forearm at the assailant and recognized the stocky man as Bishop's back up muscle from the security meeting.

Jordan tried to sit up when the man kicked him in the ribs. Searing pain rattled him senseless, leaving him gasping for air. Trying to catch his breath, Jordan used the wall to steady his body, and without anything else to lose, lunged at the bodyguard.

The two men hit the floor, scuffling, arms and legs flailing as artwork and vases crashed to the floor.

Click.

Jordan stopped as he stared into the oversized barrel of a .45 caliber gun.

CHAPTER TWENTY-SIX
Friday 2200 Hours

Douglas Easterbrook entertained his friends with lively stories as he downed his fourth cocktail, a double martini, extra dry with three olives. Impeccably dressed in a dark grey suit, white shirt opened just enough to show his tanned chest, which accented his silver hair and intense green eyes. The gregarious group hung on his every word of wild tales of how he closed one amazing business deal after another.

A young cocktail waitress with a tight pink blouse and short black skirt had her hands full with the lively group, but she kept their orders filled as the tips mounted with each visit. She smiled politely, but it was clear that she longed for something better than a service job.

Easterbrook stomped on anyone who got in his way when it came to business deals relating to technology, real estate development, and any woman he wanted. His background investigation consistently described him as ruthless and sadistic with the opposite sex.

Emily sat at the end of the bar nursing a soda water and lime on the rocks. Her location gave her an ideal vantage point to watch Mr. Easterbrook without drawing unnecessary attention. She summed up her mark carefully with his mannerisms and how he handled the crowd of admirers. She tried to formulate an accessible plan in her mind to save the overachiever from a targeted death.

"Another?" The bartender asked Emily.

She nodded. "Thank you."

Emily caught a glimpse of herself in the artisan mirror behind the bar. Hardly recognizable with dark, long hair, too much makeup, and with her only identifiable trait of her dark eyes staring back.

Several men kept their casual observation on Emily, but she made sure that they maintained their distance. The plan, as Red referred to it, was for Emily to lure Mr. Easterbrook back to his room and kill him. He explained it simply.

Rattled nerves set in as Emily's arms and legs weighed heavy, not because of the lack of regular meals, but what she was faced with in the next hour.

The collection of Bishop's photographic images of her and Rick working crime scenes after the police had ravaged the area filtered through her mind, making it difficult to concentrate.

How could she have been so careless?

Using the straw stirrer, she rattled the ice cubes in the glass.

The bartender set a fresh drink on a hotel coaster in front of her. His hands moved with grace and quickness, flipping glasses and balancing liquor bottles.

The lime skin glistened in the soda water as a continuous flurry of tiny bubbles rose to the surface. Emily watched the fizz, and blinked away all of the worst-case scenario images from her mind. She desperately tried not to think of Rick, and the fact that she was mad at him just before the kidnapping.

Voices rose in a ruckus of laughter at Easterbrook's table.

Emily looked up, and slowly swiveled her body on the barstool. She decided to turn on the charm if Red's plan was going to work. Crossing her legs seductively, she watched the target as he effortlessly engaged in another story.

He took calculated moments to admire her at the end of the bar.

Emily gave an outward vibe of disinterest, but hoped that her coyness would drive up his curiosity even more.

She unconsciously touched a small gold barrette subtly affixed in her hair, which Red skillfully implanted as a listening device so he could hear all of her conversations. On Emily's small black bag, a tiny camera lens disguised in the middle of a jeweled ornament completed her spy attire.

What Red did not know, Emily wore the silver pendant as a choker around her neck that Jordan gave her, and hoped it transmitted her location. Jordan would hopefully figure out something was wrong and come up with a plan. Until then, Emily had to give the illusion of following orders. She had to bide some time.

Four people got up from the popular table. The rest of the group followed their host's example and began to move to the bar or retire to a suite upstairs. Easterbrook made his rounds with a few friends and some high-powered associates with their outlandishly dressed girlfriends. Smooth and charming was an understatement with his flashy smile, intense eyes, but his intelligence evident with quick responses and equally matched knowledge.

Emily turned herself forward and sipped her drink with a demure, but playful reaction to the dozens of looks from the man of interest. She pushed her new long curls back from the right side of her face, fingering the strands.

The man casually inched closer to where Emily sat; he was about two people away from her when he subtly turned his back.

Staring at her glass, Emily knew she had hooked him and it was only a matter of minutes before he said something clever to her. Her explicit instructions were clear and her every move watched closely.

Like clockwork, Easterbrook gave Emily a charming smile as if he had just noticed her. He sidled up to her barstool. "I can't believe that you're here by yourself." He nudged himself a little bit closer.

"Not by choice. My group decided to go to some other bar and go dancing." Emily forced a smile, inside she felt sick.

"And you didn't want to go?"

"Not my thing. I guess I'm a little old fashioned, or boring by today's standards." Emily hoped that she wasn't overdoing her part. It felt contrived, but judging by the man's reactions, he didn't care.

Easterbrook motioned to the bartender for another drink. To Emily, "You don't mind if I join you for a quick drink?"

"Not at all." She forced a smile.

He eagerly took a seat next to Emily. Offering his hand for introduction, "I'm Doug."

"Emily." She reciprocated with a pleasant handshake. Her skin crawled as he dragged his fingertips underneath her hand in a lecherous way.

"Ah, I should have guessed. Emily is an old fashioned name."

"So Doug, what do you do?" She quickly wanted to switch gears so that he would talk about himself and she wouldn't have to engage in idle chitchat.

Emily fought to bite her tongue at times, the more she listened to Doug's stories and blatant boasting, the more she wanted to smash his face with her glass. They talked for about a half an hour. That's how long it took for him to ask Emily to his room.

* * * * *

During the ride in the elevator to one of the penthouse apartments, Emily endured Doug's hands against her back, on her waist, and down the side of her thigh as he spoke to her. She felt filthy with his inappropriate touching, but kept a smile on her face.

The target quickly opened his room door and pulled Emily inside with him. The suite was huge and could have easily been on the cover of a decorating magazine.

He whispered in her ear, "I think you would be more comfortable on the sofa."

Emily pulled away from him, "I need to use the bathroom first. I'll be right back."

Once in the bathroom, Emily had to work fast if her plan were to work. The gun was located in a lower drawer of the bathroom vanity, but the last thing she would do was kill a man in cold blood.

She looked at herself in the mirror. The plan ran through her mind. There wasn't a way for her to save both Rick and Doug. If she tried, everyone was dead.

Carefully setting down her purse, she turned it strategically where the camera faced the opposite wall. Turning the water on, she pulled the barrette from her hair, tossed it into the toilet. She slipped off her shoes throwing them into the hotel's laundry hamper.

She knew the plan was a gamble.

Taking the .22 pistol in her right hand, she moved quickly to the living room.

Easterbrook sat at the desk, body motionless; he stared out at the balcony. His posture differed from only a few moments ago, now his shoulders slumped forward and his face drawn, deeply saddened.

Emily slowed her pace as the drastic personality turnaround confused her.

From five feet away, she could see an open plain brown envelope with several eight by ten glossy photographs tossed haphazardly on the desk. She didn't need to take a closer look at the subject of the photos. It was clear that there were people dead by violent means, gunshots to the head. Even more disturbing, a photo of two boys around the age of ten was among the victims.

"Doug what's going on?" She asked.

He never moved or turned his head to look at her as he spoke. "The only thing that mattered in this world was my mom, my brother and his children... nothing matters anymore..."

"Get up Doug." Emily urged.

She pointed the gun at him.

He turned and looked at her. The fact that she had a gun didn't elicit any reaction.

"I have to kill you." The gun shook in her hand, her voice strained. She had to do something else. Anything. It was either him or Rick. There was no other choice.

He shook his head, slowly raised himself from the chair, and walked to the French doors leading out to the balcony. He opened the door. Immediately the cool breeze whipped through the room. The sounds of the city filled the air.

"What are you doing?" Emily confronted him. "Do you not understand what's going on? You have a contract out on your life." She aimed the gun directly at his head. "I have to do this..." Tears welled up on her eyes.

Doug turned and looked directly at Emily, the arrogance of the driven entrepreneur had dissolved, and a gentle human being materialized. A small smile caught the corners of his mouth accompanied by a slow nod. He stepped onto the balcony.

"Don't move!" She said.

He ignored her orders.

Emily had no other choice, she raised the gun and yelled. "Stop! You have to leave. Now!" She took a step closer. "They won't stop until they kill you."

Doug continued to walk outside onto the balcony. He paused a moment to enjoy the cool breeze with his arms stretched out wide at the side of his body.

"Doug!" Emily pleaded, slowly tightening her finger on the trigger. Her nerve weakened and she gently released her grip.

I can't...

The man took a deep breath and lowered his arms.

Realizing too late, Emily watched in horror as Doug effortlessly climbed over the railing and jumped.

He disappeared.

CHAPTER TWENTY-SEVEN
Friday 2320 Hours

The beefy man managed to get the upper hand in the all-out brawl, scrambling on the floor. The result was a six-inch barrel directed strategically in Jordan's face. The sour breath of the man almost made Jordan gag with revulsion. The distinct smell of sour milk and onion-saturated beef stunk up the close proximity.

Slowly the bodyguard got to his feet, shirt and jacket disheveled with a long tear across the sleeve. He did not speak at first, just grunted, and then used the gun to direct Jordan.

"Look, I think there's a misunderstanding here..." Jordan rose up from the floor still with his backpack intact and secured over his shoulders.

"Shut up!" The man snapped with a slight European accent.

Jordan felt that everything was negotiable, and knew that he could reason with the man even if it all boiled down to money. The man obviously wasn't respected as much as the other so-called bodyguards, and with enough time, he could convince the bodyguard not to shot him.

Keeping his palms facing the man, in plain view, Jordan said. "You know who I am, right? I was just here a few days ago with the security blueprint for Mr. Bishop."

A glint of recognition flashed in the man's eyes.

Jordan continued to push, "You know the importance of security for him?" He relaxed a bit and persisted, "My reputation is on the line, and I was making sure that everything is in working order. I'm supposed to be here. A little unorthodox I admit, but how else was I going to make sure that the system was unbreakable?"

The man looked down to the left as if to ponder on the statement.

Jordan set the trap. He was in the process of reeling the man into his line of thinking.

"Okay, the truth is that I thought I'd screwed up on one of the schematics and I wanted to make sure that it worked properly. Hey, with the amount of money that he deposited into my account, I'd be stupid not to double check." Jordan watched the eye muscles twitch on the man holding the gun, only to prove that he believed Jordan's story. At least he hoped.

Hook, line, and sinker.

Jordan celebrated on the inside, but he noticed that something strangely changed about the man.

"Move!" The burly man ordered. He flicked the gun back in forth to hurry Jordan faster.

"Look, I'm sure that you could call Bishop and we can sort out this misunderstanding."

The gun fired and a vase shattered.

"What the hell...?" Jordan cringed as he felt the bullet whizz by his head.

"I said move!" He gestured with the gun again for Jordan to go to the living room.

There was nothing else for Jordan to do, but oblige the order. He couldn't push the hired gun any harder; otherwise, a bullet would enter his head and explode out the back part of his skull. The only thought that came to Jordan's mind was that he hoped his brain matter would stain a valuable piece of artwork.

When they entered the large living room, two low watt lamps turned on giving just enough light to see the layout of the room clearly. It was the same as Jordan remembered, but a serving tray with a glass of orange juice and a dried up bagel sat on the coffee table.

Curious.

It bothered Jordan that the food remained behind, especially since the house was empty. Whenever he thought of juice and a carbohydrate filled bakery item, such as a bagel, it made him think of quick energy food or to raise the blood sugar level in the body. He estimated that the bread and juice were only about a day old by the darkened edges and spongy appearance.

Someone else was here.

"So looks like you've been entertaining some?" Jordan didn't expect any answers but glanced to his captor. The clenching of the jaw and quick, short breaths told him that indeed someone was here, perhaps against his will – or hers.

He reached the door leading to the patio surrounding the pool area. Gripping the handle, he turned it. For a brief moment, he hoped that a huge blaring alarm would sound, but nothing happened except some much appreciated fresh air.

For the first time since a fist hit his jaw, Jordan felt a constant stinging pain on his lip along with a metallic taste in his mouth.

The patio and plants were wet from the automatic sprinkling system. Jordan's shoes made a slight squeaking sound from the high rubber tread. He picked up the pace and moved toward the pool, which had a cover over it.

"Stop!" The man said.

"Look, you don't have to yell, I'm right here." Jordan took off his backpack and reached into a loose pocket.

"Drop the backpack!"

"See, you're still yelling. It's not like I can't hear you" Jordan dropped the backpack on the ground. In his right hand, he fired a hundred thousand volts of electricity from a small Taser device.

It shot directly at the man with a perfect strike to his chest. Convulsing and whimpering in short bursts, the big man's knees never buckled underneath him, he stood strong, and held firmly to the gun. The neuromuscular incapacitation wasn't working to full capacity. It only made the man furious.

Jordan held firmly to the self-defense apparatus, but incredibly, the man slowly moved toward him. The wide-eyed glare made him look primal and extremely dangerous. He kept moving closer to Jordan. The man managed to squeeze off a couple of shots with a jerky, marionette gesture.

One bullet grazed the side of Jordan's face. Another bullet struck the retaining wall on the other side of the pool. The peculiar buzz rocketed past Jordan's ears, which caused him to cringe and double over in a contorted manner. He expected the next bullets to blast through his chest and face.

The man kept coming.

Jordan held firmly to the Taser in a death-like grip. It was only a matter of time before the big man fell down.

With his free hand, the bodyguard swung his arm and fist erratically, but directly in Jordan vicinity. From the weight difference, unbalanced maneuvers, and sheer determination, both men plunged into the pool.

The struggle continued even as the pool cover slowly sunk into the deep end of the pool.

Clearly out muscled and out gunned, Jordan made a lame attempt to grab the weapon.

The battle waffled back and forth. Both men grappled.

Jordan realized that the beefy man didn't have the gun in his hand anymore. His floundering efforts caused sheer panic to spread across his face.

The pool filter reset and a low motor hummed.

With all of his strength, Jordan pushed his body toward the shallow end. He watched the man flap his arms, his head bobbed under the surface, and rise with even a more tortured, twisted expression imprinted upon his face.

At first, Jordan though the man was having a heart attack. In between gurgled pleas and wildly erratic arm maneuvers, it was clear that the man didn't know how to swim. It was barely six feet to the safety of the side. Drowning proved eminent. The movements rapidly waned as the bodyguard took one last breath before he disappeared under the surface.

The filter hummed.

The struggle had ceased.

"Crap!" Jordan managed to utter.

He quickly climbed up the pool stairs. His limbs, face, and back felt like he carried the weight of the world. His thoughts were of the Taser. Quickly scanning the pool's surface, he spotted the device floating at the far corner. Wasting no time, he fished it out.

Jordan scrambled to pick up his backpack, shaking from the adrenalin and sopping wet from head to toe. He took one last look at the man floating face down in the water before he ran to the wall where he had entered and climbed over. His heart pounded, along with short, ragged breaths, but a newfound hope that he would somehow find Emily safe – and alive.

CHAPTER TWENTY-EIGHT
Friday 2345 Hours

Even though she did not hear the body hit the street, Emily knew that it would be only minutes before the first responders and police arrived. They would swarm around the hotel and move quickly up to Easterbrook's penthouse orchestrating a mob scene.

Smashed and broken, the intended target's body gathered a horrified audience. Screams overlapped one another.

Bishop procured exactly what he wanted, just another means of death. The anger welled up inside of Emily, just as on other occasions when she wanted to kill the perpetrator instead of forwarding her evidence to the cops and letting the system take care of them. She fought a fine line of justice with every case. It proved more difficult with time.

Why go through the preliminary motions? Just kill the bastards.

Hurrying throughout the sprawling hotel room, Emily gathered her purse from the bathroom and then used a hand towel wiping off her fingerprints from doorknobs, fixtures, and anything else in her path.

She checked the gun, only one bullet in the chamber. Red thought of everything, she mused. Without hesitation, she slipped the gun into her small handbag and quickly exited the room.

The chime of the elevator interrupted the silence of the hallway.

It could have been anyone arriving on the floor, but Emily was not taking any chances. She ran to the stairs.

Immediately the cold steps chilled her bare feet as she quickly padded down several flights, feeling the extra coolness blow through her dress.

Her heart pounded in her chest, louder with each landing. She rounded another corner as Red caught her by the arm. He jerked it with such a force that her shoulder instantly throbbed with pain.

To Emily's surprise, Red's agile ability quickened as he dragged her downward with a vice grip on her arm. She stubbed her little toe rounding another set of stairs, winded, angry, but afraid she would tumble head first down the rest of the stairs if she didn't keep up with the assassin.

Her chest ached with a severe heaviness; her thoughts were of blacking out. It seemed like hours since she left the penthouse, but the recent chain of events kept summersaulting.

Muffled sirens reverberated inside the exit stairs.

Imagining S.W.A.T. in full police gear lined up in formation waiting for her and Red, kept her mind jumping from one terrifying scenario to another.

The last few stairs jarred her joints and bones. Emily felt like a punching bag and the intense workout wasn't going to be over anytime soon. She gritted her teeth, but had no choice except to descend downward.

Red loosened his grip on her arm.

Emily fought the urge to stop and rest, just to have the luxury to close her eyes for a few minutes. Exhaustion set in like a five alarm fire. Her forearm tingled as the blood flow gained momentum once again; she could still feel where Red's tight grip and fingers had encircled around her arm.

They stopped in front of the hotel parking garage door.

Red flung open the exit entry. He took hold of Emily's arm again to steer her toward a limousine parked in the corner.

Exhaust fumes intertwined with the usual garage smells as a few cars passed by and drove out.

Quickly opening the back door of the luxury car, Red pushed Emily inside. Resting on the seat were the two suitcases he had carried into the hotel, along with a pile of folded clothes.

As Emily pushed her way to the other side of the seat, her dressed ripped above the hemline.

Red shut the door.

The limo slowly backed up and eased out into the exit line.

Red tossed a pair of jeans, a white tank top, and a grey sweatshirt at Emily. "Put these on." Inside a brown paper bag was a pair of black boots that he dropped in front of her.

He retrieved her purse, opened it, and took out the gun. Without hesitation, he slipped the firearm into his jacket.

Emily waited for her breathlessness to subside and the dizziness to fade before she unzipped her dress. Normally it would bother her to undress in front of a stranger, but Red showed no interest, and changing into comfortable clothes would lessen her extreme feeling of vulnerability.

Wiggling into her new jeans, it struck her again as incredibly invasive that Red knew this much about her. Even though she was cold, perspiration trickled down her back while she quickly put on the clothes.

The lights of the city shone through the window and flashed by at a high speed. They headed northwest, from what she could tell, was the opposite direction of the train station.

"Where are we going?" She asked directly.

Red turned and stared at her.

"I did what you wanted. The target is dead." Her voice sounded tired and winded.

"You didn't do as you were told." He said flatly.

"He's dead."

After a moment, he finally said matter of fact. "I could kill you right now and throw your body out on the side of the road."

It made chills climb up the back of Emily's neck.

"You got what you wanted. Let Rick go."

Red looked out his window. "It's not up to me."

"Then tell Bishop." Emily steadied her voice with all of the strength she had left. "What do you want from me?"

"You will know when it's relevant."

"Where are we going?" She unconsciously touched the pendant around her neck.

"The airport."

CHAPTER TWENTY-NINE
Saturday 0910 Hours

Annoyed and heavily winded, the detective forged onward. Now with a new wheeze to add to his already difficultly to stabilize the moderate asthma condition, Detective Duncan took the stairs carefully down the to the medical examiner's office. It wasn't unusual that he worked on the weekend; it merely added another factor to his already heavy workload.

To take his mind off his escalating medical condition, the detective mulled over everything he knew about the arson cases. With little to no physical evidence, and without any eyewitness accounts, the cases would continue to pile up.

A sharp pain invaded his left side and then took a twisting route through the intestines. The veteran police detective waited until it subsided, and realized that he shouldn't drink five cups of coffee without eating anything. He reprimanded his neglect. He fought the consensus around the station that catching bad guys should be left to the younger, stronger, and more determined cops. He trudged forward, determined to make them eat their words.

The medical examiner's office was behind in autopsies. Nothing unusual, but it meant that important, potential clues waited as well. It also meant that the detective's arson investigation came to a screeching halt.

Duncan pushed through the door identified as *autopsy*, which was stenciled on the glass window.

The space instantly loomed with the smell of death, propelling the feelings of pain and grief. The typical cleaning aromas mixed together tried to overpower death and decay, but merely managed to mask the initial assault to the senses.

Feeling some relief in his lungs, the detective moved faster to one of the exam rooms.

Dr. Sherman hunched over the stainless table with some type of small, pointed instrument picked at the charred remains of the victim from the barn location. The burned body count rose to six, and that didn't include Judge Christensen, his daughter and son-in-law.

Sherman looked up, raised his bushy eyebrows, which peered intensely over his bi-focals. As he smiled, his short teeth looked more like a happy face on a pumpkin. For all the unique quirks of the coroner, his expertise was clearly in the forensic arena, and finding clues that many other medical examiners carelessly overlooked.

"Bobby nice to see you." He smiled.

The detective didn't mind that the doctor called him by his first name. He reciprocated. "Fred." He nodded a polite gesture. "So what do you have?"

Walking over to the desk and picking up a file, "Your vic is Timothy Dalton."

The detective held his breath for a moment. The lawyer, the defendant, and the judge from the same case all burned ... trapped. His mind leaped forward. Quickly, he accessed possible scenarios, motives, and anyone who would want all of them dead. Everything came back in his mind – the victims and families. It overloaded him.

"How'd you identify him so quickly?" The detective finally asked.

"He had this..." The doctor held up a small piece of twisted metal in a plastic bag.

"What is it?"

"Medical alert bracelet that he wore on a chain around his neck, which had melted to his sternum, but I was able to get the ID numbers."

167

"What was his medical condition?"

"Diabetic."

"Hmmm." The detective scanned the charred remains of the pedophile. It resembled a dark, twisted puzzle that grew more grisly the more he stared at it. He was unable to pry his eyes away from it.

"I have something a little more interesting." The medical examiner retrieved a box. He put it down in front of the detective. "This was the bear trap that was affixed to the ankle, but not just any animal trap.

"Meaning?"

"Meaning…" He contorted his face when he had an idea or a new clue to share. "It's an antique bear trap with an identifying number A377 and a manufactures name Out-something."

A voice piped up from behind the men, "So you mean if we find a bear trapper that wanted a bunch of people dead by arson, then we've got our guy?"

Duncan didn't need to turn from his note pad; in fact, he would rather stare at burnt bodies all day instead of dealing with Fire Investigator Myers.

"Just letting you know that the preliminary report is that the judge's house was intentionally set with multiple accelerants. This time the perp didn't care much about hiding how he set the fire." He sidled up to the exam table and stared at the crispy remains of Devlin. "Don't think anyone is going to mourn for you buddy."

The detective stared at the investigator questionably.

"Oh, I already heard it was the acquitted kiddie fiddler." He smirked and then shuddered dramatically to add more of a dramatic effect. "Word is… the Feds are going to be all over this case because of the judge, damages to city, personal property, and everything else…"

"What are you saying?" The detective asked in more of an accusatory tone.

Shrugging as he replied, "All I'm saying is that through the grapevine your investigation is going to be high jacked soon."

CHAPTER THIRTY
Saturday 0945 Hours

Emily watched the trees and hills disappear. Then they reappeared from underneath the clouds. From her shotgun seat in the single engine Cessna airplane, the countryside laid out a generous view. The aircraft shimmied occasionally, dipped suddenly every few minutes, but overall it would have been an enjoyable sightseeing tour under any other circumstances.

Red proved to be a lethal assassin, intelligent, with obvious psychopathic tendencies, and an accomplished pilot. For a man of few words, it was clear that the killer followed orders. He rarely looked at Emily, but seemed to anticipate her every move from experience and the ability to study people.

It was a long night of catching only a few restful moments until the plane took off from the Orange County Airport. The next assignment would not be as simple as the last. Emily could only sit idly by and wait.

The clear sky with breathtaking views of the mountains surrounding Lake Tahoe made Emily more uncomfortable and helpless with each second that passed. The dense forests and tranquility of the area left her isolated – both emotionally and physically. If she found a way to escape, or if she killed Red, instant death was Rick's fate – no questions asked. She longed to talk with Rick because she knew that he would be able figure a way out of the situation. His calm, intelligent manner would discover an ingenious way out.

DEAD BURN

Closing her eyes, Emily concentrated on the gentle ride of the plane's easy maneuvers as they began their descent toward the small Lake Tahoe airport. She tried to channel Rick's energy to seek some type of subtle clue that she had missed.

* * * * *

His entire life was about killing. There was little room for anything else, no family, no hobbies, and no chance of changing professions. Nothing excited him other than his next contract. The thrill of the hunt, the challenge of a flawless plan, and a perfect execution of the killing method kept Red getting out of bed every morning.

Within ten minutes, Red would land the Cessna at Lake Tahoe. It was one of the most popular destinations for winter thrill seekers and vacationers alike, and one of the last pristine areas that bordered on the California and Nevada state lines.

Red's life reduced to a precisely scheduled day. At least until Emily Stone crossed paths with the *Ones* who watched the rest of society. A dangerous move on her part, but he had to respect her on one level because she got the job done. Her motivation baffled him. In an odd twist of fate, they were two sides of the same type of personality. She on one hand, cared about justice and doing the right thing, and he did not.

He watched her struggle with her own internal demons and decisions she had to make. Most likely, she wanted to kill him, but her conscience wouldn't allow it. That was where their personalities drastically contrasted. Red killed indiscriminately with simple orders and never looked back. It's dumb luck that many of his targets were bad people, and some were just citizens who got in the way of the bigger plans of others.

He saw Emily close her eyes. She leaned against the window. Her face looked at peace, relaxed, as tension left her mouth and jaw. The unintended gestures she made with her hands and her hypnotizing dark eyes intrigued him. Red knew she was a beautiful and intelligent woman. He knew that he should feel some attraction toward her, but there was nothing but a small degree of respect.

Red had died a long time ago, and merely existed among the living. The game of killing had run its course, but he knew that the only way out was death.

The airport became visible and the tower had cleared him to land.

Red directed the plane accordingly, eased up the engine, and prepared for a landing. The only time he felt outside of himself was portraying someone else, even just for a moment, like when he piloted an aircraft.

The small plane thumped the runway with ease, slowed its approach, and taxied to a private departure area.

CHAPTER THIRTY-ONE
Saturday 1015 Hours

The reprieve lasted longer than expected. The abduction had a hint of an amateur quality to it. The strong overtones of something, or someone, much bigger nagged at Rick's suspicious nature. He kept mulling over all of the events leading up to his kidnapping.

His shoulders, back, and neck burned from the secured position in the metal chair for more than a day. He doubted that even if he did stand up, tried to fight, or run with any real skill or speed, it might prove deadly. Hunger tormented him. Whoever was behind the kidnapping obviously didn't have plans to keep him alive for long and made no provisions for his comfort.

The musty building along with the smell of an old septic system was never far away.

He knew it was morning through the tiny crack of light underneath the hood.

The nighttime had pushed his psyche to the limit; it tortured everything he thought he could endure. Screaming or pleading wasn't an option; it would only entertain his captors by forcing his pain to the limit.

Think.

Everything around him meant something vital. The sounds, smells, type of restraints around his wrists and legs. The young guard who oversaw him was an important clue to pinpoint the location, and possibly, who ordered the kidnapping.

How do they all add up?

The day grew brighter. He guessed the time around mid-morning.

If Rick strained his ears, he heard the faint but constant flow of traffic.

Think.

He shifted in his chair to relieve the pressure against his hips and lower back; the numbness had set in to his posture. Using his mental filing system, he imagined different locations around California that would be less than a mile from the heavy flow of daily traffic.

Warehouse?

Historical location?

Abandoned commercial building?

All of these locations were possible. He began to mentally tick off locations he knew well, like a closed warehouse that manufactured computer components, a historic mission, and a partially demolished apartment building.

None of these locations seemed plausible holding areas.

Think.

A low moan followed by a high-pitch squeak cut into Rick's thought process.

Slow shuffling feet approached.

The hood pulled with a quick jerk revealed some sanity again. A blinding light and circulating air rushed at Rick. It relieved his breath. He kept his head down for a moment so that his eyes could adjust to the morning light. The horrible stink swirled around the small room, but at least it moved instead of staying stagnant and trapped under the hood.

The recognizable aroma of grease took over the air. It was one of the most welcoming smells that Rick could think of at the moment.

The young man stood over him with a fast food bag and bottle of water. He hesitated, dropped the bag and water next to Rick, and then roughly released his hand restraints.

Not missing a beat, the captor backed up against the wall, pulling a gun from his waistband.

Waving the pistol, the man said. "Eat."

Rick leaned to the side and grabbed the bottle of water first. His hands shook as he twisted the plastic top off. His shoulders cramped painfully as his moved both arms in a stiff manner. Bringing the liquid to his lips, he drank hurriedly; even the rekindled stinging pain of his busted lip didn't slow him down as he swallowed more than half of the bottle.

In a whispered voice, he replied. "Thanks." Rick almost didn't recognize the raspy voice that escaped out of his mouth.

"You seem like a guy that likes beef, so I got you two burgers." The captor's eyes darted back and forth in nervous tension.

Rick nodded.

Even though he was famished, he still scrutinized the young man, staring at him with mild curiosity. It was clear that the man had done prison time, probably more for drugs or robbery. When it came down to killing Rick, the man hesitated. That was the sign of an amateur or relatively non-violent criminal, but it didn't mean that he wasn't ultimately capable of carrying out the murder.

Tearing the wrapping from the first hamburger, Rick ate the entire sandwich in five well-received gulps. It didn't matter to him that he despised pickles on his burger because it was the best burger he had ever eaten.

The feeling in his hands and fingers returned with a warm and slightly painful sensation, traveling up his arms to his tense shoulders. He didn't realize how low his energy was until he began to eat, starvation had readied itself in his body and conserved the appropriate strength for survival.

"Did you already eat?" Rick asked casually as he unwrapped the second burger.

"Yeah about an hour ago." He kept flipping the gun safety on and off.

It showed the telltale actions of an unskilled kidnapper, possibly on his first assignment.

"The burgers are awesome on the corner of El Camino, you know that place with the Hawaiian looking sign out front." Rick casually spoke and knew it was taking a chance, but he had to begin to connect with the young man on any level.

"Umm, the burgers are better on State Street, the best guacamole burgers."

"I'll have to try that one."

Rick knew exactly where the burger restaurant was located. He speculated that the man lived near there and the building would be close to that spot. It was conceivable that this building was one of the partially demoed office buildings not far from the bridge overpass and highway interchange.

"I didn't get you any fries."

"No problem."

Rick stuffed the last bit of the second burger into his mouth. He felt better, but the pain on the side of his face began to throb.

The young man fidgeted and rubbed his left wrist. It was clear that he had better places to go, but whoever was running the assignment gave him the low job of watching the hostage.

"Hey man, I need to take a piss." Rick simply stated.

The jailer pointed to a metal bucket in the corner.

"C'mon give me a break. Cut me loose so I can stand up." He paused and then asked. "Where am I going to go?"

The man studied Rick for a minute before he moved toward him. He slipped the gun in the back of his waistband and unsecured the restraints.

As Rick stood up, he thought for a moment his legs would buckle and send him sprawled out on the filthy floor. He took a couple of steps toward the bucket and then relieved himself.

Pulling the gun, the captor pushed the barrel into his back. Rick wasn't sure if the safety was on or off. He wanted to gain trust with the young man and trying to get the upper hand now would easily prove fatal.

There would be a more appropriate opportunity to escape, if his death sentence wasn't handed down before then.

CHAPTER THIRTY-TWO
Saturday 1130 Hours

The passengers at the San Francisco International Airport prepared to board the plane heading to the South Lake Tahoe. It was early enough in the year that there wasn't any seasonal snowfall, so ski and snowboard enthusiasts wouldn't crowd the plane yet. The group, combined of all ages, seemed to indicate that the flight was at half capacity. Eager faces of tourists and some business people patiently took their turn giving the flight attendant their tickets.

Entering the jet way and walking toward the aircraft's main door, Jordan pondered if he was headed in the right direction, or if it was just a technical wild goose chase emitted from a cell phone app not fully tested.

His gut told him he was doing the right thing.

The folding tunnel echoed with both light and heavy footfalls. The dome-like pathway moved slightly from side to side before he reached the actual entrance.

Looking at his seat number, the flight attendant smiled. "Welcome." She said and allotted a few seconds with him.

"Is it going to be nice weather?" Jordan asked with a huge smile and a slight fat lip.

"It's clear weather and should be a smooth ride. Enjoy your flight sir." Her eyes twinkled, but it was clear that she repeated the same sentiments to thousands people every day. Like clockwork, she welcomed the next passenger with the same enthusiasm.

Jordan quickly located his seat; thankfully, it was next to the window so that he didn't have to partake in idle chitchat from strangers. He shoved his bag in the overhead compartment, and settled in for the ride. He slipped his laptop underneath him. As luck would have it, the two seats next to him remained vacant.

Flying proved hours faster than driving up the winding roads over the mountains. The engine revved, geared up, and then the airbus sped down the runway. It smoothly left the ground, took a sweep to the left, pointed north, and headed toward the Sierras.

As the plane leveled off for the required altitude, Jordan's thoughts were never too far from Emily. His heart always did a little funny jump when he thought about her. His heart had skipped a beat when he left Sarge at the Posh Doggie Daycare and Kennel. Even though, he was a just a dog, Sarge was Emily's dog.

Jordan shut his eyes after reclining his chair. He did not care if he wrinkled his clothes, or happen to fall asleep with his mouth gaped wide open. The arsonist cases ran through his mind, the cleverness of the detailed crime scenes, the specific victims, the changing signature, and each location different from the previous.

He gently passed the time studying the cases, careful not to dwell on the uncertainty of Emily's predicament.

The plane bumped with mild turbulence, rattled the overhead compartments, and settled once again.

Turning his head and scanning the rest of the passengers, Jordan watched a teenage boy playing with a handheld computer game across the aisle. Agile fingers moved over the keypad with nonstop motion, clearly an impulsive procedure. The slim, black plastic case allowed for anytime game play, and quick photo snapshots.

Remembering the black box Emily had given him from the fire scene, he hadn't had time to fully examine it.

It suddenly hit Jordan.

That black box was a hidden camera, it wasn't live now, but it was when the victim stood at the heavy steel door before entering – a perfect vantage to watch his prey.

The arsonist was nearby, maybe not at the actual locations, but close enough to interact with the victims before they died.

Power assertive?

Obsessive compulsive?

Another bump jarred Jordan. Opening his eyes again, he hated accommodating the uneasy feeling stowed away in the pit of his stomach.

Gazing out the window, he saw the magnificent mountains of the Sierras. They were everything as described, majestic, breathtaking, and wondrous. The clouds pressed around the plane with a puffed contrast, providing a landscape foundation that made Jordan want to reach out and touch them.

That was what the arsonist wanted – to reach out and touch his victims.

CHAPTER THIRTY-THREE
Saturday 1300 Hours

Daylight dimmed as the afternoon continued. Rick knew that time closed in on his life and he had to step it up for his next challenge. Pinpointing the perfect time to strike would prove difficult, if not impossible, and there was no turning back once it was set in motion.

Time inched forward.

Subtle sounds rose and quieted with the passing hour before some familiar noises intruded.

The echoing sounds of his young guard, coming and going, indicated that there were two more rooms or common areas. Rattling of locks as a heavy chain jangled, another minute lapsed until the kidnapper was at the cell door.

Running each event over in his mind helped Rick to stay centered, focused, and not to miss any small details. Any factor increased the difference between freedom and death. He didn't have the hood over his head, which helped him immensely to scrutinize the surroundings.

Growing louder and shuffled, the footsteps came close to the cell area, but then retreated. It signified reluctance, and where there was hesitation, then there was the ability to turn the situation into your favor.

Clink.

Rick readied himself.

The door pushed open.

The man shuffled in with a plain white bag. There was no recognizable aroma permeating from it as he dropped it next to Rick.

"Thanks. What's on the menu?" Rick tried to sound upbeat, like a buddy.

"Sandwich."

The man robotically went through the same motions of releasing the restraints, settled on his gun, and targeted Rick's every move.

Slowly picking up the white bag, Rick felt his limbs much stronger as he grasped the paper wrapped sandwich oozing with mustard and mayonnaise. Tearing the butcher paper from the loaded hoagie, a pickle dropped from between the two pieces of bread and landed on the filthy floor leaving an odd imprint of cucumber juice.

"Great sandwich, better than homemade." Rick tried to start a conversation. He noticed how distracted and twitchy the young man became. Anger was just below the surface as he moved with jerky and anxious movements.

Rick could work with the personality weaknesses.

He tested the waters with his captor and mustered all his average, cool guy attitude. "Hey man, I couldn't help but notice that you're the only one that oversees this situation. What's up with that?"

The man looked at Rick, stared him down in a predatory manner, never blinking. For a moment, Rick thought he might just put a bullet in his head and be done with the entire situation.

The young man leaned forward, never taking his antsy fingers from the gun, flicking the safety on and off. It wasn't clear if he had ever fired a weapon.

Daring to continue, Rick added. "It's just that it seems like all the burden has fallen upon you, that's all." He shrugged his shoulders and looked away.

Rick waited for what seemed like an eternity for the young man to respond, with either violence or a comment.

"It sucks man."

Got him.

"Can totally relate. When I was working my first job, total disrespect by my co-workers and it sucked big time." For a moment, Rick thought he might have pushed too hard.

"You're not the right person to talk to…"

"Hey, I'm not going anywhere."

The guard stood up. He circled the room like a caged animal.

Rick knew it was only a matter of time before he wised up to the manipulation, but the human psyche always responded to someone who seemed interested in listening.

"Have you ever had someone tell you that you're nothing, and you deserve what you get?"

Rick wasn't prepared for that question, but didn't miss a beat. "They are people who feel small and take it out on everyone around them."

The man stopped and turned to look at Rick. "Do you really believe that?"

"Hey, I've got a decade, or more on you, and one thing I've learned is that *everyone* has issues." Rick shifted his weight in the uncomfortable chair, trying to relax his neck and shoulders.

"Yeah well, some people think they are better than others." He started pacing again, swinging the pistol in an erratic motion.

"They are the ones that feel the lowest."

"They just suck as people." He swung the gun up to his face and scratched his chin.

"True, but the world is filled with people like that." Rick tried not to let his sarcasm seep into his voice. Irony came to mind. How idiotic his conversation was with the young man.

Almost five minutes had passed before the man responded to Rick. Watching him with curiosity, he seemed like he was in another world. It wasn't clear if he had taken some drugs or just had a deficit of mental capacity.

"So you really want to talk?" The man looked curiously at Rick, eyes dark and foreboding, never taking his hand from the loaded gun.

"Sure, why not?"

Rick hoped that it wouldn't be his last conversation.

CHAPTER THIRTY-FOUR
Saturday 1700 Hours

Not bothering to check in to one of the local motels, Jordan decided that it was best to keep looking for Emily. Time pushed ahead and weaved a trap against him.

The early evening chilled the air. The reality of finding more information kept Jordan vigilant and hopeful as he drove up and down streets in a line search method, just like searching for evidence at a crime scene.

He had rented a standard mid-class car after leaving the airport. It had the usual pungent smell of old cigarettes masked by a putrid floral spray. He tossed everything into the trunk, except for his laptop and cell phone.

The Internet signal bounced around, depending upon if he drove up a hill into a densely wooded area, or into an open parking lot behind a casino. The security icon still showed the necklace to be near South Lake Tahoe within the approximate area of five square miles. It wasn't quite like a needle in a haystack, but it was still an arduous search.

The greenish yellow blip on the small screen pulsed with life, it knew secrets. The more Jordan watched the tedious blinking, the more it seemed to want to reach out to him.

The familiar chime emanated from the cell phone that there was a missed message. Jordan almost dropped the phone before he could read the number, but to his dismay, it was from one of his security clients confirming an appointment.

Turning into a casino parking lot, he easily found a parking place. It was strategically located where he could walk to several casinos.

The fresh air would improve his mood and energy. The hint of the clean pine smell, a sweet aroma of the woods never drifted far away, and kept the constant atmosphere of the beautiful location within arm's reach.

Pulling open the back door entrance to a casino and restaurant, Jordan stepped inside. Laughter and falling coins instantly filled the void of the darkened cave. The establishment heavily adorned with dizzying mirrors, nonstop gambling, and a carpet with a repeating, nauseating design reminiscent of a carnival bombarded him.

The jingling change hit plastic containers like clockwork, while the constant beeping, dinging, and applause of various slot machines overpowered one area after another. It boggled the mind and frenzied the equilibrium.

Jordan eyed every pretty, petite fair-haired woman, but none of them was Emily.

Why would Emily be in a casino?

He glanced at his phone again. It repeated the same alert for the necklace. It was close, maybe not in this casino, but nearby.

The process of elimination anchored Jordan's thoughts and cooled his gut instincts – at least for a few minutes. With all of the energy and thrill of the chase to find Emily and Rick, Jordan felt deep sadness.

Casually walking through the casino, he noticed all eyes focused on picture screens, cards or the dice. Many hoped of hitting it rich and all of their problems would cease. Life precariously worked in mysterious ways – it was rarely what you planned.

A pretty, redheaded cocktail waitress approached Jordan. "What would you like?"

"Nothing right now, thank you."

The lovely waitress in a short skirt with a top two sizes too small, smiled and moved on.

Jordan eased his way through one casino and then into the next, taking special care to look at the faces of the patrons and employees. He knew the investigative drill, but it didn't make his nerves slack in the least.

The second garish casino had even more sparkles, bangles, clattering of slot machines, and relentless noises than the previous one.

Glancing up at the ceiling, each mirrored tile tilted precisely in a certain direction. Jordan knew that security watched every face coming and going with high-tech computers, and communications with pit bosses and managers. If something looked out of place, they escorted those individuals to the street. Everything worked around the clock to perform seamlessly, while millions cashed in and out on a regular basis.

A woman rounded a corner in a striking black dress, but she had long brown hair. The female shape, stride, and confidence drew Jordan's attention. He recounted the first meeting with Emily and it struck a familiarity with him.

With the dim lighting and clashing sparkles of the surroundings, the woman disappeared. Jordan couldn't make an accurate identification from the brief glimpse.

Why would she be here walking around in a disguise?

Jordan faced dozens of more questions as he made his way through the crowds of people, some trying to balance their drinks looking for the next plan of attack to gain riches. He grew weary of saying excuse me to wide-eyed tourists from mid-western states and tiny towns. It was like trying to direct an unruly crowd into participating in a three-act play.

Jordan kept his focus and pushed on as best as he could under the circumstances.

A large, intoxicated man bumped into Jordan, and mumbled something that didn't resemble English, or anything spoken on Earth.

Droplets from the mixed drink dappled across Jordan's shirt.

Damn.

Vodka had been the drink of choice for the staggering man. Jordan received the strong smell of a distillery blasted across the front of his favorite shirt to prove it.

Moving through a group of meandering senior citizens straight off a tour bus, Jordan forged onward. He still didn't see the dark haired beauty, but hopefully retraced her steps.

Standing at an exit, Jordan hesitated. He looked back behind him and decided to go outside.

He burst through the door and came to another parking structure. Cars entered in a never-ending stream, quickly slipping into any available space. He doubled back around the parking area, ending up in a V.I.P area for limos, high-priced foreign cars, and celebrity acts. Several cars filled the garage, but now, it remained deserted from patrons and employees.

Dead end.

Frustrated and equally furious with himself for taking the extra time away from systematically searching the casinos, restaurants, and surrounding businesses. In his haste and annoyance, he didn't see the tall, severe-looking man wearing a black leather jacket quickly approach.

Just as Jordan turned to head back toward the casino, Red shoved him against a cement barrier and caught him off balance. He fell hard onto the ground, jarring his entire torso, clacking his teeth, which caused a weird echo in his head. He lost his breath abruptly.

"What are you doing?" Jordan wheezed as he used the barrier to regain his balance. "Look man, I don't know what you…"

Before he could finish his strained sentence, Red stepped forward and threw an impressive jab-cross combination to his face, dropping him to the ground.

Crap.

Jordan willed his eyes to open, but the only thing he saw were tiny flicks of luminous lights floating in his peripheral vision just before everything went dark.

CHAPTER THIRTY-FIVE
Saturday 1800 Hours

The restraints showed a little more slackness than before, which facilitated Rick's constant, steady movement of his wrists in order to loosen them. He would wait a moment or two to lessen the burning sensation, which caused the severe rawness around his wrists and arms. He continued with the same procedure.

"I just don't get it." The young man continued with a strange voice inflection that waned every so often, "I'm the one who goes to jail if we're caught? How screwed up is that?"

"Did you tell them your concern?" Rick tried to sound interested, but his patience had grown weary. He despised everything about the young man.

The restraints expanded a little bit more.

The captor spewed rants of persecution, and continued along with lame attempts to prove himself right. He looked up from the wall, where he had obsessively picked at the remnants of an old warning sign for electrical outlets.

"What?" He asked in an accusatory tone.

"Have you tried to tell them your side?"

Flip flopping from the whining lower rank employee to a raging psychopath, he ranted more. "What do you think? Do you think *I'm* stupid? Don't you think I know what you're doing?"

"Hey, I'm just talking to pass the time, that's all."

Just a little bit more, tugging one way, then the other.

"You think you're so much smarter than I am, don't you? You're so special that people actually want you dead."

He paced, while waving the gun back and forth. "They do want you dead, you know. After your girlfriend does what they want." He leaned forward showing his uneven teeth. "Then you're both dead."

Rick almost responded, but thought better to keep his mouth shut. The conversation headed between the fine line of ridiculous and deadly.

"And I have to clean up this shit!" He kicked debris at the bathroom bucket, knocking it over.

Dust floated around the tight quarters.

"Do you know what that's like?" He emphasized.

Rick slowly shook his head, never taking his eyes from the kidnapper. Things could go sideways any second.

Flipping the gun safety on and off relentlessly, the man used the gun as a primitive tool to scrape against the wall. Chunks of debris crumbled down the side and rested in compact piles.

The ropes stung Rick's wrists; he felt the blood running over his hands.

"It's not fair." The man mumbled more to himself than to Rick.

He worked the ropes faster.

Seconds counted.

The young man stopped raging as abruptly as he had started. He turned and craned his neck in an awkward position. His eyes unfocused and dead as he took two carefully placed steps and swung the gun at Rick's head.

Rick had anticipated the attack, raised himself up slightly from the seat of the chair, just as the blow struck his upper left shoulder knocking him over onto the floor.

Dust and old construction fragments blustered around in the air and into his sinuses.

The impact was enough to release Rick's right hand, but his legs and feet were still stationary.

The kidnapper stood above Rick, staring down.

Rick waited to hear – a gunshot.

The young man curiously leaned down and tried to grab the back of the chair to pull it up, but it was too heavy. He slipped the gun into his waistband. Using both hands, he leaned down toward Rick.

Anger fueled Rick's adrenalin. It was now or never. As the man leaned in closer, Rick blasted a punch to his throat. A direct hit landed with a harsh reality – a deathblow.

The only thing Rick could do was watch as the man staggered, gasping for air, and finally fall to the floor. The pounding heart beat and breathlessness was the only sound that radiated in his ears.

The young man lay sprawled out on the floor, wide eyed, staring at the ceiling. The ranting and raving had ceased.

Breathless and exhausted, Rick flopped back onto the filthy floor to catch his breath.

He despised the kidnapper, not for trying to kill him, but for making him take such drastic measures to take another person's life.

Slowly sitting up, Rick began the tedious task of removing the rest of his restraints. He felt lighter. The pressure of doom had been lifted; however, it didn't take away the stinging pain of the wounds sustained on his shoulder and face.

The young man's frozen position reminded Rick of how fleeting life could be, especially when emotions took over actions.

Rick took the gun and the captor's cell phone. He immediately called Emily's cell phone.

No answer.

Hastily he called Jordan, but it also went straight to voice mail.

Without wasting anymore time, Rick pushed through the doorway of his holding cell. He was surprised to see that the rest of the abandoned building wasn't as dilapidated as the small room. The entire building needed to be torn down, but it looked relatively clean. It looked as if someone had swept up.

Rick zigzagged through rooms and hallways. Finally, climbing down the rickety staircase, he found the door, which led outside.

The cool evening air welcomed him.

Freedom.

As Rick continued toward a populated area, he never saw the carefully hidden video camera, which had recorded the evening's events.

CHAPTER THIRTY-SIX
Saturday 1900 Hours

Steady up and down and side-to-side movements woke Jordan. Extreme grogginess accompanied by a crushing pain radiated from his jaw up to the top of his head. Stale vodka mixed with the stink of rubber and grease made him fight the involuntary urge to vomit.

Darkness accompanied by the occasional red flashing light, on and off, was the only view from his peripheral. The rose-colored neon lights blinked in unison, which appeared next to one another in an equal distance apart.

Nausea loomed.

Extreme discomfort telescoped throughout his body.

Reeling in uncertainty, Jordan thought he was lost in a dream, or at least hoped. The weaving motion continued, each time with a little more drastic movement that pushed his body against something solid. As a reflex, he tried to sit up from his position, but hit his head on a low ceiling. It caused a sharp pain to throb in a pounding rhythm.

Panic set in as he tried to find his way out of the dark, hitting restrictions at every turn.

Jordan's body slid to one side. It then changed directions again as his stomach heaved and dropped. It took serious concentration and will power to stop the barf process, but in the end, his body did exactly what it wanted to do. He heaved his last meal into the small confinement.

"Ahhh man." Jordan moaned. "What the hell is going on?" He gasped and swallowed hard, trying to keep another regurgitation from erupting.

Lights from an unknown source illuminated the tight confinement.

Jordan discovered the tight space was actually the interior of a car trunk.

"Hey! Let me out of here!" He banged his fists on the metal above his head, and kicked at the side of the back quarter panel.

The car took a sharp left turn, which threw Jordan's body to one side. The mysterious driver took hard maneuvers to the left, and then the right.

"Oh geez!"

Jordan tried to steady his body. Nothing else entered his mind, except for his ride to be over, and to keep what little was left in his stomach where it belonged.

"Stop!"

His fists and feet flailed in a jerky display, but no one seemed to pay any attention to him. The car made another tight turn in a seemingly endless winding road of pure hell.

"Hello!"

* * * * *

The longer he drove up the mountain road, the denser the Pine trees became. The magical quality of the forest was infectious to most. It had a calming quality to it, but to Red it didn't make any difference if it was the forest, the desert, or a state prison.

He knew the final destination. It took a little longer to get there by doubling back and driving up the roads again. His prisoner continued to shout and kick noisily from inside the trunk.

Red didn't slow the rental car, or take any special care managing one hairpin turn after another. The road narrowed. He upped the headlights as the trees closed in around the road, which gave the display of driving through an organic tunnel. The light cast shadows, bouncing back onto the road in strange streams of brightness.

No cars passed or eased up from behind. It made his job easier and less likely to have anything go wrong.

It was time to clean up the assignment and not allow any loose ends. The job had rapidly begun to turn into a saga. It would end now. He kept his prospects vigilant.

Red knew all about Jordan Smith, his previous job with the F.B.I., background with criminal profiling, recent security work, and his relationship to Emily Stone. The cleverness, resourcefulness, and intelligence pushed through Jordan's extroverted and quirky personality. It was obvious that Jordan had a crush on Emily, it was something that Red could almost relate to because of the little bit of time he had spent with her.

Yellow eyes reflected from a thick cluster of trees. As the car drove past, Red saw a large buck standing in the forest, regal and watchful. The animal reminded him again of how much he hated Bishop and his situation.

Instinctively, he eased up on the gas pedal, and maneuvered the car around to a partial clearing. The car travelled onto the wide dirt path. He continued up a hill and then made a sharp right, parked, and cut the engine.

Red kept the headlights illuminated. A causal passerby or motorist wouldn't interrupt him in at work, and no one would hear anything except for the typical mountain wildlife.

The area remained secluded.

He exited the car after grabbing a small flashlight, and checked his sidearm before he shut the driver's door. Everything was quiet with an occasional subtle snap of a twig from a small animal or a pinecone dropping to the ground.

No sound came from the trunk.

Releasing the gun safety, he sent a bullet into the chamber.

Red popped open the trunk, directing the flashlight beam into Jordan's battered face. The smell of vomit and old booze instantly clouded the air.

"Get out." He ordered in an even tone.

"Who... who are you?" Jordan stammered.

"I'm not going to say it again."

"Okay... okay..." Jordan struggled to sit up, wincing as he climbed out of the trunk. "Do you mind not directing that flashlight in my eyes?"

Red took a step back, but pushed the gun toward Jordan's face. "Walk." He motioned with the pistol in the direction of the path, which led deeper into the forest.

Jordan steadied himself with his hands up next to his head, eyes wide with anxiety. He never took his focus from the barrel of the gun. He said. "I think there's some kind of misunderstanding."

"Move."

"Who are you?"

Red walked behind Jordan, but didn't offer any kind of explanation.

"Did I piss someone off?" Jordan's voice cracked slightly as he walked further into the darker area of trees.

"Stop." The assassin ordered.

Jordan turned to face Red. His face paled, his hands shook. A distinct bruising appeared on the side of his face.

"Turn around."

Jordan squeezed his eyes shut and turned around.

"Get down on your knees, keep your hands laced on the back of your head, eyes forward."

"Hey man... you really don't want to do this..."

"Do it now."

Jordan slowly dropped to his knees. All of the energy ran out of him as he slumped forward. His breathing increased. With a violent fury, he vomited several more times.

Red moved forward and pressed the gun against the back of Jordan's head. He stood over the security expert, and watched as the man crumbled under the reality of dying.

Most people had the same reaction in Red's experience. He often wondered; if he was in the same position, if he would fold like a coward.

"You're going to do exactly what I say." Red instructed, this time his voice raised slightly in between syllables.

Taking a breath, Jordan answered. "What do you want from me?"

"Because I'm saving your life today, you'll help me when I tell you to. Understand?"

Jordan turned to look at the tall man dressed completely in black. "When... is that?"

"When I tell you."

The forest set the picture-perfect stage for the conversation between assassin and victim by growing even darker. The shadows moved. They changed sinewy shapes, which left an eerie pretext for what would happen next.

"What's your name?" Jordan asked.

"You don't need to know."

"How will I know who you are when you contact me again?"

"You'll know."

Looking at Red curiously, he inquired. "Do you know what happened to Emily Stone?"

"Yes."

CHAPTER THIRTY-SEVEN
Saturday 2200 Hours

The hotel room door burst wide open. Jordan ran toward Emily and almost fell over a table and side chair, just as they caught each other.

"I'm so glad that you're okay. I knew it was you in the casino, even with the long brown hair." Jordan rambled in a breathless manner.

Emily was stunned to see Jordan's battered appearance. The distasteful odor of day old booze and what smelled like someone's regurgitated dinner emanated from his shirt.

"Yuck Jordan, you stink." Emily backed away, wrinkling her nose.

"That's all you can say to me? Do you know what this guy put me through?"

Emily glanced at Red standing near the door. "I have a pretty good idea. Where's Rick?"

Jordan looked at Emily. "I don't know. I thought he was with you." Glancing back at Red, he said. "He's not the chattiest guy in the world, but he said that Rick's safe."

"Red?" Emily inquired.

Both Emily and Jordan looked at the man that held everyone's life in the palm of his hand. No expression registered on the assassin's face.

"So you *do* have a name." Jordan quipped. "I thought maybe it was El Diablo or Satin, or something along those lines."

Emily confronted Red. "Where is Rick? I've done everything you've asked."

Jordan interrupted. "Done what?"

"Sit down." Red ordered.

"I don't think that…" Emily started.

"Sit down." He said again.

Slowly, Emily and Jordan gave each other an inquisitive look before they complied with the demand.

Red began, "I'm going to say this once. You're going to work for me."

"What?" Emily snapped.

Red raised his gun in her direction. "First, Mr. Smith here is going to help me with an assignment that we have in the near future." He turned his attention completely to Emily, "Second, I'm going to let you live for your cooperation."

"Cooperation for what?" She asked.

"With whatever I ask."

Turning to Emily, Jordan said. "He sounds more like a Magic 8 ball, doesn't he?"

"Please…" Emily stressed. "Where's Rick?"

Red cracked somewhat of a human expression to his usual poker face. The side of his mouth had a hint of a smile. "He doesn't need rescuing."

"What?" She said as a deep pressure rammed against her chest, from the thought of losing Rick in this convoluted nightmare.

"He escaped." Red searched his phone files. He handed it over to Emily.

Jordan pushed in close next to Emily to watch the video on the tiny screen. Rick fought with some unknown man, pounding him, and then escaping.

"Is this true? Is Rick safe?" She watched Red's expression, hoping that it wasn't another trick.

"He escaped and is probably home by now."

"Is he going to stay safe?" Emily got up from the couch and stood in front of Red. "How long are all of us going to be safe?"

"Safe enough. I've bought you some time."

Emily let out expelled air. Her anger rose. "Can't you just give us a direct answer? How are we expected to go about our lives with this hanging over our heads?

"All of the information concerning you is in Bishop's private files, and it will stay that way."

"Oh, I'm supposed to trust your word?"

Red looked at Jordan, and then rested his gaze on Emily. "Yes."

* * * * *

After dialing both Emily and Jordan's cell phones, Rick had exhausted the incoming mailboxes. As a result, the phones wouldn't take any more messages.

Damn.

Luckily, a good Samaritan gave Rick a ride home after he explained that he had been the victim of a robbery. He was dropped off several houses away from his house. He didn't know what to expect, or who could be there.

Figuring out what to do next was his top priority. He would find Emily no matter how long it took, but caution was imperative.

Watching the house from a distance, he decided to call Emily's cell phone once again.

It rang a third time before she picked it up. "Hello?"

"Em, it's me."

"Thank God you're safe." Emily said with relief in her voice.

For a moment, Rick thought he might have collapsed and fallen asleep, and Emily's voice was just a dream. "You okay?"

"Yes, I'm fine. I will be home sometime tomorrow morning."

"Where are you?"

"I'm… *we're* in Lake Tahoe."

"What? Who's we?"

Emily quickly explained. "Jordan came looking for me because of the pendant. I'll explain everything when I get home."

"I am going to a motel. Don't go to the house."

"Everything is okay, for now." She said.

"Meet me at the Rancho Suites and we will figure everything out. I don't trust anyone. Understand Em?" Rick was insistent.

"Okay, I'll see you there."

"I have to figure out how to get Sarge." He said.

"Jordan put him a doggie daycare."

"Oh."

"He's fine, I'll pick him up in the morning." She stated.

Rick's mind reeled with a dozen scenarios of what had happened to Emily, but his relief overwhelmed him. "Okay." He said slowly. "Be safe and I'll see you in the morning."

She hesitated. "Love you."

"I love you too Em. Hurry home."

The line disconnected.

Rick still stood in a nearby yard, loneliness never felt so ominous. He needed some things from the house, and to get his extra car keys for the SUV, but the house needed clearance before he entered.

Without another thought, he dialed 9-1-1.

"I'd like to report a break-in." He gave them the address. "There are two men still inside." He abruptly ended the call.

Rick walked to a neighbor's house and tucked into the carport. He knew that the tenant was gone on a business trip. It was a perfect place for him to watch, but not easily seen by cops.

As he waited, his stomach grumbled for a good meal. He couldn't wait to take a shower and assess his injuries. His nose and jaw ached.

He didn't have to wait long.

By the cell's clock, two patrol cars rolled up within twelve minutes of his call. Rick knew the routine. There was a pang of urgency in his stomach, like the many times when he was on patrol. It all seemed like another lifetime now.

He watched two officers approach the house using proper protocol, followed by two more officers that went around back. Out of precaution and procedure, they drew their weapons. One officer knocked on the front door. He identified them as the police and ordered the occupants to come outside.

They waited.

It was a tense situation, emphasized by their alert body language.

The front door was unlocked.

The two officers burst inside. They were greeted within seconds in the living room by the back-up officers. All four officers did a systemized search of each room.

Rick watched the scene unfold as the cops cleared the house for him. No unwanted occupants were inside. He felt a little bit guilty about wasting the police department's time, but his safety depended upon it.

Another fifteen minutes passed before the four officers left.

Rick waited another couple of minutes after the patrol cars drove away before he entered.

With nerves and energy frayed, Rick thought about the events from the past few days. Whatever they were involved in was about to change everything. It was only a matter of time before another dangerous situation presented itself, and he didn't want to think about what could happen.

Next time, they might not be as lucky.

CHAPTER THIRTY-EIGHT
Monday 1045 Hours

The clatter of dishes mixed with the aroma of strong coffee, eggs, greasy bacon, and burnt toast wafting throughout the diner. Idle chitchat among friendly servers and fry cooks livened up the place, and made it a favorite breakfast joint among locals. With only about ten tables and a dozen booths, it kept the place hopping for business.

The curvaceous, dark-haired waitress refilled Detective Duncan's coffee with a smile. She accentuated her body with a cute swing of the hips as she walked away.

He had positioned himself at a back booth to view people coming and going.

The detective kept glancing at his watch, wondering if he had done the right thing in inviting the fire investigator for a meeting away from both offices. It occurred on him that maybe he was consorting with the enemy, but the department would instantly take the case away from him if he brought up his concerns of the arson cases.

The F.B.I. pushing in and taking over was a definite possibility. The politics of the department looked for anything to get the detective to put in for his retirement. He wanted to solve this case and have a killer in custody before he decided to sign the departure papers.

Tearing open the zero calorie sugar packet, he plopped the substance into his coffee cup to cut the bitter taste. He never quite took to coffee after his rookie year, but managed to drink gallons of java with enough sugar, and now a sugar substitute.

The detective glanced at his cell phone in hopes of receiving a message with a break in the case, but none came. He knew that the phantom detective that most cops chalked up as an urban legend was real.

He remembered the serial case that was one of the most difficult cases he had encountered in his career. The killer used a common online game that people played from their laptops and cell phones to find his victims.

The covert detective had cracked the case, complete with an entire investigation rolled out for the cops. She even went up against the killer herself. It had amazed Duncan how the details fell into place, and the story seemed more like a movie than real life.

As the detective reflected on the past serial killer case, Fire Investigator Myers slid into the booth across from him with his usual smug expression.

The detective nodded his greeting. "Lance, thanks for agreeing to meet me."

"Well, I couldn't ignore your humble request." He motioned to the waitress for a cup of coffee. "Why don't you tell me what's on your mind."

Cooling his coffee and taking a healthy drink, the detective carefully chose his words. "This serial case is complex, and the department isn't giving me any support. They just want an arrest."

The waitress poured Myers a cup of coffee and gave a quick, flirtatious smile before moving to the next table.

"Typical for any political organization that feeds the public well spun propaganda, at least more than half of the time. Well, I actually think more like eighty percent of the time." Myers stated.

"Wow, a real cynic."

Laughing and pouring more imitation milk into his coffee cup, the mixture swirled in streaks. "Well, what do you expect? Anytime the public wants a case solved, bingo, it gets solved. It could be a case that's ten years old or ten days." The fire investigator leaned forward. "You know as well as I do that cases don't get solved, they get cleared by confessions."

"I guess you have it all figured out."

"I like you detective, I really do, and that's saying a lot because I don't like many people. But this arson case is a perfect platform for lots of publicity and re-election campaigns."

The detective searched Myer's face and demeanor to see if it indicated that he was blowing hot air for himself, or if he really believed what he said. The fire investigator had good eye contact and didn't fidget when he spoke certain buzzwords. Everything about him signified that he told the truth, and truly believed what he conveyed.

Myers took a breath and continued. "Let me cut through all the pleasantries here, you want to really look at these cases, and you want someone *outside* the walls of the police department to have your back. Am I getting warm?"

"I guess whether I want to admit it or not, you're beginning to grow on me." Duncan picked at the coffee stir stick.

"It sucks to have to ask for help." Myers slurped his coffee. He eyed the detective with increasing interest.

"This is going to be one of my last cases and I want to get this guy before there are ten more victims."

"Go on…"

"You're going to make me ask in those words, aren't you?"

"Yep." Myers smiled.

"Fine." The detective broke the stirrer in half. He stared at it for a moment. "I need your help, and this has to be between us, not the departments."

"Okay."

"Okay, what?"

Myers grinned from ear to ear. "You got me at a cost. I'll help with whatever I can." He leaned in and said, "But, you have to write me a recommendation for the promotion I'm up for."

"Done."

Myers picked up his coffee mug and made the gesture of a toast. "You know that you're never going to find the perp unless he finds you first." With a big smile, he tapped the detective's cup. "Here's to crime fighting."

Duncan hoped, now more than ever, that his cell phone would alert him soon with a break in the case from the phantom detective.

CHAPTER THIRTY-NINE
Thursday 1345 Hours

Emily unpacked one of the boxes in the living room. She ripped off the heavy packaging tape, and then unloaded the contents. Most household items were neatly emptied.

The front door sat wide open.

Rick joined her, carrying a double load of packed items. "I think this about the last of everything."

Emily nodded.

She had taken to the company of silence for the past two days, trying to make sense of why Rick had kept a secret from her. It also troubled her mind when Bishop's men might strike again.

Everything made her edgy and anxious.

She felt relieved about the move and was glad that Jordan had several contacts for house rentals. Maybe a new house would do the trick.

Sarge walked into the tight living room, sniffing every inch of the area and discarded boxes. After the scent task was completed, he chuffed and snorted, exhibiting his annoyance of the new surroundings.

"Take it easy Sarge, you can mark off your territory soon." Emily patted the big dog's head.

Rick stopped her and made her look at him. "You can't stay mad at me forever."

"I'm not mad."

"Yes you are. I think I know mad, and you're definitely still mad." He smiled, trying to pull her close in a playful manner.

"There are too many things to digest right now. I'm taking my time with everything. What's done is done." She sighed. "And now, I have to get settled into a new house."

Rick took his authoritative tone by pushing his position. "I'm sorry that you're mad, but I did what I thought was right at the time."

"How can you say that?" Emily's tone reflected her resentment.

"We were right in the middle of a case." He persisted.

"We're *always* right in the middle of a case." Her voice raised in volume. "I thought we had trust, and you should know that I'd want to know if the man that killed my parents was roaming free."

Rick gently guided Emily to the couch; he quickly made a space for them to sit down. "Look, I made a mistake. I didn't want you to be upset needlessly."

Emily weakened. "How can I defend myself if I don't know about him?"

"You're right. I'm sorry."

Emily's exhaustion overwhelmed her. She felt for the first time that she needed sleep desperately.

Rick continued. "C'mon, let's put all this stuff behind us... I know that your mind is on the arson cases, right?"

She nodded.

A twinge accompanied by a throbbing pain tightened in Emily's back, reminding her of the ordeal with Red. The underlying danger would always be floating just underneath the surface. She had to be strong, focus, and continue with her investigations no matter what.

"Right?" He pushed her hair from the side of her face.

"Yes... I have some new thoughts about the case."

Rick kissed her, lingered, and kissed her again.

"Did I hear my name?" Jordan entered. His face had healed up a bit. He still had a split lip, and some minor bruising from his jawline up to the cheekbone. "I knew you guys wouldn't be finished unpacking yet."

"Almost." Emily stood up, a little embarrassed because she didn't know how long Jordan had been standing there watching them.

Rick stood up. "Hey man, thanks so much for the lead on this house. It's really appreciated."

Emily added. "It will be nice to be on the coast again. Thanks Jordan."

"Wait a minute... hold the phone... Did I hear a thank you from big Rick here?" He dramatically said with a Cheshire cat grin, followed by a chuckle.

"Wise ass..." Rick picked up a box labeled *kitchen* and tossed it to Jordan. "Don't just stand there, be useful and unpack something."

"Haven't I taken enough beatings lately?" Jordan walked to the kitchen with Sarge keeping in step with him.

Rick raised his eyebrows and said, "I think Sarge has found a new play buddy."

"Yeah, well it was that doggie spa that clinched the deal. Now Sarge only wants gourmet, all organic food."

Emily felt some relief with her talk with Rick, but she also still felt a sting of betrayal. She would get over it, but it would take some time.

After settling in somewhat, she had some specific things that she wanted to check out – alone.

Emily's next place of investigation was at the old barn.

CHAPTER FORTY
Thursday 1900 Hours

The dark, uneven road with overgrown trees arched precariously across the single lane. It added to the overall spooky surroundings, which could double as a backdrop for a horror film. Deep divots from emergency vehicles marred the path.

Emily flipped back and forth, between low and high beams, trying to determine if one was better than the other. They were both inadequate.

She eased up on the speed.

Small branches scraped across the windows and doors with a ghostly pitch. The wind picked up in velocity, weaved its way around, and in between the trees every few minutes.

The thought crossed Emily's mind that she should turn around and go home, but the intense curiosity about the specifically chosen location drove her onward.

She focused intently on the road.

Why the barn?

What was the significance to the killer?

Water from the fire trucks had flooded down the last steep incline, causing muddy tire impressions and deep groves on the outer areas of the driveway. It didn't pose any problem for Emily's vehicle as she easily maneuvered around the burn location, and parked in between a grove of trees just out of sight.

Emily tried to prepare for anything that could hinder her investigation, like partying teens, curious lookers, or some overzealous wannabe ghost hunters returning to the scene for another look.

She had told Rick that she was going out to do some shopping because she wanted to focus on the crime scene alone, without other emotions pulling her in the opposite direction. It all boiled down to solitude. She needed some alone time to get back into her normal routine, without assassins and secret government agencies interrupting her work. She pushed aside the lingering concerns about Bishop and Red to concentrate on the case. Lives were at stake.

Each new day meant that anything was possible.

Another crime scene welcomed Emily with open arms.

She took a deep breath, held it for a couple of seconds, and then slowly exhaled to steady the nerves. It cleared her mind. The pent up stress slowly seeped out of her body.

Darkness remained deep around the point of origin of where the barn had once stood, revealing a profound and mysterious existence. Even though a partial moon shone with only a few clouds illuminating the outdoors, it still gave the impression of a haunted setting. The startling contrast of black, charcoal, and grey elevated the location, and deepened Emily's drive to find answers.

Piles of dirt mixed with burnt remains of the barn were haphazardly stacked in several positions around the original foundation area. Tiny pieces that lingered unscathed added another element to the scene, glistening like little snippets of information waiting for discovery.

Emily's navy backpack with her personalized mobile crime scene kit sat on the passenger's seat. She had smuggled out her Beretta, just in case, and it rested in its ankle holster fully loaded. Learning from previous experiences, she now carried a six-inch hunting knife concealed inside her cargo pants.

Emily grabbed her gear, exited the car, and closed the car door as silently as she could. The minor sound seemed to magnify in the rural setting.

Twigs, pine needles, and burnt fragments crunched under her boots. The outdoor air amplified the sounds of the forest, and even Emily's breathing sounded intrusive in the natural environment.

She liked to search many crime scene areas at night, even though the daytime seemed the logical and easier time to locate important clues. The challenge with the lack of natural light made her work harder. It kept her observations skills on a heightened alert, leaving no piece of earth, or potential evidence unturned.

Emily stood on the outskirts of the property for a moment. Closing her eyes, she tried to empty her mind of anything that would prove to impair her impartial judgment, including the search of the old hardware store.

Every crime scene was unique.

Traces of caustic smoke still permeated the air.

As Emily opened her eyes and clicked on her flashlight, the darkened area adjusted to her vision. She could see the area where the fire had originated with the deep burn spoils with heavy blackened residues.

Orienting herself to the north and south directions, she carefully stepped away from the burn site. She estimated her grid walk to be about three times wider than what the investigators would initiate.

With each step, Emily scanned a path of about two feet wide in a systematic methodology. She made her way around the location. It angered her that cigarette butts and Styrofoam coffee cups littered around the crime scene. These items were new. They had not been drenched in water, or laid to waste by the outdoor environment.

Ignorance was not an excuse for any law enforcement investigation.

Focus.

A thin curled piece of wood caught her attention. It wasn't a part of the structural lumber. Emily picked it up and tuned it over in her palm. She realized it was a toothpick; the tiny stick had been broken four times to make a crude square. Snapped with a precision of patience and skill, it appeared new to the scene.

Was it from one of the emergency workers or detectives?

Or, did the arsonist stand at this location and watch the barn burn?

Emily took a photo from her small digital camera of the surrounding area. She made an additional footnote in a small notebook about certain behavior probabilities.

Before investigating the larger area where the barn had once stood, Emily photographed the entire crime scene space with the usual close, medium and overall documentation. The flash from the camera portrayed a detailed representation of the area similar in daylight, but actually highlighted anomalies that interested Emily most. It revealed different shades of soil, unusual divots, and small clues often missed by the naked eye.

She moved ahead and gradually made her grid walk smaller; she closed in on the point of interest. Nothing proved out of the ordinary. It had the usual deficits with the trampling of heavy shoes, wheel marks of the gurney, and scattered trash.

She studied a pair of shoeprints closely. She bent down, gauged the stride distances, and retraced the route they took. It didn't indicate to Emily that it was the arsonist, it would most likely be the homicide detective.

Carefully retracing her steps, Emily entered the burn zone. She repeated her search pattern. Her experience with arson sites remained minimal, but she strongly believed that no matter the type of crime scene searched, the approach of objectivity and thoroughness was always the same.

The wind intensified in momentum, attacking the back of her neck. Emily's body felt warm as if the sun shone brightly, not feeling the relief of the breeze.

Carefully kneeling down, she inspected the point of origin. She ran her fingers through the ash and soil, taking careful notice of any strange impression.

A specialized incendiary device wasn't the culprit, but rather something much simpler, like an accelerant to enhance the potential flammables. The area was the deepest, darkest spot at the barn location.

Snapping more photographs in a panoramic sequence, Emily supposed that this particular burn was a typical arson aftermath when something caught fire like hay or paper.

She exchanged her digital camera to her cell phone, took a couple of repeat photographs, and instantly sent them to Jordan for his opinion and analysis.

A high-pitch engine cut through the quiet evening. It continued to approach at a steady pace.

Emily grabbed her gear, stuffed it back into the backpack, and ran toward her car. The back end of the SUV stuck out too far, which posed an unwanted view from the visitors.

Crap.

Luckily, her vehicle headed in a slight downward position. Emily opened the door, released the parking brake, dropped the car into neutral, and tried to push the car forward. Inch by inch, the loose gravel and twigs crunched under the wheels until the branches hid the high-profile car.

Headlights grew brighter and lit up the surrounding trees.

Emily pushed the SUV's door quietly shut. She quickly camouflaged herself into the landscape. She knelt down, pushing her back against the trunk of a huge Pine tree. Her senses captured the strong aroma of pine and wet foliage, intoxicating and calming.

She readied her gun.

The car lights bounced around the area and then seemed to settle on regular beams heading northward. The unknown visitor cut the engine, but kept the illumination shining directly at where the barn once stood.

Two men's voices speaking in normal conversational tones exited the sedan.

Emily strained her eyes.

She dared to move forward to see who interrupted her covert search. Two figures, one heavyset and the other tall, moved in front of the vehicle. Both men were backlit. It made identification almost impossible to discern.

After a few moments, Emily realized that they were law enforcement personnel, but she found it odd that they visited the site at such a late hour. Their trained stance, typical voice inflection, and use of certain adjectives gave away their identities.

Listening to the older, heavyset man, Emily closed her eyes and searched her mind.

She knew that voice.

It suddenly occurred to her that it was Detective Bobby Duncan. She had an unusual run in with him and the high-tech serial killer case a couple of years earlier. Her life changed that day with meeting the detective and her identity became an issue. As far as Emily could tell, he had kept his promise of secrecy.

Emily found a comfortable spot to sit and wait out the investigating detectives.

CHAPTER FORTY-ONE
Thursday 2120 Hours

The laptop screen flashed one criminal rap sheet after another, while Jordan scrolled through hundreds of pages. Every kind of face and body type, tall, short, different nationalities, personal characteristics, and various criminal charges numbed the mind.

After several hours, Jordan's vision blurred. His eyeballs felt gritty as every arson suspect looked exactly like the previous one. Each face brooding, with cruel eyes as deep as a volcano pit, lacking in humanity, and with the propensity for violence rounded out the characteristics.

What began as a solid list of two hundred probable offenders with rap sheets a mile long, turned into a working list of twenty-three possible arsonists.

"It's a good place to start." He clicked a few keys and sent the file to Emily. "I bet our guy is in there somewhere." He was alone in his apartment, but it felt better for him to talk aloud.

Jordan let out a long sigh.

He leaned back in his office chair, rubbing his eyes. The dryness of his eye sockets felt crusty and irritated, which caused him roll his knuckles in a circular motion.

Even though Jordan did not work as an *official* F.B.I. agent anymore, he still had connections. There were debts owed to him, and now was a perfect time to call in some of his markers.

The computer's flat screen had grown dark. He tapped the mouse and the large viewing monitor sprang to life with the desktop's background photograph of Jordan and

Sarge. Goofing around with the sizeable black Labrador, his newfound four-legged friend, Jordan exhibited a huge smile with his arm around the dog's neck.

With a few clicks of the mouse, the background photo changed to Emily. During one of their previous investigations, he had taken a candid shot of her surveying a crime scene area. Her dark eyes, full lips, and the way the mild wind blew through her hair, made Jordan's heart skip a beat.

Jordan loved her deeply.

His entire life had stalled because of her.

A funny tune interrupted his reminiscing thoughts. An email came in from Emily, which had some photos from a crime scene.

Where was she?

Jordan studied the photos of what looked like a broken toothpick.

Interesting.

Another photographed exhibited a darkened area where the point of origin had initiated the fire.

Jordan's mind flooded with thoughts of old cases he had seen at the F.B.I. He quickly read Emily's notes about the organized and obsessive behavior theory. She indicated that the arsonist's behavior pattern was progressing and modifying with each victim.

With renewed energy, Jordan conducted more searches. He began the daunting task to cross-reference suspects associated any way to companies that install heavy security doors, either by employees, subcontractors, various companies that had bought doors recently, or with any other connection that proved too coincidental.

Jordan's evening charged into the early morning hours.

CHAPTER FORTY-TWO
Friday 1400 Hours

The doctor's examination stool swiveled and then rolled across the floor with fluidity. The man moved effortlessly from table to table, without ever having to get up and walk from one workstation to the next.

Efficiency was key.

Each roll pushed him with more determination than the last. The absolute willpower propelled him with the new anticipation of the next chosen sinner. The stool wheels aptly oiled, carefully maintained, which kept everything on track. They worked efficiently, just like everything in his life.

Take pride in your work.

The old medical chair from the early seventies was in stark contrast to the rest of the room, which housed high-tech and high-end devices. The walls remained bare of any artwork. One small window with a dark grey shade pulled tightly over it was the only decoration. Three folding tables with metal legs, a corner oak desk, two bookshelves, three lamps, and a twin bed rounded out the impersonal room.

Everything on the tabletops and bookshelves precisely angled perpendicular to the adjacent surfaces, gave an almost Feng shui symmetry. Tops, sides, and bottoms were exactly two inches from the next object and surface edge. For added effectiveness, an old-fashion wooden ruler rested on the left edge of the desk, two inches from the side, just in case certain items needed verification.

No rewards for laziness.

A scientific notebook with a brown leather cover, organized in chronological order by important dates, and cross-referenced by sin order, remained within reach at all times. The victims, described as the walking dead and recorded by sin severity, on a scale of from one through five, supported the carefully written list. Not only were the sinners marked for death, but everyone associated with them had to die too.

It was a simple equation.

The man's slim fingers caressed the hard cover. He then carefully opened to the table of contents listed by a date and a person's name. With perfect block printing, he gently traced over the names. In the process, he was careful not to crease the cover needlessly. Turning the pages with loving care, the man took his right index finger and slid it down the page, slowing as it passed over the names of Chad Bradford, Timothy Dalton, and Judge Christensen. He pushed the tip of his fingernail to indent a crease underneath their names, savoring the moment of intermission.

Fondly, he took a breath to bring the vivid images of their deaths back into view again. The pleas, the prayers, the unanswered questions, and the horror engraved on their faces once they knew that their judgment commenced.

Prepare for the inevitable.

A block number, followed by a small letter was next to every name in the index, which coded the actual fire event. It was complete with specific references of detailed diagrams and meticulous schematics.

The man, known in his own perfect world as Angel, took an extra moment to admire his future plans. The staging couldn't have been easier, or more satisfying. Each judgment stoked his inner fire, cleansing his soul, and gave him new life. It provided a chance for a new beginning as well as a new awakening.

Childhood thoughts never strayed far from Angel's mindset. Organization and cleanliness was not anything that Aunt Clara cared about in the home when he turned nine years old. After his parents had died in that fatal car accident, Angel was forced to live in a world of filth and disorder.

Immorality was everywhere.

Lack of proper nutrition and loving adult supervision made him smaller, weaker, and an easy target. He became the school joke, much more than the other students in his fourth grade class. Constantly picked on and berated became his usual daily routine, whether it was the beatings at the bus stop from the older boys, or the humiliation in the boy's bathroom from insecure bullies. Weakness eventually made him stronger, smarter, and faster than everyone else.

Angel used one of his lightweight laptops for the design schematics rehearsing the fires. It was a prototype software he took pride in designing. It had technically detailed mathematical equations and chemical compounds, in addition to others that were simplistic but effective.

The method of execution had to fit the sin.

As in the judge's demise, a man who easily let criminals back in society rose to the top of the list. He sat and watched his own family's departure before his own life extinguished.

The judgment fit the sin.

A second laptop rested to the right side of the desk, set back, in easy view for convenience, and always remained connected to the Internet. It served as his personal eye on the burn locations. The tiny cameras camouflaged in simple, but brilliant locations, watched the investigations, and on occasion, captured an interesting irregularity.

It intrigued him.

Recording movement, Angel's covert camera at the barn caught someone admiring his work. He watched the image of a beautiful fair-haired woman diligently searching the grounds alone one evening. It intrigued him as she stood alone, sometimes with her eyes closed, and other times

221

quietly surveying the areas. Her approach was soldier-like with the added bonus of determination.

She was a warrior – a She-Warrior.

She touched him.

It stirred something in him.

The woman She-Warrior struck his soul with beauty. It made his life's work deemed more important than ever before.

Angel's entire life consisted of loneliness and isolation, but he had found solace with his work writing technical manuals for high-tech devices, especially the most unusual and complicated items. He kept his life simple, never needing anything, and his employers never spoke directly to him. Money continued to grow in his personal stash through wire transfers, much more than he actually needed.

His life proved destined to rid the world of those who sinned.

With the new findings, Angel's thoughts shifted. He wasn't alone. A different feeling warmed his body with a perplexing annotate, but soon dissipated as he worked feverously locating the next sinner. Zig Rodriguez, a private investigator, now targeted for death. Next in line, Assistant District Attorney Joshua Richards and Jury Foreman Anna Sinclair waited in the wings.

Fire cleansed everything.

CHAPTER FORTY-THREE
Friday 1800 Hours

Emily tried to ignore the unsettling feeling that someone watched her. She casually found her way to the judge's estate – or at least where the residence once stood.

A strange sensation badgered Emily. A shiver spiraled down the back of her neck, down her backbone, with spiny fingertips from the unknown. Tensing her shoulders, and then lengthening her neck, she shrugged off the prickly feeling.

As usual, she dismissed it as only an occurrence in her suspicious and investigative nature. Sometimes things were just what they were, simple, straightforward, nothing devious, and nothing uncommon.

Overgrown bushes and large clusters of trees, in desperate need of pruning, worked in Emily's favor. The neighbors did not see her park the SUV near the property. She hoped that they were enjoying the dinner hour, instead of taking a walk outdoors.

Originally, she did not intend on stopping, or even slowing down, but she had to take the opportunity to walk around and take a few photos for some type of comparison.

She needed answers.

With her gun safely tucked inside her ankle holster, she slipped a digital camera and small flashlight into her jacket pocket.

Emily emerged casually from her vehicle and looked from side to side.

The private seclusion welcomed her.

She quickly jogged inside the judge's estate before someone caught sight of her snooping around without the proper authoritative badge. She didn't want to see herself filmed from a cell phone sneaking around the property to end up in a video on the Internet.

The house sustained immense damage. The exposed shell looked catastrophic in appearance. The deepest and darkest fire concentration positioned the destruction on the east side of the sprawling ranch-style estate. It developed in the area of the bedroom wing.

The arson appeared deliberate with a fair amount of planning to ensure the desired result, whether it was to flame quickly, or entice the victim in another way.

Was there a killing rating system from the killer's point of view?

Many of the beams and structural walls still feebly stood in between the charred hull.

Emily pondered the approach and the end results between the two crime scenes.

Official yellow tape crisscrossed over every standing entrance and some of the remaining window openings with an extremely heavy-handed technique.

Red papers stapled to various parts of the outside structure showed the official notice that stated penal codes for safety and condemned structures.

The ground still soggy, mixed with water and fire retardant chemicals, squished under Emily's boots. She slowed her pace, looked down as the extra liquid squirted from underneath her shoes spattering her jeans.

She frowned.

She noticed that she made perfectly formed shoe impressions around the property, making a mental note to scuff her footprints before leaving the grounds. Trudging on and making her boot prints undecipherable, she decided to enter one of the doorways that most likely had a double sliding door leading to the patio.

She spread the tape in two sections just wide enough for her slim frame to squeeze through. She flipped on the flashlight, keeping the beam low not to attract attention.

Emily directed the beam from one side slowly and then fanned it across to the other. Her mind tried to piece together a logical scenario. The holes and missing walls absorbed the light through a mouth shaped fissure, she felt like the innards of a Halloween pumpkin peering out at the rest of the world.

Strong pungent odors dominated the air. It absorbed into Emily's clothing.

Once she gained her bearings, watching her step, she noticed the house had four distinct areas. She followed the darkened trail to a large open area, and her experience told her that it was where the fire had originated.

Master bedroom suite?

Emily took several photos of the rooms, not quite sure if they would be helpful or not, but knew she wouldn't get another chance to walk through the remains before demolition.

Watching the digital screen as she pressed the shutter, Emily noticed how odd the area was next to the bedroom. At first, she thought it was a large closet, but images showed a distinct difference between the other rooms. The area in question had more standing walls with heavier construction.

After taking more close up photos, Emily took a closer inspection. Running her hands along the opening and touching the materials, she realized that the room's construction withstood more than the rest of the house.

Why?

Glass crunched under her boots.

Emily stopped. She panned the flashlight in a semi-circle around her feet.

Bits and pieces of glass were everywhere. She picked up several small fragments, comparing them to areas around the windows. They were distinctly different, but using only a naked eye did not give the individualization.

She pocketed the pieces.

Taking the flashlight and directing the beam in a circle grid, reflective flashes of light gleamed like that of a mirror.

Double reinforced construction and a two-way mirror indicated a panic room.

Was the judge already secured in his panic room?

Or, did the killer put him in there?

Emily hurried back through the home, carefully documenting anything that might prove pertinent to the investigation. Once satisfied, she hurried back to the SUV.

* * * * *

Detective Duncan sat at his desk scouring police and fire investigation reports, squinting his eyes as he kept pushing up his reading glasses. He preferred the desk lamp to the glaring overhead fluorescent lighting, but it made some paperwork more difficult to read.

Three large cardboard boxes rested on the floor beside him. The lids removed and report files organized in several stacks. More piles of files sat on his desk next to his working desktop computer.

He slurped room temperature coffee out of a paper cup that he had bought from a local gas station convenience store more than three hours ago. The microwave was his closest friend at the police station. It was his third cup of java, and it had already made his stomach rumble for food instead of another caffeinated boost.

He had received the boxes from a delivery service by way of Myers. There were arson cases the detective wanted to cross-reference with homicide cases that involved suspicious fires over the past two years. Everything was located on the computer databases, but Duncan knew that the computer operators missed details, often reference numbers and coinciding forensic analysis reports.

The detective was old school with handwritten reports that were frequently illegible. He preferred the use of pen and paper, versus laptop and electronic tablet. Many of the younger detectives scoffed at his techniques, but they always showed respect to him as a senior detective. He hated the reference as an old timer. It made it sound like the only other recourse was a retirement home and then death.

Opening his top drawer, he remembered that he had a candy bar tucked away. Not sure how old it was, but it satisfied his grumbling stomach.

He scribbled on a steno pad. The top priorities he looked for were cold case homicides involving fire, unsolved arson cases, victims trapped in a location before the fire, and recent construction of a crime scene. He was interested in the victimology of the casualties with backgrounds on occupations, such as in criminal justice system, military, stock market, or anyone associating with any high-power positions. It was a huge undertaking, but the detective hoped it led him in the right direction.

Most of the arson cases involved young men, often teenagers, and there were the usual earmarks of those crimes involving gasoline and other accelerants. The detective dismissed many cases and eventually ended up with twenty-seven cases of maybes.

He glanced at his cell phone with a reminder about other people associated with the Devlin case. Duncan couldn't help but think about the phantom detective and wondered if she was working the case.

Would she find out the name of the perp?

There was always hope.

Either way, it was a race against time.

Duncan glanced at his watch as it approached 10:00pm. There hadn't been anyone to go home to in a very long time, but his energy level wasn't what it used to be in the old days. He decided to call it quits for the night.

Tomorrow he would branch out to other jurisdictions and surroundings states to see if anything connected the arson cases through linkage.

CHAPTER FORTY- FOUR
Saturday 1000 Hours

The new house wasn't entirely unpacked, but it seemed sufficient for Emily and Rick's needs. Even though it was smaller in square footage than what they were used to, it seemed more like home.

A stack of broken down boxes organized in the corner of the living room made enough room for what was important – the arson cases.

There were three white boards rolled into the living room adjacent to the dining area. Each panel faced a slightly different angle around the remaining moving boxes. The kitchen table covered with printout of cases and pertinent photographs, laid strewn in a specific order. It was a possible sequence of motives, impulses, and capabilities of the fire suspect.

Two laptops hummed, Internet ready, and waited patiently for input instructions. A third computer communicated to a large screen that temporarily hung on the wall behind the dining table.

Colored three-inch square sticky notes in yellow, pink and blue were affixed to the glass sliding door, which led to a small backyard. The pieces of paper had information linking forensic evidence to each of the fire scenes. Yellow notes designated the possible changing M.O. of the perp, pink showed the forensic evidence, and blue had the names of possible suspects.

Sarge sat at attention, ears perked, eyes sharp, as he stared directly at Jordan stretched out on the couch. The dog gently panted in Jordan's air space.

"Why is he staring at me all the time?" Jordan mumbled.

"He likes you." Emily casually responded as she brought more photos to the table. "Don't play dumb, you know you love him."

"Lucky me."

The large dog pushed his bulky head into Jordan's hand and demanded attention.

"You should've known better than to give him gourmet meaty treats." She said.

Jordan sat up and swung his feet to the floor. "I saw the hideous dried up, preservative filled dog food he normally gets. I wouldn't eat that."

"Of course not Jordan... you have a much more subtle palate for Chinese food with MSG, and your weekly chili-cheese burgers with a rude looking French dressing, along with garlic, chili fries." Rick quickly pointed out. He sat down and typed on one of the computers.

"Hey, I'm just sayin' that the dog food didn't have *any* real food value in it."

"You should take a look at your own diet..." Rick muttered.

"Boys!" Emily yelled. She thrust her hands on her hips like a disapproving mother. "What's the problem?" She looked at each one of them and waited for an answer.

"I don't have a problem." Jordan quickly stated as a frown clouded his face.

Emily looked at Rick, raising her eyebrows. She got tired of playing mediator, especially since they were on borrowed time.

Who knew what would happen in the arson cases, or when Red might decide that they were all expendable?

"Don't look at me, there's no problem here." Rick shrugged.

Rick's tense voice accompanied by the habitual clenched jaw and ridged body language didn't convince her.

Emily decided to dismiss the entire conversation and move on to what was more important. She rejected the thoughts and feelings of anything that would interfere with the investigation.

Glancing around at the room, she realized that the arson case had more information and investigative hours than any other case she had worked to date. There were volumes of information to plow through. Between the three of them, it would be easy to dismiss superfluous facts, and focus on the evidence that would eventually lead to the killer.

She remembered clearly each step she took at the crime scenes. The differences in soil, the points of origin, footprints, and clues to where the killer stood fueled Emily's drive.

The answers they desperately needed stared back at her.

It gnawed at her every waking moment, a numbing current that ran the length of her spine, and sometimes ended at the pit of her stomach.

Was he changing his M.O.?

Were all the victims working within the criminal justice system?

She wanted to solve the case as soon as possible. She sighed, clenched and unclenched her hands, and willed all of her focus to the case. Emily transferred her energy on the physical and behavioral evidence taking up half of her new house.

"I'm pulling up Jordan's files right now." Rick announced. "And here we go..." He punched several more keys for a slide show of photographs.

Jordan joined Rick and Emily at the table. He pulled a chair out and spun it around backwards, as if he was in a country bar ready to play poker.

"Okay…" He began. "Here's the hardware store with the heavy-duty door."

The oversized image showed a steel reinforced door with shiny hardware.

Jordan explained. "… I found the exact match of the door. It comes from a security catalogue company called *AA Armed Security, Inc.* and they are the distributor for the U.S. They cater to high-end clients, you know like the rich and famous, etcetera."

Emily took a step closer to the image. "How many of those doors do they sell every year?"

"More than you would think. According to their records, one hundred-twelve last quarter."

Emily let out a breath in disappointment.

Jordan fidgeted in his chair. "You guys will want to adopt me after I tell you this."

Rick stared poker face at him.

"Well, maybe a steak dinner? Anyway, I spent hours cross-referencing the sales to actual locations where they were installed. I love being a security expert and a licensed P.I. because… I located all the doors but one…" A huge smile washed across his face.

"Who is it?" Rick asked.

"Ah, who or what?" Jordan asked.

"What?" Emily and Rick chimed together.

"You guys practice that or what?" Jordan laughed. "Martin Rover."

"Who is he?" Emily's mind searched through any of the names that she had turned up in her recent research.

"It took me a while to figure it out because I couldn't find anyone that matched the name and then… BAM… it hit me. Our arson killer has a fetish, or maybe just an obsession. Martin Rover was the pseudonym of a writer who wrote about a serial killer from the 1940s."

"I've never heard of him." Emily stated.

Jordan scratched Sarge behind the ears. "That's because it was a popular mystery novel in the early 1960s about a killer who killed all the members of his family, even distant cousins. He would devise these elaborate plans to make them look like accidents." He looked at the couple. "Clever don't you think? This writer wrote about serial killers even before the phrase was coined in the 1970s."

Rick typed in search words for the novel and the author. "There's nothing on the author. Apparently he wrote the one book, or possibly used other pseudonyms."

"Too old to be the arsonist. My guess is that the killer found this obscure book at some point in his life and then used it as inspiration. No telling how long he had been planning the murders." Emily pulled out the photographs of the black box. "I suppose there were cameras and other devices bought by the same name – all cash transactions."

"You stole my ending. I think there are small hidden cameras placed around all the scenes so he can watch firefighters and detectives work."

"Interesting." She mused. "But not original."

Emily digested everything and added it to her criminal profile. She walked to the white boards; each represented one of the three fire crime scenes.

She added to her growing list of killer characteristics:

Organized offender to the point of excessive control, age 30ish to possibly 40, male, Caucasian, no relationships, hated family life, poor experience growing up, maybe adopted or a foster child?, virgin?, voyeurism, watches others through cameras, makes judgments of others, fire represents a new start for him, high intelligence, no social skills, computer work of some type: writer, programmer, etc., anti-social but not to the point of psychopathic, has strong delusions of right and wrong, will continue to kill until caught or killed.

"So... we have a 40 year old virgin who hated his mommy, works at home, and kills others with malice?" Jordan said sarcastically.

"Why a virgin?" Rick asked.

Going through photos, Jordan piped up. "Geez poor guy, no wonder he kills."

Ignoring Jordan's flippant comment, Emily continued to brainstorm. "There's an element about relationships that seems to be at the root of his psychological needs, something that he's never received. Fear, hatred, resentment are part of him, but mostly he keeps it under control." She gestured toward the photos of the fire scenes. "Fire represents a cleansing, starting over, new, and pristine. Something he's seeking. He may see himself as pure in an impure world, but the fires are an acceptable sexual release to him."

"I'm receiving some files on cold arson cases around the state from an old working buddy of mine." Rick downloaded the files into organized desktop folders.

Jordan moved to the couch and pulled out his laptop. "I've got autopsy reports to review."

Emily looked at him questionably.

"Don't ask... and I won't tell you how I retrieved them."

Emily thought about a man who was so isolated from the world, but yet, he felt obligated to try to clean it up. She imagined him at his computer devising new firetraps for his victims, and congratulating himself after the job was completed.

As she walked into the kitchen, opened the refrigerator door, and retrieved a cold bottle of mineral water, she thought of the killer as a lone wolf of justice. At least that was how he thought about it in his own mind. He wasn't the *typical* serial killer in any retrospect; he blurred the lines of textbook killers. That's what made it so difficult, if not impossible to get an accurate read on him.

"Okay, there's a lot of work ahead of us today if we're going to catch him before he kills another person." Emily took a seat opposite her team and began to sort through photographic evidence of each crime scene.

"I brought my favorite sleeping bag." Jordan joked.

Rick looked up from his computer screen. "What about the A.D.A., jury foreman, stenographer, private investigator, and anyone else associated with the Devlin case?"

Not looking up from her notes and photos, she said. "The cops should be taking care of it. And it will bide us some time."

"I'm hungry and it's going to be a *long* day and evening..." Jordan punched a button on speed dial. "Yes, hello, I'd like to order the Number One for three please." He waited. "Yes, the works. I'll be there in twenty. Thanks." He hung up.

"*Without* MSG I presume?" Rick didn't miss a keystroke as he took another jab at Jordan.

"Dude, give it a rest..."

CHAPTER FORTY- FIVE
Saturday 1800 Hours

The late day sun cast beautiful tones of oranges, yellows, and bright pinks across the horizon. The light speckled between the trees and dappled upon the jogging trail. The workout regime, enjoyed by many, pushed the exercise level for seasoned athletes from moderate to advanced. The challenge of the trail usually deterred many casual runners from completing.

It did not take long for Stephen Caldena to make his usual evening run. The fit man pushed his endurance to the limit, apparently to achieve the runner's high, and to keep the focus on his almost nonexistent body fat.

Sidetracked by what had recently transpired in his life, Red found it difficult to concentrate as he sat in the rented car. A few emotions crept into his mind. A different feeling washed over him with attachment, and even a sense of loss. Meeting Emily made his life seem even emptier.

Was this how other people felt most of the time?

The probing question and somewhat unsettling feeling deep inside him demanded immediate attention. It was a bit unusual. However, it was better than the acid burning stomach symptoms.

A growing trepidation filled the assassin's body. After a few moments, he felt in control once again, and satisfied with the new assignment. The anger and resentment for Bishop festered with tenacity. However, as with most unsettling things, it would soon end.

Force and intensity guided Red's mission.

From two days of research and surveillance, Red knew the most opportune place to kill the mark. The man's business ventures were synonymous with dealings with the mafia, as well as other unscrupulous characters.

It didn't matter to Red what he did or why.

The scope from the high-powered rifle easily fixed on Caldena. The man slowed his pace to a comfortable jog about one hundred-fifty yards away. He stopped his forward momentum and ran in place, kept the heart rate up with each raised knee, tightened his core muscles, and simultaneously turned to enjoy the view.

Red inhaled gently and held his breath. With a modest squeeze of the trigger, one quiet thrust blew straight through Caldena's brain, exiting the forehead, and spattered the internal matter all over the nearby foliage, just before his body hit the ground.

The diminishing sunset glow accented the chunky blood droplets in a somewhat artistic manner. Beauty and death infused the macabre.

Red slowly exhaled. He sensed his body maintaining the usual sensations. He normally didn't feel any different than at any other time of his day.

But today, a little bit of relief filled him.

With the job completed, he broke down the rifle. He noticed his hands slightly shook from overexertion. Curiously, he watched the index and middle fingers waver. The sickness in his gut returned, burning and churning.

A simple job now proved somewhat of a challenge.

As Red raised his eyes and stared through the windshield, a young man and woman in their mid-twenties stood staring horrified at him. They were unable to move and unable to avert their gaze from him.

When the couple saw his eyes staring back, they turned and ran.

Calmly Red turned in his seat and retrieved a pistol fitted with a suppressor. Within seconds, he exited the car and jogged after the couple.

He hated complications, but sometimes it couldn't be helped no matter how much planning was involved.

He passed the couple on another parallel trail and cut them off.

The gun rose.

He stood in front of them with the calm demeanor of a pro. The startled couple had already begun dialing a cell phone for the police, but didn't complete the call.

Two expertly aimed bullets dropped the man and woman to the ground.

Red's favored shot, face-to-face, was straight through the heart. Simple, less mess, and dropped most people instantly.

The fair-haired couple sprawled haphazardly on the dusty path, arms and legs in peculiar hooked positions, which left a mess for the local cops to clean up.

Collateral damage sometimes happened. It was often unavoidable.

Without any hesitation as the precious seconds ticked away, Red slipped the gun into his jacket. He quickly made his way back to the car. He never saw another person or vehicle until his reached the busy highway.

Red knew the murders would quickly go cold for the local cops.

CHAPTER FORTY- SIX
Saturday 2000 Hours

Pinned up in two strategic rows were ten faces of the most likely suspects; each had their own demons and psychological needs, which dictated how they committed crimes. Their eyes seemed to follow your every move, like an intimidating portrait from inside an ancient castle. Listed next to each convict was a long list of misdemeanor and felony charges, brief backgrounds, and general physical characteristics.

The software program projected the suspect images onto the wall, but the provocative question remained for Emily and her team. Is one of these men the arson killer?

"Well?" Jordan probed his partners as he nervously tapped his pen against the side of his laptop. "Have we found the arsonist?"

Emily moved closer to the photographs. She scanned the lists, while comparing each one to the next. The glare from the hardened faces stared back at her. She knew how to focus and filter through her mind with possible scenarios of each rap sheet, imagining how and why they committed their crimes.

Her exhaustion hadn't outweighed her tenacity, even though her eyes felt weary, legs fatigued, and her shoulders tensed. She made her shoulders periodically raise and lower to relieve the stress. All the usual aches and pains associated with a tough serial killer case had bubbled to the surface.

"Five of these men don't have the intelligence to pull off this type of scenario with the elaborate planning. Look at

239

their petty stuff, definitely not the making of an extremely organized offender." Emily stated.

She paused another moment and then pointed to the five mug shots to delete. "Take these guys out."

"Okay." Jordan clicked the keyboard with effortless speed as the faces disappeared one by one. "That still leaves five potential suspects."

"At least from what we have..." Rick added sourly. "I don't know, but this is the first time where my gut says it isn't any one of these losers. It doesn't fit."

"I agree with Rick and his gut. Something doesn't seem right with these guys for those arson traps." Jordan tapped his pen in an annoying manner to a well-known beat.

"We have to follow every lead and not second guess the pool of suspects." Emily quickly added. Her right eyebrow rose slightly with a questionable expression. "I can, in good conscience eliminate three more suspects." She pointed out each man one by one. "This guy is too old and doesn't have the background. And this one is twenty-one, even though that's not impossible for him to be a serial killer, it's not him either. His capabilities are too low."

The two faces disappeared from the large screen.

"I see where you're going. The last guy has focused more on peeping Tom techniques, and lighting things on fire. Clearly not the intellect or a common motivator as our guy." Jordan added.

"Wait, leave the younger man with the last two in the group." Emily chewed her left thumbnail and stared harder at the two remaining photographs: Jonathan DeBeer and Broderick McCain. Both men were in their early thirties, intelligent, had a fascination with arson, some higher education in electronics and chemistry, no known relationships, and were loners.

"Why?" Jordan asked curiously.

"I think there's more to Sebastian Hernandez and I don't have solid reasons to eliminate him entirely."

Emily stared at all three men. She didn't want to agree with Rick and Jordan, but she felt that none of them was the arsonist. Eliminating the potential clues and suspects proved the only direction to proceed, and if they were lucky, one of these men would lead them to the real killer.

Rick sighed and directed his question to Jordan. "Have you received anything back yet from the AA Armed Security, Inc. about employees?"

"It's a small staff overall. I've check out and cleared the administrative staff, still checking on the installers and trucking companies."

Emily interrupted, "What about outside consultants, like someone who would write technical manuals or update their websites?"

"Nothing has popped yet. No one said that technology is going to solve the case right away." He smiled his toothy grin.

"If our infamous Martin Rover is using the 1940s author to hide his identity, it'll be next to impossible to track him." Emily garnered her focus at the photographs.

"It looks like we should find out a little more about the boys." Rick stated. His frown made it apparent that he felt doubtful. "What do you think Em?"

Emily searched the photos of the burn scenes for something she had missed.

"Em?"

She looked up. "Yes?"

"Let's split up and find out more about these guys. You and I can take DeBeers and Jordan can tail McCain."

As Emily watched Rick's face, strong, controlled, she was reminded of his secrecy about the escape of Leo Brown. Vivid memories flooded back into her mind of the ordeal, and the fact that the police hadn't recaptured Brown yet.

How could he do this to her?

"Okay." Emily stated with authority. "But, I'm going with Jordan to check out McCain."

Rick's jaw clenched and his eyes narrowed. It was obvious he wanted to argue, but knew it was futile, so he let it go. "Fine."

Jordan seemed to sense the tension in the room and stood up. "Cool!" He pantomimed a dance move. "Rick it's your lucky day no matter how you look at it, you didn't get stuck with me this time."

* * * * *

Cleanliness.

The makeshift kitchen transformed the corner of a single car garage into an immaculate and spotless room. Only one set of dishes resided, which consisted of a drinking glass, mug, dinner plate, small plate, bowl, fork, spoon, knife, and a serrated knife perfectly placed in the upper open cabinet. The dishes were white and the silverware simple without any decorative features, allowing for easy cleaning to wipe away water spots or lingering germs.

Organized.

Angel took off his plastic gloves, neatly folded them, every finger precisely placed vertical and folded over, before he tossed them into the garbage. Several boxes of disposable gloves took up the remaining space above the sink and small stovetop.

He didn't believe in the use of sponges or tea towels. Microbes and the unthinkable resided in them. Instead, he tore a small piece of paper towel exactly two inches square and methodically wiped the sink, counter, and faucet after every use.

After a piece of dry wheat toast and a cup of strong coffee, it required him to clean up a mess that took almost a half an hour. His mind wandered a few times remembering the beautiful woman admiring his handiwork from his videos.

Intriguing.

It should have upset him, but strangely, it did not. It proved to be a new irregularity in his life's work.

Preoccupied with his hands, nervously pressing his fingers together, Angel left the spotless kitchen and entered the workroom – at least that was what he called it. Not one other person had ever seen the room. The old abandoned garage, ideally located on the ten acres, was chosen just for him. It propelled him forward and gratified the heavy fire workload.

Before entering the workroom, Angel meticulously searched the walls, corner crevices, and window before taking a seat at his command post. He opened his favorite book, the journal of new life, an encyclopedia of cleanliness and the brilliant plans of eradicating sin.

His mission was to take down the system of sinners. The main culprit was the criminal justice system allowing these types of people to continue with their evil ways. All those involved were just as guilty and would not receive any tolerance in the burn process. Sin was easy to identify.

He saw it. He planned it. He cleaned it.

Angel's mind recalled the childhood memories deeply burned into his mind. There were no computer erase buttons to push in order to fully cleanse his detailed recollections of what *that* house was like for him growing up. He shut his eyes and dredged up one of the many days he had spent in that disaster; hoping things would change.

It had been the usual bad day for the fifth grader dealing with name calling and punching from the other boys, including some of the younger kids. Even the bus ride was horrible and torturous. Everything he endured was always right on schedule. The good news was that Angel could take the slaps, shoves, and hard knuckles pounding his frail body without grimacing or crying anymore. He knew, someday, somehow, that he would win in the end.

He entered Aunt Clara's house from the side door, since the front door was completely blocked. The flimsy, single-door construction creaked open to about a six-inch gap. Angel pushed hard with his right shoulder to budge the entrance another couple of inches.

He shoved his plain blue backpack through the tight opening and then slipped his thin body through. Shutting the door from the inside was easier and offered a haven from those who wanted to hurt him. The doorknob jiggled, wobbly in its resting place, and absent of the locking device that had long since fallen out. There were no locks anywhere on Aunt Clara's house, but no burglar would dare to enter for fear of what they might find inside the home.

Quickly grabbing his backpack from the floor, Angel slung it over his right shoulder.

He was careful to keep his footing steady. One-step, squish, two steps, crunch, as it continued when he made his way toward the kitchen.

The ranch-style home didn't resemble an average comfortable family home. Covered from end to end, top to bottom, were piles of every type of clutter, garbage, and thrift store items amassed in every nook and cranny as far as the eye could bear to see. Every precious piece purposely saved by Aunt Clara; they were cherished belongings that she would never part with as long as she lived. It grew from day to day, and week to week. Some of the walkways resembled long dark tunnels.

Angel knew that nothing had changed since he left for school that morning, but he still hoped.

"Honey, is that you?" A voice hollered somewhere between the labyrinth of filth and clutter.

"Yeah, I'm in the kitchen."

"I left you a snack on the counter. Don't spoil your dinner." She replied, this time her voice a little farther away, muffled by the walls of chaotic confusion.

The floor had a constant wet muck combination with the permanently separated linoleum from a leak under the kitchen sink. In the quiet of the kitchen, the drip sound was almost a relief, a rhythmic comforting splash.

Angel stared at the kitchen counter. A week's worth of dishes sat unwashed, flies buzzed around the dried food that had turned green, while other pieces of previous meals dried in peculiar hardened fragments. At the end of the counter was a plate where the chicken nuggets had been previously heated in the microwave, probably a couple of hours ago. The snack arranged in a tight semi-circle made an interactive playground for the cockroaches.

With an uncontrollable shudder, Angel could still see the cockroaches as if they had infested his workspace. That day had marked a new beginning. His vision cleared to the present day and he refocused to the pages of his cherished journal.

Angel lingered on the last few pages, his posture in a loving embrace, shoulders forward, a serene look etched upon his face, as his thin fingers caressed the edges of the book. Love enveloped him. He felt fulfilled with the fact that he knew his quest would never end.

Sin infested humanity.

He soaked up the image of the She-Warrior from a frozen video shot. It was an unmistakable determination and a power within another warrior that gave him never-ending hope. He ran his fingertips over her outline and then to her face. He wondered if there were more warriors out there like her. The thought tugged at his being, in a way that had never touched him before.

He wasn't alone anymore.

After lingering a bit longer with the outline of this fierce She-Warrior, Angel moved on through the carefully selected names.

A red mark notated Zig Rodriguez. The authorities hadn't found his body in the burned out car - a perfect final resting place for a sinner. Angel's thumb rubbed back and forth on the red ink to savor the moments of the screams completely engulfed in a metal coffin.

His right index finger stopped on the printed name Joshua Richards, he was the assistant district attorney that allowed crime and filth to continue to roam freely. The name Joshua resonated inside Angel's head. Joshua was a name better suited for a warrior – not a sinner.

It was time for the next cleansing.

CHAPTER FORTY- SEVEN
Sunday 1300 Hours

"Two officers need to be posted at A.D.A. Richard's house in rotating shifts around the clock until further notice."

There had been some hesitation in jurisdiction and cooperation initially, but everything was now set in motion. Better late than never, Detective Duncan thought sourly as he hung up the phone.

What else could he do at this point?

Taking a sip of coffee that teetered on three and half hours old, the detective mused over everything from the arson scenes. That familiar, overwhelming feeling plagued him. It filled his gut with frustration and the unavoidable – another victim in the near future.

His desk resembled a bomb explosion that left him with all of the gritty jigsaw pieces to clean up. File folders, computer printouts, jagged pieces of paper with handwritten scribbles, rap sheets, and autopsy reports all fought for his direct attention.

Flipping through the legal yellow pad that he judiciously uncovered from the piles, he stopped on the names of interest: *A.D.A. Joshua Richards, Jury Foreman Anna Sinclair, and P.I. Zig Rodriguez.* He took his black marker, crossed off Richards, and noted: *in progress.*

Operating in sequential order and on the assumption of previous victims, he addressed each potential target. Jury Foreman Sinclair was conveniently out of the country and didn't pose a likely victim threat, at least at the moment. He had left numerous messages for Rodriguez. Duncan's hope was that the private investigator had common sense and could take care of himself, if deemed necessary.

With a deep sigh, the detective leaned back in the squeaky and equally uncomfortable chair. A slight wheeze of his breath didn't draw his attention away from myriad of information that faced him. Sleep didn't alleviate the investigative burden, coffee didn't appease the growing fatigue, and eating better didn't allow him to solve the case any faster. The investigation sat, stalled, and he knew that there would be more bodies if he didn't come up with anything solid soon. He was supposed to have two other detectives working full-time with him, but budgets wreaked havoc on the department, and only one other detective was spared only on a part time basis.

The detective took a bite of a day old doughnut with a sticky, Styrofoam consistency, which helped to soak up the caffeine burning a hole in his stomach. He tossed the remainder of the pastry into the trashcan.

His mind wandered. The police station always seemed to have an endless supply of doughnuts, sometimes bagels, which were available twenty-four hours a day. For some reason the bakery goods would materialize magically, and no one fessed up as to who had brought them. This simple observation seemed to pick away at him.

Simple facts, simple ideas, and simple overlooked clues were often the pivotal answer needed to solve a complex case.

Duncan searched for some of the crime scene photos. Quickly sliding out files and notes as a few teetered from the piles onto the floor, he kept looking. It became an obsession. He knew that there was something he had missed. There was always something missed.

The detective flipped over the crime scene photos of the warehouse and Chad Bradford. At first glance, the scene didn't possess anything useful. He adjusted his glasses and leaned forward at the desk to view the images of the heavy-duty door at the back ally. The door stumped him. He looked past the back alley where the electrical box stood. In one outer area of the frame, there was a small black box that didn't look like anything special, but in another view, it was missing.

"What the...?" Duncan turned the photographs closer to his desk lamp examining them. He realized that the photo without the small box had been taken later by Fire Investigator Myers.

The detective sat back and scanned all the photographs once again.

Who would take the box and why?

He glanced to his cell phone. It became clear to him. He knew that Emily Stone must have been looking into these arsons. The box proved an important piece of evidence and most likely put there by the killer. Or, the killer returned to retrieve his prop. This new evidence raised more questions.

The desk phone rang.

Grabbing the receiver and toppling more files, he said, "Duncan." He listened intently and looked at his watch. "I'll be there in half an hour."

CHAPTER FORTY- EIGHT
Sunday 1930 Hours

Emily watched Jordan's face, curious and suspecting, as his eyes darted back and forth from her to the bartender. Jordan's bruises were healing on his face, but he seemed to take them as a symbol of honor.

Casually, Emily turned her head just far enough so that her peripheral vision could see the man behind the bar along with about a dozen patrons. The bartender slid the mixed drinks to a couple without a pleasant greeting, or cracking a smile. Broderick McCain continued with his usual duties, all without looking at anyone directly.

It raised some red flags concerning behavior, but nothing that would indicate the persona of a serial killer. Having memorized his rap sheet and general background, Emily tried to fit the motivations of the crime scenes and borderline genius abilities to the man behind the bar, who half-heartedly dried a glass with a towel.

After careful study, McCain didn't fit the profile.

Emily continued to watch Jordan, as he watched the bartender relentlessly.

A jukebox played pop hits from the 80s, which drowned out the clarity of any idle conversations among customers.

She leaned across the table still holding the sides of her soda water and said in a low tone. "If you don't stop staring, he's going to think that you have a thing for him." A slow smile washed across her face.

Jordan's steely blue eyes settled back on her with a fixed expression between annoyance and inquisitiveness. "Are you jealous Ms. Stone?"

"I think the better question is do you want to walk out of here with... or without a limp?" She still smiled, but her tone bordered on a serious quality.

Jordan leaned back in the booth seat, relaxing his demeanor. "I don't think I'm willing to find out. Don't forget, I've seen you fight and I know my chances aren't good."

Emily stared into her glass and watched the light reflect from the ice cubes. The multi-colored lights and décor in the outdated bar reflected a rainbow of colors inside her glass. Her arguments with Rick played through her mind. She knew that she could get beyond the feeling of betrayal, but it still left questions. It unsettled her usual toughness and determination. She hated vulnerability almost more than serial killers.

"Em, are you listening?"

She knew that it made Rick angry that she didn't want to shadow the first pool of suspects with him. It took an extreme situation for her to get mad and it took twice as long to cool off.

"Hello?" Jordan reached out and touched the back of her hand. "You okay?"

Emily retrieved her hand to her lap. She brought her focus back to the assignment and the bartender. "Yes, I'm fine."

"You were just on another planet." He downed his blended margarita and grimaced slightly at the cold temperature. "Tell me what's going on with you?"

"What do you mean?"

"Uh, I was a criminal profiler with the F.B.I. remember? I think I can read the obvious."

Emily tried not to smile as she watched the dramatic expression flash across Jordan's face. "Look, I don't... this isn't the place to have this conversation."

"Hey, I'm your friend and if you need to talk to someone, I'm here that's all. No biggee." He looked back at the bartender as his shoulders and jaw tensed.

Two new groups of people meandered toward the bar, three people sat at a table, while the others opted for the bar stools. They appeared to be friends from a nearby college and out for some drinks.

Jordan sighed and said. "I don't think he's the guy. Maybe we should catch up with Rick." His tone sounded defeated.

"Wait..." Emily quickly replied, forced a smile, and pretended she was having a good time looking directly at Jordan.

Two men in their mid-thirties walked by their table and moved to the crowded area. They headed to the end of the bar with sullen expressions. The taller man sported a zipped up motorcycle jacket and leaned into the bar, while the heavier set man with a baby face and bald head sat uncomfortably on an adjacent bar stool.

Jordan followed Emily's lead, casually observing the two men. It was obvious that they weren't the usual clientele and that they came to see the bartender. They reeked from some type of criminal activity.

Emily knew something brewed among the three men as they gave subtle nods to one another, never ordering any drinks. At first, Emily thought they were going to rob the place, but something else seemed to connect the threesome.

Jordan asked. "What do you think?"

"Not good."

"What do you want to do?"

"Nothing... yet."

"Just clue me in when you know."

"Always do."

"This guy is a con and they could be involved in just about anything."

"True." Emily casually looked around the bar as the waitress stopped at their table.

The extremely thin woman asked. "Another round?"

"No thank you, we're good for now." Emily replied.

The waitress quickly moved to the larger table and dealt out the drinks in a counter clockwise rotation. Everyone seemed oblivious to the two men that nervously watched he rest of the room.

Jordan grabbed the empty glass from Emily's hands and set it aside. "I know that I can't change your mind, but I've got your back."

Emily rolled her eyes. "You sound like a bad movie line."

"Can't help it, it's just how I feel." He smiled.

It was difficult to ignore Jordan most of the time, but equally difficult when he became relentless with his usual sarcastic chatter. Emily's anger toward Rick along with the frustration with the arson cases made her want to take these two guys outside for a beating.

Recklessness drove her adrenaline. She found it difficult not to let it completely take over and cloud her judgment.

As suddenly as they had appeared, the two anonymous men left the bar and headed toward the restrooms.

Emily stood up.

"Wait." Jordan snapped.

"For what?" She gave him a small smirk.

"Uh – you said you'd give me a heads up."

"I am." Emily left the table and walked with medium speed toward the restrooms.

"Shit." Jordan fished out some cash from his pocket to pay for the drinks including a nice tip for the waitress. Mumbling under his breath as he counted out singles, he complained, "Rick will shoot me and bury me somewhere out in the desert if I let Emily get hurt…"

Emily walked down a long hallway and past several unmarked doors that remained locked. She casually tried to turn a couple of the nobs listening for any type of voices from inside.

Nothing.

The old wooden floor complained in a high-pitch crackle under her boots as she stopped at the door with the recognizable symbol indicating the women's restroom. She stood for a moment and noted that the men's restroom was directly across the hall.

Stillness ensued, except for the muffled music lightly reverberating throughout the old walls.

Her anger had mostly dissipated. She was about to return to the bar when she heard the sound of a door creaking. The distinct sound resonated from the far end of the hallway that led into a storage area. She cautiously walked through the entryway of hanging glass beads that had once been stylish from a time long ago, but now forgotten.

A slightly open door leading to the alley tapped the frame in rhythm with the evening breeze. Streetlights flickered through the narrow opening.

"Hey." A voice whispered next to her.

She was startled by the sound of Jordan's voice so close to her ear and couldn't believe that she didn't hear him approach.

Jordan looked like a ghostly apparition with his light hair reflecting the dim lighting.

Emily motioned to him to the door leading outside.

He nodded.

The storage room smelled of moldy boxes and stale beer kegs. A gust of wind grabbed the door and swung it open with a loud crack against the building.

The outside air was a welcomed reprieve.

Jordan followed Emily to the alley. Stacked liquor boxes tied securely were the only things that greeted them. Down on the far end of the walkthrough were large garbage dumpsters. However, once out of the building, the pungent smell of refuse filled the air.

No one was in sight.

Where did the two men go?

Emily instinctively thought of her small Beretta tucked into her ankle holster. She walked to the end of the alley, not sure what she was looking for, but being thorough nonetheless.

"Em, no one's here. C'mon let's get out of here." Jordan stated simply without sarcasm, but with a slight hint of urgency in his voice.

Emily knew he was right, but something was wrong. The energy in the air felt static and foreboding. As they walked back to the outside door, the man and woman from the bar pushed their way out.

The tall man barked in her face, "Who are you?"

Jordan stepped up next to Emily and took her hand playfully. "We were just looking for somewhere a little more private, if you know what I mean."

"I saw you two in the bar. You look like cops." The woman pushed Jordan back. Her face hardened.

"Hey man, you don't have to be like that." Jordan said.

"Why were you two watching us?" She demanded. Her eyes darted from Emily to Jordan. Her gaze narrowed.

"We weren't watching anyone but each other." Jordan explained.

"Bullshit." The woman seethed.

Emily tried to move inside the building.

"Hey, where do you think you're going?" The man asked, but clearly didn't care about the answer.

"Can't a girl use the restroom?" Emily tried to sound casual.

"Nice try sweetheart." He pulled a gun out of his jacket and aimed it directly at Emily's face. It forced her to retrace her steps into the alley.

The man's partner roughly pushed Jordan up against the wall, catching him off guard. She drew her weapon and pressed it against his back.

"This isn't good…" Jordan grimaced.

* * * * *

Consecutive photographs snapped as the man and woman emerged from the car in front of the motel. The lens zoomed in close to identify the man's face as several more frames advanced.

Jonathan DeBeers stumbled toward his motel room with a skinny brown-haired woman in tow. Both laughed and giggled in between squeezing and caressing each other. The woman had on a mini-skirt too short for anything but sex.

Rick sat in the SUV and watched the couple. During the entire display, he thought that this guy wasn't a mastermind in fire setting techniques.

How could Emily be so far off with her profile?

He knew the answer.

She was pissed off at him and it clouded her judgment. He couldn't blame her. If the roles were reversed, he would probably react the same way.

What was he thinking?

He wasn't.

Now he would have to wait until everything blew over. They had been through too much to let one misstep overshadow everything they had together. All the completed cases, cryptic clues, and near death experiences with serial killers brought them closer together. They could work though anything. It would take time.

DeBeers went inside the motel room. Rick watched the light turn on and shadows pass by the window. After a few minutes, it went dark.

CHAPTER FORTY- NINE
Sunday 2000 Hours

The barrel of the gun kept Emily's focus, but she noticed the safety engaged. It allowed her an extra few seconds to formulate a plan – not a full-proof plan, but just enough time to get the upper hand. It would only work if Jordan did his part.

She scanned to her right. Jordan's face pressed up against the building distorted his usual chiseled looks, but his piercing eyes caught hers directly. He actually winked at her with the usual light humor behind it. If his eyes could talk, they would say 'go for it, I am right behind you'.

Emily's body tensed. Every twitched muscle sent the skin sensations to a magnified level, until it caught up with her racing thoughts. Whoever this couple was, it did not matter. Their next stop was jail, if Emily had anything to do with it.

She waited for the right second. Patience was not only a virtue, but also a pillar for life and death.

"Who are you?" The man demanded as he pushed his sour face closer to Emily. His teeth clenched, jawline muscles tightened.

The gun wavered slightly to the left and the barrel dipped forward.

A battle cry escaped Jordan as he cracked the back of his head into the face of the unknown woman. He scuffled with her as they both fought for the gun.

Emily seized her moment.

She took one-step back with her left foot, raised her right foot, and thrust forward in a stomp kick motion. A direct contact impacted the man's stomach. He catapulted backward with a startled expression, eyes wide, with a slacked mouth. He managed to utter only expelled air, followed closely with a weak groan.

Emily doubled up her attack with another kick to the face.

The offensive move had propelled the man even farther backward onto the bottles. The gun flew from his grasp and clattered across the ground.

Glass and liquor spewed everywhere.

Emily picked up the gun and spun around. She yelled at the woman, "Put the gun down now!"

The woman still had a look of shock imprinted on her face from the orchestrated attack, as blood flowed freely from her nose.

Gin and vodka perfumed the air.

"I have no problem splattering your brains all over the wall!" Emily never took her eyes from the woman. "You don't want to test me."

Emily stood her ground and was prepared to do whatever it took under the circumstances.

"Uh…" Was the only word uttered from the feminine half of the crime duo.

Her gun dropped to the ground.

Emily kicked the gun to Jordan. She didn't know what angered her more, being taken by surprise, or the fact that the couple was on some kind of crime spree.

Jordan composed himself, straightened his shirt and jacket. "Thanks…" He picked up the gun.

With one quick motion, Emily flipped two heavy-duty zip ties from her pocket, still aiming the firearm at the couple. To Jordan, she said, "Secure them."

"Aye-aye captain." Jordan swiftly moved inside the storage area and pushed the man over to one side, slipping the ties over his wrists. With a quick tug, he was secured but still moaning.

To the woman, Emily ordered. "Turn around and face the wall."

Not questioning the instructions, the woman turned and Jordan slipped the ties over her wrists and secured them.

A small packet dropped from the woman's pocket.

"What do we have here?" Jordan said as she stooped over and picked up a bag of drugs. "Don't you know that this stuff is illegal?"

"Screw you…" The woman spat out in disgust.

Emily watched, contemplating the next move.

A police siren shrieked and headed in their direction. Obviously, someone at the bar heard the commotion and called the cops.

"Let's go…" Emily instructed.

Jordan stuffed the drugs into the woman's pocket. He directed the woman and man into a caged section in the corner, which was a secure inventory area designed to keep high priced booze safe and employees honest. It sat empty.

"Who are you? You're not cops." The woman insisted, her eyes narrowed and filled with hatred.

Jordan shut door, affixed the lock, and kicked the side of the cage for good measure. "Of course we're not cops… duh…" He smirked and turned to Emily.

With her shirt, she wiped down both firearms. She wasn't worried that the local cops would dust for prints and identify them, but she wasn't taking any chances either.

Jordan double-checked the door of the cage.

"You're not going to get away with this!" The woman screamed.

Jordan leaned toward the cage. "I think we just did."

The sirens abruptly stopped in front of the bar.

Emily tossed the guns next to the doorway. "Let's go…"

Pushing through the back entrance, Emily and Jordan hurried down the alley and around the corner.

The radio crackling with the usual police lingo echoed behind them.

Jordan mumbled, "How'd they get here so quickly?"

"We've got to lay low until the commotion dies down." Emily scanned all the nearby structures.

Two buildings over was an abandoned restaurant that had seen better days. The front windows boarded up concealed the interior, but a side entrance had a simple wooden door that was easy for Jordan to jimmy open.

They slipped inside the empty restaurant, shutting the door quietly behind them.

The decayed stench of the old building, along with some remnants of moldy food, accosted them.

Emily stood motionless taking in her unfamiliar surroundings, making sure that they were indeed alone.

Movement from outside alerted both of them as two uniformed police officers jogged by, apparently looking for more suspects or checking out the perps story.

"What do you think, about a half an hour and then they'll all be gone?" Jordan whispered.

"Unless they really want to write an in depth police report." Emily smiled.

Jordan laughed. "Thanks again for saving my butt back there…"

"I'm used to it."

"You are… quite amazing Ms. Stone."

They stood next to the entrance in close quarters. Emily could smell Jordan's soap on his skin from his morning shower. She watched him in the dim light; his eyes remained riveted to her. Taking a breath, Emily suddenly felt warm and slightly claustrophobic. She knew that Jordan had a crush on her, but it seemed more like a strong friendship bond to her, rather than sexual tension.

"You never know what you can do until you're pushed to the limit." She rambled, feeling uncomfortable.

"Humble as well as beautiful." Jordan said with a serious tone.

Emily shifted her weight slightly and wasn't sure what she felt at that exact moment. Even with the sarcasm and wisecracking, Jordan was handsome, intelligent and capable. He understood her point of view with crime and her undeniable passion to hunt down killers.

"I… I don't know if that is entirely accurate." Emily feebly replied.

Jordan moved closer to her.

Emily didn't object or move away.

Jordan slipped his right hand around her back and pulled her close. He leaned in slowly and gently kissed her on the lips.

* * * * *

It had been twenty minutes after the sleazy couple had left the motel room. Rick still sat in the SUV determined to complete the stake out, or find something that would shed some new light on the cases.

As he waited for the suspect to return, he passed the time on his laptop. He stared at the computer file with all of the emails he had received concerning Leo Brown. He had read each one several times, but felt helpless. That man had almost killed Emily once and could still get to her at any time.

It angered him. It got under his skin and made him steam. He wanted to hunt down the killer and put a bullet in him. This person now had put a wedge in between them.

Rick looked up. He watched the motel room for any movement.

Nothing.

It was quiet and deserted. He knew that this wasn't the arson killer, but like Emily, he wanted to make sure that nothing fell between the cracks of the investigation.

With a burst of energy, Rick opened the car door and stepped out. He watched the parking lot as he approached the room. He quickly searched for anyone that wasn't supposed to be there.

Deserted.

The motel was rundown and the owner didn't see fit to update the locks to keycards. The guests didn't seem to care either. It made it easier for Rick as he fished out a motel master key from his pocket, courtesy of Jordan. If Rick was going to have to sit in a car outside and take notes on this suspect, he was going to make sure that this fire starter would pay for his criminal activity – one way or another.

Taking one last look around, Rick inserted the key and with a couple of quick twists opened the door. It took only seconds before Rick was inside the room. The smell of sweat and dirty linens made Rick's stomach churn. The sheets strewn on the floor along with empty beer cans and one mostly empty bottle of flavored vodka, rounded out the appearance of a love shack.

Careful not to touch anything, Rick systematically searched for incriminating evidence. Nothing popped out at him, but he knew all the clever hiding places in a motel room. He looked inside the Bible in the nightstand drawer.

Nothing.

He didn't want to touch anything on the bed so he took a clean looking t-shirt from the floor and made a makeshift glove before he pulled up the mattress.

No luck.

He took a quick look inside the closet, chest of drawers, and the bathroom.

Empty handed and frustrated, Rick stood in the middle of the room slowly scanning the small area. He kept coming back to the bed. Hesitantly, he dropped to his knees and looked under the bed.

The motel room door burst open and slammed shut. The outline of a tall man stood at the threshold.

CHAPTER FIFTY
Sunday 2310 Hours

Emily felt warm and safe as the dire circumstances dissolved from her perspective. Her body relaxed as she enjoyed the soft kiss from Jordan. It didn't shock her that he took advantage of their moment alone after a stressful encounter. She was surprised that he was such a great kisser, gentle but firm and commanding.

For as wonderful as Emily felt physically, her heart and spirit belonged to Rick. She gently pushed Jordan away. "Jordan, I'm sorry if I gave you the wrong impression." She realized how hollow that comment sounded after she had said it. Her sentiment seemed to resonate around the abandoned room. "I may have been giving you mixed signals." The more she tried to explain her feelings to him, the worse it sounded.

Jordan released his hold from her waist. Gently, and then slowly his hands and arms returned to his sides before he gathered his wits about him. He didn't say anything at first, but Emily could see the embarrassment and hurt behind his vivid blue eyes.

Jordan finally responded. "I'm sorry that I stepped out of line in our friendship. Some of these cases cause high emotional responses... and I guess... that I just got caught up in the moment."

Emily felt awful because she respected him. Even with his annoying repartee, she was glad that their paths had crossed. "Jordan..." She gently touched his arm.

"No need for an explanation."

"Deep down, you know how I feel about you and nothing can ever change that." She smiled.

"How do you feel?" Jordan kept his gaze even and for a moment unreadable.

It wasn't the conversation that Emily wanted to discuss. Personal feelings and relationships take away from her strong focus. More lives were at stake. She had to keep alert and vigilante at every turn.

"I don't think that this is the appropriate time Jordan." She spoke softly and carefully. "You know that we have a special bond, but that's as far as the relationship is going to go. I'm in love with Rick." She paused for a moment. "But I'm not going anywhere, at least I don't think so yet. I've always got your back." She tried to let him down gently because she knew that he wanted more from her.

"Sure… I know that you've always got my back, and you know that I would be there any time for you." He watched her forcing his voice to sound upbeat. There was still a sting of hurt in his demeanor with his shoulders slumped forward and his facial expression downturned. "I guess I was a little too late, just bad timing, but I'm okay with that." He smiled.

The sound of a police radio neared the building, chirping in between quick broadcasting lingo.

Both Emily and Jordan froze.

"I think we should stay here a while longer until the cops clear out." Emily looked around in the dark.

Jordan hesitated. He continued to stand at the previous location as if his feet were encased in cement.

Emily felt relieved to move away from the uncomfortable tension. Finding a bench, she didn't bother to wipe away some of the filth from it before sitting down. The seating was actually more comfortable that it looked. She scanned the room to keep her mind off personal feelings, and to the pass some time before they could leave safely.

Heavy dust encrusted the entire wreckage of what once was a restaurant.

Jordan took up a seat on the other side of the bench.

They both sat in the darkness, each lost in their own thoughts.

Emily tried to change the subject. "I think it's safe to say that McCain isn't our arson guy. I just can't get a solid read on this profile for some reason." She looked down, clearly frustrated.

"I don't think the profile is off, I think the perp is well hidden."

"Well even so, the suspects don't fit the profile. This case has been obstructed for lack of a better word."

Jordan took a deep breath. "If we don't go through this type of case systematically that's when we'll miss the most obvious clue."

Emily couldn't help but notice that Jordan's usual jovial attitude and sarcastic flair had faded.

The arson case weighed heavy on her. The victims not yet realized weighed heavy on her. Bishop and Red taxed her energy. There was an unending fear of the unknown. Everything competed for her attention.

The serial arsonist was her most difficult case, which made Emily's energy level plummet. She pushed harder to keep her mind on the case, and not on Jordan or Rick.

Something had to give.

As if reading her mind, Jordan stated the obvious. "I wonder if Rick is having any luck with the other suspect?"

* * * * *

Without a single word or hesitation, the tall man lunged at Rick with a surprisingly heavy force, which slammed him onto the floor. DeBeers had returned to the motel room and was hell bent on retaliation for some reason.

The clatter of bodies, arms, elbows, and feet rattled Rick's bones. It instantly reignited the injuries sustained earlier by Bishop's man. He could smell sickly sweat and alcohol of the attacking man.

Gasping for air, Rick managed to scramble to his knees using his arms to block the flying fists. The suspect never asked who Rick was, but merely kept the attack mode. The deep pain shot up through Rick's legs, as it tightened his back and shoulders with extreme anguish.

DeBeers face changed, contorted and pained. He stopped moving in aggressive overtures and allowed Rick to get to his feet.

Rick knew the look and took several steps backward as the criminal heaved with contorted thrusts. The projectile vomit rained down on the side of the bedspread and across the carpet. The stink revolted Rick.

"Get up." Rick ordered. He still felt the throbbing pain in his back.

The suspect mumbled several unintelligible words, while spitting the remnants of his puke onto the floor.

Rick stepped forward careful not to step in the vomit and pulled the man up by his arm. "Stand up."

DeBeers wavered just as his eyes narrowed, changing to pure animosity. He lunged again at Rick, but this time he averted the hit by taking a step to the side. The convict then fell forward, striking his head on the short chest of drawers before landing face down on the floor. His body lay limp unmoving, his arms rested down at his sides, palms facing upwards. Motionless.

Rick stood above the man. As he looked down, the first thought was that he was dead, and all the complications that would entail. Within moments, the slow steady breath raised and lowered the suspect's back. He was alive.

Relief swept over Rick. The problems of a wrongful death left his mind.

Thinking twice, Rick decided to drag the man and deposit him on the bed. He took another quick look around the room for good measure, looking in drawers, under the furniture, but found absolutely nothing that would connect DeBeers to the case.

Rick left the motel room.

He was relieved not to be in intimate contact with the barf and beer smells anymore. As he put the SUV in gear, his cell phone rang.

"Hello?" The connection crackled and sounded hollow.

He listened to the defeated voice of Emily as she explained that she and Jordan found nothing. At least she was speaking to him in a cordial tone and didn't sound as mad as the past few days. However, there was almost a sadness in her voice. He wasn't sure if Emily was just overly tired, or if the case proved too much.

"It's been a bust here too. Sorry I don't have any better news. I'll meet you back at home."

He pushed the end button on the cell, tossing the device onto the seat. The nagging feeling that there was more to the arsons than initially realized became more evident.

CHAPTER FIFTY-ONE
Monday 1100 Hours

The staircase snaked around to the side of the multi-level estate winding up to the large sliding doors on a veranda. The impressive views of the ocean captured the imagination. The cool sea breeze invigorated Angel's obsessive-compulsive mindfulness.

He appeared average in physical characteristics with his dark jeans and hoodie that hid his slender build. He took each step, inspecting for the proper upkeep, to insure no paint had peeled from the dark wooden stairs. His combat boots kept the efficient pace, exhibited little noise, which helped him to keep the cadence of approach and flow.

The gentle, cool breeze endured his stride like a good friend. He had forgotten what the coastline was like, clean, stimulating, and ultimately raw in nature. The surf crashed against the rocks below. It had a certain powerful tone, which helped him keep his warrior focus.

No laziness.

No uncleanliness.

It remained Angel's solace for the next ten minutes, due to the repetition of purity that hailed him.

Angel's left foot hit the landing of the deck and his shoe made a hollow vibration sound, much different from the stairs.

He stopped. With one foot on the last stair and the other on the deck, he appeared uncertain what to do next.

The area was clear of any potted plants, garden mobiles, outdoor furniture, or anything that would flutter or change colors in the wind. The deck remained sterile, empty, and void of any inhabitants. It intrigued Angel. He had to take an extra moment to admire the void; however, it didn't sway him from his urgent mission.

The job demanded top priority.

Angel stepped gently onto the deck and quickly ignored the vista of the Pacific Ocean. Instead, he slipped off his backpack to retrieve a small black box. Everything had a specific place in the pockets of the personal bag, which he had packed and repacked several times. The special organizer contained everything he needed to set his trap for the cleansing.

It only took a few seconds to attach the camera to the back siding of the house. It would allow him to watch remotely the emergency personnel hustle about their duties along with the smoke, fire, and the attractive burning embers of the house.

A prickly heat rose from his lower extremities at the thought of the grand fire tearing away the house and the inhabitants through his carefully orchestrated purification. Like tiny cold fingers making their way up his legs and torso, it excited him. It used to frighten him like an unknown parasite; but now, it electrified him at the prospect of what was to come.

Fire erased sin with a true refinement.

A computerized remote deactivated the security system of the home A.D.A. Joshua Richards. It wasn't difficult once Angel had the name of the security company. He jammed the frequencies with his homemade device with just a press of a button. The round button felt commanding, given to power that he controlled with just a thumb impression.

Angel had found out more information about the locations of all of the attorney's homes through a simple search from the County Assessor's Office. He loved play-acting; it allowed him to become anyone at any time. It was easy to disguise himself as a real estate appraiser requesting more information from the inexperienced clerk who had been happy to help.

The home had the usual minimum alarm coverage of the windows and doors, nothing else, not even security cameras. The closest neighbor had not inhabited their home in months. Angel had no fear about being spotted by curious spectators. Most people passed him on the street without a second glance or acknowledgment.

With a few quick manipulations of the lock picks, Angel popped the French door open. Out of habit, he waited for any sound or flashing of lights.

Nothing accosted him.

For a brief instant, his mind formed the image of the She-Warrior from the video screen grab. He wondered if she would take extra precautions in her work too. The thought tugged at him, punched his chest, and momentarily the prickly burning fingers clawed at his body. In all of his twenty-seven years on the earth, he had never encountered another person with his mindset.

Angel counted to fifty-seven before he entered the house. Patience was a virtue, and he strove to make it one of his finer traits. The number represented the sinners he had cleansed.

He stepped inside.

The sea breeze forced the glass door shut with a bang.

Angel startled with an adrenaline surge, goosebumps rose on his hot tingling skin. The pristine windows in the French door sparkled with the costal wind whipping around the individual panes.

Silence resounded in the home.

Stale air oppressed his senses. He gulped for more air to sustain him.

The oversized furniture in light shades of beige, pale blues, stark whites along with a few art objects in pale yellows commanded his attention. The sickening colors made Angel nauseous. He fought the urge to shred everything in the living room, smash the knickknacks through the picturesque windows, and pitch precious antiquities off the deck.

He caught his anger and turned his gaze around the room.

A white end table held several framed photographs in silver frames. He moved closer and glared at the faces staring back. Family and friends smiled dramatically from the scenes of nature, restaurants, and even from the vacant deck of the estate.

One photo caught Angel's eye in particular, a special engraved frame that said: *Christmas Vacation.* A young, dark haired boy of ten or eleven grinning ear to ear with his parents at an amusement park setting posed for the camera. It seemed artificial. All were dressed in similar sweatshirts and jeans. A large rollercoaster with eager riders with their hands raised high in the air to add to the thrill provided the perfect backdrop for the family photo.

Angel stared at the words *Christmas Vacation* until his eyes began to tear up from not blinking. Deep sadness filled him, almost too terrible to recall that event. He remembered one particular holiday morning.

Angel opened his eyes with hope that he would receive presents on Christmas morning – at least something wrapped in festive paper adorned with snowmen or reindeer. Inside he would find a new toy, book, or even a cool t-shirt. When he was six, his parents had presents for him. That was the last time. The car crash took his mom and dad from his life, but he knew that they were starting over, somewhere again.

As he lay on his mattress staring at the ceiling, he memorized every inch of the few posters he had found tossed away in a neighbor's garbage can. The colorful photos kept his gaze away from the clutter and garbage that had oozed into his tiny bedroom.

The house stayed quiet.

Christmas morning had officially begun for the neighborhood. He imagined children squealing with delight at all the presents nestled under the tree and stockings stuffed with candy. Parents groggy, sipping the first cup of coffee.

Nothing would ever magically materialize for Angel, but he patiently waited for his time. The promise of his new beginning drove him to survive another day.

He knew that Aunt Clara slept, as she always did most of the day and nighttime. She rarely checked on Angel, and never asked him to clean up his room or to do his homework. He was alone and grappled with the usual pre-teen angst of growing pains and daily concerns – isolated.

As Angel's room became lighter, he sat up, rolled to the side immediately touching the floor. He stood in silence staring at the wall of refuse standing tall before him. He made sure that he wore at least two, sometimes three, pairs of socks before he ventured from his room into the rest of the house. He tiptoed through the dwelling; hopeful something had changed, but he knew that everything was the same as it was the night before.

He stood at the threshold of his aunt's bedroom - watching. She lay on her side with a plaid blanket covering her body, knees drawn up toward her torso. Her chest raised and lowered subtly as she dreamed – hopefully of better places. Her short dark hair in tiny twisted curls had streaks of grey.

Huge stacks of clothes, boxes, magazines, and newspapers towered all around her. Angel envisioned that she was a queen in her royal bedchamber. The recyclables were the towers all around her, a magnificent castle, protected by a moat with alligators, and the clothes were her trusted court and guardsmen.

Aunt Clara slept.

Poor Aunt Clara, a miserable woman of this world. She couldn't get out of the way of sin and disorder. She desperately needed a new start of a life, a new beginning, a do over.

Angel knew it was a miserable situation, but he didn't feel any sadness. He tried to muster some emotion, feelings of gloom, a tear or two, but nothing ever came. He felt nothing, except the need to clean up an impossible mess.

In the very back of a cluttered cabinet in the kitchen, he found the items with the answer. He knew it was a sign directed at him. The feeling of strength like a warrior superhero consumed him. The empowering feeling took over his body.

It was time.

As Angel stood in the doorway with a can of lighter fluid in his left hand and a book of matches in his right, he knew it was the right thing to do.

Angel closed his eyes, squeezed the lids tightly, and then reopened to find that his present vision restored. Looking at the happy faces of the lawyer and his family did not detour him from his mission.

He retrieved a folded piece of paper that had a schematic diagram of the estate, along with intricate notes of the weaknesses of the electrical and gas lines to the home.

He systematically got to work.

The cleansing would commence soon.

* * * * *

The charred car sat alongside the country road halfway in a ditch, just off the roadway, and burned beyond any identifiable semblance of an automobile. Twisted and blackened to the point of disturbing. Most horror writers could not conjure up the shocking vision any worse than what premiered in front of Detective Duncan.

The car and driver were the victims of a chilling branding by a serial killer. The car registration showed the name of a private investigator by the name of Zig Rodriquez.

The case hadn't been deemed a serial case. It didn't definitely confirm a connection between the other arson cases, except that all of the recent victims had worked on the same court case.

The arson investigation was assigned to another detective who would begin to run down the minimal amount of clues, about cases the P.I. worked, any threats, drug affiliations, and the company that he had kept. Duncan knew that it would lead to nothing. The department barked up the wrong proverbial tree once again.

The detective stood and watched the scene unfold. It was the first time that he felt more like a fly on the wall than a homicide detective. He reached into his jacket pocket, pulled out a cigarette, lit it, and enjoyed the feeling of the smoke in and out of his lungs. Irony fit the situation perfectly in a morbid way, but he didn't care. He needed something to steady his increasing anger because more bodies would continue to pile up.

The familiar sound of rattling morgue wheels stopped suddenly. For a moment, everything became quiet, except for the wind twisting through the dense trees.

Two coroner's technicians pulled the body out of the car. They set the remains inside a heavy-duty bag on the gurney, struggling a moment to make sure the limbs stayed inside the sack.

Two forensic specialists completed their documentation and packed the few specimens into their crime scene unit vehicle.

Duncan looked to the area of trees that had the best view of the car. He had a hunch, call it an instinct, due to the years of walking through all types of crime scenes. The perps always wanted to admire their handiwork, even to the point of arrogance and obsessiveness.

The uneven road sharply dropped off into a dirt turnout, which led into the trees. Scattered paper items and garbage blown into crevices littered the exterior of the emergency parking area.

The detective stepped into the dirt, took one last hit from his cigarette, tossed the butt on the ground, but careful not to contaminate the surrounding area around the crime scene. Nearing closer to retirement made him more reckless, but it didn't change his dogged pursuit of finding the bad guy.

Three large Pine trees in between a grove of Eucalyptus trees grew in a semi-circle. The spot appeared to have the best view of the car. If the perp could not afford to be seen at the crime scene, there were simple ways to still watch the handiwork of the cops.

Breathless and tired from the lack of sleep, Duncan plodded over to one of the Pine trees. He found a small black box fixed to a tree trunk a little higher than eye level.

The detective yelled in the direction of the forensic technicians. "I need photos along with video documentation over here now!"

A chime from his top pocket averted his attention. He quickly grabbed the cell phone and found it was a text message from a record's clerk.

CHAPTER FIFTY-TWO
Tuesday 0830 Hours

The small blue and white cottage barely larger than a modest studio apartment sat hidden in the trees on the quiet street. Overgrown shrubs and dead grass all needed tending long ago, which practically dwarfed the little house. No direct views from the neighbors added to the secrecy of the surveillance and covert activity.

Emily leaned over Jordan's shoulder to gain a better perspective. "Park over at an adjacent street." She motioned to the area. "It'll be the best area to sit for a while and it looks like most neighbors aren't home."

"Aye-aye captain." Jordan eased his sedan to a parking place in between two trees. There was a still a view of the walkway leading to the cottage.

"And stop saying that." Emily stated. She studied the surroundings, squinting her eyes to see if anyone looked out their windows.

"It's better than Ma'am."

"Don't say that either."

"See, you don't leave me many choices."

"What you think?"

"About what?"

"Jordan…"

"What?"

Emily steadied her annoyance, partly due to what happened between them, but mostly because she was edgy and suffered from the extreme lack of any restful sleep. Slowly, and with the nicest tone she could muster, she asked. "Do you think that the cops have already been here?"

"Are you kidding?" He smirked.

Emily stared at him.

"Okay, I'm sorry. No, I don't think that the cops have been here." Jordan sighed. He placed his hands on the steering wheel and pushed his back firmly against the leather seat. "They just found the P.I.'s torched body yesterday and their hands are full with the whole arson thing."

The sun scattered the morning rays through the dense trees. The bright beams reflected into the front seat of Jordan's car. Emily shaded her eyes with her right hand. She tried to ignore Jordan's demeanor. He was usually amped up and ready for anything, but now he looked like someone had punched him in the stomach and kicked dirt in his face.

"It's my turn." Emily readied herself. She made sure that her Beretta was loaded and tucked in her ankle holster – just in case.

"Wait."

Emily met Jordan's gaze. A twinge of guilt invaded her mind.

"I mean... Rick will be pissed off if I don't do the recon this time."

"I've been doing this a lot longer than the two of you combined." Emily hated that she sounded insensitive, but it had to be said. She wasn't in the mood for any discussion about it. "I think I can handle this..." She fitted the small headset to her right ear and adjusted the microphone. "Don't worry, I'll be in contact with you every step of the way."

Jordan's eyes looked pained as he studied her face. He copied Emily's example. The headset was in place as he double-checked his cell phone too.

Jordan made a silly salute.

"Wish me luck." Emily smiled and exited the car not waiting for a reply.

She wasted no time and hurried toward Zig Rodriguez's house. The investigator didn't have a private office; he only borrowed the use of an extra cubicle at the courthouse. By the process of elimination, Emily knew that the cases he worked on were at his residence. It was quiet and on his own turf.

The distinct fragrance of honeysuckle caught hold of her senses, sweet, pleasant, and a reminder of the beautiful things in the world. The wild vine had taken over the side yard, moved along the fence, and up the side of the house. As lovely as the scent was, Emily couldn't help but think about the burnt smell of the private investigator's car and what a horrible way to die.

The real question tormented her.

Was the P.I. killed as a part of the serial killer's plan, or was he killed because of something he uncovered?

Emily walked around to the back yard. It was completely dirt, no patio or deck, and the fog and drizzle made it soggy and uneven beneath her shoes. Pieces of mud adhered to her boots. She lightly stomped her strides to loosen it.

The back door of the cottage looked more like a closet door than the back entrance. She tried to turn the nob, but found it locked. Scanning around the immediate area, a ceramic snail sat alone with a goofy cartoon smile on its face. It was the only thing clean from dirt in the yard. Swiftly picking up the caricature, a house key tucked up inside the tight crevice dropped to the ground.

Within seconds, Emily stepped into the cottage.

"Has the eagle landed?" A clear voice in Emily's ear disguised with a British accent asked her.

Emily took a moment and quickly inventoried the cottage. "I'm inside."

"It's all clear out here. Just a black cat jetting across the street. Is that a bad omen?"

"Not from where I'm standing."

"Oh, good."

"Give me some silence while I look around because I can't concentrate with you in my head."

With a chuckle, Jordan said. "How do you *really* know that it's not *all* in your head? Maybe you have all kinds of different voices resonating in your head, and none of us really exist."

"I wouldn't be so lucky…"

Emily heard Jordan exhale air that sounded more like a windstorm whipping around in her ear. She ignored the remark and focused on her search.

The house seemed like a carbon copy of someone living in a motel too long, or a dorm room after a party. Due to the small size of the dwelling, clutter dominated most of the living areas. Beer bottles sat on every available surface, dishes stacked in the sink, clothes draped over the backs of chairs, and the thrift store furniture lent to the image of a divorced man.

Emily cautiously weaved around the furniture, sometimes in extreme tight areas. She hoped that she didn't track mud inside.

On the other side of the room, a corner computer desk appeared from the mess, neat, orderly, and everything had its own place. A drastic contrast compared to the rest of the cottage. To her dismay, she could not locate a computer, high-tech tablet, or any type of an electronic device.

On two of the walls were numerous framed photographs, some of Rodriguez in a police uniform, faded newspaper articles about a large drug bust, and various vintage family photos. She got the impression that there was a sadness, or feeling of homesick by the abundance of family generations displayed.

Emily knew that Rodriquez was a police officer for twenty-two years, then held down several security positions until he began working for the district attorney's office. By the appearance of the home, Emily surmised that he was divorced and most likely had children he rarely saw. The background information she viewed earlier from the computer didn't say one way or another, but he seemed to take pride in his work and enjoyed the challenges by the appearance of his work area.

To the left of the desk, a jumbled display of knick-knacks, but not the usual kinds, sat facing outward. These items were idols, creepy looking and carved out of various types of wood. Emily shuddered. She kept searching.

Her mind wandered back to the arsonist. She wondered what he had planned for the next victim. There was a brilliant quality to the killer, but she knew that the arsonist wasn't just beginning his kills. There were many more victims in the plan.

Flipping through files and steno pads, nothing appeared out of the ordinary with the private investigator. Background checks on witnesses and suspects from a variety of cases ranged from fraud to murder. Rodriquez conducted his business in an old school way. He wrote on paper, all written out long hand with a surprisingly beautiful script of penmanship.

A bang hit the window. Emily jumped. She immediately turned and saw a stunned bird flapping in the backyard. Imagination was the worst enemy when you were in covert mode. She shook off the nerves and continued her search, cautious not to touch anything that would leave her fingerprints behind.

Glancing back at the strange carvings in the corner with oversized heads and bulging, beady eyes, she shivered. Her fingertips chilled to an icy fervor as she sorted small pieces of paper with numerous phone numbers and names.

Nothing jumped out at her.

"It's been twelve minutes. Do you know where your sneaky detectives are?"

"Shut up Jordan..." Emily rolled her eyes, but couldn't stop a smile. She was glad that he couldn't see her face.

"Find anything?"

"Not really, but I found something that you might like to add to your apartment decor."

Emily snapped a photo of the idols from her cell phone and sent it to Jordan.

She continued to sift through paperwork looking for something that would give her a clue or an answer, or at least another lead to chase down.

There had to be something in Rodriquez's house.

"Ewwww... nice hobby dude." Jordan's voice competed with the static that roved in and out of range.

"I just thought of you." She continued to focus on the files, moving paper to her right once she viewed it. To the far left side of the desk were fancy colored brochures of ski resorts, vacation homes, and security systems.

The items intrigued her.

The phone rang inside the house.

Emily stopped. Her headset gave a weird crackle and she lost the connection with Jordan. In a whisper, she spoke. "Jordan? You still there?"

Nothing.

The landline phone rang in a dull tone.

Ring... Ring... Ring...

No answering machine picked up, so it continued to ring, seven, eight, nine times...

* * * * *

"Em? Hello? Hell-OOO? Those freaky wooden things didn't come to life... hello?"

283

Jordan sighed. He pulled the headset off. "Technology sucks."

He retrieved his cell phone from atop the dash and looked at the photo from inside the cottage again of the demonic faces. "Geez." Scrolling through several saved photos on the cell phone memory screen, he stopped on a photo of Emily smiling directly at the camera. Jordan admired it for a moment.

He glanced at his watch and gave Emily five more minutes before he went in after her. They had spent too long parked in the neighborhood. Someone might notice Jordan's car and jot down the license plate number.

Jordan stared out his driver's window and let his mind wander. His thoughts came back to Emily's face in the abandoned restaurant and the way the light cast across her face and hair. Her intenseness and intelligence captivated him. He loved to watch her eyes light up when she used her deductive reasoning skills and pieced together the clues that the cops could not solve. The difficult challenges drove her, which was one of her most attractive qualities.

The passenger door opened.

"It's about time. I was going to…" Jordan was about to go into a long dissertation about the importance of safety.

Red got in and shut the car door.

"What the…" Jordan was shocked to see the assassin in the seat next to him dressed entirely in black. He looked as if he hadn't shaved for a couple of days.

Jordan stammered and then asked, "How did you find me?"

"Easy."

"What do you want?" Jordan tried not to sound frightened, but he knew it wasn't good that the hit man materialized out of thin air. Even worse, he wanted something from Jordan. That alarmed him in so many ways.

"Drive."

"What?"

Red grabbed the cell phone from Jordan and slipped it into his breast pocket. "Drive. I'll tell you where I want you to go when we get moving."

"I can't leave Emily here. I need to at least tell her that I'm leaving."

"She'll be fine, at least for now." Red looked straight ahead and didn't bother to use the seatbelt to strap himself in for the ride.

"What do you mean for now?"

Red turned his penetrating gaze and stared directly at Jordan. "You think that she will stay safe for long after she has been targeted?"

"But... I thought you said..."

Abruptly, the assassin answered. "You thought wrong."

"You said that she was safe and that you were taking care of it." Jordan let his insecurities take hold and his voice hit a higher octave.

"I bought her time that's all."

"Time?"

"I don't think you completely understand. Once she has been targeted, there's nothing changing Bishop's mind – ever. Now he wants her dead because she escaped." He paused and then said. "Time's up."

Jordan tried not to gasp in alarm. A million scenarios jumbled through his mind with assassin commandos coming after Emily by the hundreds. He thought that once they had escaped, and that Emily and Rick had moved, everything would go back to as it was before. He shook his head. Nothing was ever going to be the same again.

"Drive." Red ordered.

"So now you're kidnapping me?"

"No. Drive."

Jordan turned over the engine and his high-performance German sedan hummed. "This is where you cash in on that favor from me, right?"

"Yes."

Jordan eased the car away from the curb. "Well at least I don't have to ride in the trunk this time."

CHAPTER FIFTY-THREE
Tuesday 0930 Hours

The air in the corridor leading to the record's division made Detective Duncan's sinuses congest with extreme pressure, resulting in a nagging headache. He had walked more in the last couple of days than in an entire month. Many of the staff members at the police department were sick with colds and flus; the virus was probably already invading his system, he thought sourly to himself.

The detective turned the corner and entered a large room where several open work cubicles occupied the records clerks. Everything in the room etched a sickening beige color. The exception was the personal items on each desk, containing photos of kids and dogs, small figurines, and occasionally fresh flowers, which only marginally brightened the workspaces.

Phones rang at several desks transferred by clerical operators from the main incoming lines.

A couple of women hurried into adjacent rooms carrying background information for police detectives and patrol deputies.

The ache in Duncan's knees and ankles screamed at the excess weight he hauled around, but he wasn't going to let it slow him down now. He could feel the squeeze as time ticked away. After the case closed and a suspect was in custody, he would take some of his vacation time and make plans to put in his retirement papers. The thought reenergized him, pushing him to move faster.

He had received a text message from Jenny. She was the record's division supervisor and a good friend. Duncan trusted the impeccable work during her fifteen years of service. She undoubtedly understood law enforcement and investigations. Even with all the difficulties and personnel cutbacks, she focused, and dug in to find information that detectives like Duncan requested.

The detective smiled, raised his hand in a friendly gesture at a couple of the clerks, and walked to a small room where a blonde woman sat behind a desk. The woman was thin and pale, but her intense green eyes radiated behind her glasses, which moved around the computer screen in front of her.

"Hey Jenny, what do you have?" Duncan asked with a winded strain to his voice.

She looked up over her glasses and smiled. Her sparkly eyes danced   "Detective I didn't expect to see you until the end of the day or tomorrow morning."

"They didn't need me anymore at the arson site… besides, I wanted to visit you instead." He smiled. For a moment, he thought Jenny blushed.

"Grab that chair." She motioned for him to pull up a chair that sat up against the wall.

"Wow, I have to sit down for this?"

"You bet. You need to see the progression of what I found. You can be the judge." She cleared some manila file folders and various color-coded paperwork from her desk. She piled them on a shelf behind her.

It was a tight fit, but the detective managed to squeeze into the small space. A faint smell of jasmine surrounded Jenny and it was a nice distraction from the horror of crime scenes. He admired her simple beauty that most would miss until they had a second look. Even though she was in her late-forties, she had a way about her that was youthful and fun.

"Okay, lay it on me." The detective settled in after he put on his reading glasses.

"You know how I love puzzles and mind teasers, right?"

"Yep."

Jenny split the computer screen into several window sections. "Here's the photo of the black box and a partial identification number MRE... and here's a photo of the steel security door and the manufacturer numbers that begin with STE and INT."

"You've lost me."

"Hold your horses, I'm not done yet." She adjusted her glasses and clicked the mouse several times. "I did a little digging on the Internet and found that there are only two companies that specialize in this type of door. They are experts in the mechanisms and installations. Other companies can order this door, but they don't have the same knowledge and experience." She shifted in her seat and inadvertently bumped Duncan's arm. "A small mom and pop company started out twenty something years ago, Robertson & Sons, and now the company is called AA Armed Security, Inc. DBA Robertson & Sons."

Jenny opened the window of the security website. Professionally organized, top-notch photos with expertly written descriptions contributed to the credibility of the company.

"I shop catalogues, not online, but with physical catalogues sent to my house." She gestured to the small stack of mailers behind her. "There's one thing that I have noticed when I'm calling in my order. The items generally begin with ITM or something that coincides with a specific type of collection or season."

Duncan followed her breadcrumbs of logic because he knew that Jenny was one of the sharpest people working at the sheriff's office. He let her continue and didn't interrupt.

"Every time a specific security item was referred to with a STE, the coinciding item on the website had this image." Jenny waved the mouse cursor over the item number and a symbol appeared that looked like a brand with a swirled "S" in it. "I remembered that case from ten years ago where the rapist wrote those letters to the D.A.'s office and always signed with that peculiar symbol."

Duncan followed her logic. "You know Jenny, it's a long shot that the killer is the copyrighter."

"Okay. Then check this out." Jenny opened a pdf file of the security company's catalogue; every item that designated a STE had the same symbol hidden in the text.

The detective's mind spun in several directions. His thoughts were of obsessive-compulsive personalities. He had encountered these types in past investigations. They were meticulous in how they committed their crimes. The arsonist reeked of this type of personality.

The high-tech security company didn't mean anything definite, but it was a lead and another way to take the investigation. A rumble in his stomach made him think about eating, but food would have to wait a little longer.

"We need to get a list of people who are technical writers, copyrighters, or anyone who worked on the website and catalogue for this company."

"I'm already ahead of you." Jenny handed the detective a printout of outside consultant employees. "I had Doug run this for me." She smiled and stared at the detective over her reading glasses.

Duncan leaned in and gave Jenny a kiss on the cheek. "You're a true gem Jenny... you should have been a detective." He rose to leave, which took a few extra seconds and as he carefully squeezed between the desk and bookshelves.

"It's always my pleasure detective." Jenny's smile brightened up the entire office long after Duncan had left.

* * * * *

It was almost time.

Angel wanted to be there to see all the glory of the fresh cleansing, no matter how long it took. He sat in the small room – waiting and watching. Every fire he had watched, never missing any of the intense heat, the overwhelming smoke, the blackened scorch, or the way that the flames danced to their own tune just for him. The ballet of the beautiful music eradicated the old and welcomed the new beginning with open arms. He loved the fire. The sin actually left the blaze, floated up high and dissipated. He witnessed the cleansing on many levels and yearned for more victims.

His mood, now chipper, and even a small smile crooked at the corners of his mouth. He tapped his mechanical pencil softly against the notebook, not feeling so alone anymore. The emptiness that usually plagued him every waking moment seemed to lessen in its grip on him. Something big was about to happen. Usually that would disturb Angel, the thought of something out of the ordinary, but not today.

A copy of an old paperback novel written by Martin Rover, missing the cover flap, earmarked on numerous pages, proved one of his most prize possessions. The book travelled everywhere with him. It too, had witnessed every fire. The story was about a young man who killed everyone in his family, including distant cousins, and anyone who knew or dated any of the family members.

He gazed at his laptop computer that was slightly askew on the small table, which never happened in any of his missions. Now he lived dangerously, even for just one day. The image on the screen was of the woman, the She-Warrior, small, powerful, and intense. It excited him. She knelt down examining something from the remnants of the fire. Angel felt in harmony. Even though he did not know her name, he knew it must be an important name – fit for a warrior.

Angel remembered the power he had received that special day from the high after the big fire. It filled him with a calmness and hope. He still celebrated that day on December 25th every year. It was better than any birthday or holiday; it was the day he freed himself from the filth and personal turmoil of society's sins.

"We have another victim over here!" The firefighter yelled through his protective mask.

Angel overcome by smoke could not get out of the house before he collapsed, just before he reached the side door. As he lay there, he remembered hearing a loud repetitive crashing noise as the firefighters broke down the door, along with part of the wall in order to get to him.

The next thing he remembered was floating high above the fire; carried away on the flame's shoulders as a true hero for everyone to see. As hard as he tried, he couldn't open his eyes to witness the epic event. He could only enjoy how his body and spirit felt.

It had been so easy.

The solution materialized in a supernatural way.

The answer to his continuous question of how he could get out of his filthy, sinful situation, to start over again, presented itself cleverly. He remembered fondly as he carefully walked around his aunt's bedroom early Christmas morning squeezing the lighter fluid. The toxic fumes tickled his nose. He moved faster and knew that once a fire started it would only take minutes to ignite the rest of the house.

The light of the match mesmerized Angel. He stared at it turning his hand slightly to get a better look, and felt a strong bond with the fire. It was a kinship. Something he had never experienced before. Everything about the mini inferno consumed him deep inside, the flame, the gentle flicker on the end of the match, and the deep range of color from yellow, red, to orange.

It was beautiful. It was the answer to his life. It was the cleansing of the bad to bring in the good.

He had tossed the match into his aunt's bedroom.

It took seconds to engulf the room in a wonderfully systematic way. He ignored the terrified screams. The dance of the fire inspired him, which kept his full attention.

Standing and watching with attentive curiosity, he didn't gauge the effects of the smoke and how aggressive the fire pushed through the piles of garbage, walls, curtains, furniture, newspapers, and old carpet. It was like pulling a string on a magical toy before flying off to another new world.

He played the fantastic sequence over in his mind as he lay on the gurney.

He forced open his eyes to an amazing new world. The oxygen mask placed over his nose and mouth made him feel like he was in a wonderful dream, a noble king, in a knight's helmet watching over his kingdom.

The firefighters hurried to the blaze with high-powered hoses shooting tons of water, while the ambulance drivers fussed over him.

It proved he was worthy. He loved all of them. They changed his life forever. He could now go to a new home and begin again.

Angel did not realize that he could feel that happy again.

Until now…

CHAPTER FIFTY-FOUR
Tuesday 1030 Hours

"What were you thinking?" Rick raised his voice as he stood in a confrontational manner.

"I don't know what the problem is? I'm following through with the investigation as usual." Emily tried to keep her anger under control, steadying her voice, but lately she felt on the verge of losing everything.

"I thought we were working this investigation together?" His eyes cooled matching his demeanor.

"We are. Jordan and I checked out the P.I.'s house." Emily moved to the kitchen followed closely by Rick.

"And?"

She took a cold bottle of mineral water from the refrigerator, twisting the cap off. "Nothing new, except I found some interesting brochures."

"Brochures?" He snapped.

"Yes brochures." Emily took a sip of the water.

"Where's Jordan? He's usually following you around like a puppy dog." Sarge barked. "No offense big guy."

"I don't know."

"What do you mean you don't know?"

"I don't know." Emily hated the use of interrogation techniques for her own actions.

"Didn't you guys go in his car?"

"Yes... but he took off."

"Great... what's his problem?"

"He sent me a text message after I got a cab and said that he would meet me later." Emily felt trapped and wanted to get on a plane, to go anywhere else. Taking a few breaths, she said. "I don't know what was up, but I don't think we should worry unless we don't hear back from him today."

Rick calmed down. "Did he say anything?"

"Just his usual stuff... you know Jordan. Everything was fine. Then when I came out, the car was gone."

Emily thought of the kiss in the old restaurant and thought better of telling Rick about it. Jordan seemed sad, but fine. She knew that he wouldn't leave her stranded unless there was something important that needed his attention.

"I'm sorry Em, it's just that things have gone a little sideways the past few weeks and I don't have a good feeling about this arson investigation."

Emily weakened. She knew that it was difficult for Rick to talk about his feelings. "I know, I'm sorry too."

She hugged Rick tight and didn't want to let go. It was difficult because she was burdened with too many emotions all vying for attention. She was apprehensive that any misstep in the investigation would cause the arson killer to claim another victim.

Rick looked at Emily. "I'm really sorry about everything."

"I know..." It still pained Emily that he didn't confide in her especially with everything they had been through. She fought back the tears and concentrated on the next step.

"What do you want to do now?" Rick's anger had disappeared and his typical resolve came into focus.

Emily moved back to the living room where she had left the brochures.

"What's that?" Rick asked.

"The investigator's house was just a work office for him and everything seemed typical. But, I found these brochures of exclusive resorts, security systems, and high-tech watches."

"Someone he was trailing or a suspect background check?"

"I'm not sure, but all of these brochures are written with the same type of language. It's like they were written by the same writer."

She flipped open a laptop and keyed up the first website from the brochures.

"Looks like the same copyrighter." Rick read the information over Emily's shoulder.

"It may have nothing to do with the arson case at all, but…"

"What a perfect way for any criminal to remain anonymous. This is a dream job if they work as a copyrighter and submitted their work by computer."

Emily frowned as she scrolled through the websites.

"What's the matter?" Rick asked. "I know that look." He managed a smile.

"It's just that this particular killer or arsonist goes to great lengths to create these snares for his victims, and then burns them." She glanced back at the white board. "He may be naive in some ways, but he wants some type of notoriety or something that separates him for the rest world…"

"Like serial killers that write letters to the police or leave their signature symbol at the grisly crime scene?" Rick perused through the brochures once again.

Emily moved the cursor over the security descriptions and inadvertently positioned the mouse on the item number. A strange symbol appeared and then disappeared. "Did you see that?" She slowly moved the computer cursor again and the "S" symbol appeared with a triangle.

"What is that? I've never seen that before." Rick concentrated on the text.

"I don't know, but it's on most of the items identification numbers." She quickly toggled through more item numbers. "There it is again! Is doesn't stay long." She grabbed a piece of paper and quickly sketched the image.

"It looks like an artist signature... coat of arms... some type of ancient text... It actually looks like a snake image..." Rick surmised.

Emily stood up straight to relieve some of the tension in her lower back. "But why would the private investigator for the prosecution, mainly doing background checks, have these brochures? He definitely wasn't in the market for a high-tech security system or a ten thousand dollar a night luxury spa."

"Something he found during a background check?" Rick contemplated. "Has Jordan checked out the employees, specifically the outside consultants for that security company?"

"He hasn't sent anything yet."

Rick scrolled through existing files on his cell phone.

Emily sat down at the kitchen table. She poured through arson photos again. She felt her heart sink. Nothing was coming together as it usually did. They were getting closer, but the how and why overwhelmed her.

"You need some sleep. Take an hour and just relax." Rick seemed to sense her stress, partly caused by the pressure she put on herself.

"I can't..."

"You need to refresh yourself, you'll think clearer."

"Wait." Emily retrieved the piece of paper with the symbol.

"What are you thinking?"

"Isn't there a symbol for fire? You know like an ancient symbol?"

Powering up his laptop, Rick typed in several search words and waited. "Here..." He pointed to the screen. "The Greek element sign is a triangle. See here..."

The screen showed all the elements and the signs that represent them, fire, water, air, and earth.

"Okay, that's half our symbol. What about the snake or weird backwards "S"?"

Rick took a moment to search more specific symbols for fire. "Here. The triangle represents the alchemy symbol for fire, but there's another one too."

Emily read the description. "It represents the fire symbol that corresponds with southern directions in a practical ritual, the season of summer. This emblem also signifies connections made within the realm of transformation, with the point meeting in the center, where both are connected and affecting each opposite end."

"I think we might have found our guy."

Emily processed the profile in her mind and said. "He sees himself as an avenger of sorts? But what motivates him?"

"Experiences, traumas, brain damage?"

"There's something driving him where he feels that there is no other choice." She hesitated. "Is he destroying or helping victims in his mind?"

"We need that list from Jordan."

Picking up her cell phone, Emily tried calling Jordan. It went directly to voice mail. She left a message. "Jordan, we need you. Call as soon as you get this."

Rick grabbed the notes of the other possible victims from the table. "If we can't find out who this guy is yet, then we'll have to wait until he finds us."

CHAPTER FIFTY-FIVE
Tuesday 1130 Hours

Jordan waited and helplessly watched. His nerves pushed his curiosity forward only out of sheer survival. He couldn't keep his hands and fingers still as he resisted the urge to run like hell. He wasn't sure if Red was a man of his word, or if he would kill him after he got what he wanted. The drive to the small airport made him uneasy, but Emily's life and freedom were much more important than the arson case at the moment.

Red moved effortlessly in the hangar with the preciseness that had few flaws, if any. His solemn face, dead eyes, and a serious directness made him a force unto himself. He was a lethal weapon when called upon. Checking the Cessna, he went through the typical maintenance routine, while devising his scheme.

The impressive aerodynamics of the flying machine did not give the plane justice from a distance; but up close, it reeked of opulence. Jordan had only been this close to a private airplane once during his career in the F.B.I. It was an undercover mission, which involved three special agents posing as drug dealers. They had used a private plane as their mode of travel.

Flying wasn't Jordan's optimum choice of transportation, but Red gave him precise orders. He worried and stressed about the plan, but there was nothing else he could do to change what was already set in motion. He ran his hand along the side of the Cessna, sleek, perfectly proportioned, as it helped to steady his rattled nerves.

It made Jordan wonder how an assassin could live a lifetime fulfilling death contracts, and not feel any remorse for what he had done. It was living a hollow existence. Red seemed a different type of psychopath forced to believe that it was all in a day's work. Jordan saw a flicker of light; perhaps hope in the man's eyes as he told him about the best way to free Emily for good. There was *something* behind Red's cold, calculating facade that provided hope and understanding.

Not knowing what else to say to Red, Jordan asked. "Do you need any help?"

"No."

"I don't know much about planes, but I could squeegee the windshield." Jordan paced uncomfortably. He hated long silences when there were people around because it made him ramble on with extreme sarcasm.

Red stopped and looked directly at Jordan. He did not say a word. The stare was like the scope of a rifle.

"Hey, just trying to help." Jordan shrugged and looked away.

The assassin slipped out of his leather jacket and shirt. He put on a compact parachute and redressed himself, this time with a heavier jacket that helped to camouflage the bulkiness of his attire.

Jordan opened his mouth to say something, but decided to keep his comments to himself instead.

Red walked up with purpose, Jordan thought for a moment that the assassin was going to snap his neck or stick a shiv into his gut. Instead, he said. "It's time." Red gave Jordan a folded piece of paper. "You understand?"

Jordan unfolded the paper and read the instructions. "Yes."

The hit man reached into the plane and pulled out a small duffle bag. "Everything you need is right here." He looked at his watch. "You have forty minutes to get to the location."

Jordan grabbed the bag. It was heavier than it looked. "Then I guess I better get my ass moving..."

He rushed out of the hangar.

* * * * *

It had taken him almost half an hour to pack the rations of food and water that he would need to sit out the time. However, time to Angel was relative. It was something that people worried about constantly, but he found it to be invigorating with the possibility of a hopeful new beginning.

With the information he had gathered from the county assessor's office and the security company, the family would visit the home at least once a month, usually twice. Sometimes it was just the lawyer and other times it was the family, which included a few extra friends. It didn't matter whether it was one person or a dozen casualties, the outcome would still be the same.

A perfect end with the ultimate cleansing.

Angel continued to make himself comfortable in the confined room, but his direct view was the master suite. As soon as the sinner arrived, he would be able to see his face. The stench of sin would be apparent.

He hoped one day that he was able to see the aura of sin on anyone he passed on the street. Imagining how it would waft around the body and exit out of the top of the head. It wouldn't be beautiful, but sneaky, and ugly to gaze at the murky colors. It existed. It needed his help.

Sin must stop.

He unzipped the dark blue plastic lunch bag and retrieved perfectly sliced pieces of cheese. Angel only ate American cheese. Other cheeses were too soft and spongy, while others tasted of moldy garbage. He adored the orange color and the texture of the dairy product, which made it easy to cut in perfect two-inch squares.

Organization was crucial.

He popped the small wedge into his mouth and let it sit on his tongue. He tasted the sharp, tangy flavor that filled him with energy. The deli food would sustain him until the show began.

The thought of the fiery image, flames taking control to devastate everything in its path, changing shades to push through anything that tried to squelch the power, completely energized him. Soon it would be five down and two to go before moving on to the next mission.

The warrior waited in hiding.

CHAPTER FIFTY-SIX
Tuesday 1230 Hours

Several cop cars swarmed around the assistant district attorney's home, a few parked precariously, while some police officers chatted with one another waiting for further instructions. A large, heavyset man, assumed to be the detective in charge, lumbered toward the home and up the driveway, gesturing to some of the uniformed officers.

Upon closer inspection, Emily immediately recognized the detective; it was Detective Bobby Duncan. Her mind catapulted back to two years ago.

"Looks like the first time that the cops beat us here." Rick sarcastically stated as they cruised on by the residence.

No one paid them any attention.

Emily remembered her conversation with the detective. He was stern, but respectful. She would always remember what he did for her. Jail was the obvious conclusion to the outcome, but he let her go so that she could continue her never-ending undertaking as a phantom investigator.

A few chills slithered up her spine as she reminisced all of her narrow escapes in the past. Sometimes she woke from a deep sleep frightened by what could happen at any time, but whatever was in store for her remained a secret.

"Em?"

Emily quietly answered. "Yeah, I think the cops have it covered. It didn't look like A.D.A. Richards was home."

She watched the neighboring homes and dense trees pass by the passenger window like obscure objects in a repetitive painting. Finally she asked, "Did you check out if the A.D.A. has other homes?"

"I left the list at home, but I'll double check again. There might be a corporation name recorded as the owner for tax purposes. I'm sure he has a condo or maybe a summer beach home." Rick drove to a nearby shopping center and pulled into a parking place.

Shoppers hurried to their favorite stores unaware that more pressing situations of life and death floated all around them. Emily watched a woman animatedly talk on her cell phone as her red hair blew around her face. She pushed the shopping cart full of groceries, which ended abruptly at the back hatch of a large sports utility vehicle. She still chattered away about trivial topics.

It amazed Emily that most people were oblivious to what went on around them.

"This is going to take a few minutes." Rick worked efficiently with the tiny keyboard on his phone, keeping his attention focused.

Emily watched him work. He knew exactly how to conduct the most complex investigations. She wondered if he missed working on the job as a police detective.

A staggering man appeared from around the back of a restaurant. He interrupted her thoughts. He swayed and stumbled every other step, but kept going with absolute determination. The suit he wore looked like something that a salesperson or an office manager would wear.

The surrounding people paid little attention to the man.

Emily kept her watchful eye on him, something did not seem right.

A twenty-something man rode by her car window on a bicycle. It wouldn't seem strange except the guy made subtle gestures to the staggering man. They were an obvious odd couple, but if you looked closer; they seemed about the same age, build, and just the wardrobe appeared different.

"Did you hear anything I said?" Rick asked.

Emily turned and looked at him. "I'm sorry, but there's something weird going on in the parking lot."

Rick averted his attention from the Internet, quickly scanning the parking lot to see Emily's concern.

She continued with her suspicion. "I think there's going to be a robbery or theft."

Searching for shopping center security cameras, she only found one at the bank and grocery store. Emily then quickly grabbed a navy hoodie from the back seat. "I'm going to slow them down or at least make them move on."

"What a minute Em. You can't do that."

"Funny, I feel the same about them." She zipped up her sweatshirt and pulled up the hood. With one hand on the handle release, she said. "Get a photo of them to email to the burglary division for ID."

Before Rick could respond, Emily jumped out of the SUV causally heading toward the men.

Emily carefully watched where other shoppers meandered. At the moment people seemed to be inside the stores and not wandering around the parking lot. She was relieved that it was a Tuesday instead of a weekend.

The man who had staggered into the parking lot gazed into various cars for a quick inventory. Emily watched as he made a casual gesture with his left hand to the person on the bike.

Tricky communication techniques, but she was prepared to stop them. There was another type of criminal that she hated; it was the opportunist who gave grief to the average person.

Not today, she thought.

The man in the suit pressed up against a small sedan, peered into the windows, and then turned to lean on the car.

Obviously, he checked to see if the alarm remained engaged or not.

Emily thought she would play her own game.

"Excuse me? Hello? Sir?" She quickened her steps. "Have you seen a small dog run by here?" It was difficult for her not to laugh by the startled look on his face, eyes wide and face paled. She continued as she walked toward the man, "He's a really sweet, small, brown and black puppy with a leather collar." She realized that the man was no more than eighteen.

He turned and ran.

Something inside Emily snapped. She felt increasingly angry and wanted to unleash her rage onto someone else, anyone else, her teeth clenched, jaw tightened, and every muscle constricted to the breaking point. The frustration of the arson case and the feelings of uneasiness about Bishop and Red didn't mix well together. She felt out of control. The two thieves were no big deal, but she wanted to make them pay for their stupid decision to rip off property from others.

Emily moved with purpose.

When she reached the back of the buildings, no one was around. There were several garbage dumpsters surrounded by areas of cement and a straggly patch of yellow green grass. She walked around the dumpsters expecting to see a hiding perp, but no one waited. He was obviously more cunning than she had first realized. He must have had an escape route, and was no doubt long gone.

Emily's guard lowered as she turned the corner in between two large dumpsters. The guy from the bike materialized, he took a step forward and shoved her backward. She lost her balance and tried desperately to regain her footing to no avail; instead, she fell against one of the dumpsters smacking the back of her head as she went down. A dull ring radiated around in her brain. A searing pain telescoped down her spine.

Calming her breath along with her rapidly beating heart, she tried to gain her balance. Emily watched for her attacker to make another move. She saw his face, intense, full of hatred, and there wasn't anything redeeming about his demeanor.

The perp stood over her, leering, and ready for any counter attack. He didn't seem surprised that she was a woman under the hoodie, instead he moved with a slight swagger as if he was proud and was going to make her pay.

Emily took the few extra seconds to catch her breath, even the ringing in her head subsided. She knew that the criminal thought she was a weak opponent. As if hearing what she thought, he lunged forward and roughly stood her up.

He finally spoke a few words, "You think you're so tough bitch? Maybe I need to see how tough you really are..."

Emily stared him in the eye. She sensed some hesitation in his approach of attack by her unwavering attitude, or maybe it was something about her driving courage that spooked him. He was about her height. It would make it easier for her to fight back and keep him at her level.

She laughed.

It felt good to let go, the happy utterance was a release that felt better than crying. All of her cases from the past, and the new ones she hadn't studied yet, merged into a monster that she could fight. Now the monster was a petty thief that stood in front of her.

Disbelief shadowed the young man's face.

The surge of adrenaline pumped through Emily. She used that moment for her attack. She handled an effective uppercut boxing move, and made a direct hit to the attacker's groin. He instantly went down to his knees in agony.

"Never, ever, judge anyone by how they look..." Emily kicked the guy on the right side of the head; he flopped down to the ground semi-conscious.

She readied herself in an attacker's stance. Taking her left foot back, she prepared herself for another frontal assault.

"Hey!"

Emily looked up expecting to see the partner in crime.

"Stop!" Rick yelled as he confronted Emily. He used his body to block her.

He leaned down and helped up the stunned man. "Get out of here!" The man limped away, still with a look of horror on his face.

Emily walked past Rick without a word. She wasn't sure how she felt, but she didn't want to be psychologized now by anyone.

"Em..." Rick jogged up to her with a look of concern on his face. With his voice even and soft, he said. "What's going on? Are you okay?"

"I'm fine. He jumped me and I had to defend myself."

"You were going to kick that guy's face in."

"Maybe now he'll just get a job."

"What do you want to do?"

"Did you have any luck with more addresses?" Emily quickly changed the subject. Her mind was already back to catching the arsonist.

Slowly, Rick answered. "I found a house up north."

"Let's go."

CHAPTER FIFTY-SEVEN
Tuesday 0130 Hours

The Cessna taxied down the runway, gained speed, and eased into flight with the grace of a large predator bird. The aircraft glided easily into the west and then made a sharp turn southward along the picturesque coastline.

The spectacular views enthralled the senses. The clear crisp day lent to the sparkling waters below and the pristine visibility. Only approaching clouds in the distant west muddled the vista.

The plane lowered its altitude and set the cruising speed to a comfortable pace.

It was one of Red's tasks to fly Bishop to special engagements and meetings. He automatically checked all gauges, estimating that it would take sixty-seven minutes to fly into the Los Angeles area.

Under normal conditions, it would be a perfect day for Red's plan. Precision and efficiency was crucial. Nevertheless, it was not ideal, which in turn left his stomach in an acrid stupor. He had meticulously planned for this day and nothing could have darkened the outcome or his mood, except for an additional passenger.

He hated changes in well thought out plans – it boiled his nerves. The anger continued to build as it seethed beneath his cool demeanor, causing his stomach to flip flop. He noticed that his left hand wavered slightly from stress. It was the first time that the normal pressure of the job began to push his limits. He drove his personal health issues from his mind and concentrated on his next task.

The man that sat next to Bishop was tall and beefy with his shirt buttoned up too tight for his meaty neck. The guy wasn't the smartest thug in the litter, but he was heavily armed. Only known as Rush, it was one of Bishop's occasional bodyguards. Bishop rarely had a need for one of his henchmen to accompany him on a short trip because Red usually pulled double-duty as pilot and bodyguard.

It was never a problem – until now.

If Red was going to execute his plan, he only had nine minutes to make up his mind. He heard Bishop's voice prattling on about something with his usual high-minded attitude.

The assassin curled his hands into fists and made his decision.

Securing the autopilot, he emerged from the small cockpit and stepped into the passenger area.

"All smooth sailing I presume?" Bishop held Red's stare. A practiced concrete smile he used on so many occasions. It made you know that he had the upper hand at all times.

"Nothing out of the ordinary." Red said.

Rush smirked, turned his head to look out the window, and ignored Red's intense look with a disrespectful defiance.

Red quickly looked at his watch.

Two minutes… thirty-seven seconds…

"We're right on time." Red said.

Bishop's eyes narrowed and changed to a murky grey. He scrutinized Red closely with an air of curiosity.

Two minutes… fifteen seconds…

Red casually slipped his right hand into his bulky jacket to retrieve a knife. It had a double-edged blade and was seven inches in length. With extreme efficiency and speed, he lunged forward, sunk the blade into the left side of Rush's neck, and gave it a quarter turn twist.

Blood gushed profusely and sent fountain spurts spattering the inside window and luxury leather seat. The startled expression of the now bug-eyed bodyguard remained secured on Red. No question imprinted on his face, but rather a peculiar glare.

The man clasped his thick hands onto Red's forearms in a death grip as the last bits of air gurgled from his mouth. His hands loosened slowly and fell away. The remaining blood flowed out as the man crumbled forward, falling onto the floor.

Within a few seconds of the attack, Red stood up and turned to face Bishop with a calm manner.

His boss, still seated in his seat, remained calm, and showed no reaction to the horrific scene. Several droplets of blood had made its way across the aisle, which left dappled dots on the sleeve of Bishop's jacket. His darkened gaze fixed on Red.

Two minutes… five seconds…

"Bravo." Bishop bluffed.

Red stood quiet. The bloody knife felt superb in his hand. It had been a while since he had killed someone with a blade.

"Is there something we need to discuss?" Bishop casually asked.

"No." Red replied.

Bishop laughed. "I guess I may have underestimated you *and* your abilities."

Red stood his ground. That familiar ache in his hands and shoulders fought for his attention, but he gritted his teeth in response.

"Am I to presume that you didn't kill Emily Stone?"

"I fulfilled the contract." He flatly lied.

One minute… forty seconds…

Red had to move quickly if he was going complete his task.

311

Bishop leaned forward and grabbed a hidden pistol with surprising quickness. He aimed the gun directly at Red and fired.

Trying to anticipate Bishop's next move, Red hit the floor hard and rolled his body out of immediate firing range.

The splitting sound of the gunfire pierced the air, rattling around the cabin.

The bullet managed to blast into his left shoulder, pain radiated immediately, and continued to grow in intensity. He felt his left hand and forearm go numb. Grappling to take cover and hoping that more bullets didn't puncture the body of the plane, Red's body rolled again as he retrieved his own gun.

Bishop squeezed off another round.

One minute…

* * * * *

Jordan fidgeted with his wetsuit before he left the Monterey Bay harbor in the zodiac boat. He loved the water and realized it had been too long since he had been scuba diving, or even body surfing. There was nothing more invigorating than participating in a one-on-one with the ocean.

The mist of the water lightly sprayed his face as he glided along with increasing speed. The sunny day made it even more inviting if it had been under any other conditions. In the distance, clouds threatened to bring a storm.

He embarked on a secret rendezvous mission. He never dreamed when he woke up that morning he would be partaking in something so dangerous and even a little bit devious. It was the hair-raising activities and dare devil antics that entertained heroes, not an ordinary security person.

As Jordan thought about what Red had asked of him, it made him yearn for more undercover assignments. The image of Emily's smiling face flashed through his mind frequently and their undercover investigations together. He would formulate a life plan once everything was over, and when the smoke had cleared – if he lived that long.

An uneasy feeling crept into Jordan's mind. It was the same type of eeriness that plagued him when he was on an undercover operation back at the F.B.I. that something could go wrong – and usually did.

What happened after he fulfilled his obligation with Red? He knew too much. Was it just the case of eliminating the loose ends and Jordan would be the next target?

Jordan didn't have a choice. The events had already been set in motion.

He swallowed the lump in his throat and tried to concentrate on the amazing blue water. He shot past two small scuba boats, which marked the divers in the water exploring the breathtaking marine life. As he thought of the great oceanic adventure, envy wormed its way into Jordan's mindset.

It did not take long to distance himself from the harbor and the coastline. He read his compass and knew that he was heading northwest into no man's land. It was the deepest part of the bay with an underwater canyon depth of approximately one mile.

By Jordan's estimation and current speed, he would arrive at the location directed by Red in less than ten minutes.

* * * * *

The second bullet had grazed his earlobe, but didn't catch anything meaty on his body like the first round. The trajectory of the slug pinged, bounced behind him, and did not ricochet back. The aircraft still maintained the proper altitude; otherwise, the firearm would have penetrated the shell of the cabin, causing the plane to drop and air pressure to diminish.

Glancing to his right, Red saw the large pool of blood left behind from the bodyguard.

No sound emitted, except the low hum of the plane.

Less than thirty seconds...

There was no turning back now. From a crouch position, Red readied his gun, took aim and fired. The bullet smashed into the control panel, sputtering, crackling, and a small fire erupted as the plane made a gut wrenching drop.

The floor banged and slammed like an amusement park ride out of control, but with deadly circumstances. Everything inside the cabin battered against Red's body.

Fifteen seconds...

Red kicked at the emergency door. He missed several times trying to gain his bearings.

The plane lurched sideways and barrel rolled. Everything in the plane tossed around like a blender in a dizzying somersault.

Two more gunshots buzzed by Red's head.

With a final kick, the door opened with such a force that it blew him backward. Wind whipped through the cabin with a force of a banshee in a hurricane.

The noise was deafening.

Several pings of Bishop's bullets battered around the cabin.

Red tried to gain his balance and prepared himself to exit. He clumsily unzipped his leather jacket, shed it as fast as he could, and revealed the compact parachute. The wind thrashed the discarded coat in a mad tornado and pasted it up against the wall.

The aircraft stopped spinning for a moment, and then continued to whirl in a turbine-like motion.

Using all of his strength and fueled by instinct, Red gripped the edge of the doorway. The plane continued to roll.

He thought he heard a voice yelling, but the wind held strong to center stage.

As Red observed the infinite blue below every three seconds, a gunshot exploded into his shoulder again. The sound seemed small in comparison to the drumming heartbeat inside his head. The last thought that entered his mind was that his arthritis didn't hurt anymore.

He disappeared out the exit.

Three seconds...

Two seconds...

One...

The Cessna headed downward at an extreme angle before it collided into the deep water with a horrendous force.

The plane sank immediately.

* * * * *

Jordan watched the planes harrowing descent just before it slammed into the ocean. It was like nothing he had ever witnessed before and for a few seconds he thought the plane would land right on top of him. The waves churned with choppy cutbacks in the swell after the plane made contact with the water. A shower of seawater blasted a radius of at least two hundred feet.

Before the Cessna had made a sharp nosedive, spinning as it fell, Jordan saw a body fall from the aircraft. He knew it was Red. The form took a free fall before the parachute opened, but the body looked like a lifeless ragdoll as it floated down and pitched into the water.

Opening the outboard motor to full throttle, Jordan rushed to the aid of the assassin.

As he approached, the scene looked grim. Red's body floated, unmoving, and he had the look of a wax mannequin. The chute had tangled around his legs and made the entire display look even more shocking than it previously did from the distance.

Jordan maneuvered the boat next to Red. For the first time, he saw the blood around his shoulder and arm.

The sea began to build velocity as the waves churned, lifting the boat up and down. Jordan's stomach matched the water with an unsettling motion; it wouldn't take much for him to hurl his breakfast overboard. He fought the tightening of his gut in order to focus on his orders.

He leaned over and touched Red's back. The hit man flinched under his contact and rolled to his side. The normal calm stare of the expert killer, now looked rattled and in a moderate amount of pain.

"You okay?" Jordan managed to ask.

Red nodded. He clumsily climbed into the boat. It took a little bit of extra effort, but he managed to sit upright, grimacing in agony.

Jordan helped to free the chute from his legs and body. Upon closer inspection, it was obvious that Red had suffered gunshot wounds, which had entered and exited the body.

"We need to get you to a hospital."

"No." Red replied. "Go."

Jordan hesitated for only a moment, but then nodded in agreement.

He turned the zodiac around and headed back toward the harbor as fast as the boat would carry them against the current, bumping and fighting the waves.

He glanced at Red every so often during the trip, wondering how he would explain his own participation in the premeditated murder and crashed airplane. What bothered him even more was, if he would be Red's final contract. He doubted that authorities or emergency personnel would find the body or the Cessna, but stranger things have happened.

316

The journey seemed to take forever, but in actuality, the return trip made good time despite the tide. Jordan steered the boat east away from the main harbor and up toward an adjacent river.

Jordan tried to make some small talk with Red, but the hit man only stared at him and didn't offer any further information.

With his stomach still churning, Jordan realized that he hadn't eaten anything in hours. He thought better, a strong drink would do the trick if he made it back to shore.

The zodiac taxied along the deserted shoreline where a car and pick-up truck waited. Instructions were that Jordan was to drive the truck back to his car, wipe it down for any prints, and leave the vehicle parked.

It was a welcome sight to get to land, but he knew that there was the possibility that his mission wasn't over – yet. When he saw the shoreline, his thoughts turned to Emily again.

"You know that it would never work."

Jordan turned to Red in surprise. He felt that his feelings had overflowed and now everyone could read his deepest, most intimate thoughts.

"She won't ever love you, at least in the way you want."

"Who are we talking about?"

Grimacing as he moved and slowly got out of the boat, Red said. "I know people… I read them well… and she doesn't love you."

"What are you my personal therapist now?" It stung Jordan to hear those words because he enjoyed every little bit of his time in denial.

"Move on."

"Oh, and I'm going to take advice from a…"

Red stopped and stared at him. With an intense, steely-eyed glare, and even with at least one bullet wound, he still looked quite formidable.

"What I mean is… what makes you so certain?" Jordan clarified.

"It is what it is."

Jordan looked down at the bottom of the boat and saw blood. "And what about her life?"

"There's no contract."

"I have your word?" Jordan inquired.

"Yes."

"And what about me? My debt is paid, right?"

Without another word, Red turned and walked away.

Jordan watched the assassin as he got into the car and slowly drove away. He kept watching until the car disappeared from his view. There was more to the Red than just killing, thought Jordan, but he hoped that he would never see him again.

CHAPTER FIFTY-EIGHT
Tuesday 0330 Hours

Emily sat in silence on the ride up the coast. She watched the landscape become more rural with the occasional house dappled across the countryside. The estates became larger and more sprawling the closer they approached the attorney's summerhouse.

A soft rumble reverberated among the dark clouds, which approached from the west. It was unusual weather for the beginning of fall, but not rare. The brewing storm took precedence and kept the attention away from the actual turmoil that loomed inside Emily.

Her mood softened as the miles added to the journey. She felt bad that she had vented on Rick, but kept her feelings quiet. She sensed her controlled demeanor return, but something had to give. She struggled even harder to maintain an average sanity in the relentless hunt for killers. Things had a way of getting worse before they settled back down.

Emily could only wait.

"It should be the next house." Rick announced. He didn't look directly at Emily when he spoke.

Emily strained her eyes and could see a long driveway with an iron gate. The house camouflaged by extensive bushes and trees sat protected and private. Quick snippets of blue flashed in between the trees, but it quickly turned to more of a dark silver grey as the sky shifted into storm mode.

Rick drove on past the home and took two quick hairpin curves before he spotted a place to park. Gravel crunched under the tires as the vehicle hugged close to the inside barrier. Dust rose in murky clouds, drifted up into the air above the SUV and gradually settled. Rick cut the engine.

An uncomfortable silence filled the car.

Emily's eyes remained fixed, watching straight ahead at nothing in particular. Her mind raced and mulled over all of the events from the past few days. For a brief moment, she almost forgot why she pursued some of the most violent killers.

"Do you want to check out the house?" Rick interrupted. "Everything looks quiet."

He watched Emily.

"We're here. Let's go have a look."

"If we found the house so easily, the arsonist could find it too." His voice lowered before he finished his sentence. He turned to open the car door.

"Wait." Emily touched his arm. She noticed that he tensed; obviously, he didn't want to talk about the strained communication and edgy relationship issues. She gently pushed, "I don't want things to be like this… I'm sorry for all that's happened."

Rick studied her eyes. "Em, it's not your fault."

"It's *always* my fault. I'm the one who pushes these investigations. How could I not think that something would go wrong?" She looked down.

"No one is holding a gun to my head."

She looked up at him and thought carefully before she spoke. "Because of me, and what I've chosen to do, you were kidnapped and tortured…. and…" Tears welled up in her eyes.

"I'm here now and all that is behind us." Rick spoke softly.

Emily knew that he meant what he said. "I just don't like the secrets."

"Let's see this case through. Then we can figure out what to do about Leo Brown. Okay?"

Emily was quiet for a moment as she stared through the windshield at the winding road. She nodded adamantly. "Okay, we'll figure it out together."

Rick leaned over and kissed her on the lips, long and gentle. Emily instantly felt the passion and love that had always been there between them. The incident with Jordan made her rethink her feelings, but there was nothing to rethink any more. Her relationship with Rick was something that she would never take for granted again.

"Let's check out the property." Emily stated with more strength in her voice. She had more energy and felt her concentration sharpen. The dull headache she sustained softened to an acceptable level.

"You got it." Rick cracked a warm smile before he opened the driver's door.

Emily exited the vehicle, took a long look around at the surrounding area and marveled at how peaceful and serene the location appeared. She immediately caught the sea air, clean, refreshing, and comforting.

She walked around the car thinking about her weapons. Only her ankle holster carried the Beretta – one gun instead of her usual two. She tapped her pocket to confirm that her cell phone was nestled in a safe place and operational. Pulling the device from her pant pocket, she saw that she barely had one bar showing for signal strength. She also noticed that Jordan had not returned any of her calls or texts and wondered if he was taking some time off to nurse a bruised ego. She hated the thought that they might not be friends anymore, because she valued his expertise and opinions.

"I think we can enter from this gate." Rick announced.

Emily saw that there was a wrought iron garden gate that hadn't been used in a while. Tucked back with tall brush along with snaking vines, it had blocked part of the property view. Most people would not notice the entrance unless they looked specifically for it.

Rick wrestled with the gate until it moved, first a couple of inches, and then it screeched open a little wider than a foot. He pushed back the overgrown shrubbery. Within a minute, there was an opening wide enough for them to access the property.

"Are there any security cameras?" Emily asked concerned.

"I checked before we got here, and it showed, at least from my sources, that the outside security is inactive."

"Inactive?"

"They aren't paying for outside security cameras, probably only inside ones." He looked at Emily. "What's the matter?"

"I don't know… something seems wrong here."

"Let's just take a quick look around to make sure that no one has tampered with the house."

Emily hesitated. "Okay. A once around the property would be helpful."

Rick smiled again. "It's just like any other location we've searched in the past. Piece of cake."

"You're sounding more like Jordan every day." Emily joked.

"Practically everyone is a comedian these days." He replied with a sarcastic tone.

Emily followed Rick, she was watchful of the entire area.

The couple made their way around to the side of the house for a closer look.

* * * * *

The Saltine cracker emphasized the creaminess of the pasteurized cheese. Angel allowed the salty texture to sit on his tongue as long as possible in order to impart patience and reward. Nothing crushed an incentive faster than by acting too quickly or too impulsively. He kept that simple mantra, repeating it in his mind continually.

The cracker slowly disintegrated into a soggy texture that reminded him of a wet paper towel. During one of his school bullying experiences, three boys had shoved his A+ science paper into his mouth, clamped his jaw shut, and then made him eat it. Students laughed hysterically during the entire episode. He shuddered because the image seemed so vivid and alive, like it happened yesterday. He popped another piece of cheese into his mouth to help forget the vision.

He looked at his computer.

The laptop screen was small, but it still told a story as it sat on a small corner of the floor.

Two people approached the house.

Something inside told him that he would see the She-Warrior again, but this time she had brought an outsider. Someone who didn't fully understand the fires. His newfound respect for the unknown warrior dwindled rapidly.

How could she do this to him?

Angel watched as the couple made their way across the front yard, hesitating every so often, as they scrutinized the area. He imagined a hulking creature with huge fangs from another dimension leaping from the bushes and devouring them. It would tear each of them limb from limb, leaving nothing, not even blood or bones.

He lingered on the thought of the bloody massacre a little while longer. It was almost as satisfying and cleansing as fire – but not quite.

He watched the couple walk up the same stairs he did earlier.

It's kismet.

They didn't respect the stairs by keeping in a straight even line, or traveling in the middle of the steps.

They mocked him.

He could almost hear the kid's voices in elementary school chanting their hateful insults and ridicules.

A frown washed across Angel's face as he watched Emily and Rick approach.

* * * * *

A faint smell of paint wafted around Emily every few steps on the staircase as she gazed at the tremendous view. She kept in sync and followed Rick.

Glancing from side to side, everything appeared in pristine condition around the grounds and home. Despite the occasional whiff of paint, the fresh air amplified by the crashing waves, calmed some of the nervous energy that she felt rising up throughout her body. Most of the time, these strange, tingly sensations had served her well, but now it gave her mixed signals.

Emily stepped onto the deck landing and the entire panoramic view came into focus. She and Rick stood for a moment.

"Wow, what a view." Rick admired.

"I never get tired of looking at the ocean."

"What do you think?"

"Everything looks okay…"

Something caught her eye, Emily walked to the set of French doors and one of them was open by a few inches. She turned and gave Rick a quizzical look. Her instinct was to leave, but her drive made her push forward.

"Wait." He motioned to her. Retrieving his cell phone, he punched in a few numbers and waited.

Seconds later, the phone inside the house rang. The pitch seemed higher than the average phone as it continued to ring. The sound made Emily's skin prickle.

The phone persisted until Rick ended the call.

"Did they just leave the door open?" Emily said, but in fact, highly doubted it.

"How do we know for sure that no one is home?" Rick looked through the glass, careful not to touch anything.

Emily searched Rick's face. She could see that he had the same thought she did. In a low tone, she said. "Should we call it in to the local cops?"

"We should... just to be safe." He said as he readied his phone.

As he pressed the number, a crash came from inside the home. A strained whimper came from another room.

"I'm going in..." Emily pushed the door wider and stepped inside. She half expected the alarm to blare, but nothing happened. She stood at the threshold of the living room.

"Wait." Rick said with urgency in his voice.

"What?" She turned to face him.

"My entire cell went dead and there's no signal." He stepped inside the house next to her.

Emily quickly checked her phone. It was dead, like the battery had run out, but she knew that it was fine only a few minutes ago.

Rick looked over her should and saw her phone too. "What the hell?"

The door slammed shut behind them with a startling crash.

Emily went to try to open the door.

"Stop!" Rick stressed.

Emily halted.

Her instincts fully kicked into overdrive as that familiar tingly sensation waved a red flag deep within her core. She turned slowly with eyes fixed on Rick.

She stood in anxious silence.

He gestured to the frame of the door.

There were a couple of unusual wires attached to a tiny blinking plastic box.

"It's rigged to…" He gingerly followed the wires, which led to a small odd-looking device.

Emily stood quiet, very still, grounded firmly to the hardwood floors as she watched Rick take careful steps to follow the two wires.

He turned and looked at her, face stern, before he said. "The windows and doors are rigged to explode."

CHAPTER FIFTY-NINE
Tuesday 0430 Hours

Detective Duncan sat at his desk at the department lost deep in thought. Most of the other detectives were already gone. It was quiet with few interruptions.

His cell phone rang.

It interrupted his mental process, which tried desperately to link the forensic evidence to one of the computer programmers, or at least to the copyrighters from the security website. Once on an investigation, his thoughts rarely ever wandered away from the case.

He fumbled for the cell from his inside jacket pocket, still feeling weak from not eating anything all day.

"Duncan." He listened with a growing glimmer of hope that he might get a lucky break. "Thanks." Hanging up the phone, he slipped the device back into his pocket.

He jotted down on his small notepad: *139 Whitewater Road*

Food would have to wait a little longer.

A strange 9-1-1 text message came in from an unidentified source about a possible break in, located at Assistant District Attorney Richard's house. Duncan had already checked out the house, but kept the local PD on speed dial. If there was anything unusual, they were to notify him immediately.

The detective stood up from his desk and a slight dizziness washed over him. He steadied himself until his vision cleared. Making a mental note, he would grab a sandwich on the drive up to the attorney's house.

This serial arson case wore an unrelenting groove on him. Something had to break soon.

As he drove north, he called in to the local dispatch to find out if patrol had reached the house yet and if there was anything to report. As usual, there had been a violent disturbance that took precedence, and patrol was more than forty minutes away.

Weaving through traffic at a cruising speed of eighty-five miles per hour, the detective blared the sirens when he deemed necessary. He easily sped through any congestion of traffic.

Most cars scattered, braked, moved to the slow lanes, but the looks upon the faces of the motorists were comical, startled, and often uncertain. A cop car speeding with sirens flashing provoked all types of emotions with the general public.

The dull unrelenting headache ensued. He rubbed his forehead with his fingertips and felt a slight perspiration that had covered his face and scalp.

He chomped on a turkey and Jack cheese sandwich, loaded with mustard, mayonnaise, and pickles on dark rye bread. With some relief, the blood sugar level in his body balanced out, but his sweaty outbreak persisted.

He blared the sirens again in quick bursts as he drove past a cluster of SUVs trying to jockey for the lead.

The detective had made great time as he took the cutoff to the northern bluff areas. It was where the rich and entitled people had their second or even third homes. The road became windy after a few minutes, which caused Duncan to hit the brakes frequently. He stabbed the gas pedal at every opportunity, sliding a bit into the vacant oncoming lane.

The left and right sharp corners of the road made him nauseous, especially around the exceptionally tight curves. He thought for a moment that he would have to pull over and throw up, but he fought the urge and figured the upset stomach would pass. Suddenly his sandwich didn't sit well.

Glancing at his GPS, he knew that there were several cross back roads before he hit Whitewater Road. The detective pushed the speed harder as the Ford hugged the corners to the best of the automobile's engineering. He never saw any traffic in front of him as the countryside turned more rural, allowing for more decadent homes all competing for the picture-perfect ocean view.

The sedan cranked a tight left corner on Cobblestone Avenue; he continued to speed along the deserted road as the engine roared into high gear.

His chest felt heavy and strange as his arms buzzed with a peculiar energy.

The unmarked police car took the next right too fast and all tires squealed in unison. The detective hit the gas pedal with continued force.

From his peripheral, two local patrol cars approached from an adjacent street. He knew that they had been dispatched to the estate. His mind spun with many questions about the curious call.

Pain shocked him from his left shoulder, down his arm, and crushed his chest with a horrendous force. He gasped for air as his vision blurred to a narrow tunnel focus. The tremendous agony overrode everything in his body as he made one last effort to gulp fresh air.

He passed out.

Never releasing his foot from the accelerator, Duncan plowed into a power pole with a deafening crash.

The cop car came to an abrupt stop. The lines broke in half, bucked, crackled, and forced a spattering display on the road and into the heavy brush.

The roadside quickly ignited in a fire.

CHAPTER SIXTY
Tuesday 0445 Hours

Emily's whole body went numb. The strange feeling travelled out her fingers and down her arms. She stood absolutely still, staring at the wires fixed around the windows and doors. Her mind came to an abrupt stop. She could not respond immediately to what Rick had said to her.

"Em?" He asked with urgency in his voice.

She did not respond right away. They had ventured into a killer's snare. It was her worst nightmare, caught in an unknown territory without any means of escape.

She finally spoke. "What do we do now?"

Rick replied calmly. "We need to find another way out." She could see the deep concern in his eyes.

She bent down and retrieved her Beretta. It felt good in her hand to have something that she could defend herself with in an emergency.

"No…" Rick motioned to her to put the gun away. "If you have to shoot, it could set off one of these trip wires."

Emily holstered her weapon with displeasure, but she knew he was right. Before she moved from her position, she looked at everything in the living room, at every piece of furniture, from top to bottom, and around the edges of the rugs to make sure that there weren't more traps.

"C'mon, we can find a way out of here." Rick interrupted the silence with optimism. He gently touched her arm.

"Okay…" Emily hated the unfamiliar surroundings, not just being inside someone else's house, but also not knowing what could happen.

Rick took immediate control, strong, capable, and with a determined diligence. He searched the room systematically.

Emily watched him methodically investigate areas around the walls, floor, and furniture. Her eye caught sight of something shiny. She saw a small pair of silver sewing scissors sticking out from underneath a couch cushion. Stepping carefully toward the couch, she pulled them out and slipped it into her pocket.

"It's clear in this room." Rick stated. "I'm so glad that my buddy Randy from bomb squad taught me a lot about bombs and tripwires when I was on patrol." His voice had a tone of relief.

"Do you think that anyone is here?" Emily looked to the next room and down the hallway.

"We heard voices, but my guess is that it was a recording of some kind." His face turned suspicious.

"Someone is here." Emily stated with confidence. That tingly feeling surfaced again throughout her body. It reminded her that the Jack-in-the-Box would pop up at any moment.

The couple slowly walked down the hallway, pausing only to take a brief stance if someone were to burst through a door. The training they both had received as cops instinctively kicked into high gear on their approach.

A small winding staircase, which led to the bedrooms below was at the end of the long hallway. They headed in that direction.

Emily felt a chill, gooseflesh prickled on the back of her forearms and neck as she inched forward. The familiar paint smell permeated the air once again, this time it was the freshly painted white walls along the hallway. The paint was recent; there were no pieces of art hanging on the walls yet.

Four small black boxes about two inches square placed in each corner of the long corridor made Emily remember the hardware store.

"Wait." Emily stopped. She spoke softly. "A painting or maintenance crew has been here recently. So when were the wires installed?"

Rick didn't immediately answer.

Emily could tell that he thought the same thing. The trip wires were newly installed and maybe the perp was still inside.

"If this is recent…" She began.

"The She-Warrior has found me." A voice stated.

The clear, unknown voice interrupted Emily and Rick's search. They stopped, stood motionless for a moment, and looked for the person that belonged to the unnerving tone.

The man's voice came from above.

"What is your name?" The voice asked. There was a juvenile quality to the timbre.

"Who are you?" Emily probed.

"You don't have the right to ask anything of me." The voice had an almost computerized sound to it, but she knew that it came from the killer's own undistorted voice.

"I like to know who I'm talking with before I introduce myself." It sounded lame in Emily's mind, but she wanted to communicate calmly and conversationally.

Silence.

Rick gave her a subtle nod to let her know that she was doing the right thing.

"May I know your name?" She asked as she put her hands on her hips trying not to show how helpless she felt. As she rested her fingers near her pockets, she pressed the tips of her nails into her hips to steady them.

"I've had many names, good and bad, mostly bad."

The answer perplexed Emily.

"Well, what do you like to be called?" She tried to smile and relax because she knew that the man watched them. It reminded her of some of the nightmares she had in the past, where the killer was always just out of reach. She couldn't see them, but they still continually pursued her.

Emily and Rick waited for an answer.

* * * * *

The emergency vehicles parked a safe distance from the accident scene. It resembled the aftermath of a hurricane and fire all rolled into one horrifying incident. Additional police officers evacuated close neighbors as the firefighters blasted the trees and shrubs with gallons of water.

One of the patrol cars had already radioed into the power plant to shut off the electricity within the necessary grid area, so that they could clear the accident and render first aid to the man inside.

Radios blared from both the fire and police dispatchers.

More emergency personnel arrived at the scene.

Chatter among professionals was that a police detective was still trapped inside the car.

No car or any type of vehicle could get through to the other streets, even in a dire emergency.

* * * * *

Emily couldn't just wait for an answer, she had to do something. Wrestling with every possible scenario that her mind could conjure, she took a carefully placed step forward.

"Stop!" The voice ordered.

For some reason, it reminded Emily of a kid's game, *Red Light Green Light*, as she stood still, but wanting to continue in order to win the game.

"Okay, but can we meet in person?" She didn't know what else to say.

In Emily's peripheral, she saw Rick trying to deduce everything in the hallway for some type of escape route, or possibly, where the killer might be hiding.

"You are a warrior..." He stated.

The question struck Emily deeply. The word *warrior* made her feel that her mission in life had made a difference. To hear this description from a killer disturbed her.

She decided to try to reach him in some way – in any way. "You are a warrior too. What's your mission?"

Silence.

She continued, "It's a tough job to do it alone, and people can't understand why you do it."

Emily felt her heart beat faster as she turned to observe Rick. She knew that he wanted to kick down all the doors to get to the killer. His hard stare, strained lips, and unsettling shift of his body weight gave it away.

"I know people say this a lot, but I know how you feel. I've been there and I've chosen to hunt bad people ..." She let her sentiment sink into the mind of the killer.

The couple waited.

"People spread sin... it's like a cancer... it eats and eats...it's never satisfied." The arsonist replied. His voice slowed in speech, almost in a juvenile-like stutter.

"Yes, yes they do. I've seen it firsthand." Emily took a breath and said. "Please, can we meet you in person?"

"He's not one of us." The robotic tempo of the killer's voice returned.

Emily gestured to Rick. "Yes he is. I couldn't do what I do without him. He understands more than you think." A deep pang hit the pit of her stomach as she thought about all the cases that Rick was there for support.

"Go down the stairs. Enter the room on your right." There was an ominous quality to the simple instructions.

The couple took a step in the direction of the stairs.

"Stop!" The man ordered. "Just you…"

Rick began to object, but Emily stopped him. She gently laid her hand on his arm. She gave him the knowing look and glanced down where her ankle holster rested. His eyes darkened and a stubborn tenseness filled his character. He understood.

Emily took another moment to study Rick. She wanted to tell him that she was sorry for getting angry about Leo Brown. She knew that he would never do anything to hurt or deceive her. A small smile washed across her face as she turned to head down the staircase. She tried to ignore the tension in Rick's arms and fists; she knew he wanted to switch places with her.

She descended the staircase. Each step felt strangely spongy beneath her feet. Emily concentrated on her steps in order to not stumble or take a header down the stairs. The staircase narrowed and twisted, leading downward to another living area of the house. The architect was mindful to squeeze every inch of the fantastic view into the design at all levels.

Waves crashed outside, from down below and against the jagged rocks. The late afternoon sun struggled to shine in between the fast approaching storm clouds.

For the first time since they had entered the house, she heard a low rumble of thunder.

Reaching the bottom, Emily scanned the room that seemed to be a study or family room. The old uneven hardwood floors gave away the age of the original portion of the home. A few rugs adorned the center of the room revealing the different shades of wood.

One door was open and revealed a small bathroom with white and yellow towels, while another door remained closed. She searched the usual spots to make sure that there weren't any wires or booby traps before moving forward.

Looking back at the living area, she calculated in her mind that they could escape through one of the small windows.

Emily stood at the door. She rested her hand on the silver doorknob. Her mind flashed back to the remains of the crime scenes and the aftermath of the fires.

Would she be next?

Tensing her right arm, she pressed her hand on the knob and opened the door.

* * * * *

With the official okay from the police that there was not the threat of live electricity, paramedics and additional firefighters rushed to the Crown Victoria and attempted to open the passenger door.

All four doors were smashed in like a crumpled piece of foil. The roof and windshield had pushed back into the vehicle with an inside out twisted metal display.

One of the firefighters smashed the side windows. It took about sixty seconds of maneuvering and teamwork, but the crew pulled out the limp body of the detective. They swiftly laid him on the ground and paramedics began CPR procedures. Three professionals hovered over the heavy man as they pumped air into his lungs and compressed his chest in proper sequence.

After a daunting fifteen minutes, one of the men shook his head. They officially called the time of death with sorrowful expressions of losing one of their own.

Detective Bobby Duncan was pronounced dead at the scene.

* * * * *

As Emily pushed open the door, she saw that it was the master bedroom decorated in the typical beach style of all whites and light blues.

The room sat unoccupied.

The bed was made and the comforter carefully smoothed out with perfect edges. The room wasn't as large as she thought it should be for the master bedroom.

The eerie quietness spooked her. She was about to turn and leave when one of the full-length mirrors shifted. She immediately stood in a defensive stance expecting the worst.

Sliding just wide enough for a person to fit through, a thin young man appeared, dressed in dark clothing with a sweatshirt hood pulled up over his head. He stood at the opening in partial darkness and looked no more than sixteen years old by his stature and choice of clothing.

Emily changed her stance, remained silent, and caught her breath because the appearance of the young man surprised her. She contemplated her case profile, and mentally assessed him as he stood barely six feet from her – many aspects of the crime scenes and various clues now made even less sense to her.

He moved slowly into the bedroom from the safety of the cleverly disguised panic room. The dwindling light cast a partial shadow across the side of his face, the other cheek covered by his sweatshirt. It was clear that he was in his mid to late twenties.

Finally, his face completely emerged into the light, sickly pale, skin translucent but flawless, and eyes as dark as coal.

The young man never took his eyes away from her.

Emily found her voice and said to him. "I'm Emily." Her tone sounded hollow and a bit stilted.

He showed no reaction, as no expression displayed across his slim face.

For a moment, Emily thought he was deaf. His shoulders seemed bony and rounded, but he stood motionless watching her. She couldn't ascertain if it was curiosity or a fundamental hatred.

"You are a She-Warrior... I've seen you..." The high-pitch of his voice broke the silence. Even as he spoke, his facial expression never changed.

Emily forced a smile. "What's your name?"

After hesitating a few seconds, he finally said. "Angel."

"That's a strong name for a warrior." For the first time, Emily noticed that he had two remote controls in each hand, along with some type of device secured to his belt. "Angel, what are you doing here?"

He blinked for the first time since their face-to-face meeting. "Destroying the sinners."

"How do you do that?"

"Fire cleanses everything."

CHAPTER SIXTY-ONE
Tuesday 0545 Hours

Jordan relived his harrowing adventure numerous times in his mind as he drove back to his car – legs slightly shaking from the huge adrenalin rush. The relief he felt after starting his vehicle, by the fact that it didn't blow up, made him a little more at ease.

Sitting on the passenger seat was his cell phone. He quickly picked it up to check his texts and emails. It still had a few signal bars. There were several messages from Emily. His heart skipped a beat as he listened to the messages. It was unusual that she didn't just leave a text message, her voice sounded strained and distant, instead of pissed off that he had left her at the scene.

Quickly, Jordan hit send and dialed Emily's cell phone, which immediately dumped into her voice mail. He tried several more times with the same result. He even dialed Rick's cell and it went to his mailbox too. Both cell phones were off. It was something that rarely, if ever, happened.

He felt a need to see Emily, but also to check in and fill her in on the situation with Red.

Before he realized it, he turned the car around, and headed in the direction of her new house. It only took about fifteen minutes to get there. His friends SUV was gone.

With his usual intuition, Jordan parked and got out of his car. He studied the house. It appeared quiet with nothing obvious out of place.

Jordan chose to enter the couple's house from the back in case a nosy neighbor panicked and called the police. Out of habit, he looked for anything out of the ordinary, or anything that had been disturbed. Everything gave the impression of the usual routine.

He knew where Emily hid the extra key, which was behind the flowerpot, in between a piece of wood, and wedged next to the vent underneath the house. He retrieved the single key and inserted it into the door.

As he opened the back door, he had twenty seconds to enter the security code. He quickly punched in the four-digit code. Quickly, the green light flashed for entry.

A bark reverberated from the other side of the house. It only took three seconds for Sarge to bound up to Jordan just as he stepped inside.

"Hey buddy..." He shouted a greeting. "Anyone home? Hello? Ready or not here I come..."

The dog spun in circles, tail wagging furiously, banging the wall and the washer and dryer in between slobbery licks.

"Okay, okay... give me some space. Where's your mama big guy?"

Jordan moved through the house inspecting everything as he went. Again, it seemed normal. He went into the living area with Sarge in tow.

The photographs of the three arson suspects were still affixed to the white board, now with a pen strike through them. He saw the brochures on the table of high-end vacation destinations and immediately he thought of the security catalogue. The same sleek layout, the same copyright wording, and upon closer inspection, the same watermark symbol were in common.

He murmured aloud. "What else did you find?"

The happy snort and wet canine muzzle pushed against his hand. He scratched the big dog's head as he looked around for anything that might give him a clue as to where they might have gone.

Shuffling through paperwork and notes, he found nothing that he had not seen before. Jordan became frustrated and pushed the papers and photos aside. A small notebook dropped to the floor.

He bent down to pick it up. Jordan stared at several penciled addresses in Rick's handwriting. One in particular caught his attention. "Bingo."

It read: *139 Whitewater*

"Where have I seen this address before?" He searched through other lists until he found a reference to *Whitewater* and A.D.A. Richards with possible addresses. "Gotcha."

Without wasting another second, he flipped open one of the laptop computers and punched in the address for an Internet search of California. Two of the search attempts were in central cities, so he narrowed the search to more affluent areas, both north and south.

Settling on the north coast, Jordan clicked on the satellite image of the street. He toggled around the front yard, the road, and just as he traveled up the road, he saw the black SUV parked.

"Damn, I'm good!" Jordan congratulated himself. "Glad they update the images every few hours."

Sarge looked up at the sudden outburst.

Jordan was about to close the computer when he had a second thought. He quickly keyed up the California Highway Patrol incident page for the area.

As he read the listing of traffic accidents and road hazards, he sucked in a breath. A serious single car accident reported involved a Crown Victoria and a fire outbreak. It looked like from the emergency radio codes that it was a fatality. There was an extended road closure in effect, which involved the street where the attorney lived.

"Crap!"

Jordan slammed the computer shut.

Sarge barked in response to the sudden noise.

CHAPTER SIXTY-TWO
Tuesday 0615 Hours

There was a big difference between creating a criminal profile based on behavioral evidence, crime scenes, and autopsy reports and facing the actual serial killer in person. Emily's instincts told her to take the arsonist out, but there was another side to this damaged young man she wanted to try to understand.

Somewhere along the line, Angel most likely fell victim to severe abuse, identity confusion, and environmental turbulence. His well-intended actions, from his own mind, distorted to the point of psychopathic. Ordinary things in his life skewed basic reality. His intricate obsessive-compulsive behavior conveniently convinced his psyche that the only way to survive was to take the lives of those he deemed unfit. He adamantly believed that he was doing right.

Emily did not want to kill him, but the situation may not offer her any other choice. "Angel..." She began slowly. "Sometimes people are forced to do things that don't seem fair."

"There's right and there's wrong."

"I agree with you, but people have to answer to rules and laws, and to higher authorities."

"It still doesn't change anything."

Emily took a carefully placed step closer to Angel.

He cringed and pushed one of the black boxes out in front of him. "Don't come any closer!"

She took a deep breath. "Please, you don't have to do that. We can make the sinners pay, the right way. I promise you."

343

"There's only one way – a complete cleansing."

His voice chilled Emily. The simple tone without any inflection slithered its way into her consciousness.

The storm brewed outside with a booming thunder that surrounded the house. It felt like it would encapsulate them inside a cocoon.

Emily watched Angel become agitated, his eyes darted from side to side, and he rubbed his fingers along the remotes.

She patiently persisted. "Angel you don't want to hurt another warrior like you, do you?" She decided to try a different angle to get through to him.

He did not answer her. Instead, he groaned and paced in a perfect square.

With a slow movement, Emily dared another step toward him.

"STOP! You are a fraud! You are not any kind of warrior!" He pressed a button and there was a strange crash, a muffled growl, followed by a crackling sound.

Emily spun around and looked up at the winding staircase. A popping sound erupted within the walls and across the top floor of the house. She instantly smelled smoke from an electrical fire. The blaze blocked any access to the staircase.

No. Rick...

Trapped...

It was only a matter of minutes before the house turned into a full-blown inferno.

Two loud crashes erupted from overhead.

Anger overwhelmed Emily's judgments. A boiling rage bubbled to the surface, infusing every nerve and muscle inside her body. Turning to face Angel, who looked more like a scared child, she slipped the scissors from her pocket. Without another thought, she lunged at him.

The five-inch pivoted blades from the scissors plunged into Angel's chest. He tumbled backward, pulling Emily with him. They smacked heads from the fall. The impact jarred her body and rattled her skull, impairing her vision. For a brief moment, the tiny room spun like a merry-go-round.

Angel had dropped the remotes. He lay still. His eyes closed, blood oozed from the puncture, and the extreme frailty of his body looked like he should have been on a slab at the morgue.

Emily pushed herself up from the floor, legs wobbly, with her hand and hip throbbing from the impact. It was difficult to catch her breath as she staggered through the doorway of the small room.

She glanced up the stairs. The fire had already taken over the hallway. The flames dipped and swirled, gaining a furious momentum.

"Rick!" She yelled.

There was no answer.

Gaining her balance and wits, she went to the two small windows. There was no patio or deck, except from the story above. A retaining wall was the only means of escape. The ocean churned below crashing against the jagged rocks, building in velocity every few seconds.

She grabbed a small lamp, tore off the shade, and used the base to smash out the windows.

The storm rushed into the room.

Taking a throw blanket, she tried to remove any pieces of glass from the sills.

The mounting smoke with nasty tufts of branch-like talons crept its way into the room, snuffing out the refreshing ocean air.

Emily coughed repeatedly, trying to regain some of her breathing space.

Suddenly, a sharp pain hit her thigh and she went down on the hardwood floor. Blood gushed from the wound, quickly saturating her pants. With a survival instinct, she held her right hand on the side of her leg and pressed firmly.

She looked up through the greyish smoke.

Angel stood above her with a huge hunting knife between his hands in an ominous prayer stance. He slowly raised the knife above his head.

A strange low rumble emitted throughout the house.

* * * * *

Rick heard most of the conversation between Emily and Angel. He knew that the killer would ignite his clever incendiary devices. Luckily, he had backtracked his steps quickly just as the black boxes exploded in the hallway.

Forcing himself through the smoke and fire, he tried one of the doors. It was only a closet.

The next door was locked.

He took a step back and used a stomp kick move to kick the door in, hinges splintered, the frame cracked easily upon impact, and the door fell down flat inside the small bedroom. One twin bed and single dresser proved the only furniture small enough to fit inside the room. A window barely two feet wide was just above the dresser.

Without wasting any time, Rick scaled the dresser and smashed out the window with his elbow. The room was adjacent at a forty-five degree view away from the ocean.

The flames approached and caught the bedspread on fire.

Smoke filled the room.

Rick's eyes stung, tears welled up making it difficult to see, and his chest felt heavy as he gasped for any available air.

The suffocating plumes of smoke kept charging into the room. It pushed his physical endurance to the limit. He took brief moments to breathe deeply at the window opening.

As he tried with all of his strength, he couldn't wedge his body through the small opening.

* * * * *

The stare of Angel's eyes alarmed Emily. They were cold, bottomless, and the iris changed from a brownish black to a sickly grey. They no longer resembled the eyes of any ordinary person, but a demented predatory animal. Angel's frail body, thinning hair, and translucent, pallid appearance, seemed to morph into a sinewy monster shape. His mind roamed with demons as he channeled his energy to burn sinners.

Fits of coughing took over Emily once again. She rolled to her side, trying to catch her breath and escape the killer. Excruciating pain radiated from her leg as she turned out of the way.

Angel slammed the knife downward, missing Emily by mere inches. The long hunting blade stuck deep into the hardwood floor. The young man savagely tried to pry it loose. Groans and inhuman wails escaped his lips, his arms moved in a savage exhibition of an animated beast.

Her leg numbed.

Her hands wet with blood.

Emily grappled for her Beretta in her ankle holster. Any available strength dwindled from her body. Her vision blurred from the smoke as the fire crackled in a deadly path, heading directly toward them.

After manipulating the knife back and forth, Angel managed to free it. His chest heaved trying to capture a breath. Blood soaked through his sweatshirt.

Left handed, Emily balanced the gun as best as she could. She pulled the trigger, firing one shot.

A direct hit to Angel's chest stopped him. It wasn't a look of surprise or anger that washed over his face, it was relief. He stood motionless with his arms down at his side dropping the knife, staring at Emily. His lips moved, but the words were lost in the noise of the raging fire.

A growl in between the raging fire shook the floor. It came from the walls, ceiling, and across the floor. The deep growls emanated from everywhere.

The unsetting rumble around the house shifted to a deafening roar. A loud hiss accompanied by a thunderous stampede gained the momentum of a runaway freight train.

Emily readied herself to fire another shot. Instead, she realized what was about to happen. She grabbed the blanket, covered her head, and curled her body into a tight fetal position on the floor as small as she could manage.

Angel stood still as a statue.

Emily pushed her body into a corner, closed her eyes, and pulled the blanket tighter over her head and face.

It was time to pray.

The loud booming roar of a gigantic fireball travelled through the house, down the staircase, and headed right toward the oxygen from the windows. The intense heat and powerful speed of the burning inferno lapped up every ounce of air with a thunderous commotion. The backdraft made one last ditch effort with a hissing sound before it retracted its flames.

Through a tiny crack of the blanket, Emily saw the enormous fireball propel Angel's body out through the window. Blood spatters around the frame of the window remained the only remnants left of the arsonist.

The immense heat had slammed above Emily's body, catching portions of her torn pants on fire. She quickly extinguished the flames with the blanket. There wasn't much time before the fire returned – with more vengeance.

Angel was gone.

She quickly looked around the room. Charred fixtures and furniture remained the only reminder of what once was a family home. Smoke swirled around the rooms. Millions of small fires searched relentlessly for air to grow and erupt even bigger.

Emily struggled against the wall to gain her balance and stood up. The plaster felt warm and rough underneath her hands. Dizziness overcame her, but she pushed her body to climb out the window.

Flames flicked its tentacles around the walls and crept closer.

The massive heat took her breath away.

Her mind would not cooperate at first, frazzled, images of recent events seemed to appear in staccato, but finally pure instincts kicked in as the blustery cold wind hit her face.

Emily hoisted her body through the opening. A shooting pain and debility tortured her right leg. A welcome rain battered her face.

She landed hard on the retaining wall. Lying on a narrow ledge, Emily succumbed to fits of coughing.

The roar from deep inside the estate built momentum once again.

Emily crawled on all fours toward the structure's foundation just as another thunderous fireball blew out the windows. A combination of intense heat, cold rain, and a searing breeze hovered a few seconds above her.

Fresh air comforted her, but the dizziness returned. She automatically gulped the refreshing, clean oxygen.

Emily thoughts returned to Rick. Her anxieties probed the question of whether or not he was still trapped inside the blaze.

Loud explosions of windows and various items deep inside the house filled the night air.

The early evening weather turned dark.

Emily felt the increasing rain pelt her face.

Trapped on the ledge, the absolute helplessness terrified Emily.

A hundred foot sheer drop-off below, a burning inferno behind, and no access on either side, pushed her survival skills to the limit. Five feet down, several jagged rocks would allow a possible path toward the stairs. She might be able to reach it.

Everything she had been stressing about seemed so insignificant now. Emily bullied herself to move forward. She could make it.

Another huge crash reverberated from inside the house and made her tremble.

She let out a yell, cursing her hesitation and lack of courage. Sitting up, she immediately looked down at the crashing waves and inaccessible cliff, which made the vertigo factor intensify. Contrasting white foam and the reflection from the dwindling dusk transformed the tide into the bowels of hell.

Looking down at the rocks below, she saw some of the grisly remains of Angel's shredded, broken, and burned body.

Not wanting to take her hand away from her leg, she forged on despite of her injury. She sat with her legs dangling over the edge, rolled to her side, scraping her stomach on the cement barrier, and slowly eased her feet down to the closest rock.

A crash blasted above her head. Pieces of embers swirled around in the wind. The burnt stench permeated the air.

A little bit farther... and she touched her feet to the rock. Hanging onto the flat ledge, she used the remaining energy left to hold herself steady, as she shimmied carefully toward safety.

Her weight pulled down hard and her fingers numbed. The rain picked up momentum, but the blaze still burned strong.

Wet from the rain and blood, Emily inched her way to another footing, not knowing what she would find. Her balance wavered. She couldn't find another solid foothold.

She hung helpless.

This was how her life would end.

The wind picked up in huge gusts.

Emily thought she heard a voice several times.

"Over here!" She yelled. "I'm here!" Her own voice sounded hoarse and weak.

She couldn't hold on much longer.

A strong hand grabbed her wrist and pulled her up.

"Em!" Rick's voice competed with the wind and sounded hollow. He pulled her close and hugged her. Noticing her condition, he immediately took off his belt and affixed a quick tourniquet. "I think we can make it to the staircase and get out from there."

Her pain intensified, but her relief was even greater. Rick was alive. He had minor scrapes and abrasions, but he was in one piece.

"Angel's dead?" He asked.

"Yes…" Emily replied. "But I don't think I can climb anymore." Her words were lost in the wind.

"If we can beat the fire to the other side, you won't have to…" He grabbed her hand firmly and they climbed to the base of the house.

The supports of the deck above rattled and creaked with an ugly sound.

With just a little distance to go, Emily and Rick moved closer to what remained of the house.

An unexpected burst of heat encircled them.

Emily's chest felt tight, restricting her breaths. Her footing slipped on the second narrow ledge. She knew one of her next steps would prove fatal.

The wind whistled underneath the deck supports creating a fun house effect.

Rick kicked numerous times at the bottom side of the wooden staircase, which was still intact. He took out a couple of the lower steps, so they could climb through to safety.

The heavy rain slowed the fire's progress.

A splintering commotion overrode the blustery wind and fire. The deck above crumbled, slowly at first, and then it balanced precariously.

Rick looked toward Emily in horror.

He moved quickly to pull her to safety, when the patio deck plummeted. Part of lumber and supports hit Rick and slammed him to the ground.

Emily shielded her face as the noise of the crash caused her momentary deafness.

Half of the deck hit the ground at a forty-five degree angle, leaving a makeshift shelter. She inched her way to Rick, he lay partially on his side, not moving. His arm bent in an awkward position, no doubt broken.

"Rick!" She cried.

All of her emotions rose to the surface and tumbled out. She wanted to cry and laugh, vent her anger, but didn't know which one to emote first.

She rolled him carefully onto his back. He was alive and semi-conscious, blood and mud encrusted his shirt, face, and arms. He mumbled some incoherent words as he came around.

"C'mon Rick, you have to help me. Get up, we've got to get out of here now." Breathlessly, she said. "It's only a little bit farther."

Emily sat him up and pulled him to his feet. Her leg felt strangely dead and she couldn't feel the ground beneath her feet. Her main concern was Rick. With his good arm around her neck and shoulder, they managed to clumsily climb through the open steps, and stagger down to the path leading to the driveway.

Concentrating intently on getting to safety, Emily didn't hear the sirens of fire trucks and paramedics approach through the deafening thunder and heavy downpour.

They fell several times, hurrying toward the road. Each tumble sent a new debilitating pain throughout her body. They pushed through the gate to safety.

Once they reached the road, she collapsed onto the street still holding onto Rick. Emily couldn't remember if she cried aloud, or if it was in her own mind. She had left a part of herself back inside the house; her psyche now built a wall against the rage and war of killers. Something had changed inside her.

She looked at Rick who seemed more alert, but in extreme pain. Her world seemed to make less sense than ever before, as they lay on the quiet street, bleeding, burned, and partially broken in the pouring rain.

The fire had lost some of its earlier wrath, but the dense smoke continued to fill the air. The intense heat mixed with the humidity made peculiar clouds drift around the property.

The large emergency vehicles arrived. Men hurried to their duties, hoses were hooked up, and water immediately blasted into the smoldering structure.

Two firefighters and two paramedics came to their aid. They quickly assessed the couple's injuries.

Emily was loaded onto a gurney as they tended to her leg. She closed her eyes. Exhaustion riddled her body and her mind drifted off.

CHAPTER SIXTY-THREE
Two Weeks Later

The gentle waves lapped up along the beach, moving the sand back and forth. The coastal sounds were hypnotic and the warm sun equally inviting.

A green tennis ball glided down the beach and bounced once. Sarge ran effortlessly along the coastline, wet from the waves, snapped up the ball in a full run, turned, and proudly galloped back to Rick.

The large dog dropped the wet ball at his feet.

Rick used the long plastic launcher to snatch up the ball. He hurled it again. His left arm in a sling, abrasions visible on his arms and face, but were well on their way in the healing process. He laughed as the wet Labrador skidded in the sand.

Emily walked with Jordan in the opposite direction. She still limped slightly from her injury, but her abrasions, minor burns, and lacerations marking her hands and arms had already begun to repair. However, her emotional trauma would mend at a slower rate.

"I still can't believe that you managed to scare the crap out of me twice in one month." Jordan said matter of fact. "And you closed a difficult serial case."

"Well, I've learned my lesson. I will always wear my pendant from now on." She smiled and touched the necklace around her neck. She looked at him seriously. "Thank you Jordan for erasing the contract on me. You gave me my life back. Well… at least my way of life."

Jordan changed the subject and gestured to her leg. "No chance that you'd remove that bandage and let me count the stitches?"

"Nope."

"Didn't think so."

The sun lit Emily's face, showed off her amber eyes, and the subtle scar she wore like a badge of honor on her cheek.

Emily stopped and faced him. "So what's on your mind Jordan? You have been different since the fire."

"I've had a lot of time to think."

"Sounds serious. Think about what?"

Emily was intrigued and hoped that he still wasn't hurt about their kiss. She had never seen Jordan so serious for so long before.

"My life has been... let's just say in a holding pattern and I need to figure out where to go to from here."

"You going back to work for the F.B.I.?"

"Hell no!" He flashed his smile.

"Then what?"

"I'm going to be gone for a while. I have a friend up north near Red Bluff ."

"What's her name?" Emily teased.

"It's a he..."

"Oh."

"Very funny." He made a face at her. "It's my old college roommate. He needs some help remodeling his cabin, and I thought it would be good for me to take a break and gain some perspective for a while. It's quiet. The fishing is good."

Emily laughed. "I can't picture you fly fishing..."

"Hey, if I can hunt serial killers, I think I can throw a line into the water and catch a fish."

"How long will you be gone?"

"I don't know."

Emily stared at Jordan for several moments.

Emptiness filled her. She knew that he would not always be there to help. She cared about him and considered him a good friend. It would be strange not having him around, and not being able to run criminal profiles by him on a whim.

Jordan looked uncomfortable. "You can always send me any profile or photographic evidence. If you really need me, I'm only a few hours away."

"Okay."

"Just promise me to be careful. Send me a text every Wednesday and Saturday, so I know you're okay."

"Yes sir, will do." She forced a smile.

"Good. I'm off to pack." He stood awkwardly and hesitated.

Emily leaned in and gave him a quick kiss on the cheek. "I'll miss you. We both will."

"I think Rick could live without me."

Emily turned to leave. She didn't want Jordan to see that her eyes welled up with tears. "Yeah maybe, but Sarge will sure miss you. Take good care of yourself Jordan."

Emily turned and walked back to Rick and Sarge. She didn't know how long Jordan watched her, but now she felt, more than ever, that things seemed to be slipping away and out of her control.

She caught up to Rick and placed her arm around his waist.

"Everything okay?" He asked.

"Yeah, he's just leaving for a while."

"Oh." Rick threw the ball into the water.

The dog happily chased the ball, swimming in circles until he latched onto it, and began his run back. "And how are we?" He asked.

Emily smiled, leaned in, and gave him a long lingering kiss.

She said. "Better than okay."

THE END

CPSIA information can be obtained at www.ICGtesting.com
Printed in the USA
LVOW13s0759250913

353740LV00005B/1/P